NAKED SCREAM

NAKED SCREAM

Andrea Douglas

ATHENA PRESS
LONDON

NAKED SCREAM
Copyright © Andrea Douglas 2006

ISBN 1 84401 629 3

First Published 2006 by
ATHENA PRESS
Queen's House, 2 Holly Road
Twickenham TW1 4EG
United Kingdom

Printed for Athena Press

Chapter One

The scream was human. Or was it a wounded animal crying in torment? It split the night into fragments, like a bullet breaking glass. Where did the noise come from? It was *me*! I was that animal. Suddenly I was laughing, cradling myself as you would a child. I am alive. I looked down at my chest, expecting to see blood, and my hands felt for the wound. There was no blood, no wound; the bullet must have ricocheted as it hit the window. The assassin failed, I am still here.

Lights everywhere and people talking! My room door burst open, with Tania, my key nurse, tumbling through it. 'What's all this commotion? You naughty girl, you have woken the whole corridor.' Tania looked concerned but angry.

I just couldn't stop laughing, it bubbled and burst to music in my head!

I was alive! Was I in prison? Gently, she rocked me as I began to loosen the grip on my knees, swaying to and fro in a soothing rhythm. 'Tell me what happened, Angelica.' She smoothed my wet hair and kissed the top of my head, holding me as my body began to tremble uncontrollably.

There were no words, only pictures in black and white, flashing across my vision like an old-time movie. How could I tell anyone what I had seen? Who could explain it? How that face would haunt me as it laughed, the wicked sardonic smile wrapped in a black balaclava.

Tiredness overwhelmed me as she laid me down beneath the soft duvet. I asked my lips to move but they held their secret tightly behind closed doors. The dream was trapped inside my head, if it was a dream. One day I would be able to talk about it. Perhaps tomorrow would be that day. Would tomorrow ever come? I felt a sharp prick in my arm and could taste sweet almonds. Sleep enfolded me like a sheet as I slithered down into the arms of oblivion… all memory gone. Dream world now took control.

I was alone in a sightless tunnel, deep beneath the earth. The sides of the tunnel were not solid and were moving towards me and away from me as if they were breathing. I walked lightly, almost floating in the air, deliberately going forward, being propelled by an inner energy. One side of the tunnel, to my left, was dark and forbidding, almost black. The right side was lighter, like a dense membrane, but I dared not reach out to touch it. A voice was trying to persuade me to look up and see the light and smell the beautiful flowers; instead I continued, remorselessly, down the stone tunnel in search of the way out.

In the blink of an eye the end appeared before me, the narrow tunnel widening into a circular amphitheatre, having three rows of stone seating in tiers. From the far end of each tier faceless people emerged from door-less anterooms to take their seats.

I chose one opening at random and ventured into it. There was a square-shaped pool into which naked men and women were stepping, silently, obediently. No, not me... am not willing... will *not* give in. I couldn't breathe, my chest heaved, my head spun. What was this weight dragging me down? I didn't want this. I would not surrender. Who was the unseen enemy? Then there were hands pulling at me and there was a rush of noise and an explosion of light. Air gushed from my mouth as if I was being crushed, so I gulped fresh air to replace it.

My eyes were wide open. This was my room, my bed, my flowers.

'Well, hello there, sweetie.' Tania's smiling face was hovering above me. 'Boy, oh boy! You're a tough one. I didn't think I was going to wake you today. Another bad dream? That's two in one night, you poor child. Do you remember last night and all the commotion you caused? Hee-hee.' She giggled and raised her hand, pretending to smack me.

'I'm so sorry, Tania.' I winced at the thought. 'Please apologise to the nurses' station and to anyone else. I suppose it was just a nightmare.' I was wrung out, exhausted.

'No worries, sweetie.' She laughed. 'It's all part of the scheme of things. So how are you feeling this morning?' she said, as she handed me a phial of pills and a tumbler of water.

'OK, I think!' I spluttered as I had a mouthful of water.

'Do I still have to take these tablets? They make me feel so peculiar, sort of spaced-out, and my mouth is like a sandpit.'

Very gently, this tall, buxom nursing sister took my two small hands in her large capable ones and sat beside me on my single bed. I studied her brown face, thinking she must be Jamaican or Bahamian, with skin that glowed like roasted chestnuts. She always smiled as she spoke, her black eyes dancing. I knew she was there before I heard her voice because she smelled of warm honey – or was it vanilla? She could only have been about five years older than I was, but I felt like her child. I think she enjoyed holding me and calming me as much as I did – a reciprocal pleasuring of souls.

'Well, it's like this, sweetie.' She pushed me forward as she heartily plumped my pillows, the effort making her bottom wobble.

'You are doing very nicely so far, but you have only been here a few days and—' I cut her short.

'And what?' I blurted out. 'What comes next, Tania? When do I get to see Dr Michael, this medical magician? How is he going to make me right again?' I swallowed hard as I could feel the tears choking my throat, searing hot water behind my nose then overflowing down my face.

'No! No! No! No more! Please, no more tears!' I screamed aloud. 'Pull yourself together, you stupid cow!' I yelled.

'Now then, stop this self-abuse, you silly girl,' Tania rebuked me, but I was no longer listening.

Too late now, the waterfall would engulf me until the fountain ran dry. I would surrender to lethargy and apathy once more.

Tania had left me to conquer the latest bout of waterworks. Once it abated, I threw the duvet back and staggered into the bathroom. God, I looked a sight. I showered, dressed in T-shirt and shorts and tried to repair the swollen blob that used to be my face. I was shakily trying to fringe my red eyes with waterproof black mascara when I heard a gentle tapping at the door. The clock was showing 9.05 a.m., perhaps it was one of the kitchen staff bringing my breakfast. I called out for the person to enter and was astonished to see the man who was standing in the doorway.

I was aware of a great affinity towards this stranger, the arrival of a dear friend. At first glance I saw the largest, all-knowing brown eyes behind smoke-tinted lenses, iron-grey hair, medium height, stocky build and a nose and mouth chiselled by the gods. His skin was the colour of dark caramel, giving him the look of an Egyptian. He was wearing a lightweight cashmere suit and carried a black leather clasp case, which he was holding against his chest.

It seemed an eternity before a word was spoken; we were both so intent on that initial reaction that words would be superfluous. A smile broke over his face and he said, 'Mrs Reeves, how do you do? I am Dr Michael. May I come in?'

'Of course, please do, will you have a seat?' I said, quickly taking my handbag from the chair.

I suddenly felt ill at ease, which he sensed immediately.

'I have you at a disadvantage, Angelica,' he said warmly.

'May I call you Angelica?' He had a very disarming smile.

'Yes, that's fine. I think I know you but I can't remember from where or when.' I sat on the edge of the bed, confused.

'Let me enlighten you. We met, quite briefly, a few days ago when I was called to your house to talk to you. Do you remember now?'

He said this not looking at me, but while he was opening his case and arranging papers on my small writing table.

Slowly, I went back in time. Through misty eyes, I saw that he was wearing an Aquascutum tracksuit in a soft navy fabric. His face was unshaven but those eyes were the same, and the over-whelming feeling of tranquillity and understanding entered me.

'Yes, I do remember! You were kneeling beside me as I sat on the stairs in the hallway of my house. I was exhausted and distressed and you told me not to be afraid any more because you had come to rescue me. That's right, isn't it? Please tell me I'm not losing my mind.'

Involuntarily my hands were reaching out to him. I needed him on my side. I needed someone to hold me.

'Well, Angelica, perhaps not in those precise words, but the meaning is the same.'

He looked at me with an indulgent grin, reminding me of a well-loved teddy bear. I could drown in those eyes, so hypnotic. I didn't feel uncomfortable any more, in fact I had this compelling urge to sit on his lap and fall asleep against his chest.

Did he know what I was thinking? I could no longer look at his face; instead I watched my hands rhythmically tracing lines from my knees to my groin. Back and forth, back and forth – so comforting – no pain.

'Angelica!' Dr Michael called to me sharply, pulling me back. 'We are now going to take down some background history so that I can prepare a programme for you. I will start by asking you for your family history and then move towards more personal details about yourself.'

He looked at me directly as he said this, without moving any part of him except his mouth. I could only see his mouth and was overcome with the spaced-out weirdness again. The questions came, followed by my answers, monotonous and robotic. I could hear my voice as if I was listening to a recording tape. It was so far away and yet I was totally aware of Dr Michael as his pen travelled across the paper, line after line, and his wonderful, sensuous mouth.

'Excellent, Angelica. You have done incredibly well,' he said with candour. 'I think we deserve a refreshing cuppa, don't you?'

My mouth had dried up, so I nodded in agreement. Really, all I wanted to do was sleep, to drown in oblivion.

Brr… Brr… Brr… The telephone rang, breaking the silence.

'Excuse me, Dr Michael,' I said as I picked up the receiver.

'Hello, Angelica, this is Ann Amery. If you haven't heard my name before, I am your occupational therapy coordinator, or OTC for short. Is Dr Michael with you? I should like a word with him.' She sounded very brusque and efficient; it was like taking a cold shower.

I handed the receiver to Dr Michael and quietly sat back on the bed, just watching him. He spoke quickly as he methodically packed away his papers. I felt as if I had been dismissed, no longer important. He placed the receiver back into the cradle and gently touched my arm as he opened the door to the corridor. Stay with me! Don't go! I pleaded silently.

'We shall meet again tomorrow. I'm afraid we shall have to have a rain check on our cuppa as Ann Amery would like to see you now,' he said, smiling.

'Don't look so worried. Together, Ann and I will help you regain your equilibrium.' With that he nodded goodbye and closed the door.

I stood looking at the door handle for ages, expecting something to happen. Brr... Brr... Brr... The phone rang again, snapping me out of my reverie.

'Hello, Angelica, it's me again, Ann Amery. Could you find your way down to the main reception desk on the ground floor? Ask Archie Dickens, the reception clerk, for directions to the OT unit. I shall be waiting for you. Don't be long.'

She didn't wait for my reply; all I heard was the click as she hung up. That sick, uneasy feeling had returned. What was happening to me? Would someone please switch off my brain!

OK, this was a test. No more pussyfooting around, just open the door and find this Archie Dickens. Opening the door was a breeze, then into the corridor. Now for the hard part – which way – left or right? I could feel the prickles across my face and down my arms and there was no air to breathe. How long was I motionless? Come on, get going, it's only a corridor. That's it! Fine! Not the lift! Take the stairs! My legs were like jelly.

Faceless people passed me. I kept my eyes to the ground. I didn't want to be recognised. Start at the second floor – keep moving – first floor – ground floor. Success, I could see the entrance lobby and a small man in a blue uniform sitting behind a desk, reading a newspaper. Had I been this way before? I couldn't remember. I approached the man and was about to speak when true panic set in. I had forgotten where I was going. He saw the fear in my eyes and quietly rose from his seat, stepped forward and took my hand. All I wanted to do was return to the safety of my room.

'You must be Angelica,' he said kindly, still holding my hand. 'I believe Ann Amery is waiting for you. Would you like me to take you to meet her?' he said, watching my face intently. Too many questions. Why was I so cold and yet so hot in my head? Why couldn't I find my voice? Suddenly I was six years old and wanted to cry or scream, but I struggled to keep my composure and slowly nodded in reply.

As he guided me towards some swing doors the rushing noise gradually subsided and the feeling of nausea died. I needed fresh air and desperately wanted to be outside in the daylight, hearing the birds and the wind in the trees. I so wanted to *scream!*

A door opened and a stout, middle-aged woman stood in front of me, with her hand extended towards me. I didn't want to touch her hand. 'Thanks, Archie,' she said in a dismissing tone. 'Angelica is going to be with me for a while.'

With this remark Archie turned and walked away and I was alone with Ann. The door closed and we walked to a pair of softly padded armchairs. Ann gestured for me to sit in one and she sat facing me. Instantly I felt ill at ease. I didn't like this woman with her short, cropped hair and stern face. She reminded me of a teacher I had when I was at grammar school, who took great pleasure in singling me out to humiliate me. She would tie my hair back with string, then make me recite in front of the class, 'Beauty is only skin deep and pride goeth before a fall.' I wasn't proud. I was a pretty child, wilful but not bad, and she tormented me because she was as ugly as a grey spider with decaying teeth.

But this was another person, who was probably understanding and not malicious, so I must not pre-judge her. I was finding it difficult to focus on her. Neither of us had spoken and I wasn't sure what was expected of me. Ann was reading from a file of notes in her lap and not once in that first five minutes did she glance my way. I let my gaze fall on the folds in the curtains, which were cream in colour, adorned with bunches of vivid red cherries; through the windows I saw a vast lawn edged with vibrant purple rhododendrons and tall, majestic oak trees like dependable sentries. I was compelled to return to the room and I found that Ann was now staring at me with pale, blank eyes.

What was this game, a battle of wills? What did she want from me? Wasn't she here to help me understand my grief? There was no kindness or empathy in that stare, just emptiness. A human refrigerator whose light had gone out.

She cleared her throat and said, 'Let's begin, Angelica. I want you to tell me why you are here wasting my valuable time and patience!'

It's going to happen again, I thought, another spiteful bitch of an ugly woman who wants to humiliate me and finally destroy what little confidence I have remaining. OK, play the game, concentrate, no tears. I could feel myself wavering. John, my husband, would do this to me, staring but not talking. He was a master at the game.

My hands began to trace the route from knee to groin. I sang a lullaby in my head to soothe me. A small voice was saying, 'You won't beat me, I shall win in the end.' Don't cry! Don't cry! You must not cry! Stop rocking! My mouth opened and I heard my voice saying, 'I came here at your invitation today. I came here for Dr Michael to help me adjust to tragedy in my life. I came here because I am sad and lonely and afraid. I came here because I am exhausted. I came here to seek sanctuary. I came here because my children need me to be strong for them but I am so tired, so very tired!'

I was outside myself, looking in. I could see my chest heaving to gain breath and I saw her eyes following the rise and fall of my bosom. This woman of stone sat there impassively, studying my face, her soulless eyes boring into mine. Something savage grew within me, how I wanted to slap her face for trying to belittle me. Then suddenly her composure broke and she smiled. The corners of her mouth and her cheeks dimpled, but the eyes remained cold and empty.

'OK, Angelica, round one goes to you!' She almost chuckled. So this was some kind of test. Was there a camera secretly recording my reactions? 'Now let's get down to the real reason behind your pretty facade.'

She rose and was relocating herself behind her desk. You battleaxe, I thought, I can't do this any more.

'I have the general history of your family and how long you have been depressed and tragic too.' She said this, I am sure, to taunt me. Why use the word tragic? It is so melodramatic. My life isn't a drama, it is real.

'I do not understand why you are so hostile. I thought you were going to help me!' I shouted at her. Oh! No! The hot water stung my eyes.

I turned away to hide the shame of crying again. I felt like a trapped bird without wings to escape the foe. She could destroy me piece by piece and play with my emotions at will. I was no longer in control.

'Come now, Angelica, dry your eyes. Here, look, there are tissues at your elbow.' She pushed the box towards me.

'I'm too tired for any of this.' I sniffed and wiped my nose. 'Life is already beating me up. Why do you want to battle against me too? I am confused and helpless, so help me, please!' I tried to find a response in those pale eyes.

'Angelica, be calm now and listen.'

My body slumped as I sat and waited for the next attack.

'You are going to be strong and you are going to get very angry. The anger within you is trapped and that is the reason that you cry. So, I will teach you to turn water into fire and then manage the anger in such a way that will give you your freedom and joy back. Our main aim here is to guide your thought processes from negative to positive, then the energy within you will rekindle and grow from strength to strength.' She finished her speech by saying, 'Do you trust and believe what I have said?'

'Yes!' was my immediate reply. I was hypnotised.

'Well, *don't*! Trust yourself! You own your own pain, your own happiness and your own destiny. So go and get it back! Don't allow others to take it from you!' She almost spat the last words. This woman was to be nicknamed – Boadicea – for when she spake forth she withered everything in her path. She was one angry woman.

With notebook and pen, we then began the arduous task of journalising the events that preceded my visit to The Abbey Park Care Clinic.

My name is Angelica Reeves. I am married to John, a high-flying City businessman. We live in a secluded village in Kent and have three, gorgeous children. To the outside world: a normal, middle-class, hard-working family. To all intents and purposes, this was correct. I am forty-three and John is forty-eight and we have been married for twenty years. I would love to say it was a wonderful, contented partnership, but that would be untrue. True happiness had not visited our union; there were too many secrets. Life is a sequence of questions and answers and sometimes we fail abysmally. The Reeves family entered into the ritual of life until about four years ago when an alien entity seemed to invade our world. It began with just a feeling of foreboding – an unpleasant curdling in my gut – and it grew. John became even more reclusive than usual, not wanting to join in our family events, shutting himself away in his den and only finding spare time for his solitary pursuits of fishing and golf. He looked haunted and grey.

We had been happy, almost blissfully, for a short time. Then, piece by piece, John took bits of our jigsaw away without explanation, so I filled the gaps with fantasies. The man I married was a chameleon, strutting his stuff arrogantly and performing his marital duties with panache. I was his prize possession, a trophy to be seen and admired but not touched; and he was living a lie.

I blossomed and bloomed and in 1976 Jason was born. My firstborn was the most beautiful baby I had ever seen, with huge blue eyes, white-blond hair and an enormous pair of lungs. Did I transfer my love to him and lose touch with John? Yes, I did! John was jealous of Jason before he was born and slowly the poison seeped into his brain to ferment and grow and Jason became my world. John would make excuses for his absence at home and I learned to be a single parent, reluctantly at first, and then as a normal practice.

For a brief period in 1978 we became lovers again and the twins were born. I truly believed the dark clouds had lifted and revelled in motherhood and family harmony. It didn't last! John reverted to his obsession with money and became morose and distant, only venturing in our direction when it suited him. All the time I could sense him watching me, envying my innocent joy with the kids and my passion for dancing to wild music.

I tried to include him in everything, but he was belligerent and uncooperative: work, fishing and golf came first and we were the runners-up. He provided the candy and we were grateful. The twins were oblivious to atmospheres as they had each other, but for Jason it was hard. Anything he achieved went unnoticed, which made him try even harder to please his dad, until the day he was accepted into a private boarding school. Jason jumped at it! John sighed, almost audibly, as if a great weight had been lifted from him, and I was devastated.

How could I survive without my little soldier? That's when the rot set in for me. I let Jason go without a fight. I let him down. I believed that if he were away from his father's negative attitude it would help him. He did flourish and actually hated coming home. He preferred the company of his friends. So I arranged trips to see him, sometimes taking the twins, when John was away on his golf tournaments.

For the twins it was a battle for attention at all times. They were a competitive pair and at fourteen the world was their playground. Rebecca was my princess, a true born-on-a-Sunday child, having all the attributes to go with the saying – bonny, blithe, good and gay. Academically, she achieved through application and hard work and she was a dolphin in the pool. Sean – born on a Monday – only one hour after his sister, was fair of face – he had the 'boy next door' good looks. He was brighter academically and only did the minimum to achieve the grades. You could say he was a bit lazy with the books, but he was happy. They both swam for their local team and Sean played football for the county and his school. Life for them was a breeze. Doesn't it all sound too good to be true? Well, there was always a hidden agenda, which was going to rip our world apart. Oh, if only I had hindsight. Could I have changed it all? The crunch came last year, in 1992.

Jason was sixteen years old and an adolescent. Dad was just the old fart who paid the bills and occasionally showed interest in his achievements – or lack of them. He committed the cardinal sin of being caught in possession of marijuana and was expelled. John's reaction was lethal. He sent him off to his brother Toby in New York, as he couldn't bear to look at him. That was when I passed the point of no return. My dislike of John became loathing and I retreated into myself when he was around, and he would lock himself away in his den.

My body sank down. I was exhausted.

'Sorry, I can't think any more today.' I could feel my shoulders collapse and my mind slid downwards into a very dark recess. It was then that my pencil took on a life of its own. The next writing was my signature, etched into my soul:

My mind is like a whirlpool I cannot comprehend
The pain and anger that I feel never coming to an end.
Thoughts broken like a jigsaw not fitting close together
Unwanted fear is pushing me to the end of my tether.
The scream has not awoken it lurks somewhere below
Then like the lava bursting forth the pain begins to grow.
Salt water spills from my eyes obscuring thoughts and vision
Overpowered by lethargy, as grief becomes my prison.

I heard a voice, my voice crying out.

'Will someone please help me?'

A great weight enveloped my head and I was aware of hands lifting me and then laying my body somewhere soft and warm, and a voice in the distance saying, 'Yes, I'll keep her still and comfortable until you come. Yes, Dr Michael, there is far more trauma than I first thought. I agree, we must let her rest more before she attends therapy. This little lady has hidden great anxiety for a long time.'

Then silence, a long foggy walk, floating, breathing, smiling, a small prick in my arm and a sweet taste in my mouth and emptiness.

Chapter Two

I awoke feeling wonderful. The sun was streaming into my room, painting golden fingers across the floor. My small table was almost hidden by so many beautiful flowers and there was a pile of unopened envelopes. I felt like a star.

I tried to get up, but my body refused to oblige. What was wrong? Where had my strength gone? I reached for the red bell-cord and pulled, hoping to see Tania's lovely face peering around the door, my human sunbeam. Instead, a diminutive figure appeared, a tiny Chinese nurse with black hair piled on top of her head so high that it looked like a beefeater's hat.

'Hello, I am Sam Liu, your new key nurse,' she said with a refreshing smile and a bobbing action, like a startled bird.

'Oh, no! Where is Tania then? She is normally here until 4.30 p.m. and it is only 11.15 a.m.,' I said with ill grace.

'Tania is on holiday for two weeks. So sorry, you have to put up with me!' she replied, still smiling.

'I didn't mean to be rude, sorry, I just feel odd and was hoping to talk it over with Tania.' I was still desperately trying to sit up in bed.

'Here, let me help you,' she said, as she popped me up like a cork out of a bottle.

'How did you do that? I must be a dead weight,' I said, looking at her tiny frame.

'It is easy when you know how, and you are very light.' She grinned, looking at me through lowered lashes. She was as bright as a button and reminded me of a frisky kitten.

'Tell me! Why have you let me sleep so late? I should have been on a walk two hours ago. Yesterday, I walked with Joanna from 9.30 a.m. to 11.30 a.m.'

'Angelica, you have not been too well and therefore we allowed you to sleep until you woke up naturally. You have slept for forty-eight hours.' She watched my face for a reaction.

I couldn't take it in. Forty-eight hours asleep! Where did all the nightmares go? My mind was a blank. What should I be remembering? I should be walking! I shall soon be home with the twins – oh, my babies! I will phone Jason in New York! I'll run with the dogs in the wood! I was getting ahead of myself.

'I think I feel happy, sort of new, different,' I said. 'My head is awake, but my body won't respond.'

'Shall we see if you can eat something. You haven't eaten very much since you arrived here, so we must encourage you to eat more or you will become weak and disorientated.' She said this as she was reading my notes. She had a sort of American accent with a hint of Far East. Her eyes were like jet beads, full of strength and something I couldn't describe. I knew I was staring at her, but she was like a magnet; she must have studied in America, I mused to myself.

'Actually, I am starving! Can I have scrambled egg on toast? Is that OK?' I asked.

'You bet you can, Angelica. I shall order it straight away.' She grinned and walked to the door.

'While I am gone, could you try to get up and wash at the sink? No shower yet! And *don't* go back to bed! Do this for me, please!' She gave me my orders as she closed the door.

Easier said than done. My body didn't seem to belong to my head; they were not working in harmony. With slow, deliberate movements I rolled out and off the bed and wandered, erratically, into the bathroom. Clinging onto the sink, I washed without falling over and could not stop giggling at my reflection in the mirror. I jiggled like a puppet on a rubber band. My waking feeling was usually one of disquiet and fear of things yet to come, so this warm, humorous anticipation was so refreshing. How long would it last?

The prospect of getting dressed without mishap was daunting. What was making me feel this way? Surely not just lack of food! I looked for the puncture marks in my arms, but none were obvious, only freckles.

Crash! I now resembled a broken frog, but the giggles just kept on coming. No good, I need some help, so I'll wait until Sam returns. The sun's rays were still delighting me with their kaleidoscopic mosaics around the room. Someone had hung a beautiful crystal in the centre of the window and the radiance glowed from it.

A gentle tapping and Sam reappeared in the doorway.

'Goodness me, Angelica, I think the clothes would look better on you than draped around the floor.' She laughed as she arranged my breakfast on the table, overseen by the array of flowers.

'Eat first and your energy levels will increase dramatically, then I will help you to dress,' she said as she helped me from the floor to the table.

I munched into the scrambled egg, but found I was full very quickly.

'Sorry, I can't eat all of this, I'm not as hungry as I thought.'

Sam inclined her head in acceptance and handed me a phial of pills and a tumbler of water, which I took. While I ate she had sped around my room like Mary Poppins, so it was looking tidy again.

'Thanks for doing all of this. I feel so useless at the moment. Am I drugged with an antidepressant or is it something else?' Needless to say I was a little confused.

'Let me help you dress and then I shall try to fill you in with what has happened since you joined us here six days ago.' She held out my underwear for me to put on. 'Very pretty undies! Are you expecting to go out somewhere nice?' She grinned.

I almost fell over again as I giggled and struggled out of my nightie and into my favourite, oyster-coloured silk bra and panties. When the material touched my skin it was like the tenderest caress. Ooh! Memories! My legs were less like jelly and I almost gracefully stepped into Capri pants and, finally, a soft cream silk top.

All this while, Sam watched me. She didn't speak, but was intently studying all my movements. I didn't feel embarrassed or uncomfortable, as she offered no physical threat. As I finished, we both sighed and laughed in unison.

Sam patted an adjacent space on the bed and I gratefully sat down beside her. She reached out for my hands and inspected them on both sides, finally pressing the fingernails.

'What fortune do you see for me, Sam?' I asked.

'Angelica, I am going to help you to see yourself as you really are. We are going to break through the protective shell and let the butterfly emerge and find her wings.' She said this while holding my hands.

'To do this, you must follow a simple pattern of life, which will involve lots of sleep, plenty of exercise, which you can choose to do, and good food. You can walk, jog, swim, play tennis, yoga, meditation, all here at the Abbey. We would like you to drink at least two to three litres of water a day and have your meals in the dining room with the other... residents...' She hesitated as she said the word residents.

'Don't you mean... crazies?' I said in mocking jest.

'Angelica, you must never degrade yourself in this way. This is a place of healing. People come here, because, like you, they cannot deal with the decision making. Their way of life has become confusing and possibly harmful to themselves and others around them.' She said this with such sincerity that it had to be true.

'Over the next few weeks we shall discover what has weakened your strength and help you to accept the facts, deal with them and rebuild your confidence.'

As Sam was talking to me in this melodic way I drifted off to another time and place where life was good. To the Comfort Zone.

Chapter Three

Oh, how I loved my car! She and I were a team. She was a drophead coupe in creamy white, with dark-blue leather interior, and I had christened her – Orgasma. Everyone laughed at the name, but I didn't need anyone when I was alone in my car – she was my partner. We bonded together like a perfect trinity: my car, the open road and me, especially on a Sunday. When I first saw her in the showroom, I adored her. After sitting on her upholstery and hearing her responsive, throaty rumble, we purred together. She was my very own phallic car.

I was escaping reality for a while, on my way to the health hydro for four days of indulgence. Mother-in-law would be installed to supervise the twins and John was who knows where – I no longer cared. A thought I may live to regret.

Only two hours of driving and I would be turning into the driveway of the 'magic kingdom' of Hydro-Plicity. There were seven of us altogether, who met up every year for four days of pampering. A motley group of friends from very different walks of life.

Jeannie and I came from the same village in Kent. She was dark-haired and petite, a local publican and closet alcoholic, even though she wouldn't admit it. She had two children, of similar ages to mine, and a very naughty husband, Mike, who ran the pub with her. We were both in our forties, going on twenty-five, and relished our playtime together.

Vanessa was some years older than us – about fifty-five – a columnist for a national newspaper and a famous author of many biographies of the rich and infamous. She was divorced, rich and bitter, and a fountain of knowledge with an uncanny knack for discovering the truth.

Hermione was lovely and Vanessa's best friend. She was willowy, in her early sixties and a widow. Hermy – as we called her – was a stunning woman, with an abundance of intriguing stories from her classy past. She had been married for forty years to an aristocratic man of indecent wealth, who had died tragically and left her very well provided for.

George was a London stockbroker who lived half his life in Surrey with his wife and the other half with his secretary in various locations. He was fair, grossly overweight, laughed like a drain and drank like a shoal of fish. He was about fifty and would probably die much too soon of liver malfunction, and he said 'fuck' all the time.

Susie was George's secretary and was always with him for the four days. He actually stayed for seven days, the last three he shared with his wife, who arrived in the wake of the mistress. Back to Susie. Well, she was mid-thirties, single and had a huge bosom, nothing special to look at, but obviously very necessary to George. If she wasn't around she wasn't missed. This was an observation made by the group and not a bitchy remark. I said there were seven of us and the *pièce de résistance* was Simon.

Oh! What an Adonis! He set many hearts thumping during his four-day visit – including mine.

Simon was tall, dark and stunning to look at, about forty-seven – no, he was forty-seven – and totally in control. He wore his hair long and curly, his eyes were dark brown and he had a cute mole on his left butt cheek! How did I know that? He had his own hairdressing salon just off the south side of the M25 and was separated from his wife. He had nicknamed our gang the Hockey Team – don't ask me why – and he was the Chief Coach. He had many skills and most too naughty to mention.

Only Jeannie and I kept in regular contact, but we all had an understanding that we would meet up at the same time and place every year. The moment was nigh. I was tingling with anticipation.

The hydro itself was a *premier cru* location, but our gang elevated its grandeur. The aura we created was almost visible, so much so that we had 'cling-ons' appearing during our week each year, forever trying to be in 'our' gang. There was always a buzz among the therapists, hoping for some juicy gossip from Vanessa's confidants and willing to trade any titbits they had gleaned from celebrities who had passed through their hands during the year. Indiscretions not read in the tabloids.

I peeled off the road on to the pebble driveway, greeted by

10 mph signs on either side of the ornate entrance pillars. There in front of me emerged the grey stone facade of an ageing stately home, now converted into a health hydro for the rich, not so rich and hopefully aspiring body beautifuls.

It was only 2 p.m., but all the rooms were illuminated, as the day was cold and very dark. The month was February and snow was in the air. I made a quick scan of the car park, to find that I was the first to arrive – unless someone had changed their car. I tooted the horn outside the office window and Chas looked out – he was one of the regular doormen. He beckoned for me to use the office staff car park, which was a bonus as it was adjacent to the front door. As I straightened up to pull forward, two light beams swung round alongside me and there was Simon, in his Audi, grinning at me from ear to ear. He buzzed the offside window down and shouted across space, 'Long time no see, Angel. Let's go light some fires.' What a star! I couldn't help laughing out loud.

By the time I had pulled my suitcase from the back seat he had disappeared through the front doors, like a genie from a bottle. 'Thanks for giving me a hand,' I said to the empty air. What a cad!

Chas came out to greet me, all ruddy-faced where he had been sitting by the fire.

'Hello, flower, I know you'd be here first. You can't wait to give me a hug, I knows it!' He took my case and crushed me to him, all in a single movement.

'Chas, you are like a prickly hedgehog,' I said, pulling his whiskers.

'Are you all gonna behave yourselves this year? No more sneaking off down the pub, flower!' He hustled me inside, propelling me towards to reception desk.

Simon was lounging against the mantelpiece with a glowing wood fire beneath. He was surveying his prey, like a tiger waiting for the opportune moment to pounce.

'No point in ringing the bell, 'cos they're all in a meetin', so's I'll sign you in,' Chas said as he grasped his spectacles from the top of his head and found space for them across his nose.

'Here we are, flower, you has number 56 as usual, best room that one for a special lady as you are.'

He didn't know that Simon was sticking two fingers down his throat in the mirror and ended up choking until his eyes watered. He really was a shitbag at times.

'Chas, you are a darling, thank you. What would we do without you?' I pushed a note in his breast pocket, giving it a friendly tap.

He gathered up my bags and ambled off upstairs. 'You doin' yer own, Mr Carter!' he called over his shoulder, more as a statement than a question. I went to join Simon, by the fire, for our 'hello' hug. He pulled me down onto the sofa and as my head fell against his chest I was overcome by the all too familiar smell of Aramis.

'Oh, Angel, I have been dreaming of this all week.' He was gently kissing my hair and I was trying to untangle myself from his arms and compose myself for the imminent onslaught of reunion hugs. We didn't have to wait long before George and Susie exploded into the foyer, bringing cold air and snowflakes with them.

'You fucking bugger, Carter! See, Susie, I said he'd beat us to it!' George roared with laughter and started a mock battle with Simon. Susie and I smiled in greeting. Suddenly, heads appeared from every doorway to investigate the rumpus. The manager's meeting had come to an abrupt end. Bellboys seemed to pop out of cupboards, rounding up suitcases and golf bags and door keys.

Poor Susie looked as if she wanted the floor to open up and swallow her, when we were saved by the entrance of Queen Hermione. She quelled the situation with one withering look in George's direction.

'Good gracious, George! What has the last year done to you? You are even more rotund. You should have got here sooner!' Hermy was such a tonic. No one had her command or her control. George looked deflated, like a naughty schoolboy.

'Keep your wig on, duchess, we're going up!' He grabbed Susie's arm and pulled her towards the stairs, exiting the skirmish with a nod in all directions.

'Well, that's livened up this extremely cold afternoon. We can always depend on George for entertainment.' Hermy grinned at me as she tapped her highly polished nails on the reception counter.

'Hello, Angelica, you are as lovely as ever,' she said, blowing me a kiss. 'And you look as raunchy as ever, Simon!' She winked at him, provocatively. In another time and space she would have used him outrageously.

'You are a sexy siren, Hermy. Where is your sidekick, Vanessa? Don't you normally travel on a tandem broomstick!' Only Simon could get away with that sort of remark. Hermy aimed an imaginary missile at him and he ducked, involuntarily.

'She should be here soon, darling. You know how she likes to make her grand entrance.'

One never knew if Hermy was being straight or facetious. She was often too witty for the company she kept. Chas was back in reception and caught my eye. He was jangling my door key as if to say it was time that I left reception and went up to my room.

'I shall leave you two reminiscing for a while. I'm going to unpack and have a pre-dinner swim,' I said gaily.

'Aren't you going to wait for Vanessa to arrive, you minx! You know how she expects an audience.' Hermy was definitely in an acid mood.

'Sorry, Hermy, I'll catch up with her at dinner. She won't miss me as long as Simon is still here,' I purred in his direction.

'Actually, I'm gonna have a swim too and more besides, if I'm really lucky.' Si ran his tongue across his top lip in a very lascivious way.

'Go then, you are dismissed!' Hermy waved her hand with a royal flourish and a wicked grin. Was she aware of our body language?

'Come then, Chas! Help me to my suite, if you please. I shall not wait either.' And with a swing of her hips Hermione had vacated the reception area with Chas in attendance, towing her luggage.

'OK, Angel! The first one to the pool makes the fun begin. By the way, where is Jeannie?' he said as he swung his bag over his shoulder. It was now 3 p.m. and five of the infamous seven had arrived.

'She will be here by dinnertime. We travelled separately because there is trouble brewing between her and Mike, so he decided to bring her today.' I didn't elaborate and Si wasn't the type to pry.

He caught hold of my hand and yanked me towards the door to the basement games room. It sprang open as if by command and we hurtled down the wooden staircase. It was pitch black and smelled musty. You could still distinguish the yeasty aroma of old beer barrels and stale ale. In its previous existence it was probably a well-used liquor storeroom. But the fragrance that invaded my airways now was Aramis.

Simon was like a man possessed, a thirsty nomad and I was his oasis. His tongue traced a line from my eyes to my nose then my mouth. I felt as if I were diving into a bowl of crushed fruit and sucking on the fleshy delights.

My nipples stood erect against my dress as his hands caressed my body and I could feel his viper so hard on my belly. My mind was in a turmoil, half of me was saying, please push your fingers between my thighs where I am becoming so hot and wet, and the other was saying, praying, urging, 'Oh! Simon, I can't wait!' I groaned.

His reply was graphic, to only the damp air and cold walls, as he slid into my pulsating tunnel.

'White, hot Willie meets red, hot Fanny!' he rasped into my ear. 'Thank you God I have now entered the kingdom of Angelica – woweeee! Sorry, Angel, I couldn't wait.'

With a banshee whoop he exploded and we both shuddered together like trains hitting the buffers.

'Well, this definitely beats swimming hands down,' he said as he zipped the tired viper back into its cooling-off compartment and gently smoothed my woollen dress back to the sides of my legs.

'Oh, my Angel, why do we wait so long?' He sounded so needful, and expectant of an answer, but we had played this game before, each of us waiting for the other to make a sign of commitment, but life always threw a boulder between us.

'Simon!' I had no words to reply, just a longing that was insatiable. I took a deep breath.

'We are two lovers flying high on the wings of passion, but we fly away in opposite directions.' I looked at him in the dark and saw a man I wanted and who wanted me. Could we survive together?

'For three years we have indulged in our fantasy for four

incredible days. We phone a few times in between and meet briefly on a train or in a car park and pretend that something special is about to happen, but we never jump that last hurdle and we never will.'

I said this and quickly covered his lips with my hand. There was no answer.

'Let's do us both a favour and cool off in the pool, loverrr.' I pulled him towards the stairs.

'How I love it when you roll your arrrse!' He pushed his hand between my legs where hunger still abode. He was back to saucy Si and ready for action.

As we climbed the stairs I was aware that I was leaving my dream world and slowly coming back to the wicked world of *now*. But I would return to the balmy days of the hydro when I needed the Comfort Zone. As my eyes opened to the real world I felt expectant, possibly because my memories at that moment were so erotic. On my table, someone had laid out a meal of fruit and a selection of cheese and crackers, accompanied by a thermos in the guise of a teapot. I looked at the clock, it was 4.35 p.m. Gracious, where had the day gone?

For the first time in twenty-four hours I dared to think of my family and home. My phone hadn't rung at all, unless it was an internal call. Had they diverted my incoming calls or had my family and friends been advised not to call? I suddenly felt so alone and vulnerable. What was happening to the twins? My eyes strayed to their photos by the bed. Please try to forgive me for being so weak.

Had I fallen off the edge of the world, never to be seen again? Would I be brainwashed and reprogrammed to begin a new life as someone else? So why did I always return to my fantasy world, my life wasn't that bad, but I just couldn't cope. It seemed that as soon as I had one problem licked, another popped out of the cupboard just to give me a final kick.

I looked across at the fantastic array of flowers, wondering whether they had been lovingly chosen, but I wasn't up to reading the messages that accompanied them – not yet. After I had eaten I would tackle the pile of envelopes and attempt to read the cards.

Why did my mind panic and my stomach curdle at the thought of someone communicating with me? I have to face my fears eventually – so why not today?

Uncurling myself from my sleeping pose, I persuaded myself to sit at the table to eat. Sam had propped a note against the teapot: 'Hope you had a good sleep. Now try to eat the *small* meal I have prepared for you.'

'OK,' I said to the empty room, 'I'll have a go.' As I began to eat I gazed out of the window at the lawn below.

The month was June and we were being blessed with a glorious summer. Overhead the sky was a perfect blue and the heat of the sun must have registered around seventy degrees in the shade.

There were three people on the lawn attempting to rig up a badminton net, two men and one woman and a lot of determination. Eventually, it was erected and they then tossed a racquet into the air to see who would play first. It appeared to be the larger man with silver hair who had lost out. He ambled to the side and lay on the lawn, propping himself up on one elbow. I couldn't quite see his face, but I imagined that he was about fifty-ish and had an angular fluency of limb, like a golden retriever.

The other man was much younger, thirty-five-ish, with a stocky build and less tall, probably around five foot nine inches and his hair was the colour of burnished copper, coarse and unkempt. He was definitely overdressed, already looking flushed and sweaty.

The woman was about my age, but much more muscular than me. All my muscles were in my arms and my boobs. She had very short, shiny, brown hair with blond highlights that caught the sunlight, and she was wearing tight luminous blue cycling shorts and a white crop top, which accentuated her trim figure.

They began to play in a very light-hearted way, neither wanting to overplay their hand for fear of upsetting the other. The window frame created a kind of theatre and I was the audience. She shrieked and giggled and bounded around like a hare, very soon to be victorious. The older man hauled himself to his feet, already resigned to defeat.

I munched away, not even realising I was eating, being too involved in the game below, when she must have become aware of my watching her, because she looked up, straight at me, and waved. I gulped with embarrassment, as I was snooping, but she yelled, loudly.

'Come on down and join us, we need a fourth, then we girls can slaughter the men!'

I pushed the window open and smiled back. 'Can I join you tomorrow? I'm a bit fuzzy today.'

The men looked up and smiled in understanding, but she shouted, gaily, 'Too much wacky-backy, I'll bet!'

I waved and stepped back into the room, not wanting any more conversation, not today. Resuming my seat at the table, I was delighted to see how well I had done with my food. I poured myself a cup of tea and was startled by the knock at the door. As expected, it was Sam, but I didn't expect to see Dr Michael with her.

'Hello, Angelica, may we come in?' he said warmly.

'Hello, yes, of course, come in.' Why did he make me feel so flustered? Sam blew a quiet whistle and applauded as she cleared away my tray. 'Well done, see you later.' She nodded to Dr Michael and left the room.

He stood against the window, letting his gaze fall across my flowers and the unopened cards and the sun's wondrous patterns dancing on the walls. His eyes saw everything. I sat, nervously, on the edge of the bed, waiting for him to speak. (It is customary for the patient to fall for their shrink.)

'Angelica, we have been concerned about you. Can you remember anything that happened? Do you recollect going to see Ann Amery or returning here to your room?' He moved towards me and sat on the chair, facing me.

'Yes, I went to her room and immediately felt threatened by her. I became upset and felt dizzy. She went on and on at me until I couldn't breathe. I wanted to scream, but I couldn't do it. Then everything went black.'

I could feel the fear taking hold again as I watched my hands repeat the familiar journey on my legs. Dr Michael's hands covered mine to stop the movement and he said very quietly but forcefully, 'We are going to introduce you to some other patients here as we feel you have been in your room, alone, for far too long.'

'I can't, I'm not ready yet! I don't know anyone.' I felt the tears in my eyes and in my nose.

'Sh! Sh! Angelica, it will be fine, trust me.' He took a tissue from the box and handed it to me. 'I have devised a little programme for you and we shall see how you do. Tonight, Sam will not bring your supper to your room, but will take you to the dining room and introduce you to some other people. You will have a light meal and then come up to the day room, perhaps to watch some TV or…'

'No! No! I won't be able to do it!' I shouted.

'Yes, you will,' he said firmly and patted me on the hands.

He stood up and, looking down at me, said, 'Tomorrow you will thank me for this and we shall discuss your progress after the morning walk, when I shall show you your new itinerary for the week.' He walked to the door, then turned. He was about to take something from his pocket but thought better of it and said, 'You will do this today, Angelica, or tomorrow may be a very difficult day for us both, OK?' He smiled and left.

'Shit! Shit! Shit! Why now?' I had started to feel better and now I felt like *shit*.

Sam came into the room and sat next to me on the bed. 'Come on, Angelica, it's not so bad. Don't be afraid, I am coming with you and I'll stay as long as you need me there.'

I tried a watery smile but had no inclination to talk. For God's sake, where was my spirit?

It was now 5.45 p.m. and I had to get ready to go to supper. The evening meal was from 6 p.m. to 7 p.m., and it was served in the ground-floor dining room. I had read the times on the back of my door.

'I have to change my clothes, Sam, and have a wash.'

'I'll help you. Do you want to choose or can I?' She was rifling through my few outfits in the tiny wardrobe while I washed.

'You choose, I can't be bothered.' The shock of having to leave my room was getting to me.

Sam had picked a pretty, banana-yellow jersey dress – it just so happened to be my favourite colour – soft, supple and easy to wear. I let her slip it over my head and I caught my reflection in the mirror. All I saw was hollow eyes and fear.

'Oh! You look beautiful. You are such a cute lady. We must

get the sunshine in your smile as well as on the walls.' She spun me round and took my hand.

'Best foot forward! Let's go!' Sam opened the door and we stepped out into the corridor, together.

There was lots going on and the atmosphere was welcoming and not hostile. To the left were other doors and further down an open door with a light above it saying 'Nurses' Station'. The room at the end of the corridor had two glass swing doors, which were wedged open to show an array of comfortable chairs and coffee tables. This was the second-floor day room. Coming back down the corridor, on the opposite side, were three more doors, all closed. We turned right and walked towards the stairs. We passed four more doors, two on either side, then reached the stairwell. The corridor continued further, with doors on one side and windows on the other, overlooking a quadrangle, but we were going to go downstairs.

Voices and people were toing and froing like worker ants, some in white uniforms and some in daywear. I tried to look interested, but I felt like a blind person being led to water. Suddenly, a giggly laugh attacked my ears and there she was, blocking my path. The badminton lady grinned and said:

'Well, hello again. I'm Petra, inmate number 38, just next door to you. See you at dinner. Shan't be long!' And with that she trotted down the corridor and disappeared. She was going to be a fair-weather friend.

Sam looked surprised. 'When did you two meet?'

'Oh, we haven't actually met, I was watching her and some men trying to play badminton earlier and she looked up and waved to me.'

We were now on the ground floor and walking towards the entrance lobby, which was always kept locked and had to be accessed by a password. It kept the inmates in, and the outside world out. Just before the lobby we turned left into a recessed anteroom, which led into the dining room.

Sam squeezed my hand and pushed me forward. Groups of faceless people were sitting, eating and talking. It reminded me of a railway buffet car, too much noise and not enough seating. My mind was shutting down as I tried to stay focused on the self-service counter. I felt as if I was underwater as all the voices seemed muffled, then an explosion:

'Ugh!' My huge intake of breath was preceded by a hearty slap on the back.

'Hiya, said I'd be back!' Petra, oh, lovely Petra, snapped me out of my numbness.

Sam almost looked relieved at her intrusion.

'Oh, hi! I'm Angelica, I'm new here.' I sounded like an imbecile.

'Let's find a pew.' She then whispered loudly enough for Sam to hear, 'Get rid of your babysitter as soon as you can.' She grinned like a Cheshire cat.

She found us some seats and told anyone interested enough to listen that those seats were now reserved. What was she on? Her mood was so high it was dangerous! She was a human dynamo. At the counter, I chose a minute helping of cottage pie, with some carrots and a chocolate milk drink. I hadn't had one of those for years; it was Rebecca's favourite. Although I had eaten only a snack, a couple of hours ago, I was still not hungry. The smell of the food made me nauseous. Please let me get through this without embarrassing myself. We three sat down together, complete strangers sharing the same space, all with our selection of problems carefully disguised. Sam was brilliant. She made polite conversation and allowed me the time to come to terms with my first visit to the dining room.

Petra sparkled and smiled and ate very quickly. She consumed her double portion of pie, plus an apple and custard dessert, in the same time as I digested only a few mouthfuls. Did she do everything at breakneck speed, I wondered? Very soon she had finished and was gone, shouting, 'See ya!' over her shoulder.

I looked at Sam with incredulity. 'How does she eat so much so fast and not have chronic indigestion?'

'Do not worry about Petra, she has her own way of dealing with life. You must try to eat a little more and when you are ready we will go up to the day room so that I can introduce you to some other patients before they go to bed.'

'I think I have eaten enough tonight. I can't manage a dessert, so can we go now, please?' The room was too noisy and claustrophobic and I needed some space or to escape, but where would I go?

We walked back into the corridor and I remembered Archie at the desk. He looked up and smiled as I said hello, using his name.

'How are you tonight, Miss Angelica?'

'Oh, much better thank you, Archie.'

Was I any better? I couldn't work out what I was doing here or even how long I had been here. I just needed to sleep and not to have to think any more. Where had Angelica disappeared to? Who was this other person who had monopolised her body? Where had my life gone?

'Sam, before we go upstairs, I want to ask you something.'

'OK, ask away.'

'What have I been given to make me so listless and unbalance because at this moment I am lost in a fog and it's frightening.' I was clinging on to the stair rail for support and trying to look composed.

'Angelica, we have given you some mild tranquillisers to help you sleep and a small amount of antidepressant to control your state of mind. This will only be for a short while.' She smiled into my eyes and loosened my hands from the rail.

'Come along, up we go. There is nothing to be afraid of, at least not in here.'

She added the last remark as an afterthought. How much did she already know about me? She can't know anything! No one knows! Was it just a flippant remark? Do they know about the 'Voice' and his evil threats?

We had reached the second floor and were heading towards the day room, passing my door. I had the overwhelming urge to go in and close the door but the swing doors beckoned to me. The room was spacious and welcoming. A lady, wearing a bright floral housecoat, was pushing a trolley on which were an urn, cups and saucers and an array of beverages. Sam found us a pair of armchairs beside a coffee table, lit by an amber lamp. I sat down gratefully and accepted a cup of tea. The pleasant woman was asking me a question.

'Do you want sugar, lovey, or are you sweet enough?'

'Oh! Yes please, I do take two, thanks.' I helped myself and stirred the hot steaming liquid.

As I looked up, I recognised the two men from the badminton party, sitting at the far end of the room, with a chess set between them. They both looked across at me and smiled. The older chap pointed to the chess pieces and laughed.

'We are about as good at this as we are at badminton.' That was the cue to get up, walk over and introduce himself to me.

'My name is Harvey and that is Alex. I am pleased to meet you.'

He took my hand and for one brief moment I thought he was about to kiss it, instead he gave it a gentle pat. He was full of olde worlde charm.

'I am pleased to meet you too. I am Angelica.' I smiled up at him and across at Alex.

Harvey, reluctantly, returned to his chair and I looked around the gathering to see if Petra was there – she wasn't.

'I wonder where the woman from room 38 is? Do you think she'll be in for a drink, Sam?'

She shrugged her shoulders. 'She may come in. I think she listens to music in her room, sometimes. You will meet her tomorrow on the morning walk. I know she is booked to go.'

Gazing around me, I saw nothing of interest, so decided to retire to my room. Sam accompanied me to the doors and said goodnight. I nodded to Harvey and Alex and walked the few yards along the corridor to number 36. As I passed room 38, I heard Vivaldi playing, very quietly. It sounded serene and restful.

I opened my door, stepped inside, closed it and switched on the light. Leaning against the door, I surveyed the room. For a while, this was to be my sanctuary. It was a pretty room, with pale yellow walls and an ochre carpet. There were two windows at the corner of the room, almost creating a balcony. They would only open a couple of inches in order to protect the wayward patients. The curtains were apple-green, with buttercups dancing over them, and a matching throw covered the bed, which sat against the wall.

The bedside table, writing table and chair were in yew wood, which harmonised with the warmth of the room. To the right, the en suite was totally white, with lemon flowers on the shower curtain and a lemon-coloured shower cap hanging on a hook. I was aware of my head becoming clearer and my breath cooler. I suppose the drugs were wearing off. At a given time the night sister would come in to give me fresh water and some more tablets, so if I was going to do any writing, I had better do it now.

My diary and notebook were in the desk drawer. The diary had six blank pages, which I didn't want to think about, so I quickly returned it to the drawer. I turned the pages of the notebook to scan the lines of verse. These pages contained the very being of my soul, both tragic and funny. Perhaps one day someone would read them and understand me.

While transferring my latest poem, 'Despair', into the journal, Sophia, the night sister, knocked and entered. She was the only staff member I had met so far who was without a personality. If someone had said she was an android I would probably have believed it.

'Hello, Angelica, I'm glad to see that you are in the world of the living tonight.' She didn't appear to be ecstatic about it, but I accepted the comment.

'Would you take these tablets now, with the tumbler of water, and I shall then leave you in peace.' She placed the plastic, miniature cup containing the tablets in my hand and held out the tumbler of water for me to take.

'Thanks, Sophia.' I threw the tablets to the back of my throat and swallowed them with the water.

'I had better get ready for bed before these little monsters start to work.'

Her reply was non-existent. She obviously had other things on her mind. She took the tiny pot from me and left silently. I wondered if the night-duty staff were picked for their ability to float in and out quietly, without disturbing the patients. No, that can't be true, because Tania was a belly-load of chuckles and had been on duty at night. I finished the poem, had a quickie wash, changed into a nightie and jumped into bed.

Click. The top light was off and the bedside lamp on. I snuggled down under the duvet, hugging my pillow. I could still hear Vivaldi, *The Four Seasons*, gently playing through the walls. Pictures of Sean and Rebecca and Jason journeyed through my mind. I hadn't seen or spoken to them for a week. Do they miss me? Please miss me like I do you! Poor Sean is probably still trying to make sense of the prostrate figure of his mum on the bathroom floor. What was it he said? – 'Mum, you sounded like a wild bird who had been caught in a trap.' He was so frightened. He saw my inert body, mumbling and wailing. I still remember the pain in my head and the scream that exploded from my mouth, continuing without need for breath, like a siren, seeking every dark corner in which to expel its strident wail of grief. I must forget the tragedy of that day and hope that they could too, otherwise I really may go crazy. Forget the harsh thoughts and the menacing telephone voice and that sardonic face in the black balaclava.

Chapter Four

Sink into dreamscape. Go where only those invited could play a part in my fantasy – the Comfort Zone.

I was back at the hydro. The door opened into the rear lobby and Si peered out, surreptitiously.

'The coast is clear. Let's go, Angel.'

We ran quietly down the corridor towards the archway, which led into the therapy studios and the pool. At this time on a Sunday, the therapy areas would be hushed in silence. The therapists worked a six-day week and the on-call doctor would have seen his last client long ago.

Sunday was transition day for the weekly guests. If leaving, they were gone by midday, and those arriving came from 2 p.m. onwards. The majority arrived around 6 p.m. and went straight into dinner, like having the Last Supper. As luck would have it, we had the turquoise water of the pool to ourselves.

Simon shed his clothes on a poolside lounger and dove commando-style into the water.

'Come on, slow coach. I want to taste your nectar mixed with chlorine.' I guiltily read the sign above me as I lowered myself, step by step, into the pool – PLEASE SHOWER BEFORE ENTERING THE POOL – Oh, well, it's only love juice, I'm not covered in oil.

Si tugged at my undies. 'What have you got these on for? There's no one around.' With that, he turned me upside down, pulling off my panties in one movement. So much for the graceful entrance of the swan, I now resembled a choking chicken.

'You bastard! I'll get you for that!'

His arms thrashed the water, with five foot two inches of human torpedo tearing along behind. As he reached the wall, I expected him to stop, but he somersaulted in the turn and disappeared.

I stopped, treading water, only to be held from beneath by a human octopus. Simon's mouth, like a limpet, had found my labia and was ravishing me like a shark. Heavens above! I could not move. I didn't want to move. In a split second my body had been transformed into a love machine, its juice being drained by a water demon. What an acrobat! He must have been standing on the bottom.

His grip on my thighs released as he exploded out of the water with a shriek. 'I have just tasted the ambrosia of the gods and I shall die in peace.'

I swam around to see his gorgeous face and convulsed in laughter. He was wearing my knickers on his head. We clung to each other and sucked face until our mouths were as red as ripe berries. Slowly, making our way to the steps, we heard a gentle coughing from above. The lighting was so dim that we couldn't see who it was.

'Well, well, well, Cupid definitely shot his arrow up your arse, Simon, old man!' he chortled.

'George, you sneaky old fart. How long have you been there?' Simon was holding his masterpiece as he rose out of the water and I struggled into my knickers to retrieve some of my modesty.

'Long enough to know yours *definitely* don't shrink in the water!'

We all three screwed up with laughter, holding our sides. Somehow, it helped the situation and I no longer felt quite so embarrassed. Even the jacuzzi seemed to gurgle with mirth.

'Well, little lady, I shall look at you in a new light from now on. I think I shall crown you, Andromeda, a true goddess from the deep.' Making a royal flourish he handed me my clothes and we went by way of the back stairs to our rooms to dress for dinner.

George left us on the first landing. I kissed Simon and found my way to my room on the second floor. Simon whistled his way onward and upwards to the top floor, two stairs at a time.

Room 56 was unique because it was built over a huge curve in the original stairwell of this fabulous Georgian residence. This meant that the four-foot bed was encased in a low-domed ceiling and surrounded by a one-foot wooden edging on three sides. Making the bed was extremely difficult. There were two gothic-shaped doors opening into a cupboard space and one other door which led into the en-suite shower room. The furnishings were elegant and minimalist. The only window was slightly dimpled and overlooked the roof of the pool below.

I loved this room. It was my dreamscape, a pleasure-dome on earth. All mine for four days of escapism. I put my clothes and toiletries away and dialled Jeannie in number 60. After a few rings, I was about to replace the receiver, when a breathless Jeannie answered.

'Where the hell have you been? I've been ringing for fifteen minutes. Chas said you got here ages ago.'

'Slow down, Jen, I'm here now. I just went for a swim with Simon and George.'

'Liar! Liar! I saw George and he said that he would go and find you.'

'OK! OK! I lied. I was making erotic, exotic love with Simon, naked in the pool!'

'Don't be daft! You weren't, were you?'

We both sniggered, but for totally different reasons.

'George said we are meeting for tonic cocktails in the coffee room at 7 p.m. I'll tap on your door at 6.45 p.m. Hey, honey, are you OK? Did Mike bring you?'

'Yes to the first and yes to the second and – no comment for anything else – ugh! See you later.' Click. She had disappeared from the line. I dropped my clothes on the floor and studied my nakedness in the mirror. How different my reflection, now, this minute, to any day in the past year. Was it my imagination, or did I look sexy and beautiful and so alive? Or was it because I was sexually revitalised and the animal within me was electrified and waiting to feed?

Aloud, I exclaimed. 'Oh, Goddess Andromeda, your shower awaits!' With a wry smile, I stepped behind the curtain to allow the cascade of water to warm me.

I awoke to another balmy summer day. What time was it? 8.15 a.m. This was the first time that I could remember, since my arrival at the Abbey, that I had woken refreshed and not nauseous. I lay, listening to my heartbeat, trying to work out how many days

I had been here – possibly seven, but who's counting? I wallowed in the memory of my wakening dream and was wonderfully aroused. Who needs a man when, in dreams, I can have what I want, without repercussions or any chance of deceit.

What had Dr Michael said? Today I would be given my weekly programme of rehabilitation to the real world, one step at a time. As I got up and started to wash and dress, the unease grew. Was I supposed to go down to breakfast, alone? Should I pull the cord and ask for help? Being asleep was so easy; there were no decisions to make.

I was having a conversation with myself but it was in my head. If I go outside now someone may be passing my room, or I could go to the nurses' station. I did it! I opened the door and turned left and there was my answer, right next door at room number 38.

I knocked once and the door opened, just a crack. Petra was standing there, bleary-eyed and dishevelled – no bounce – no sparkle – no recognition!

'Yes? What?' She rubbed her eyes.

'Sorry, Petra. It's me, Angelica, from number 36. I thought we could go down to breakfast together.' I was perplexed; she just stared at me.

'No, not now.' She shut the door. I was alone again.

Sam was standing by the nurses' station, watching the performance without interfering. She walked towards me, holding out her hand.

'There is no easy way of finding out people's frailties, Angelica. Sometimes one has to jump in and swim. You see, Petra, like you, is not always what she seems.'

'Sam, you are talking in Chinese! I don't know what you are on about! I realise Petra has problems, otherwise, why would she be here?'

'Perhaps we could go down to breakfast together,' she said gently. 'Petra will probably join us later.' We began to walk.

'Actually, I was in two minds whether to knock on Petra's door or to find you, but attempting to be strong I chose the first option,' I said as an explanation.

'That's fine, Angelica. You have conquered one fear, so allow me to approach the next hurdle with you.'

We walked towards the stairs and descended to the ground floor. I took a sideways glance at Sam and wondered how she kept her mane of hair so neatly coiled – there was so much of it.

'I'll take it down one day and you can watch me put it up.' She grinned mischievously.

'How did you know what I was thinking?'

'Just put it down to sympathetic telepathy.'

This little Chinese sprite intrigued me more each time I saw her.

We arrived at the breakfast room and Sam gave me an enquiring look.

'Just today, please.' I voiced my answer.

The French doors were open and the adjacent table was free. We turned our cups the right way up and I stood a teaspoon in mine to show that the table was occupied.

The sight of food still churned my stomach and the smell of cooking was even worse, but at barely eight stone I knew I couldn't afford to lose any more weight, so I must eat.

'Why not try some fresh fruit and muesli, with a little yoghurt.' My little telepathic sprite offered the suggestion.

'I shall go for that.' I pointed to the pieces of kiwi fruit, grapes and raspberries. 'And I shall have Jordan's Hawaiian mixture with a vanilla yoghurt on top. Are you having something, or have you eaten?'

'I love your choice and probably would have had similar, but I had my breakfast at 7 a.m. I'll join you and take some tea.' She spoke to the boy behind the counter to order a pot of tea for two.

'Do you have a preference, Angelica?'

'Yes, could we have Earl Grey, if that's OK with you?'

'That's fine!'

Sam ordered the tea and we sat at our table. There must have been twelve to fourteen people dotted around, some on their own and others in groups. I didn't recognise anyone, so I returned my attention to the dish of cereal.

The French doors opened out onto a small cobbled courtyard, which was of the original paving. The stones were rounded and dimpled through centuries of labourers' feet and horses' hooves. Directly opposite was an ancient building that used to be the coach house, with two huge, black, painted doors, large enough to house a Georgian coach and pair, I should think.

Sam followed my gaze and remarked, 'That building has been dramatically renovated and reconstructed and is now the occupational therapy art studio.'

'Isn't it wonderful that they have left the original facade. I can imagine what it was like a hundred years ago,' I said dreamily.

'Angelica, you really are a sad romantic.' She winced, as she wanted to take back her choice of words.

'Sorry, sorry, I didn't mean to call you sad – it was a stupid adjective to use.'

'I won't take offence by it, that is exactly what I am – A Sad Romantic –but at least I have managed a whole twenty-four hours without tears.' I gave her a watery smile and finished my cereal.

The waitress delivered our tea and Sam accepted the 'mother' responsibility and poured. The courtyard clock struck 9 a.m. and as if by magic the room was suddenly alive with people, like a swarm of bees. Harvey and Alex sauntered in with another young man in tow who looked as lost as me.

'Good morning, Angelica,' Harvey said with a bold smile.

'Ditto, Angelica,' from Alex who was taking a huge mug of coffee to another table and concentrating on missing stray bodies and feet and bags.

The young blond-haired man looked directly at me and locked eyes. They were searching, wild and steel-blue. He didn't blink and neither of us smiled, but we automatically knew we would have a special bond.

He sighed, deeply, and looked away, only to look back immediately.

'I know you are Angelica because Harvey has told me two hundred times already. He's crazy, you know. Well, I am Iain, nice to meet you at last.' He pulled a lock of his hair, like a naval salute and almost grinned. I liked him.

'Might see you on the walk? It's round the shrubbery today. Who knows, tomorrow they might let us walk on the common – on leads, of course!' The grin was shallow as he turned towards the servery. Our conversation was at an end.

I sighed aloud as I concentrated on my cup. 'He was very

strung out. I wouldn't offend him in a hurry!'

'Angelica, you are very perceptive, but you must try to focus on yourself and not be too interested in the grievances of others. Are we finished? Let's go and I shall show you where to meet Joanna for the walk.'

We made our way through the tables and I said, 'Bye for now,' to Harvey's group.

'I need the loo and to change into trainers. Shall we go upstairs, first?'

'No, you go, I'll wait here by the desk as I need to speak to Archie.'

I hurried up two flights to the second floor and hesitated before going into my room. Should I knock on Petra's door or not? No, I can see her later. I don't want to miss the walk and she should be there too. I freshened up, went to the loo, put on some lippy and changed my shoes. My reflection in the mirror looked different today. It was almost a look of awareness, rather than emptiness. I realised then that I had escaped the intake of pills this morning.

The clock was saying 9.25 a.m., so I had five minutes to get to the lobby. As I approached Archie's desk, I saw the retreating figure of Dr Michael. He turned into the IC unit and was gone. Sam was studying some notes and smiled as she saw me.

'All ready for the walk? I think the others are waiting in the breakfast room. When you get back, come to room 10, just along there and I shall be with Dr Michael. He has your weekly programme and would like to discuss it with you.'

'OK, I'll be there about 11.30 a.m.' We parted company and I entered the breakfast room.

Take a deep breath and turn the corner, I said to myself. So I did. There was a gaggle of people in one corner and a few standing by the open French doors. I headed towards the faces I knew.

'Hi there, Angelica. Good of you to join us.'

'Oh! Hello, Harvey, Alex, Iain. May I walk with you this morning?' I remembered this curdling feeling in my gut when I first entered the playground so many years ago.

Before Harvey could step in and take control, Iain gave me his arm and said. 'Milady, I am at your disposal,' mimicking the chauffeur in *Thunderbirds* with me as Lady Penelope.

We all laughed at Harvey's dropped jaw and, thankfully, he joined in too. 'I am truly honoured, thank you, Parker!' I bobbed a mock curtsey and we followed the small groups of people into the courtyard. 'Thunderbirds are go!' he cried.

Once Joanna had ascertained that we were all on her list, we walked through the yard along a narrow cobbled path, overhung by blue wisteria, and arrived at a wooden gate which led into the shrubbery.

Iain and I walked along side by side, still linking arms. How strange that two people who had barely spoken a dozen words between us appeared to be such comfortable friends. Is this what happens when we are in need of comfort and human touch – two lost souls holding on to a lifeline?

Like the tale of Noah's ark, two by two we passed through the gate into a field as large as a football pitch, subdivided by a maze of prickly hedges. In each small plot were rows of neatly tended fruit bushes, raspberry canes, runner beans climbing poles in the shape of wigwams and lines of green vegetables.

At the very centre was a small loggia with fruit baskets piled high along one side. As we approached the loggia, Joanna grouped us together.

'I hope you are all in the mood for picking! As you can see, we are surrounded by strawberries, just aching to be picked, so grab a basket and fill it up!'

'This is like a school outing.' I felt the giggles coming on.

'The little ones are the sweetest!' Iain said as he took up his basket and was suddenly on all fours, pretending to sniff them out like a bloodhound. Harvey and Alex wouldn't be outdone, so they did likewise.

I watched them play, like three performing seals, it was so refreshing. Of course, for each one in the basket one had to be consumed. It was compulsory.

Joanna came beside me, laughing at their antics. 'Isn't it great to be outside on such a lovely day?'

'Oh, yes. It makes me grateful for being alive,' I said, taking a huge breath of air. Why did I say that?

'I'm sorry you haven't been too well since your first walk, Angelica. How are you settling in now?'

I had to swallow hard before answering as the numbness started to creep behind my eyes and around my neck. What was happening? One question and I was panicking! I found my voice and replied, 'This is not real! It's all just a game! I don't know why I am here with these strangers. I want to be at home with my kids.'

I had tears in my eyes, but I wasn't crying. Joanna took my basket from me and led me to a seat, quietly.

'I shouldn't have interrupted you, I'm sorry. You seemed to be enjoying the company.'

'Yes, I am.' I was in control again. 'I think I have just forgotten how to have fun and not feel guilty about it. All of this seems so irresponsible. Grown adults acting like juvenile delinquents!'

'Yahoo! Yahoo! I have won!' Iain yelled aloud. Everyone was clapping and laughing. Joanna tipped her basket into mine. 'It's OK, no one noticed,' she said, winking.

'OK, smarty-pants! But I bet Angelica has as much as you.' The challenge was made. Every basket was taken to the loggia and weighed. Surprisingly, there wasn't much of a difference between each one. Harvey bounded over, like an overgrown puppy, with what he thought was a great suggestion.

'It's Wimbledon fortnight, so why don't we have our own strawberries and cream garden party?' There was an overwhelming silence. 'Well, that went down like a lead balloon, old chap!' Alex said, while slapping him on the back. 'Why don't we take these baskets back to the kitchen and ask the chef to make us a superb trifle for tonight and tomorrow.' Joanna suggested. Then there rang out a chorus of – tomorrow and tomorrow and tomorrow, as we all joined in.

Thankfully, my small panic attack had passed unnoticed and I was on the rails again. The strawberries were unceremoniously piled into an antiquated wheelbarrow and someone was elected to guide it back to the kitchen. Iain regained his position by my side and we ambled our way through the vegetation, back towards the Abbey.

'You threw a wobbly back there, didn't you?' he said, without looking at me. He didn't wait for an answer but carried on, as I watched my feet.

'I know you have only been here for about a week, it takes time to acclimatise. I've been here for ten days and am only just getting the hang of things.'

I thought, Parker to the rescue, and it was working. I pushed my hand through his arm and gave it a squeeze. It was muscular and strong. 'I'm not sure who I am any more, like a yoyo on a piece of string. There is so much crap going round in my head and I can't stop visualising the most awful happenings. I suppose it's the same for everyone!' I looked sideways at him for a reaction.

He nodded, saying, 'Just take things easy. Come and find me if you want to talk.' I had found a friend.

The gate was ahead of us. 'After you, Milady, Penelope.'

'Thank you, Parker,' and we passed through together, laughing. Harvey and Alex came up behind us. Harvey dropped his head between us saying. 'You two look very conspiratorial, you'll have people talking!' 'Don't take any notice, Angelica, he's just feeling left out.' Alex gave us a rueful grin, simultaneously knocking Harvey off the pathway.

We arrived at the courtyard and everyone disbursed in all directions. Alex suggested a coffee in the lounge for anyone who hadn't a pressing engagement, so we walked along the corridor together.

'The Four Musketeers unite!' Iain offered a new role for us.

I was about to climb the stairs when Alex suggested that we use the downstairs lounge, which he said had a more secluded ambience.

'I see, I see, we have been dining on dictionary-speak!' Harvey teased him.

'Whatever!' And Alex walked through the doors, arming himself with a steaming pot of coffee. Harvey was obviously wearing thin.

This room was identical in shape and position to the second floor lounge, but the decor was less welcoming. The lounge above was gold and amber, full of warmth, where this one was in blue and decidedly cold. I preferred the upstairs, this room gave me the creeps. I shuddered, involuntarily, noticed only by Iain.

'What's up, Doc? Are you cold?'

'No, just a strange shiver. I probably need caffeine, that's all.'

'Coffee with two sugars, madam?' Alex handed the mug to me.

'How did you know, or was it a calculated guess?'

'I'd like to say it was telepathy but the truth is I was being over-observant last night.'

I looked puzzled, not realising the implication, but accepted it.

'Last night, you remember, in the lounge upstairs!'

I thought back and it twigged. 'Ah, yes! Sherlock – the cup of tea from the trolley – well, thanks, anyway.'

I walked towards the doors, overlooking the lawns, sipping my coffee. It was truly a wonderful outlook. Then two precocious animals caught my eye.

'Oh, look! Aren't they gorgeous squirrels? They are playing with the leaves.' I was captivated.

'Bloody vermin, if you ask me!' Harvey retorted.

'Well, I'm not, you cold creature, they're sweet.' He looked hurt. 'Sorry, Harvey, I didn't mean that. I'm sure you are just as loveable as those furry things.'

We linked arms and watched through the windows.

'Crumbs! It's 11.30 a.m. I must go. Do you know where room 10 is, anyone?'

'Yep! Right next door, on your right. The psyche room!' Iain added with a grimace.

'Best of luck. Go in peace!' Alex made the sign of the cross. I left them chatting, walked to room 10 and knocked.

The door opened and Sam stood to one side to let me pass. Dr Michael was sitting in a high-backed leather chair, positioned in a deep alcove, surrounded by windows.

'Hello, Angelica, how was your walk?' He stood, gracefully, took my hand and led me towards the leather chaise opposite his chair and I sat, obediently.

'The walk was enterprising, I think we picked enough straw-berries for despatch to the local store,' I said with false gaiety.

Sam had resumed her seat at the desk and was writing notes. Dr Michael was sitting with his hands in his lap, gazing out of the window. He seemed to be collecting his thoughts.

I broke the silence by saying, 'This room must be almost directly below mine as the view is mostly the same, only at a different angle.'

I was waffling to combat the silence, then relaxed and looked out of the window too. There was no danger here.

'Angelica, how long have you been at the Abbey?' His look was indulgent as if he was playing for time.

'About a week, I believe. I don't seem to have any concept of time. I have spent long periods sleeping, as you are well aware!'

He looked startled at my sharp response.

'Are you angry with me?'

'Of course not! I am frustrated with me because I have got lost somewhere and I have no comprehension of when, why or how. I am here with complete strangers, who all have the same... look!'

'And what – look – is that?'

'I don't know, sort of zombified.'' I suddenly laughed out loud and it surprised all three of us.

'The whole episode is so funny, it's tragic. I don't know how I can accept who I am and I am so pissed off with crying and nightmares and being afraid and not being me any more that I want to scream and scream and scream until it goes away!'

I was now agitated, clammy and trembling. Calmly, Dr Michael knelt beside me and handed me a piece of crumpled paper, which he took from his pocket.

'Do you recognise this poem, Angelica?'

I flattened the paper and read the first word – 'Despair'.

'No, no, no, no, no!' Was I screaming or was I crying?

'The important line is "The scream has not awoken it lurks somewhere below".' He read the line and pulled my hands away from my face.

'Don't fight it any more – *scream* – this is your repressed anger. Let it go!'

'I can't do it now! I am so tired!' I was trying to get myself under control.

'Please lie down on the couch – be calm now!' He retreated from me.

I lay down and my breathing became slower. Sam was motionless, behind the desk, still writing, with her head down.

My outburst hadn't moved her; she didn't even look my way. I felt alone, so desperately alone.

Dr Michael was seated back in his armchair and was inspecting a small tape recorder in his hand.

'I need to have some information from you, Angelica, and this is the easiest way to remember it. Is this OK with you?'

'Yes, I suppose so.' Just acquiesce, I told myself. Go with the flow.

Chapter Five

Click. The machine was activated. Dr Michael was now my shrink. He turned to the machine and spoke very clearly, watching the coloured dials bounce at the sound of his voice.

'This is the first recorded interview with Mrs Angelica Reeves. The time is 12 noon. Before we begin, would you like a glass of water, Angelica?'

'Yes, please.' Thinking a vodka and tonic would be better.

Sam poured the water and placed the glass in my hand, giving it a gentle squeeze.

'What led up to your breakdown and instigated the writing of that poem? How did you become so very sad? Take your time, we shall go as slowly as you wish.' His voice was almost musical, it floated through me like a balm.

'I remember:

'It was early, about 7 a.m. John was sitting on the bed, his shoulders bowed and there was the telephone receiver in his hand. I asked him who was on the line. He said it was the Samaritans. He wanted to take his own life and needed someone to stop him. I looked at him but didn't really see him. He could no longer intimidate me – I was numb and had no words to comfort him. I had already died inside and could only hang up the phone and tell him that everything would be OK. I would stand by him for the sake of us all and he must try to be strong. I backed away from him in disbelief. We were strangers locked in our own house of horrors. I went downstairs, not knowing what to do, when the phone rang. It was his mother, she was weeping and wailing, saying I must support him and stay with him even though he had been stupid and almost wrecked our lives. If I left him she would want to end her life. Die! Olé! Everyone wants to *die*!

'I replaced the receiver and turned to go upstairs. The noises of the house had disappeared and I was walking in a dream. I remember going to my bureau and taking out my notebook. If I wrote down how I was feeling, I would be OK. My vision started to blacken and I had to hold the walls on the landing and fumble my way to the bathroom. Where had everyone gone? I needed help and no one was around. Something in my stomach heaved and I shrank down by the toilet as I thought I was going to be sick. Where were the children? Please don't let them see me like this! There was no air to breathe, I was dying, I couldn't fight it.

'Then *it* happened. My neck and chest constricted and this horrendous noise erupted from me. It was hollow and echoed in my throat like a ship's siren. I knew it was happening, but I couldn't stop it.

'Then the floods came – I cried and cried and cried and the water just kept flowing. I tried to hide behind the toilet because I was out of control but the space was too small. The crying ceased, followed by sobbing that seemed to tear my head apart and then I had the most evil spirit pull my body in two and I was screaming – screaming – *screaming*!'

'There, there, there. That's the worst over.' He was cradling me and I was wrapped in his arms on the chaise. My face and his trousers were wet from my tears as I had lain across his lap. Dr Michael's face was a picture of sadness and empathy and I knew that he would help me to find my way back.

Sam was talking to someone at the door. 'No, it's fine now. Really! Yes! She was a little overwrought, but is now fine.'

She closed the door and resumed her writing at the desk, not once looking in my direction. It was not her role to take any part in the first Awakening of Anger – the bonding was between Dr Michael and me.

He disentangled himself from my grasp and sat back in his chair, looking deeply into my eyes. 'Have some water now. We shall not go any further today as I think the ordeal would be detrimental to your healing process.' His understanding enveloped me like a soft blanket.

'I must look like a frog in a wig,' I said lamely.

'You are truly an amazing woman. In grief you still manage to see the funny side.'

I grimaced as my head was drumming.

Click. The machine was deactivated. He was studying my face and shaking his head in disbelief. There was a low cough and Sam spoke quietly to him, not wanting to break his train of thought.

'Excuse me, Dr Michael. It is 12.30 p.m. and you asked me to remind you of your next appointment.'

He smiled at her and thanked her.

'Now, Angelica, what are we to do with you?' He looked thoughtful.

Sam then interceded with an impromptu suggestion. 'If you agree, Dr Michael, I could have lunch with Angelica – perhaps a small picnic in the gardens, somewhere where she can wind down?'

'What do you think, Angelica, is that a good idea?' he asked hopefully.

'As long as I don't have to attend any classes this afternoon. I am exhausted.'

'No, it's Friday, and your programme begins on Monday, so this afternoon you can rest and Sam will be on call if you need her.'

'OK, Sam. I'll break bread with you, but only if you promise to let your hair down!' We both smiled, a secret shared. Dr Michael looked confused and relieved at the same time.

'Sam has your programme written out for you, so I shall see you Monday, Wednesday and Friday.' He was getting up from his chair and his forehead was furrowed. He walked towards me looking very pensive.

'Normally, I would let you go home for the weekend, but you are not ready yet. I shall phone your husband to break the news.'

I sighed with relief. I couldn't face anyone yet, especially John.

'But, there is always a but! I will suggest that he comes here, for a visit, perhaps tomorrow, yes?' I was stunned. What would we talk about? A million things were whirling through my brain. What if they didn't want to see me! What if Becca and Sean were too ashamed to come?

'What if they are embarrassed and too awkward to come?' I was panicking.

'Of course they will want to see you, they love and miss you,' he said, reassuringly.

My head was dazed and my mind bruised. I stood and walked to the door where Sam was waiting. 'I'll have some lunch prepared for us in a picnic basket and I shall meet you in fifteen minutes by the reception desk.'

'Go to your room to refresh yourself, Angelica, and enjoy a peaceful afternoon.' Dr Michael touched my cheek and cuffed me under the chin. He turned away and returned to the desk where he began to make a phone call. I was dismissed and still had this fear of rejection.

I walked down the corridor towards the stairs and Iain popped out from nowhere. He took my arm and I felt warmed by the comfort and support. 'We heard you next door, that was a tough ordeal for you. It will get better, believe me.' He gently squeezed my arm. 'Do you need some company? I have a degree in mimicry and jokes.' I had to smile. 'That's the way, Milady.' He was my champion.

'Iain, I have to join Sam for lunch, to have a cooling-down period, but I would love to join you for dinner, and the others too.' I didn't want to get too familiar, knowing it would be only too simple to lose myself in the attention he was giving me. Wrong time, wrong place, wrong man.

'That's great, see you around 6 p.m. in the dining room.' He did the cute salute and left me at my door.

I hadn't seen or heard anything from room 38. I wondered why Petra hadn't joined us for the walk. Perhaps she had gone home early for the weekend? Anyway, I didn't have time to enquire, only enough to wash my face and grab my baseball cap to protect my head and put on my sandals.

Sam was still wearing her whites, but had taken off her belt and loosened her hair. It hung down her back almost to her bottom in a thick braid. She swung a basket towards me. 'We have a picnic fit for a queen!'

We walked out onto the patio, which preceded the lawns. Iain and Alex were sitting on a swing seat, both gazing into space. Alex looked across as we passed. 'Are you OK now, Angelica? We were quite concerned!'

'Yes, thanks, Alex. Sorry to have caused you to worry.' I said the words, but still felt quite numb. The answer was more instinct than emotion. Iain looked up and nodded, two lost sheep waiting to be rounded up by Harvey.

We sauntered across the lawns, heading for the shade of one of the huge oaks. There was hardly a noise to disturb the country park setting, just a faint rustling of leaves from the tepid breeze and the call of a bird. Sam threw a blanket down in the shade and opened the basket. Piece by piece she laid out an immaculate fare, even down to condiments and napkins.

'I am impressed, I can't believe that this is provided by the Abbey,' I said in disbelief.

'Of course you are right, the hamper is mine and I filled it myself from what was available in the kitchen. Do you approve?'

'I am speechless. Presentation is the key to titillate the taste buds.' That was my truth.

'Ooh la la! What praise!' She twinkled with pleasure.

I lay on the blanket, watching the swaying of the branches above me, laden with thousands of leaves tussling with each other and sheltering their rich crop of acorns. Was it any wonder that the squirrels delighted in this habitat? Snapshots of the past hour jumped across my vision to mar this tranquil setting, but I would slowly learn to deal with it. Hopefully, my mind would repair itself sooner rather than later. One thought was real.

'I'm starving, Sam. Shall we begin?' Sam was perched on her folded legs, ready to pounce. I rolled on to my side and retrieved a plate, napkin and leg of chicken. 'Bon appetit, Sam, my little Chinese sprite.'

'Tell me, what is a sprite?' She looked intrigued.

'Sprites are mischievous fairies, full of fun but very intelligent.'

'I am extremely flattered and embarrassed.' She was blushing, which was charming.

'Why are you embarrassed?'

'Angelica, my duty as your key nurse is to become your guide and your support for a while and to use my knowledge to understand you. I believe that you are a very spiritual lady with immense intuitive powers and have probably eased the burdens of many people by giving of yourself unreservedly. I have to make you aware of this and tell you to *stop* for a while, because you have to heal yourself. I am embarrassed because I feel humbled when I read your reports and see how strong you are. It has taken a toll on your well-being, but you are a survivor.' She looked at me directly while she talked and used her whole body to express herself.

'Thank you for that. I didn't realise you had undertaken so much research on my account. Have they spoken to John? How much do they already know?'

'We know some of your background, but in order for you to go forward you must release your anger by writing it out, speaking it out or using creative artwork to expel the torment.'

'So this is why we are out here today?' I gave her a knowing look.

'In one word, yes!' She looked at ease now.

'Where do we begin?' I asked, logically.

'We have already begun. I have admitted to you that we know a little but we must know the whole truth to create the picture.'

I sat up and crossed my legs to ponder what she had said. We both enjoyed our meal and pretended that the sparkling water was vintage champagne. My fantasy world always won over reality.

It was nearly 2 p.m. and the sun was high overhead. Apart from us, and the sleeping squirrels, there were only three other people in the grounds. One person was stretched out on a bench with a newspaper across his face and the two other people were women who were sitting near the patio under a parasol. The sun was a ball of orange in a clear blue sky and it was extremely hot. I thought of the kids, larking around in the pool with their friends, trying to out-swim or out-dive each other.

I knew the time was fast approaching for us to talk. Something I was not relishing. I was exhausted and finding the exposing of my intimate thoughts degrading.

'I sense that you are apprehensive, Angelica. Please try to be at ease, I just need to go over your programme for the next week and then I shall leave you to relax for the rest of the day.' She pulled out a timesheet, with each day allocated to a different therapy.

'Will I still be able to have my walk with Joanna every day?'

'Yes, that won't interfere with the OT programme from Monday to Friday.'

'What happens at weekends?' I needed confirmation that we were expected to go home at weekends. My kids were as essential to me as water; the fear was seeing John.

'Except for this weekend, when you are remaining here, we hope you will be at home with your family.'

'When will I be told if I am to see John and the twins tomorrow?' I was sick to my stomach when I thought of the ordeal ahead of me.

'We should know by dinner tonight. I shall let you know, personally, before I leave.' She fidgeted to make herself more comfortable.

I sat and hugged my knees. I didn't have to relive painful memories right now.

'Before we begin I want you to take this one tablet to help you to relax.' She handed me a little blue pill.

'The magic Smartie,' I said as I swallowed it.

She then began to read aloud. 'Monday is art therapy in the courtyard studio from 11.30 to 12.30. Your afternoon is free until 4 p.m., when you will see Dr Michael. Tuesday is art therapy, again, from 11.30 to 12.30.'

'Who takes art therapy, would I know the person?' I butted in.

'Yes, it is Ann Amery, she is the OT coordinator. She takes art and self-awareness classes.'

I grimaced without realising and an icy shiver laced my spine.

'Do you have a problem with Ann?' she asked openly.

'First impressions are probably insanely overstated, but she was cold and belittling. I was quite distressed by her stark approach, she made me feel insecure.' I couldn't have been more honest.

'I see. Ann is the head of OT and has a very direct approach. You will get used to it.' The comment was made more like a statement than an explanation.

She continued with the agenda.

Tuesday afternoon was an open invitation to yoga for beginners, horse riding or free choice of exercise. Wednesday had a self-awareness class from 11.30 to 12.30 and Dr Michael at 4 p.m. Thursday would be meditation or yoga from 11.30 to 12.30 and after lunch there would be an outing to the local sports centre.

Friday was another self-awareness class from 11.30 to 12.30, followed by two hours of pottery or needlecraft from 2 to 4 p.m., and then to Dr Michael, when he would assess if I should go home for the weekend.

My head was spinning. The dread of confronting the source of my pain was looming. Was this paranoia? The prickles started to march down my arms and I was finding it difficult to swallow. The dam was about to burst again but I *must not* let it happen. Evidently the inner turmoil was etched on my face. I could hide nothing from Sam.

'Take a deep breath and transfer your thoughts to music and dancing. Imagine yourself doing what rocks your soul. You are the whirling gypsy on that African shore. Let the image take you.' Sam's voice charmed me and the visualisation was working. She seemed to know who I wanted to be.

'Lay down now and sleep. You are perfectly safe here. Indulge your fantasies and let your inner self rebuild.' Her voice drifted away and once again I was in my dreamscape – the Comfort Zone.

Chapter Six

It was a delicious feeling as the soft warm water cascaded over my body, washing away the traces of chlorine and Aramis. I was exhilarated. I stepped out of the shower and wrapped myself in the thick towelling robe. With deft fingers I curled my hair to let it fall around my face and into the nape of my neck, then a touch of mascara, creamy bronze lipstick and to complete a fine mist of Anaïs Anaïs.

I chose an ivory, woollen, ankle-length dress, exposing my shoulders for, hopefully, the desired effect, and to complete the ensemble, silk panties and cream shoes. Voilà! Je suis prêt. One twirl in the mirror and it was time to meet Jeannie.

I rapped on her door and she sprung out at me like a jack-in-the-box.

'You hussy! What's the juicy gossip!' She was anticipating the gory details.

'You are incorrigible, Jeannie! As if I would divulge my lusty adventure to you.' We laughed our way down to meet the others.

'How are things with Mike? Any improvement?'

'Oh! He makes me sick! One minute he is going to change and his illicit goings-on will stop and the next minute I am a dried-up old hag and he *has* to seek solace elsewhere.' She almost spat the last words. She shrugged her shoulders and we bounced into the coffee lounge to be greeted by:

'At last! We are now complete!' Queen Hermione twirled her hand at us in regal salute.

There was a tray of non-alcoholic cocktails to be taken at leisure, all full of fruit, umbrellas and multicoloured liquid. I chose one called Subtle Surprise and Jeannie took Rumbustious Red.

Simon was in deep conversation with George and broke away just to say, 'Hiya, Jeannie, long time no see.' He slid a tongue across his lips, sent in my direction. Discreet, Simon was not! We walked over to Vanessa, who was looking stunning in a black Versace creation.

'Vanessa, you look a million dollars!'

'Thank you sweetie, it cost about that too!'

'Nice that you can afford it. How is the latest book coming along?' I thought I would ask her before she went into minute detail about her current project.

'All finished, sweetie, and at the publishers.'

'Another best-seller, I expect!' Jeannie wanted to put in her twopenn'orth.

Vanessa smiled broadly and spanned her hands heavenwards. 'God willing, it will be successful.'

Just a touch OTT, but one had to admit that she was amazingly brilliant at sewing a story together. Hermione had been chatting to Susie and was now bored stiff and ready to eat.

'Simon, you delicious man, please escort me to the dining room!'

'I would be honoured, Ma'am.' He swept the floor with one hand and gallantly proffered his arm. What a colourful couple they made, the Queen and the troubadour!

There were two dining rooms, one for the 'Regular Eaters' and the other was the 'Special Low Calorie Suite'. Tonight, we were in the 'Regular' room and had our reserved table waiting for us, situated in the bay window, overlooking the courtyard and famous cherub fountain. There were seven cherubs, either blowing water from their mouths or from their penises; the number seemed ironic, as there were seven of us. Spotlights traced the trajectory of the water, which was quite spectacular.

George never failed to make some banal comment to lower the tone.

'Anyone for "Golden Showers" in the light of the moon? What about you, Andromeda? Isn't it your turn?' he said with a raucous chuckle and a wink.

Would we ever live down our escapade in the pool.

'If you are game, George, I'm sure Susie will accommodate you.' I whispered against his ear. He just grinned.

The food gallery was as inspiring as ever. There were huge bowls of salad, fruit and vegetables from every corner of the world. The cooked meats and fish were magnificently displayed, adorned with edible flowers. It was a culinary delight and made the taste buds overflow.

'Don't they make it difficult to calorie-count. Do you think we could cheat, just for tonight?' Hermione was piling her plate in precarious heaps.

'Hermy, you are like a golden-headed swan. You hardly need to slim!' I retorted in envy.

'And you, you little beauty, are going to be chased everywhere by a certain special fellow, so you can lose those few pounds also without counting calories. I am so jealous! Sexercise for ever!'

'Shh! Hermy. You are outrageous!'

'Oh, I know, isn't it a hoot!' She gracefully took the head of the table and waited for her entourage to take their places.

Simon seated himself next to me and pulled his chair as near to mine as he could. He slid his hand up my thigh, his fingertips penetrating my primary erogenous zone.

'The hidden valley is wet and warm. How glorious it is to welcome me in such a moist manner!' he leaned across and purred in my ear, while retrieving the salt.

I stopped his fingers intruding any further and said, probably too loudly and definitely too huskily. 'Let's toast the Hockey Team, reunited!' And I raised my glass to hide my blushing face.

'The Hockey Team!' voiced in chorus to the clink of glasses.

Simon swallowed deeply from his glass and very deliberately sucked the tips of his fingers of his wandering hand. The man was in his element and savouring every tantalising second.

The conversation ebbed and flowed and gradually we caught up with each other's pursuits over the past year.

'What is your husband doing now, Angelica? Isn't he some kind of money speculator in the city?' Vanessa was probing again and speaking too loud. I could feel my blood freezing before it reached my head. Did my face betray me or was the painted smile still in place.

'Nothing changes where he is concerned. He is still working hard in the City. He probably doesn't even realise that I have disappeared for a few days.' I finished with a brittle laugh, but I knew that the inquisition would be inevitable. She was like a ferret and would hassle until she had the answer.

'Are you still writing your poetry? You should find a publisher, sweetie. They are really quite good, if not a little sad.'

Vanessa was very intuitive and I could feel her dark eyes boring into my soul.

I shivered, involuntarily, which was observed by Simon.

'You OK, Angel? You look a little pale.' He squeezed my knee.

'Must have been a ghost walking over my grave.' Or just the nearness of you. I was purring inside and, thankfully, distracted.

Call it telepathy or anticipating future events out of my control, I didn't know, but something extremely unpleasant was unfolding and I had no power to stop it.

'Anyone for bridge?' Hermy was a master at the game and was hopeful of a rubber tonight.

George, Susie and Vanessa volunteered like lambs to the slaughter. Susie was a follower and desperately wanted to partner Hermione to increase her knowledge of the game.

'Shall we all find a cosy corner in the main lounge? You four can play and we can harass and exasperate, in that order!' Simon was in a mischievous mood.

Hermy rose to the bait. 'Watch your tongue, Simon, or I may have to remove it with my teeth!' She would love to try.

Simon spread his long arms and enfolded her like a swooping eagle, hustling her out into the corridor. We all followed.

'Angie, you have retracted into your shell! What's up? Are you missing the kids already? Give yourself a break!' Jeannie, sweet Jeannie, was concerned. She knew me too well.

We were walking quite a few yards behind the others, so I hesitated and pushed her into the aromatherapy lobby and said in a hushed tone.

'They won't miss us for a while. Jeannie, I have this awful feeling that something dreadful is happening with John. Mike and John are bosom buddies. Do you know why I should feel the way I do? Something is going down in town and I must know what it is!' I stood and waited.

She looked down at her feet and slowly, deliberately, made the decision to tell me the little that she knew.

'Look, I don't know much but I believe John is in serious trouble with some villains in the East End. Mike let it out the other day and then swore me to secrecy. He said you cannot know for fear of involving you and the kids.'

'I knew it! God, damn it! I knew he was hiding something. Fuck, fuck, fuck! Shit! I really do feel sick now. I've got to go home, haven't I?' I was trembling with emotion and fear.

It was about time that I confronted him. 'Ignorance is bliss' is not a truth, it is an excuse! How dare he jeopardise our lives again with his clandestine dealings!

'Don't be stupid, Angie! What could you do? Whatever it is, he can deal with it. Let's face it, he has got out of some scrapes before and survived, smelling of roses.' She didn't sound too convinced but I needed time to think clearly.

Perhaps I should have a good sleep and phone home in the morning, as I had promised.

'OK, Jeannie, you're right. Things have been awful at home lately and I must admit I have been too scared to ask any questions because I couldn't cope with the answers.'

'Come on, silly, let's join the others before they send out a search party.' We linked arms and marched towards the lounge.

The room was buzzing. All the new arrivals seemed to have grown voices in unison, so conversation was impossible. The energy would change once they were on their starvation diets and high aerobic exercises. This small community would then become quiet and thoughtful and less vociferous. The designer outfits would become robes and slippers as they disappeared behind closed doors in search of revitalisation.

The Hockey Team had draped themselves around the piano, where George was entertaining his friends with a Liberace impersonation. All thoughts of the bridge game had evaporated. He really was quite good and very soon had the entire room joining in. If the directors of the hydro were within earshot, I would take a bet that the piano would be spirited away by tomorrow, for repair.

This exhibition would have been detrimental to the holistic approach of beauty therapy, and so on, and so on. In other words, no ciggies, no alcohol, no sex *and* definitely no frivolous fun!

As much as I would have loved to snuggle into Simon, I caught his eye and signalled by 'head on hands' that I was tired and ready to retire to my room. He dropped his bottom lip, blew me a kiss and returned to his karaoke with George.

'I'm going up too. I fancy a nightcap, or two, do you want to join me?' Jeannie teased me, conspiratorially, as we inched towards the door.

'Jeannie, you're as bad as Cynthia Payne! Didn't she get kicked out for boozing, a few years ago?'

'Yes, but that was something else entirely! She turned that cellar room into a raving disco. So the story goes, one of her Rolls-Royce, turned up with a boot full of champagne and even the therapists got legless!'

'What a riot! Is it true, though?' I said, not quite believing the story.

'Who knows! It's like Chinese whispers, by the time it's been recounted a few times the story is unbelievable. Anyway, as we are now at your door, do you want a nip of brandy or not?' She hesitated for a moment.

'OK, you twisted my arm. Shall I come to your room?'

'No, I'll be back in two ticks.'

She ran along to her room and by the time I had kicked off my shoes and thrown off my clothes, she was back.

'Look, Angie, I won't stay as I have some work to catch up on. Here's your belly-warmer.' She gave me a huge tooth mug, half-full of Remy.

'Grief! I won't drink all that!' My eyes widened at the prospect.

'Go on with you! It'll do you good. Make you sleep. Night! Night!'

She returned to her room, which she called a closet as it was so small.

I knew she would get through at least a quarter of the bottle tonight. That was why she didn't want me around. She and her addiction were a private affair.

I closed the door and readied myself for bed. It was only 9.30 p.m., but I needed to sleep, to lose myself in nothingness. I took a large slug of the brandy and perched the tumbler on the wooden surround, snuggling down into the carved bed. As I closed my eyes I saw Jason, Rebecca and Sean, playing as children do.

They were teenagers now, but when I wanted to feel near to

them I would conjure up favourite memories. Jason would be clicking away with his treasured camera and blowing me kisses. Becca would have her head in my lap, sucking her tongue, as I stroked her ears and hair. And Sean, oh, fun-loving Sean, would be charging around on his Peewee motorbike, chasing the dogs and laughing his head off. John crept into my mind! Well! He wouldn't be there at all. Why did I stay with this man who spent all of his time searching for a better deal and no time with his family. I stayed with him because I loved him once, a long time ago, when I felt appreciated, but now I was expendable. I was almost an intrusion into his dark world of finance and faceless people.

Tomorrow, I would phone home to ease my mind. Tonight, was to forget!

There was something furry brushing against my hand. I opened my eyes, slowly, not daring to move and was in wondrous amazement. A pretty grey squirrel was nibbling crumbs from my plate and its fluffy tail twitched, momentarily touching my hand. It must have sensed my wakefulness as it darted behind a tree.

Very gently, I eased myself to a sitting position and waited. I could feel its eyes inspecting me and courageously it returned to sit beside me. After a few moments it trusted me and began to clean its mouth with its tiny front paws, then inched its way forward to peer into my upturned basket.

It made a cute clicking noise and magically was joined by three other squirrels. They took no notice of me but jumped in and out of the basket, discovering titbits and trophies to take back to their secret hiding place.

The vibration of approaching footsteps sent them scurrying off in all directions and I was dismayed.

'Can I join you, Angelica?' It was Alex, sauntering lazily towards me.

'Of course you can.' I patted the ground next to me.

As he lay out full length, he let out a sigh and pushed his fingers through his hair.

'Is that how you feel today, Alex?' I waited for him to reply.

'I hate Fridays because I have to face going home to the same

64

trauma every weekend. I have a gorgeous wife and baby daughter, who love me and want me back, but I am lost in my fear and just want to be here, alone.' He looked so full of despair but managed a watery smile.

'How long have you been at the Abbey?' I asked.

'About four weeks, this time. They have a room with my name on it.' He laughed, sarcastically.

'Do you want to talk about it?' Here I go again. What was I doing, I wasn't a shrink! He looked so haunted.

'Angelica, has anyone ever told you what a lovely smile you have? You have a wisdom and gentleness that radiates from your eyes, as if you know the answers.'

'I wish that were true. If I knew the answers, I wouldn't be here, would I?'

I turned his arm to look at his watch and he said, 'It's 5 p.m., give or take. I have been watching you sleeping. You looked so peaceful, curled up like a kitten until the squirrels woke you. They were so aware of you too, you are like a magnet.'

'I expect it's because I am a newcomer, they are just inquisitive.' I pushed myself to my feet and started to gather my things together.

Alex lay there, with his eyes closed to the world. His pose was hiding the violated child that had secreted itself deep within the bowels of the man. I touched his nose and he looked up at me.

'Is it four of us for dinner at 6 p.m., or have you seen Petra to make it five? We could be the Famous Five Revived,' I said almost gaily.

'No, I think it'll be four. Petra has already been collected by her brother.' He got to his feet and we walked across the lawn to the patio.

The sun was still warm, a balmy afternoon. I would have liked to have stayed out longer, but I had to return the empty hamper to Sam and find out if John and the twins were coming to see me tomorrow. Thankfully, Jason was in America on vacation with his uncle. I didn't want to worry him as he had gone through enough unpleasantness this year at school. When would all this end?

'You are deep in thought,' Alex said as he pushed the door open for me. 'See you tonight at dinner.'

'Sure thing. Bye, Alex.'

I climbed the two floors to my corridor and saw no one. Where had the people gone? I was quite unnerved by it. As I approached the nurses' station I could hear the chatter of nurses in conversation and was relieved that I was not alone. A sudden screech of laughter made me stop in my tracks and a head appeared in their doorway.

'I say, I am so sorry. Did we make you jump? Come on in, Sam is here too.' She was a young blonde nurse whom I had seen around.

Sam looked up from her desk and smiled.

'We are just completing the handover for the weekend and that noisy laughter was all due to a very tacky joke by Polly.' She pointed to the blonde nurse who was grinning broadly.

'I have to have a shower before dinner, so could you call in before you go off? I'll leave your hamper just here.' I pointed to a corner that was free of clutter.

'OK, I'll be there in about fifteen minutes.' She resumed writing and I went to my room.

I threw my clothes on the bed and wandered into the bathroom. Oh, the joy of warm water sliding down my body was a tonic. I dried myself quickly, buffing my skin with rapid movements and neatly folded the towel. Once I had rehung my clothes, I slipped into an ankle-length crêpe dress of burnt orange, reapplied lipstick, brushed my curls and focused on the growing pile of envelopes nestled against the vase of flowers.

I can't keep putting this off. Now is the time to read the words of love and comfort. One by one I slit the envelopes to reveal the card and the sender. The lines of verse would remain unread, saved for another time. I was a doting cat-lover and was amazed to find all but three had pictures of frolicking felines. My friends really do care!

Tap! Tap! Without waiting for a reply, Sam was there beside me. She peered round to view my face.

'Good girl! No tears! I am so pleased you have now taken time to welcome the kindness of those people who love you.'

'The tears are there, but I am keeping them at bay for now.' My voice was straining to keep control.

'The news is good.' She held my fingers so tight that it hurt.

'John, Rebecca and Sean will be here for lunch on Sunday. I have booked a table for four with the chef and you will be dining at 1 p.m. It is all arranged.' She spoke quickly and deliberately to give me strength.

'Whew! That's better than tomorrow.' I sighed with relief. 'It gives me another day to compose my thoughts.'

'Right, I'm off now until Monday. Here is your itinerary for each week. Polly will be around and Carmel, the duty sister. Take things easy, you will be among only thirteen people who remain here for the weekend, everyone else goes home, to return on Sunday evening. So you are not alone, OK!' She was through the door and free of her duties.

It was 6 p.m. Luckily I didn't have time to think about anything but rushing down to join the others for dinner. I could feel my heart drumming against my chest and needed to draw in deep breaths. Down to the ground floor and there was Archie at his desk.

'Hello, Archie, time for dinner!' I called, briefly, as I passed.

'Enjoy your meal, Miss Angelica,' he said and smiled.

It was already 6.15 p.m. I was a little late. I turned the corner into the dining room and was surprised at its emptiness. Alex, Harvey and Iain were sitting at the table by the French doors. They all rose to their feet as I approached and Harvey pulled out a chair for me.

'Good evening, Angelica.' Alex and Harvey, in chorus.

'Milady Penelope.' A subtle grin from Iain.

'Good evening, inmates!' I giggled to see the reaction from other patients sitting on adjacent tables. I felt like a celebrity.

There was a lady sitting by herself in one corner and I sensed a great affinity towards her. She had the palest blue eyes and a smile that would make the Mona Lisa envious. I acknowledged her by returning her smile.

'Well, shall we select one of the chef's masterpieces, now we are together?' Harvey pulled out my chair. I was looking forward to the next hour, getting to know a little about these three men who had chosen each other as preferred company and thankfully adopted me into their circle. By the end of our stay we would know each other more intimately than one could imagine possible but the revelations were on the horizon, yet to come.

'Lasagne with beetroot, carrot and rocket salad, please.' I made my decision quickly.

Harvey was close on my shoulder and seeing my selection said, 'Very colourful. Do you choose by taste or colour?' He was intrigued.

'Both would be the truth, but I try to satisfy the gourmet first and my artistic side second.' I smiled at his old-fashioned charm. It was a long time since I had been interested enough to make pleasant conversation.

The three men all chose meat and three vegetables, in large proportions, floating in a sea of rich spicy gravy. The sight of this had a very unpleasant effect on my stomach. I had such a poor appetite lately and was longing to regain my enthusiasm for eating. But as my nan used to say, if you don't put fuel in the boiler, the fire will go out – and that was exactly the case. I had no energy and wanted to sleep all the time.

'As I am the latest arrival, may I ask some questions?' I scanned all three faces.

'You may not get answers!' Alex spoke up first and looked non-committal.

'That's OK, nothing serious or intrusive, just how long have you all been here?' I smiled at three guarded faces.

'This time I've been here two weeks and was unfortunately here for a spell last year, but don't worry, I have a family history of mental imbalance.' Harvey said this in such a matter-of-fact way that I wanted to laugh and only just managed to hold it back. So impolite!

'This beef is truly succulent!' Iain laughed loudly at his own remark and we all joined in.

'How about eating and trying to forget where we are.'

'I'm sorry, Iain, I was stirring up bad vibes. Are you all going home for the weekend, or will someone be keeping me company?'

'Julie's picking me up at 8 p.m. tonight. She's my wife.' Iain didn't seem too happy about it.

'Me too, Laura will be here soon and I'll probably be back

tomorrow evening. You see twenty-four hours is about as much as we can take.' Alex looked like a defeated child.

'Well, you're lucky young lady, as you can have me for the whole weekend.' Harvey was about to achieve a coup de grâce. 'You see, my wife left me last year and now lives with my ex-business partner, so I am an outcast.'

Harvey had now taken on the guise of a well-used shabby teddy that had been dropped in a bin.

'Be gentle with him, Milady, he bruises easily.' Iain was as sharp as a razor. I believe his prickly wit was his own defence system.

Harvey threw him a look of reproach, but managed a grin too.

'Have you been given an agenda by your shrink, yet?' Iain asked just before he filled his mouth with Yorkshire pudding, with gravy running down his chin.

'Yes, it looks as if I'm booked in for some OT every day, some days it's two sessions. Is that the same for you?'

'Pretty much, I would guess. Perhaps we could compare charts on Sunday evening in the top lounge?' Iain suggested.

'As we are all fairly recent arrivals they could have grouped us together. I know there are a few openings in my awareness class, with Ann the Android.' He obviously wasn't a fan.

'I didn't like her too much on our first meeting. Is she always so unpleasant?' I looked from one to the other.

'In chorus, boys! *Yes!*' They all roared and I did too.

We had all gradually become more at ease and less aware of each other, offering cameos of ourselves and snippets of information relating to our illnesses.

Iain was suffering from tinnitus in both ears. Sometimes he hit his head against anything hard to try to stop the noise invading his mind, or he would get drunk until he passed out. The noise had increased in volume over the past year and after exhaustive tests he had been referred to a specialist at the Abbey. He went to only one of Ann's classes and walked out, too angry to participate.

Harvey had declared he was a hopeless case of depression, due to matrimonial collapse and betrayal. He was trapped inside his self-pity. Voluntarily, he had become an EST patient, which allowed the IC unit to send certain amounts of electricity into his brain. This was too much information for me to handle, so he attempted to lighten up and chatted about the forthcoming weekend interlude.

Alex was very guarded still and only offered the fact that he had been undergoing therapy in the outpatients department for a year, which was going nowhere, so was admitted about four weeks ago and had a room on the East wing where the long-term inmates were housed. He didn't have to attend any specific therapy classes as he had a one-to-one session with his own counsellor, three times a week. This structured counselling suited him as he was a self-confessed recluse and preferred his aloneness. Eventually, a little magic would set him free from his cell.

I said very little, except that I cried on a regular basis after having panic attacks and that I wanted to be somewhere with my children that would not include my husband. I had to regain my confidence.

Four sets of eyes watched me while I spoke, all showing growing interest. The pair of hypnotic eyes that I sought were those belonging to the foreign lady who sat alone in the corner. Her stare was almost tangible, with a trance-like quality that enveloped me.

The boys sensed the interaction and looked to see who the intruder was. 'Keep well away from her, my dear, she's definitely disturbed. I cannot understand why she is allowed to be here.' Harvey looked protectively at me.

'That is Françoise Le Fevre. She is a French artist, based in London. A touch Bohemian and suffers with delusions. Her art is fantastic and demonic and she has a knife phobia.' Alex added this information as if he was reading her history from notes.

'Is she dangerous, Alex?' I asked. 'You seem to know a lot about her.'

'I have talked to her, on the odd occasion she is communicating, and I have visited her room to see her paintings. Mostly, she keeps away from everyone. She is a very complex character and hears voices that command her to end her life. She is only hospitalised when she abuses herself and needs supervision. And, no, she isn't dangerous to others or she wouldn't be here.' He took a long drink from his glass then looked at me and smiled. 'Actually, I think you'll like her,' he added.

'I find her appearance fascinating, like a gypsy in gossamer layers.'

I looked towards her again, but she had gone.

'Time for me to go, folks.' Iain rose from the table.

'See you Sunday sometime, Milady.' He grinned, kissed my hand and left.

'I think he fancies you!' Harvey said petulantly.

'Oh, don't be so pathetic, Harvey. You really get on my nerves.' Alex pushed his chair back and left without further comment.

'Don't take offence, Harvey, we are all a bit strung out. They are going off to face something that worries them and we are stuck here, too afraid to leave.' I gave his hand a sympathetic tap.

His spaniel look became a doting smile and this human shaggy dog escorted me from the dining room to the upstairs lounge. It was approaching 7.30 p.m. and for some peculiar reason I thought of the TV, not that I missed watching it, in fact exactly the reverse was true. I was amazed that for the week I had been here I hadn't thought of it once.

I walked beside Harvey, musing on what an attractive couple we would make. Goodness me, what a strange thought! A more bizarre match was not possible. I was five foot two inches, petite, with dark, soft, curly hair and in normal conditions considered to be vivacious and pretty. Harvey was six foot one inch, quite handsome, in a battered way, with an abundance of pale-grey hair and dressed in Harris tweeds.

Glancing at his profile I saw – I want to be your puppy face or perhaps dog in the manger. He would be a non-effectual door-mat. I then looked at his hands dangling from his sleeves and his huge, size thirteen feet, and before I could arrest the thought I pondered whether he had a huge willy, too. I couldn't suppress the giggle.

'Giggle! Gurgle! Squeak! Oh, excuse me. I don't know what's come over me.' I glanced his way, holding my lips to try to quell the laughter.

'It's nice to hear you laugh,' he said, not looking at all uncomfortable.

I was the one feeling disturbed, as I had believed my thoughts were visible. We had reached the top lounge and I was delighted to see that it was bathed in evening sunshine.

The two ladies I had seen earlier in the gardens were ensconced in armchairs in front of the TV, which was on far too loud.

'Do you mind if I turn the volume down a little?' Harvey had stepped forward and touched the remote control before they had time to form a reply.

Well done, Harvey, I thought. There was no response from the two ladies as they resumed their silent vigil in front of the screen.

We chose to sit as far from the TV as we could, at a group of four armchairs with a central table and the nearest to the beverage trolley. The same affable lady with the floral apron was the champion of the trolley and guarded it jealously. She offered us both a mug of steaming coffee, which we accepted gratefully.

'You two have a nice cosy chat, eh!' She manoeuvred the trolley on its journey across the lounge, giving us a wink.

'Have you any plans for tomorrow?' Harvey asked the first question.

'If it's as lovely as today I should like to do the woodland walk and then laze in the gardens after lunch and perhaps do some writing. How about you?'

'I have to go into town to collect some dry-cleaning. Why don't you come with me?'

I felt my body freeze at the very thought of it and spoke before I had properly formed a reply.

'No, no, I couldn't do that! I'm not ready to go outside and *not* with you!' I couldn't stop the anxiety overwhelming me or the gremlins beginning their march down my arms and legs. When would this stop happening?

'Don't get in a flap! It was only a suggestion.' He looked forlornly at me and strangely enough it acted as a healing agent. My tremors subsided as I saw this poor disconsolate man. I was sorry for him.

'I overreacted, Harvey, sorry! I just can't imagine going outside, doing normal things, or being involved with ordinary day-to-day activities.' My hands held fast to the warmth of the mug and I watched the two ladies locked into the TV screen, like zombies.

Silently, the Bohemian lady approached and nestled herself into a chair, facing me. The electricity between us was amazing.

'Hi, I'm Angelica, I saw you at dinner. This is Harvey.'

He nodded.

'Bonsoir, Angelica, I am Françoise.' She all but glowed, radiating such intensity.

Harvey had been excluded, immediately, and was obviously uncomfortable. In a few gulps his coffee had been drunk and he rose to leave. 'Excuse me, ladies, I'm off for a stroll. See you tomorrow.'

'You are an extremely beautiful woman and if you permit I should wish to paint you. You will sit for me, yes?' Her voice was deep, almost masculine, with a hint of earthy resonance.

'I am speechless and really flattered. Perhaps I could see your work sometime?'

'Tomorrow! If you are not going home, I shall find you, yes?' She leaned forward and touched my face with her fingertips and sighed.

'You have such a spirit, such knowledge!' She uncurled herself from the chair and floated out of the room.

I remained in a state of wonderment and disbelief. The two ladies, watching the TV, witnessed only the flickering of the screen.

Polly put her head around the door and smiled in my direction.

'You OK, there? Or would you like some company?' She came and sat next to me.

I recounted to her the encounter with Françoise and she listened with interest.

'I think I'll go to my room now. Would you look in later, if you have some time?' I rose to go.

'Yes, of course. I have some tablets to give you before I tuck you in.' She walked with me as far as the door and I continued the few yards to my room.

I sat by the window and watched the cavorting of the squirrels as the night sky descended over the gardens below. My mind was whirling and I couldn't focus on one thought.

Now was the time when I could talk out my nightmares and agonies, hopefully, without diving into fear and despair. But there was no one around to listen. I could not relax enough to sleep as I remembered the happenings of the last few months. A strange inner strength gripped me and I knew I would recover.

I paced my small room, opening the desk drawer to take out my notebook, then putting it back, taking my jacket from the wardrobe and discarding it on the bed. The energy within was increasing as I paced the floor. The need to sing, shout, talk, walk was unbearable – I was about to burst!

A gentle tap and Polly was there beside me. 'What's up! I thought you would be ready for bed.'

'Polly, I am about to explode. I have so much buzz inside that I cannot sit down!' Would she understand? Was she prepared for this or would I be sedated until someone senior was available?

'OK! Let's walk, talk, whatever. Have my shoulder to lean on for a while. I'm going to square it with the sister now, so just wait for five minutes till I get back.' She pushed me down on the chair by the window and left.

I was so excited and breathless as jumbled visions popped in and out of my mind. If I could make sense of this macabre jigsaw, perhaps I could start rebuilding my life.

'I'm back. Shall we go outside and sit in the garden?' She took my hand and together we almost ran into the stillness of the gardens.

'Not here on the patio, under the oak tree, over there!' I pointed to where I had sat earlier in the day. We walked across the lawn to a wooden bench and sat side by side.

'I have permission to record your voice on this machine. Is that OK?' Polly held a small tape recorder and pushed a button to show a red light.

'Yes, that's what I need, some proof of what I saw and heard. Where shall I start?'

'Say whatever comes into your head.' She was eager and expectant, my confidant.

'I keep seeing the same face in the balaclava, mocking me, taunting me. This man wants to kill me but he couldn't because it is John, my husband. He loves me, so why does he try to shoot me. Then, I see him frightened, crying in his hands, contemplating suicide and his mother, whining, whining, whining, blackmailing me to stay or she too will take her life. The imploring faces of my children, telling me to stop crying and making that awful noise! *Stop* it!... *Stop* it!... *Stop* it!... Don't go away! Come back! Where have you gone? Don't look like that! Mum, you are frightening us!'

I was trembling with emotion and Polly was rubbing my hands.

'Do you want to go on?' Was she out of her depth and hesitant?

'Yes, I must say more.' I hugged my knees. 'I have to return to the lodge, that's where the horror began.'

'John had been arrested, I was away at the hydro and the twins witnessed it all. They are only fifteen and it was too much for them to bear alone. The officers arrived with John, in squad cars, and plundered my home. They were looking for evidence and my poor children had to see this and try to understand. If only I had been there!' I sobbed a painful sigh but this time – no tears.

I took a moment to look at the Abbey with lights in some windows, standing resplendent with the moon and stars as a backdrop.

'The tape is off for a moment. Are you warm enough or would you like me to get your jacket?' Polly was indulging me while I tried to compose myself.

'No, I'm fine! Can we go on?'

'If you're sure, the tape is back on.' She also hugged her knees and we sat toe to toe – like bookends.

'They took him away, leaving my children at home, alone. I should have been there to protect them. I remember Rebecca saying that she had told the Flying Squad Officer that I would be home soon, so he left a telephone number where he could be contacted. Sean said that his dad looked pale and defeated and he told them not to worry – it was all a *big* mistake and he would explain later. It was a Sunday. Whatever did they think? His mother should have been with them but John hadn't collected her. That wasn't going to happen as he had already been arrested in the City. I had the phone call on Monday evening, as I was about to go into dinner. They had spent twenty-four hours alone, trying to piece together what had occurred. I had such a fabulous day, full of massage, mud baths, jazzercise, swimming and sauna. I was so relaxed. The world was warm, wonderful and I would have phoned home as usual, at about 7.30 p.m., to hear how they were enjoying themselves without me, but I *didn't* phone! Instead, I got a call from a very distressed son at 6.45 p.m. on Monday and our world became black, degrading and full of evil men.'

I began to cry, very gently, not heart-rending as before, but a slow flow of a mother's grief, mourning the loss of her family. It would never be the same again for any of us. We would have to live a life of fabricated stories, courtroom dramas, prison visits and shame, in a place where friends forget to call and enemies knock at the door.

Polly sat very still. She had stopped the tape. She watched and waited for me to decide what action would follow.

The tears stopped. The ebb and flow of my hands ceased the rhythmic motion on my legs and I took a deep, healing breath.

'Thank you, Polly. I needed that. I think I am now ready for bed.'

We approached the patio, leaving dark shadows, behind us. In the outside world I would have been afraid of shadows but not here in sanctuary. Something inside me recognised this feeling. Was I born afraid? Did I have this chapter of life preordained!

The stairs were climbed in silence. I was totally exhausted. The welcoming sight of my bed was immediate. On taking my pills, I allowed the misty, tumbling sensation of sleep to comfort me.

Chapter Seven

I heard a faint scratching noise and opened my eyes. The room was dark, with light seeping in under the door, where a piece of paper lay. I got up, took the paper and read the message by the bedside lamp.

I am protecting your door, like a knight on heat. Please let me in! I opened the door and there was Simon, lying full-length, in the doorway.

'Get up, you idiot! Come in before anyone sees you!' I pulled him inside, furtively glancing along the corridor.

'Angel, I missed you! Don't be angry!' He was adorably, drunk.

'I'm not angry, just sleepy. Look at the time, it's nearly 1 a.m. Where have you been to get so tiddly?' I slithered back into bed.

Simon didn't stand on ceremony. He vacated his clothes and nestled in beside me.

'George had some brandy, so we drank a couple of tots.' He spied my half-full mug by the bed.

'Did he give you some too?' We both laughed as he pulled me into the shelter of his arms and rocked me.

'You're my Angel, my beautiful Andromeda and I adore you.' His kisses were uncontrolled, like a lion devouring his kill.

I was being encased, by my human tree. His arms and legs entwined with mine and his strength overpowered me. Our hair mingled together on the pillow like merging rivers as the warmth of his breath on my neck began to fan the fire growing within. This gentle giant caressed my body as if I was made of the finest silk. He gasped as he found my secret place and crooned against my eyes, my lips and my ears. Pulsating rapture had engulfed our senses as we tossed together in perfect rhythm until our passion was spent, then lay as one, newly baptised in our love. Two souls cocooned in our heaven. Sleep was a peaceful reward.

I watched my Romanesque creature in the dim light, cuddling the pillow like a favourite toy and knew I would write about this night. I drifted off to sleep to the sounds of gentle snoring, the odd endearment then punctuated by a volley of bottom burps.

The shrill ringing of the phone woke me. It was Jeannie.

'Hiya, honey. You awake?' She sounded too chirpy.

'Well, I am now! What time do you call this?' I was looking round for any sign of Simon. He had disappeared without a trace.

'At the third stroke, it will be 8 a.m., precisely! Peep, peep, peep!' She giggled.

'Right, let's get down to breakfast for 8.30 a.m. See you outside my door.' I hung up and turned over in bed again. I spread my legs wide to find a cooler area and instead I found a tell-tale damp spot. Ooh! What hunger and thirst was satiated there! It wasn't just a dream. It was Sexy Si.

I thought of Hermione and said aloud, as I showered, 'Sorry, Hermy, he's not for you, so eat your heart out!' I sang at the top of my voice. Heaven, I'm in heaven and the problems that surround me through the week. Seem to vanish. Brrr! Brrr! The phone obviously didn't appreciate my vocal talents and insisted on an answer.

'Hello?' One hand held the receiver, the other the towel.

'Good morning, you goddess of lust.' His voice was husky through booze and lack of sleep.

'When did you leave me? I woke to find all I had left was a wet patch and bruised lips.'

'Oh! Angel. Which lips were bruised? Can I kiss all four better?' This thirsty man definitely needed water.

'Simon, you are insatiable! See you in twenty minutes at breakfast, bye!'

I set the receiver down and finished drying myself.

Today we had weighing and an in-depth chat with the sister (in her regulation blue uniform), followed by the receiving of our programme and inclusive therapies.

I wore a comfy tracksuit, leather pumps and no undies (for easy access). My hair was tussled into an unruly mop of curls, tied in a scrunchie and my lips were painted with bronze lustre. I was ready for action.

As I opened the door, I found Jeannie, reading the paper, sitting on the window ledge.

'Where's your bag, you LouLou?' she chastised me.

'Oh! Shit! Just a minute.' I dived back inside and collected my holdall. 'OK, Jeannie with the light-brown hair – let's move on out!'

We bounded down the spiral flight of stairs, down the corridor into the dining room. Diane, the head waitress, beamed at us.

'How lovely to see yous two, I'm so glad. Is it just the two of yous this time?' She was so pleased to see us.

'Only us for breakfast, but the usual crowd are here.' Jeannie wanted to eat and pushed me in the direction of a corner table with only two chairs. 'Would yous ladies like this table?' Diane pointed to the one we were aiming for.

'That's great, Diane, thanks. Can we have a full English breakfast with everything?' I said with a wink.

'Oh, yous are a wag! Yous know the ropes. The choices are all set out with the amounts of calories and this morning yous can have porridge.' She walked to the kitchen to get our juices, clicking her tongue like a mother hen.

'Yummy, yummy! Let's get stuck into all this fruit and muesli and nuts and we can fart all day.' Jeannie was not amused. I gave her a reproachful glare as I selected my fruit and yoghurt and tried not to laugh when she came up behind me, saying, 'Too much fruit makes your bottom burps silent but deadly and too many nuts makes them explode like a pea shooter with the hammer jammed.'

That was too much information and we giggled and spluttered like escapees from St Trinian's. I couldn't look at Jeannie. My sides ached and my nose and eyes were streaming.

Diane returned with our juice and freshly squeezed lemon and said.

'Oh! It's such a tonic to have yous here. Yous always cheers the place up. I won't ask yous for the joke 'cos I knows it'll be a rude 'un.' She wandered away, musing on her fledglings.

We were being surveyed by superior beings with pink, permed hair and moustaches, owning huge diamond rings, worn even in the pool. A few people coughed and shuffled their chairs and as our laughter subsided so did the uncomfortable atmosphere.

'Now the hilarity has subdued, how do you feel about John

and the underlying problems?' Jeannie was brutally subtle.

'I don't know what he's mixed up in and I pray it's nothing too serious, but I shall have to demand an explanation when I get home. I dread going home; it's like entering a graveyard for all the warmth and conversation there. Luckily, the twins are rarely around and Jason gave up on any support from John when he got into trouble at school. You remember that drug-taking scenario, when John totally lost it and turned his back on Jason.'

'Grief! I'd forgotten about that.' She looked at me with pity. 'Poor thing! Did he get expelled? Was anything proved against him? I can't remember.'

'No, not really, but as he had finished his A levels they suggested that he and a few others left and continued their education elsewhere.' I didn't need reminding of this too. I couldn't be any more depressed. Why wouldn't she shut up?

'Is that when he went to John's brother, Toby?'

Why was she bringing all of this up?

'Yes! John washed his hands of him and shipped him off to the States, out of sight, out of mind, and Jason was pleased to go. There was no love lost between them, but it broke my heart!'

Enough was enough and I rose, almost crashing into Simon as I shoved the chair back. He stood there, expectantly.

'Sorry, Simon. I was going to get a pot of herbal tea, sorry.' I backed away and found Diane in the kitchen.

'Everything OK, lovey? What can I get yous?' She smiled willingly.

'A pot of your wonderful raspberry tea, please, Diane.' I stood by her table taking in deep breaths while she prepared the pot.

'I'll bring it in for yous, no need to wait.'

'I'd rather wait, Diane. I wanted to have a breather.'

She gave me a nod and a wink, knowingly, so she thought. I gazed around the fantastic, stainless steel kitchen, glowing with cleanliness and order. The chef prided himself on culinary expertise and a great team of sous-chefs and gofers.

'All ready, lovey. Crikey, yous was in another world.' She placed a small tray in my hands, with the teapot and cups perfectly balanced.

I had myself back in control and greeted Simon with a sheepish grin. He had joined another lady on an adjacent table and was chatting merrily.

Jeannie made space on the table for the cups.

'I've got a big mouth, Angie. I prattle on without thinking. I have verbal diarrhoea and I'm sorry!'

'No hard feelings! Let's drink our tea, then go and get weighed.' I wanted so much to revive my joie de vivre, but the air of foreboding had re-entered my head. A good workout would soon set me back on track. *Smile*, I told myself and let the veneer develop.

We left the breakfast area with short greetings to faces we recognised and made our way to the pool.

'See you in a mo, ladies,' Simon called as we passed.

The waiting area was packed with newspapers held aloft to shield faces and multicoloured designer outfits, blue rinses and, of course, fingers and wrists sporting huge rocks. The elite definitely had to wear their wealth like a uniform – it gave one status – and *red* lipstick was essential, but only worn by the females.

We found ourselves a free white table, next to the jacuzzi, which was steaming and frothing like a cappuccino, only smelling of herbal essences. 'They've given the place a face-lift! I didn't notice it last night,' I said, innocently.

'Aw! Come on! You weren't actually inspecting the decor last night, more like Simon's block and tackle!' Jeannie was actually correct.

The giggles took hold again. We were so in tune with each other, blood sisters without the bloodletting.

'We heard the uproar this morning, even though we were being punished in the diet room. What devilry is afoot, you munchkins?' Hermy and Vanessa stood gloriously before us, like two dowagers from *Vogue* magazine.

'And good morning to you too, Hermione. O, Wondrous One!' I could not resist the tease and she pulled at my curls as she sat down. 'Hello, Vanessa, I see you have just a few papers for light entertainment.'

'Coals to Newcastle, darling, I can't desist. It would be like embarking on a cerebral diet as well as a body fast.'

Jeannie was about to make a fatal remark when, thankfully, her name was called and she toddled off to see the sister.

'Have you brought any of your poems with you, Angelica? I was impressed with the sample you showed me last year. I should like to read them.' Vanessa was being indulgent, but she was a literary genius.

'I have written some and they still seem to emerge from my dark side. I would really appreciate your comments.' Her sponsorship could be invaluable if I was to publish.

'Angelica Reeves. Please come to room 11.'

The voice of authority saved me from further interrogation.

Consultations went on all morning, which slightly disrupted the dilettantes, already immersed in their routines. The newcomers monopolised most of the poolside tables and loungers and became a nuisance.

Once we had been overhauled by nursy, we were ready for immediate inclusion in therapeutic pursuits. I was salivating at the thought of Tim, the masseur, who could manipulate my body into total submission. I had only to wait until 11.45 a.m. and he was all mine for thirty minutes.

Elevenses were taken in the coffee lounge, which had the ambience of an indoor garden centre. It was beautifully floral, with trellises hanging from the ceiling, creating decorative individual booths for semi-private conversations.

The Hockey Team grouped en masse, to vent our feelings on the diagnosis of the saintly sister and the strategy we would adopt to improve our fitness and health. All except Simon, who came here with an athletic physique, mind and morals. His aim was pure fun!

I had twenty minutes to imbibe a refreshing glass of orange water and then I was off to see Tim, my holistic masseur. Simon was there beside me before I realised. I was still visualising those tantalising moments, yet to come, as Tim's fingers probed my muscles, encouraging the tension and stress to leave my body.

'Angel, where did you go to, my darling? Your eyes are misty, like pools of cloudy water.' He had a way with words! Not!

We both broke the spell with bubbles of belly laughter.

'Simon, you say the daftest things.'

'Well, I had to drag you back the best way I knew how!'

'I'm off in five minutes to meet with my man of mystery.' I purred in his ear.

'But I haven't made my plans yet, Angel. Where are we going?' He looked intrigued.

'As she said in that famous old movie: "If you need me honey, just whistle. You know how to whistle. Just put your lips together and blow."'

George was trying to eavesdrop on our conversation and threw his arm around Simon's shoulder to get closer.

'Juicy, juicy, juicy! You lecherous pair! What naughties are afoot? Can Susie and I join in?'

'Sorry, Georgie. I'm off to see the magical masseur, Tim. You two reprobates have misconstrued the plot.' I winked at Simon, leered at George and called goodbye to the gang.

'See you later at the pool.'

I grabbed my bag and almost ran down the corridor. Oowee, I could hardly wait.

Tim's massage studio was set away from the other therapy rooms, which circled the pool. I had to walk through the pool area and up a flight of stairs where one would find the gym, aerobic and fitness rooms and only two massage studios, one of which was Tim's – just the elite.

I arrived and my pulse had quickened in anticipation. My eyes fixed on the brass door handle. What a child I was: it was like Christmas and the expectation of Father Christmas and presents.

'Angelina, Angelina, Angelina!' He sang his arrival as he pounced up the stairs behind me.

'Tim! You man of healing hands! It's *Angelica*! And don't you forget it.'

'I know, I wanted to sing to you and the song is already written. Please enter my Chamber of Horrors. Hey, did you notice the fabulous plaque by the door.' He pointed to a small brass plate with his name emblazoned upon it.

'You have definitely arrived. May I knight you, Sir Timothy!'

'Get your clothes off, you hussy, and lay yourself, dutifully, on my couch.'

He turned his back while I derobed and lay my body down in sacrifice. I pulled the white fluffy towel up to nipple level, closed my eyes and waited for the hands to descend upon my flesh.

'Do not utter a sound! Keep your eyes closed and let me ease your tension!' He walked around to my feet, gently folding back the towel to expose my legs, and began to oil my body.

He used a combination of oils to suit each client and for me it was eucalyptus, bergamot and ylang ylang. The fragrance invaded my senses and I was away, far away, floating in harmony with his hands.

'Time to turn over please, Angelica.' He fluttered the towel to obscure his view of my naked body and laid it back down across my torso, only exposing my legs, and began a similar routine of effleurage, kneading, lifting, circling and gently cuffing my muscles.

'Now for the part you love the most!' he whispered, almost sensually, as he pulled the towel down as far as the two dimples at the top of my bottom, now exposing my back.

'Oh bliss!' I couldn't help the throaty groan escaping from my mouth.

'Shh! People will think that something else is going on in here and they'll want some too.' He pushed the corner of the pillow towards my face.

'If you feel an urge coming on – suck on the pillow!'

Even his mocking couldn't break the spell. I was captured. Too soon it was over.

'When you are ready, get up slowly and dress and look at the new frame behind you by the window.' Quietly, he left the room and I pushed myself up onto my elbows to find his new wall hanging. How lovely and so flattering. He had framed a poem I had written for him last year, heralding his expertise. I read it aloud.

> Your wandering hands weave a spell.
> Knowing my bodily needs so well.
> Briefly finding erogenous zones.
> Forcefully kneading skin and bones.
> My body awakens under your touch.
> Raw nerves pleasuring in this so much.
> Tension ebbing from every pore.
> Muscles aching but wanting more.
> Time has elapsed the treatment ceasing.

Slowly the pressure of hands easing.
All breath dispersed unable to speak.
Breaking the spell and leaving me weak.
I peel my body from your table.
Reaching the floor when I am able.
Head for the door with great sorrow.
Farewell my friend until tomorrow.

I opened the door and met his glance. He raised his eyebrows, encouraging my comment.

'Tim, I'm truly flattered! What made you display it for all to see?'

He looked at me with a warming smile.

'No one has put into words exactly how my massage affects them. It just made me feel exceptionally gifted and humble. Praise like that is worth more than money!'

'That's good, because I am broke!' I swung my hips and with a wave of my hand, descended the stairs.

'Until tomorrow, Tim.'

Jeannie leaped out on me and hugged my oiled body. 'You bitch! You're soaking wet!' I cried.

'That's what water does to you.'

She scampered off into a cubicle to dry and dress before I could retaliate. Her little rascal face peered over the door.

'Are we going into lunch now? It's almost 12.30 p.m. and I'm starving.'

'OK, I'll wait by the jacuzzi with George and Susie. I can see them up there.'

I walked in a daze towards them when a stream of water hit my feet. Simon was playing dolphins in the pool and spat water at me as I passed, much to the amusement of his viewing public. He always had admirers. I pushed his head back under and he disappeared, to re-emerge by the steps as I arrived there.

'You are going to upset your fan club if you keep singling me out. I'm sure certain onlookers think you are Tom Jones, even though you are taller and much more handsome and possibly *sexier*!'

'What do you mean – *possibly*? You know I am!'

'Go and get changed if you are joining us for lunch. You've got five minutes!'

He jogged to the men's cubicles and I sat with George and Susie.

'Hail, Andromeda! You are glowing!'

George was sitting like a Buddha, very red and smiling from ear to ear. 'Hi, you two. We all look as if we have been prepared for frying. How are you, Susie?' I directed my gaze at her, hoping to get more than a monosyllabic answer. She looked at me through lowered lashes.

'I'm fine, thank you.'

'She's hunky-dory, aren't you, babe?' George gave her thigh a resounding slap, which made her blush. Conversation with Susie was hard work.

'I could eat your arm, George, nicely seasoned and roasted to a crisp!' Jeannie arrived with food on her mind. He chuckled and scooped her up, throwing her across his lap and paddling her bottom, loudly.

Our little gang was noticeably riotous and understandably irritated a few people. Simon joined us, so now we were five. Hermy and Vanessa kept their distance during the day, preferring more sedate company, but loved our free-spirited night-time antics.

Diane had reserved our regular table in the bay window and fluttered around us through lunch. The topic of conversation was mainly diet and alcohol and the programme of events for the afternoon.

George let us know what he was going to do.

'I'm gonna fuck the knickers off my woman!'

Poor Susie was so embarrassed, so Simon launched into George. 'That's enough, George, there are ladies present.'

'Where? I can't see that toffee-nosed Hermione or the stuck-up Vanessa,' he blustered.

'Hey! Come on, George! Have you swallowed a scorpion?' I couldn't sit and say nothing.

'Come and give me a kiss and I'll behave,' he retaliated.

'On your bike, you rogue.' Simon interceded with a rueful grin and sparring fists.

'Is anyone going to Leon's jazzercise class at 2 p.m.? Jeannie and I are going.'

'I should like to go. Can I tag along with you?'

'You are more than welcome, Susie. It's a great laugh and good exercise too. He performs like Mr Motivator.' I was pleasantly surprised she had wanted to join us.

'He's got a lovely bum, too. That would motivate any hormone-deficient woman!' Jeannie was always ready with a saucy remark.

'Sorry girls, you can count me out. I don't fancy watching his bum or prancing about like a deluded fairy. I'll challenge you to a game of pool if you're keen, George?' Simon rubbed his hands encouragingly.

'You're on, Boyo. I'll whip your arse,' George retorted, amiably.

We vacated our chairs and walked into the pool area, which was always our assembly point. Simon came up behind me and whispered against my hair.

'Slide your hands to the back of your waist and see how your presence moves me!' He pushed himself against my hands and his viper responded with magnetic force.

'Can *he* persuade you to dance with *him* instead of Leon?' Simon crooned in my ear.

'What's all this quiet talk, you two? Let's all hear it!' George was eager to intervene.

'Actually, George, Simon was saying how it would be a cold day in Hell before you would beat him at pool!'

Simon shoved me so hard that I almost toppled over, then swiftly pulled me to him and kissed me full on the lips, soft, luxurious and wet.

'There, you little minx! That's for telling porkies. I shall have to deal with you later.'

Yes, please, I thought. I could hardly wait.

We went our separate ways, the boys to the pool-room and the girls to the dance studio for a workout with lovable Leon. We stripped off to T-shirts and shorts and formed neatly spaced lines with room to move. Leon was already there, prancing about like a black panther.

'OK, ladies and gents, for those who don't know me, my name is Leon and we are about to have thirty minutes of fun with a capital F – and don't forget your water!'

He glanced around the room, recognising some faces.

'You, you and you, come here to the front! These ladies are experts, so you others can take their lead.' He grinned.

Jeannie, Susie and I dutifully moved to the front and so we began the rhythmic warm-up routine.

Leon was a black American who had graduated from his 'Fame' school of dancing in New York and had decided to tour the world. He had stayed at this hydro in England for four years, with no desire to move on. In his words, this was Heaven. He was single, fit and good-looking. He could have a different babe every night of the week with no questions asked and the pay was excellent. Life was his for the taking.

His class was easy-going and he made us laugh. The music was perfect too, soul songs from the forties, fifties and sixties – music to get down to. After about half an hour most of the class left, but a few of us stayed for the more funky stuff, fifteen minutes of high aerobic dance.

At the end of this session we fell around the floor, hoping for oxygen or the kiss of life. We got neither, just a cup of water.

'Bye, bye, ladies! You'll were real good for honkies!'

Someone threw a shoe at him as he disappeared through the swing doors. 'Well, I'll take that as a compliment!' one lady said.

Susie looked at me for guidance, she was really lost without George.

'OK, girls! Who is for a sauna, swim and a frothy jacuzzi?'

'Ooh! That sounds lovely! We can get even more sweaty, then very wet and finally brewed in herbal essences!' Jeannie was knackered, but would not give in. I believe pure alcohol was oozing from every pore.

'I am looking forward to this. It is so nice to be my own person once in a while.' This revelation from Susie was breaking new territory. It suited her.

We headed down to the lower therapy areas around poolside and booked some space in the steam room and sauna cabinet, which were all currently busy.

'Just enough time for a leisurely shower and swim!' Jeannie held open the doors for us.

We had a communal shower, put on our cozzies and swam. In the afternoon most clients did their own thing as the therapists finished by 1 p.m. Some chose golf, others horse riding or just using the facilities at their own volition.

I swam for pleasure, not for exercise, and nestled into a steady stroke. I could see Simon, George, Vanessa and Hermy in deep conversation, sitting under the indoor palm tree by the jacuzzi. Each gave a wave and carried on their conversation.

At this point all I wanted were my private thoughts, trying to unravel the complicated decisions I had to make. All I could think of was – *out* – I had to make a better life. How could I stop this inner scream that was lurking somewhere beneath the surface. My heart had gone cold long ago, this pain was much lower, in my gut, in my back, in the core of me. I had to keep control for the kids, they were my world, the very heart of me! Oh! You stupid, stupid *wet*! Those lyrics were written for foolish romantics – like *me*!

I almost drowned as I laughed at the maudlin choice of thoughts. Get a grip! Girls just wanna have fun! I spied Jeannie and swam under her, trying to dislodge her bottoms. She was too quick for me and submerged so we were in face-to-face combat. The initiative was hers and she zapped my top.

Urgh! Splutter! I surfaced amid coughing and spluttering and much screeching. Luckily, my toes were now on the floor of the pool but my top was floating away.

'I'll save you, my little Chickadee!' George sort of dived or exploded into the water like a loaded Zeppelin, causing a huge tidal wave. Susie, Jeannie and I clung onto the sides in hoots of laughter.

George surfaced, eventually, with my bikini top strapped to his head, like a volley ball player.

'Isn't this how yours are worn this year, Andromeda? Or is it just the *knickers* on the head?'

I hung round his huge neck, kissed his head and retrieved my top.

'That's enough, George, or I shan't let you play in my team again.'

'I stand rebuked, fair lady, and shall desist furthermore, even though your hard nipples are piercing my skin!' He hauled his robust body from the pool, leaving me to become respectable.

'We ladies are now going for a sauna and will join you for a quickie in the jacuzzi before dinner!' I sneaked a glance at Simon, who was still immersed in conversation, so I went for my sauna.

Susie and Jeannie got there first and there were three other ladies, already cooking, so I was relegated to the lower level, which I hated. It was too hot.

'I'm only staying here for five minutes, today,' I excused myself.

'If you can't stand the heat! – and you know the rest.' Jeannie, always the smart-arse.

If I did five it was only barely. I couldn't breathe, it was much too hot.

I seemed to stand under the shower for an eternity, letting the cascading jets refresh me.

'Come on, Angie. Let's hit the jacuzzi and end up like prunes!' Jeannie flicked my bottom with her towel and ran.

As we glided along the poolside to the far end the lights dimmed in unison. The huge antique clock above the men's changing room was showing 4.30 p.m. We all saluted the clock and George said, 'Only half light now, me hearties! You are now entering the time warp of the Marie Celeste. In an hour we will all disappear – Ahaa! Ahaa!'

At this time of year we were encouraged to vacate the pool area by 5.30 p.m., so the lights were dipped as a reminder. The Hockey Team had thirty minutes to commune in the hot tub.

'Hermy, please take that awful flowerpot off your head!' Simon was halfway to pulling a floral rubber hat from her head.

She removed it herself and chided him with a wet slap.

'I'll have you know that these were très chic in the sixties.' She grinned.

'Well, I would rather see you like this, sort of tussled and tarnished and *tarty*!'

Vanessa gasped. She could not control her anger. She had swallowed the prince and was left with a very outrageous frog.

'Say something, Hermione! Don't let Simon speak to you in that fashion!' She had gone scarlet.

We all screamed with laughter, especially Hermione.

'Oh! Don't be so tight, Vanessa! He was just funning. Thanks for your defence, but I thought he was rather humorous.'

Hermy tried to give Vanessa a cuddle, but she huffed and puffed her way out of the jacuzzi, mumbling as she went and probably feeling slightly embarrassed. She walked into the shadows.

Needless to say everyone was subdued for a second, looking from one to the other for a lead.

'Oh! Fuck it!' Good old George to the rescue.

'Trust you, you old fart.' A good retort from Jeannie.

'You can talk, you bottom-burper!' I couldn't resist.

'I have to say it George, you are very *loud*!' Susie was amazing, instantly blushed and George looked bemused.

'That settles it! *Brrrrump*!' Simon's rear end exploded and we all jumped out. The laughter, then, was uncontrollable.

'How did we come down to this level? Vanessa was only saying earlier, how we would have to find an alternative spa as this one no longer satisfied her sensibilities.'

Queen Hermione was attempting to compose herself by fluffing her hair and fumbling with her towel.

'You shouldn't have worn that dreadful cap, Hermy. It made you look like the Bad Queen in an *Alice in Wonderland* spoof!' Simon could hardly speak, his sides were hurting so much.

'Do you think they have put laughing gas in the water, or, perhaps we are all mad!' That was the most audacious statement Susie had ever made, and without any help from George. We sat there stunned and in silence, looking at Susie.

A black face peered around the corner, followed by Leon's lithe body, at a very opportune moment.

'I might have guessed it was you lot! What the devil is going down? This is a respectable establishment, not Butlins!' He was joking with us, of course, and sat on the lounger next to Simon.

'So how's it hanging, man? Any juicy gossip in the celebrity hairdressing game?'

'Leon, if I divulged any secrets it would make your hair stand on end!'

'OK, my man! Ain't you noticed, I have *no hair*! So where's the party tonight or are you playing it straight this time?'

Leon and Simon could play with words for hours, so we females decided it was time to put on our posh frocks for dinner.

I stood first and the others followed, making our way to our respective stairways and rooms. Jeannie left me at my door. We were both exhausted.

'See you at 7.25 p.m., honey!' I called as she opened her door and looked back with a grin. Susie was right, I thought, we are all mad!

I threw myself down on the bed, looking up at the ceiling. I was so tired, but nicely so. No! I can't do this! Shower first and then I can rest for a while. It was 5.30 p.m., so I had plenty of time.

The shower was exactly what was needed. Refreshed and clean, with shining hair, I began the refurb. Loads of mascara to make my eyes look feline, and tonight I would wear the slinky black number with the opening from my neck to my bottom dimples.

'*Brrr! Brrr! Brrr!*'

'Hello, this is room 56,' I said coquettishly.

'Hello, room 56, this is room 90. Which one shall we spoil tonight?' Simon was in dominant mode.

'I think we should waste yours, my sheets are already imperfect.' I purred in reply.

'OK, Angel. See you at dinner.' The phone went dead.

By 6.30 p.m. I was ready, so I decided to write in my diary and then select a few new poems for Vanessa to read to try and make my peace.

'*Brrr! Brrr!*' I thought Simon was impatient as I picked up the receiver.

'Hello, may I help you?' I sighed into the mouthpiece.

'I have an urgent call for you, Mrs Reeves. I'll just connect you.'

The operator left the line and the next voice I heard was Sean.

'Mum, you must come home! They've taken Dad away!' His voice broke and he began to cry.

My heart was racing and I sat on the floor, holding my throat, completely stunned at what he had said.

'Speak to me, sweetheart! Please don't cry!' What was going on? I was cold and trembling.

'Mum, it's me. Look, this is awful. The police have arrested Dad. The place is upside down. Nan didn't come, thank goodness! What shall I do, Mum? Can you come home?' Rebecca was now crying, too.

'Listen! Can you hold out for two hours and I'll be there? Just hold out for me! Can you do that? Speak to me, darling, please!' I waited for them to calm down. It seemed for ever.

'Mum, I'm OK now. It was so hard telling you that I got uptight, sorry. They took him last night and we haven't heard anything all day. They were real bastards, Mum. It's taken us all day to tidy up. They treated Dad like a criminal. What's he done? We thought he would be back, so we didn't call you sooner. Please come home!' Sean was now strong and back in control.

'Sweethearts, I love you all so much and I'll be there in two hours. Be brave! Keep yourselves occupied and phone my mobile every fifteen minutes so that I know you are OK. I'm on my way. Don't worry, I'll sort it out! I replaced the receiver and saw my reflection in the mirror. Suitably I had chosen *black* for mourning.

Chapter Eight

A light touch on my forehead woke me and I opened my eyes. Polly was standing there smiling at me.

'Don't rush! It's only 8.15 a.m. I was wondering if you would like to walk on the heath with me. I have squared it with the boss and she has given the OK.' She looked hopeful.

'Shouldn't you be off home by now?' I replied as I pushed myself up on one elbow.

'No, I'm here on the weekend watch. We stay for forty-eight hours to attend to the few patients who remain here at weekends. It is only a skeleton staff and it's not hard work. I can grab an hour or two through the night.' She walked to my closet and began rehanging my clothes, discarded from last night.

'So what's the verdict? Shall we go?' She swung around to look at me.

'The verdict will be guilty and we shall all pay the price!' No tears now, just a blank nothingness.

'Oh, crikey! Wrong words! I am so sorry.' She sat on the bed and took my hands and we stared into space. Every now and then a numbness overcame me. The words took a long time to form in my mouth. Sometimes I thought my lips were the dam and if I opened them my life would gush from me, so I kept them closed as long as I could.

'I checked on you at intervals during the night and you were so peaceful. In fact, once I found you smiling and thought I heard you laughing in your sleep. It must have been a comforting dream!' She talked to cover the silence, while I composed myself.

Polly was astute and empathetic. So far my key nurses had been equally attentive, but their attendance was so different. Tania was motherly, warm and bountiful, ready to hug away my tears or chastise if necessary.

Sam, the Chinese sprite, was a tactician, with understanding and full of intuition with the artistry of ancient healing.

Polly was a listener, a gentle genie, there to guide and also learn. Each had a part to play; the only ingredient was the patient and their need for life balancing.

Now calm again, I smiled and nodded. 'Let's go! I should like to get some fresh air. I'll shower and be ready in fifteen minutes.'

'What about breakfast? You must have something!'

'I'll take some fruit with me and grab a bottle of juice from the dining room. Is that OK?'

'That's fine. Be back at about 9 a.m.' She left.

As I showered, I remembered how particular I used to be with my clothes, hair and make-up. Now I had lost interest. The clothes stopped me from being naked and I suppose I still liked to be clean and emerge with some self-respect. I couldn't remember the last time John commented on my appearance. Once I stood naked between him and the TV, he smiled benignly and asked me to move as I was blocking his view. He preferred porn movies to me!

Polly was back. We collected some drinks and left via the courtyard, taking the lane, which led to the heath. The space and freedom was exhilarating. I kept turning round to see if the Abbey had disappeared – it was totally obscured by the woods.

'Do I look different, Polly? Would anyone know I came from the Abbey?' She sat down with a bump and laughed.

'You are silly. You look no different than I do. We are both casually dressed and to all intents and purposes are two friends having a Saturday morning jog.'

I sat down beside her and had a huge gulp of my drink.

'Follow my finger and I shall point out all the landmarks for when you jog out on your own.'

I leaned on one elbow and was relieved and interested at the guided tour Polly gave me on the locality. How long would it be before I had the confidence to go out on my own?

We walked a little, jogged and talked. She was surprisingly eloquent, had left uni with a 2:1 in Sociology and Psychology and was hoping to go to the States to study. Until then she was agency nursing and had chosen an assignment with Dr Michael at the Abbey for six months. I began to get a bit peckish and suggested we sat against a tree while I ate my banana.

'Out of all the trees to pick on this parkland, why did you head for the oak tree?' She rested her back on the trunk and watched me.

'I have always had a fascination for oaks. They give me a feeling of protection and strength. It all goes back to when I was young. We had a beautiful oak tree at the bottom of the garden and my dad hung a swing on the lowest branch. I would stay there swinging for hours, creating stories. I used to call the branches "hugging arms" – I think that is what I am searching for, someone who is strong and resembles an oak tree.' We both laughed in unison.

'You have a vivid imagination, perhaps that is why you suffer, you are still living in your childhood.'

We both lolled against the tree, locked into our separate thoughts and daydreams. The sun was almost overhead and painted fabulous patterns on the grass around us as its rays pierced holes through the lush foliage.

The comfortable silence was broken by Polly.

'Angelica, do you realise how strong and diverse the human mind is? With the advantage of guidance and carefully chosen stimuli we can repair a damaged mind just as we can heal tissue. You have the power to emerge from your trauma as a bright new butterfly.

'Start today! Confront your demons, understand where they are coming from and walk away. It's not going to be easy, but you can do this!' With a little cough she jumped to her feet, took my hands and hauled me to my feet.

'What's up Doc?' I felt apprehensive.

'The treatment starts now! You have to try to beat me back to the Abbey!' She ran like a rabbit, darting and zigzagging across the grass, then checking to see if I had accepted the challenge.

'Yahoo!' I yelled.

I was surprised at my new-found energy. As I increased my pace I was reeling her in. How contrived was the scenario? Was Polly allowing me to overhaul her in order to increase my self-esteem? I didn't really care. I was enjoying myself for the first time in ages and if I found the gravel drive of the Abbey first, then that would be a bonus.

As we entered the woodland, I lost sight of Polly and thought I had turned the wrong way at the fork, but lo and behold there was the outline of the Abbey in the distance. My knees were beginning to burn so I considered slowing down when I caught sight of a bobbing ponytail ahead of me. We hit the stone pathway together and landed in a heap of breathless giggles.

'Angelica, you are amazing! Believe me now, you are *not* going to fall off again. I'll have you hitting that punchbag with a vengeance, before long. That's when you will address your anger. The room with the punchbag is waiting for you at the end of your corridor, so when you feel the venom rising, just let rip!'

We sat side by side, regaining our breath and watched a black BMW pull up beside us. A young man with floppy blond hair got out, with an older woman fussing at his side. She touched and prodded and whined at him like a dog worrying a bone. The young man was wide-eyed and defensive, seeming oblivious to the harrying of the woman.

They were joined by an older man, who had dragged himself from the driver's seat and was approaching the main door. To an onlooker it could have been a domestic interlude, visiting relatives, to a Georgian estate, buried in the depths of the Kent countryside. But it wasn't! They resembled a family torn apart by fear and misunderstandings. Could the doctors within help readjust their lives?

The wisteria-covered porch beckoned them. They waited, patiently, for someone to acknowledge their arrival. It was Saturday and lunchtime. There was a good possibility that the intermittent call sign had not been heard or seen, so Polly offered her assistance.

She tapped the authorisation code into the panel and we all gained access.

Briefly, I looked into the faces of these people, each one locked into their own torture chamber. The older man was holding himself erect, but was tired and resigned. The woman seemed to be in control of the situation, but her hands were agitated and her eyes bore pain. Now, the young man was an enigma, he was tensed like an athlete waiting for the starting pistol and his easy way of walking lied about the confusion within.

My being there was superfluous. I waved to Polly and took myself off to my room. It was already ordained that the new arrival and I would become as close as kinfolk.

As I stood beneath the shower with my eyes tightly closed a reawakening of my inner self had begun. Perhaps it was a cocktail of sunshine, fresh air and exercise, or was it the emptiness in those grey eyes that sparked a memory in mine? The newcomer had that 'look'. We all had it at times.

At that moment I wanted to sing. I loved singing. My tummy grumbled in harmony. I was really hungry. A light had been switched on inside me and I wanted to rejoin the world. The date on the calendar seemed significant. It was the 4th of July, a landmark in modern history. I dressed and hurried down to the dining room, hoping this positive feeling would last.

The corridor leading to the dining room was empty and the building quiet and at rest, but I didn't feel lonely; instead I felt expectant. I wanted my future. I wanted my life back!

Harvey was sitting alone, in our usual place by the French doors. He was looking downcast and jumped to his feet at my approach.

'Oh, how wonderful that you are here, Angelica!' He pulled a chair out for me and I sat facing him.

'Have you eaten yet, Harvey? I'm starving!' I smiled into his face.

'No, luckily, I was just about to choose.' He was really staring at me.

'Do I have a spot on my nose, Harvey? You are staring at me!' I started to rise.

'Actually, Angelica, you look stunning. You are like a rose in full bloom. Have you had some good news?' He was getting too close, almost hanging over my shoulder. Too close for comfort.

'No! I just had a great fresh air escape with Polly and have returned feeling rejuvenated, refreshed and zingy. I walked back to the table with a humongous salad, leaving Harvey to digest what I had said and finish deciding what he was going to eat.

Before he could launch into an interrogation, as he resumed his seat, I asked brightly, 'So how did your morning go, Harvey? Did you take your trip into town for your dry-cleaning?'

'Yes, I looked for you at breakfast, to see if you would go with me, but you weren't around.' He had that hangdog expression and I wanted to shake him, instead I quietly recounted my morning's exploits.

Poor, sad, Harvey! He so needed to get a life. I couldn't afford to let him bring me down. I said I was going to sit in the gardens and hopefully write some more prose while the distractions were limited. Inwardly, I was begging him not to ask to accompany me. He didn't read the telepathy.

'May I sit with you if I promise not to be intrusive?'

This was hopeless. How should I say *no*?

'Yes, of course, we can keep one another company.'

I offered him a weak reassuring smile, inside it was a grimace. My eyes strayed around the room: only two other people were eating, both gazing at the patterns on the tablecloth in front of them. The chef came out from the kitchen and caught my eye.

'How's the salad? Did you find enough choice?'

'Oh, yes, it is excellent, my plate resembles an artist's palette.' Don't go back in the kitchen, stay and talk to me, I thought.

My buoyant mood was evaporating. Thankfully, someone heard my silent plea for support. The entrance of the young blond-haired man and the elderly couple gave us food for thought.

He headed for an empty table, of which there were many, and sat down heavily, dragging the chair out by using his foot. This young man was acting like a spoilt child. His voice was loud and petulant where his father's was quiet and calm. I was engrossed in the performance and tried to look away, but the theatricals were magnetic viewing.

The mother (I had assumed they were his parents) joined them at the table carrying a tray of tea and a selection of cheese-cake and gateaux. 'For Christ's sake!' The young man forced his chair back and the tray became airborne, launching edible missiles in all directions and making puddles of tea on the floor amid shattered crockery.

Without any apology he stormed across the room, exiting via the French doors. His eyes showed hatred, or was it fear? Harvey leapt to his feet.

'I'm going to offer my help.' He was beside the couple in a trice, the Good Samaritan helping to put everything back on the tray. I watched the young man stride towards the stable block. He halted at the wall, turned and slid down until he was resting against it, balancing on his haunches and staring into space.

I didn't want to get involved, so I left as unobtrusively as I could, heading for my room.

'Hello, Miss Angelica, how are you today?' Archie was sitting behind his desk.

'I'm feeling good today, thank you, Archie. I just love this gorgeous weather.'

I was now at the stairs and flew up the two flights. Once inside my room, I took a deep, steadying breath. It was unnerving recognising that, small insignificant incidents could topple my equilibrium. The answer was: *stay focused*.

With my shoulder bag stuffed with pens, pencils and note-book, I retraced my tracks to the lobby and burst upon the unsuspecting quiet of the Abbey lawns. Secretly, I hoped that Harvey would not find me.

What a glorious day! In another time and space it would have been idyllic. Right now I had decided to play truant from my life and take on the guise of a fictional character. After all, who was around to witness the birth of the chameleon?

I swanned over to my favourite place under the oak tree and marked my territory by laying my blanket on the ground. The sun was at its zenith. It was tanning weather. My skin was taking on the colour of *café au lait* and I was aware of the inner glow produced by the warmth of the sun.

Cross-legged I sat on the corner of the blanket, so that my body was in direct sunlight and my head was shaded by the canopy of leaves. Wearing baseball cap and dark glasses, I was incognito, ready to set my pen to work. I stretched my neck in praise of the sun.

Gazing across at the main building my eyes rose to the second floor and I focused on my window, then scanned back as I glimpsed a face at the next-door window: it was Petra. I hadn't seen her for a couple of days and assumed that she had gone home. She looked tired and spaced-out and retreated when she saw me. That's OK! I wasn't in need of company. I just wanted to chill out and be creative, to do my own thing.

A tiny, whiskered face popped out from behind a bush and rippled across the lawn towards me. *Food* – I heard its thoughts and could have sworn it was smiling at me. It perched, boldly, only six inches from my toes and pretended to wash its face, but I knew it was inspecting me.

'Hello, little squirrel. Have you come to keep me company? I wish I were Dr Doolittle and could talk to you!'

He hopped around me and cheekily peered into my raffia shoulder bag. I pushed my hand inside and found a packet of crisps. He patiently waited for me to burst the bag and shed the contents. Of course, I obliged. Did I imagine my furry friend clapped his hands in anticipation.

A clicking noise erupted from its mouth and, amazingly, the entire family descended upon the scene. It was obviously, the scout leader and had told them that it was safe to approach. I would love to think that we shared a special bond.

What a commotion! There must have been a dozen of them, brazenly cavorting around me, stealing the crisps and pulling at my clothes. As if by magic, they disappeared. Something had disturbed them.

'Oh! Quelle dommage! I am so sorry! I have ruined your party!' The throaty exclamation of Françoise melted over my head.

I looked up to see her face silhouetted against the sun. Her golden hair spun away from her head in tendrils, giving her a supernatural appearance.

'Please don't fret! They have had their munchies and I was being sorely distracted. As you can see, I have my notebook and pen in hand and have written nothing.'

'I will sit with you – yes?' It was a rhetorical question and Françoise sat beside me.

'Now I will make sketches of you for your portrait and I will not be a nuisance. You will not know I am here – yes?' She was dressed in a flowing robe of rust, green and turquoise that billowed around her like an autumn garden. I found her presence calming, almost mesmeric, and together we addressed our arts.

An hour passed so quickly with neither of us speaking. I wrote two poems with ease. The first was 'The Palomino', conjuring up thoughts of my sister and her husband and their lifelong parallel with horses. The second was 'The Songbird', who proclaimed his love of life and need for flight.

Occasionally, I felt a penetrating stare from Françoise and was tempted to interrupt her, but thought better of it. She would invite me to look when she was ready. Perhaps our thought patterns collided because she spoke while she was sketching.

'Are you not a little afraid of me, cherie?' She turned her head at an angle so she could see the reaction in my eyes.

'Let's face it, Françoise, all institutions have gossips and whispers and, before you ask, the answer is yes, to your next question. I have been told a few unsettling things about you.' I remained comfortable and at ease as she lay her sketch to one side and sat closer to me.

'I am a very bad woman and have dreams that torment my soul that make me do bad things to myself. This is true! C'est vrai, mais je ne suis pas un goule! Pardon! I am sorry, I forget I am in England, sometimes.'

'Look, Françoise. You don't have to explain anything to me. My head is upside down and I am afraid of my own shadow.' I held my hands towards the sky in mock surrender.

Françoise looked puzzled, saying, 'Your head is very much normal and perfect to be drawn. Do not be worried for I will not make you hideous!'

She began to sketch again, so I closed my eyes and remained still, allowing the warm sun to saturate my willing body.

Occasionally, Françoise spoke, very quietly, telling me about her way of life in Paris and her love for her husband and her two children. Michel and Lauren were being cared for by her mother in France and David, her husband, was close by. He was attached to the French Embassy, being on overseas duty for another six months and then they would return to France.

This was the third occurrence of her illness. On the two previous occasions she had cut her arms and had been taken to a psychiatric hospital just outside Paris. She pulled her sleeves back to expose the many lacerations on her forearms.

'Oh, my God! You poor soul!' I couldn't stop the feeling of empathy.

'Contrary to belief, I have not hurt my babies or my husband, I just hurt the bad part of me which needs to be cleansed.'

She smiled, with angelic purity; she was totally surreal. My mood was so relaxed and soon I was nodding, lulled by the warmth of the sun and the gentle company.

'I have prepared enough sketches and will now leave you to your slumber – au revoir, ma cherie.' She stood up and floated across the lawn to be swallowed by the shadow of the building. I lay, curled on my blanket and entered the world of dreams – my Comfort Zone.

Chapter Nine

Was this going to be the end of my fantasy? Was this the last time that I would visit room 56, with the beautiful square carved bed full of delicious memories?

I had to gather my thoughts at electric speed, no time to delay. I ripped off my dress and pulled on a sweater and jeans. Dial the number!

'Jeannie! Don't speak! Just listen! I am in desperate need of you right now, please come to my room!'

I dropped the receiver onto its cradle and pulled my case from the cupboard. Everything was crammed in without ceremony and the entrance of Jeannie halted nothing.

'*Stop! Stop! Stop!* What the hell are you doing?' Jeannie stood with curling tongs in hand, looking like a deranged woman with an electric gun. 'I have to go home, *now!* The kids are distraught and *John* has been arrested and is being held in some police station in London. *I feel sick and my chest hurts.* How could he do this to us, Jeannie? The kids were there, they saw it all!'

Jeannie's mouth hung open and her hands flew to her face to halt the scream that was about to come. The curling tongs fell to the floor and I couldn't help thinking how ridiculous her appearance was.

'Look, please help me. Make some excuse at reception to cover for me. Say anything you like, but make it realistic Jeannie, *please*! Do it now!'

I ran into the bathroom and grabbed at everything that wasn't attached to the walls, stuffing my holdall to bursting point. How many minutes had elapsed? I could hear Jeannie on the phone and the click as she finished. She held my shoulders as I appeared at the bathroom door and forced me to stand still.

'Calm down, Jelly!' She fastened her eyes on mine.

My body was trembling and I resisted the tears that were welling in my eyes.

'Oh, you cow! You haven't called me that for years!' I sniffed loudly, shaking myself free.

There was a loud bang at the door and Simon was standing there beside me.

'What are you doing here, Simon? I can't deal with this now!'

He looked so handsome and suave, my very own swashbuckling hero. Calmly, he folded the entire contents of my case and repacked my vanity bag, while I stood there, speechless.

'Angel, Jeannie called me. She explained the whole thing. I shall deal with the enquiries that will follow and settle your bill, trust me!'

'How can I thank you both for this? I wish I could turn back time, but I can't.' I kissed Jeannie, leaving her alone in my room, trying to make sense of what was about to happen. Simon took my hand.

The door of room 56 closed and in silence we headed for the back stairs. An encouraging glance flew my way and I held tightly onto his hand as if he were my lifeline, the transfer of energy I needed to carry me through the next few hours. As we approached the emergency exit, my phone rang.

'Hello, my darling, I'm on my way, just getting into the car. I shall phone you in a quarter of an hour. Are you and Becca OK?'

Simon pushed the door open for us and wrapped his body around me in the shelter of the doorway, as the cold air hit us.

'We're OK, Mum. Don't worry, just drive safely!' I slid the phone back into my pocket and relaxed for a second in the comfort of Simon's arms.

Our breath froze in the air like white mystical dragons, and although it had stopped snowing, the ground was covered completely in a milky shroud, with crisp peaks twinkling in the moonlight.

'Sweetheart, I'll walk you to your car and then go to the manager's office. I'll tell him that you have had a family tragedy and have had to leave.'

'Simon, I will get my family through this, won't I? I feel so sick! Oh, I don't know how I feel!' My words were constricting my throat. I had so many visions careering through my mind that I was beginning to doubt that I could drive the two hours through the snow. But I had to, my kids were depending on me. Please, if there is a God, get me to my twins safely.

I clung onto the back of Simon's jacket as we skirted the building. How quirky the mind is. I thought of Simon as my very own 007 and immediately dismissed the character and replaced it by a long black tunnel without light.

The night interpreted my darkness and telepathically the car park lights awoke, illuminating the frozen cars and snapping me back to reality.

'Stand there in the porch and I'll get your car warmed up.' He guided me into the dimly lit porch and began to clear the frost from the windows of the car.

I looked inside to where the log fire was roaring and a few people were gathering to chat before going into dinner. Oh, shit! Why was this happening to me? When does the struggle ease? Silly girl! This is only the beginning, if you can't handle this then you might as well surrender now. Who will protect your kids then?

My mind was having a two-way conversation. I had to remain calm or I wouldn't be able to function. Don't ask yourself questions, just get on with whatever has to be done. OK! I looked across at Simon. The windows were clear and he had reversed the car out, ready to drive away. I stood and shivered. Was it a ghost or merely the cold?

'All done, my Angel.' He pulled me fiercely into his arms, I could hear his heart thumping against my ear.

'I'll let you know what's happening as soon as I can. Make some plausible excuse for me, I'm relying on you, Simon.' I saw pain in his eyes or was it the cold air?

'Take care, darling. Please, please drive carefully. You know how I feel about you!'

I got into the car, checking that my bags were sitting safely on the back seat and my phone was sitting on the seat next to me. All the dashboard lights were indicating that the car was ready to depart.

I blew Simon a kiss and gently pushed down on the accelerator. The tyres crunched on the frozen gravel and I took one last look at my action man, standing tall against the brightly lit stone entrance porch. The picture resembled a stately home awaiting the guests and he was the host.

That was the last time I was to visit the wonderland of the health hydro, but I wasn't to know it then. As I drove towards the lights of the main road I had one fleeting thought. If Simon really loved me, I wouldn't be making that journey alone, he would have been there to support me. For once, I should have been the priority. I suppose I understood his reluctance to commit, but life doesn't wait for the faint-hearted. This was one chapter in my life that I had to do, alone. The lioness was returning to her den. No creature would protect her young with fiercer determination.

So, thanks Simon, thanks for chickening out. Come, Orgasma – get me home – safely!

I felt a chill shudder through me and opened my eyes. I had fallen asleep on the blanket and the sun had dipped below the rooftops. Tears clung to my lashes and I sighed as I remembered the last view of Sexy Si at the hydro. That was six months ago and my life had disintegrated since then. He is not so eager to see me now and who can blame him, certainly not me. Even my so-called best friend shunned me. Isn't it strange how people believe that misfortune is a transmittable disease?

I could sense eyes watching me and expected to see one or two squirrels hiding close by, but none was evident. Then I saw movement by the patio doors. Someone was swaying to and fro on the swing seat, his face was hidden by the canopy.

Deliberately, I gathered my things together and threw the blanket across my shoulder like a Mexican bandit. The seat continued to swing as I approached. The atmosphere was decidedly hostile. Should I speak or not?

'Hi, we must be the only patients enjoying the fresh air.' My voice faltered as I saw the steely look of indifference that was projected at me.

The icy feet of a thousand ants climbed my legs and arms and camped at the base of my skull. I knew that look, John had stabbed me with it so many times. It was a mixture of fear, love, hatred and indifference. Why was this young man so hostile? He couldn't be projecting his anger at me!

'Sorry, I was miles away. We haven't been introduced, I'm Chris.' He jumped to his feet and extended his hand. He was tall and solid, attractive in a boyish way and had silky, foppish, blond hair.

I stepped back, involuntarily, he had caught me off-guard. The eyes were blue and the mouth, now, smiling. How could he change from cold steel to sky blue geniality in a split second, or was it all in my imagination?

'Hi, I'm Angelica. It's a bit of a mouthful, I'm afraid. Have you settled in OK? It's a touch daunting at first.' I was rambling to cover my embarrassment; this man had unbalanced me and I wanted to get away.

'I've been allocated a room downstairs, number 11; it has French doors that open onto the fields. They evidently put you there until the witch doctors have assessed you. Needless to say, the doors are locked and bolted. Can't have Neanderthals roaming the countryside, can we?' He was primed, ready to implode, so I must stay calm.

I smiled and turned away, preparing to go inside. I was uncomfortable with the sarcasm and negativity exploding from this man.

'May I ask you a question, Chris?' I said with inevitable curiosity. He hesitated and took on a sulky, defensive pose.

'I suppose so. What?'

'Did you arrive today with your parents? The people with you looked very concerned!' He recoiled from me as if he had been stung.

'Yes, that's who they are, the fine doctor and her husband!' His face contorted and he looked as if he was about to vomit.

He was so angry, not with me, but with himself. I ventured towards him to try to repair the balance, but there was no way he would now allow me to invade his space. An invisible barrier had been erected. This was all too confusing and too tiring and *not* my problem, so I made my retreat.

'See you later.' I tossed over my shoulder. The reception area was empty, as was the corridor leading to the lower lounge, all except an unsupervised floor-cleaning machine, which was vibrating against a wall.

I was about to climb the stairs when the swing doors to the

ICU hushed a sigh as the suction pulled them together. A tall, foreign-looking man in green aprons walked towards one of the rooms. He casually looked in my direction and smiled. I wondered who he was as I went up to my room. I must be improving if I'm becoming curious. Turning the corner, I almost bumped into another new face.

'Hey, little lady, and who are you?' She smiled broadly and steadied me with her soft, warm hands.

'I'm Angelica Reeves, room 36. Hello!'

'And I'm Carmel, the weekend duty sister. How do you do!'

She linked arms with me and opened my door, allowing me to go in before her. She was short, tubby and glowed like a kitchen maid. I was instantly relaxed, expecting her to take on the guise of my favourite aunt.

'Have you had a good day, Angelica? You're not overdoing it, are you? You must have lots of rest.' She pushed me down on the chair, held my face in her hands and studied me, intently. She then popped a thermometer in my mouth, held a timepiece with one hand and took my pulse with the other.

'I'm an old-fashioned nurse, so I am, you'll be pleased to know. I take your temperature with one of these and not one of those space-guns and I love talking, too!' She paused for breath.

'Well, how am I doing, Carmel? What's your prognosis?' I said with a laugh.

'Ooh! La! You're the lady who writes the poetry and has a way with the words, so you are.' She gave a small curtsy. 'I am pleased to say your pulse is very low, which is good, and your temperature is just a little high. Nothing to worry about.'

'It's only 5.30 p.m., so may I have a long cool shower before dinner? Do you think that will ease my flushed head?'

'You bet it will, so it will. You know where I am if you need me.' And with a wink she left the room.

I stood under the shower, letting the tension evaporate. Tomorrow would be difficult, seeing John and the kids for the first time in over a week. We would all be nervous and over-anxious. Please, God, get us through the day. Did He hear me? I shivered. Time to get out of the shower and down to dinner. The encounter with the angry young man was forgotten.

Oh, no! How am I going to support an evening with Harvey. Poor chap! I felt flat and a cover of melancholy wrapped itself around me. Perhaps Petra would be down for dinner tonight. I closed my door and looked at hers. No, I wasn't in the mood to be snubbed, so I will not knock. Perhaps I shouldn't have chosen green to wear, not exactly a mood-enhancing colour. Too late to change now, so be positive!

A song from *South Pacific* sprung into my head as I descended the stairs and I fairly bounced into the lounge, and only fifteen minutes late.

'Better late than never, Milady!' Iain was grinning as I approached. Did he look too pleased to be back? Avoidance was a technique we had all learned to master.

'Well, there's a surprise, Iain. I didn't think you were due back until tomorrow?' I was relieved and delighted to see him. Harvey was holding out a chair in readiness, so I sat next to him.

'Truth is, Julie and I argued from the moment she picked me up so she was glad to offload me.'

'That's sad for both of you. I have my first meeting with John tomorrow and I'm a bit queasy about it.' I smiled at him.

'Shall we eat and talk about something more interesting!' Harvey was tetchy and hated being left out.

'Good idea, Harvey, let's see what's on offer.' I squeezed his arm. My mood had lifted at Iain's return.

There were more people dining tonight, which created a better ambience. The two spinster ladies were huddled together, nibbling at their food. Françoise was in deep conversation with a very dark, middle-aged man in one corner, then, next to our table, was Chris. He sat in silence, as did his parents. They were intent on their plates and kept their heads bowed. I wondered why they were still here? Chaperones were not encouraged.

'So, what did you do this afternoon, Harvey?' I hadn't seen him since the lunchtime drama.

'I spent some time with Chris's parents. They are extremely worried and apparently devoted to him. His mother is a GP, you know, an astute woman with high standards – she wants me to keep an eye on him!' He was puffed up with self-importance and flattered by her confidence.

'She must be out of her tiny mind! You're not a *doctor*, Harvey! How could she be so stupid as to ask *you* to look out for him!' Iain was annoyed and gave her bowed head a penetrating, reproachful stare. It did seem to be an irresponsible request for a GP to make.

That was like a wet blanket. No one spoke for a while. We finished our meal in silence, each one reflecting on hasty remarks. If I could have a one-to-one with Him upstairs, I would definitely want to know why everything was so complicated. I would ask him for a time capsule and to be transported to a future where everything had been resolved.

There was an enormous thunderclap, which made everyone jump. The air cooled and the rain came down in torrents.

'One banana, two bananas, three bananas.' I counted out loud. ''Scuse me, Milady! What's with these *bananas*? Is this some kind of fruity game?' Iain looked seriously amused.

'No, it's a way of knowing the distance of the storm. You see a banana is the equivalent to a second and a second is the relative time for a mile, so three bananas between the lightning and the thunder means the storm is approximately three miles away.'

I hadn't realised that everyone was listening to me and there was a roar of laughter to match the booming of the thunder.

'There! It's getting louder, it's only two bananas away!' I added quickly. 'You really are crazy – or should I say going bananas!' Iain was on good form.

'Oh! Ha! Ha! You fickle friend, Parker.'

A couple of blue-and-white stripey-legged boys came out of the kitchen and asked us all to leave the room, as they had to secure all the windows. The wind was fierce, smashing the rain against the windows and turning the cobbled courtyard into a river.

'Let's go up to the lounge.' Harvey was already unseating me from my chair.

'Great idea, I love storms!' I said as I swung myself free of the table. I remembered sitting in a darkened room with my three babies huddled around me. The curtains were fully open as we sat in awe watching the gods above hurling white fireballs at each other across the black skies and roaring in anger as the thunderclouds burst.

Iain had preceded us and was a few paces ahead. He put his

hand to his ear, shaking his head. As I caught up with him, his grin had become a grimace.

'What's up, Iain? Are you in pain?'

'It's the tinnitus. The pressure seems to be building, like a pressure cooker about to blow off steam.' He was wild-eyed and sucking the air through clenched teeth. He bounded up the stairs like a clockwork toy, leaving us far behind.

The two elderly ladies passed us, almost running, I had never seen them move so fast. I heard one of them say to the other. 'Turn it off, dear, then you won't hear the thunder.' One of the women had a very visible hearing aid.

'Poor old dears, I expect they are frightened of the storm.' Harvey was forever thoughtful, bless him.

'They're probably desperate to get the best seats in front of the TV,' I said in reply.

'Crikey! What happened then?'

Harvey threw himself against me and we both landed in a heap, trapped against the wall. The lights fused and I could not inhale or see a thing. 'Bloody hell, Harvey! Get off me, please! I'm suffocating!'

'Oh, sorry Angelica, that was an almighty bang. It must have blown the electrics.' He yanked me to my feet.

We were dazzled then by an enormous beam of light and Carmel's lilting Irish brogue.

'Well, that was a mother and a father of a thunderbolt. May God bless us!' She was carrying a large torch and we followed her into the lounge.

'Now, is everyone OK? How about you two ladies, all OK? Good! Well, what we shall do is this. We'll have a nice cup of tea, to steady ourselves, and I'll go and see if we can get some more light, so I will.'

She counted seven of us and the lady with the tea trolley made eight.

'Mrs Dighton, you shall have this nice big torch and I'll use this little one.' Carmel took a penlight from under the folds of her apron and rushed off down the corridor, like Mary Poppins without her umbrella.

Mrs Dighton then took control. She herded us into a convenient group of sofas and dutifully rewarded us with a steaming cup of tea.

The lightning forked and the thunder replied, just as angry as before, as the rain poured, relentlessly. Iain had both hands over his ears and was making a strange noise. Concerned, I knelt beside him and spoke into the back of his hand.

'Can I do anything to help? Is it so bad?'

He lifted his head and was red-faced with laughter. The strange noise he was making was stifled giggling.

'So, Parker, what's so funny?'

'Your prediction was correct, Milady. I got to half a banana and all Hell broke loose. You really are a spooky lady!'

We laughed and laughed and the storm swirled around us. The gods were definitely at war.

Very dimly, the lights flickered, then came to life. Harvey and another man extinguished the overhead lights and left just two table lamps glowing. A young student nurse informed us that the generators were working and the mains would soon be back.

I saw Françoise and her guest leaving her room and approaching the lounge. They were enveloped in each other, merged into one person.

Their conversation was in French and she broke free to introduce us.

'Bonsoir, mes amis. This is David, my husband.' They obviously adored each other and I was jealous.

How juvenile! I tormented myself. Stop comparing yourself with other people. I tried to smile, but I was overcome with envy. How many people experienced that kind of bond. I wanted it. I wanted it so badly. Why couldn't I have unconditional love?

The room became claustrophobic. My throat swelled and ached with the pain of holding back the tears. I was going to burst, so I stood up and fumbled my way down the corridor to my room. Sanctuary!

The storm was rumbling in the distance and someone was calling my name, but I couldn't turn around. Once in my room, the dam burst. I slid to the floor with my back against the door. Who was I crying for? What was I crying for? I was crying for *me*, the poor soul locked outside of *love*.

'Angelica, it's me, Iain. What's the matter? Are you crying? You are, aren't you! Let me help, please!' The handle turned and he pushed, gently, but my weight held the door closed. He didn't persist and I was relieved to be alone.

I hadn't cried for days. It's strange, what triggers the emotions. The release was exhausting. I don't know how long I sat there, tasting the salty tears. The storm had moved on and the evening sky softened. It wasn't time for the stars to speckle the night, so I waited.

There were lights showing from most of the windows, so I assumed that the power was restored. I could hear Vivaldi playing and realised that I still hadn't seen Petra, even though I had glimpsed her briefly at the window. Had she chosen to secrete herself away or was she too unwell to venture out.

Carmel knocked once and walked in.

'Well now, you are going to have my undivided attention, so you are.' She went into the bathroom and I heard her running the bath. She was humming an Irish ditty to herself.

'Come along, my lovely, the bubbles are waiting!' She hustled me out of my clothes and into the warm water. It was all a dream. By the side of the bath was a small dish of pink petals, floating in fragranced oil and beside this was eye make-up remover and two cotton wool balls. Carmen knelt by the bath, holding a vanity mirror to my face.

'Do you want to do it yourself or shall I do it for you? Can you see how the mirror is steaming up? Aw, go on, I'll do it!'

She didn't wait for a reply, just took hold of the cotton wool and very gently applied them to my eyelashes until all of the black was removed. I no longer resembled a panda.

'I'm gonna leave you for five minutes while I go to tuck in my other babes, then I'll be back for you.' She took the bowl of petals and sprinkled them across the water, then very casually pulled out the plug. 'Just so's you know, I'm in charge!' With a wink and a roll of the hips, she was gone.

I lay there, watching the water subside, leaving the petals stuck to my skin. There was a 'stillness' inside where the ache had been. The softness of the towel dried my body and my bed beckoned to me.

Carmel appeared with a cup of chocolate and my knockout pills but there was something else with her. I looked down at her feet and she was wearing bunny-eared slippers.

'Carmel, you are a true leprechaun!' I was laughing.

'Thank you, sweet Jesus, for giving her hope! It's good to see you laugh. I thought you'd lost your giggle, so I did!'

'Carmel, how did you know I had lost it? It was as if I was watching a play with strangers and I had to join in and couldn't. Do you know what I mean?' Suddenly, I had verbal diarrhoea and was gabbling at the speed of light.

'Hush now, everything will be all right. You are overwrought, one step at a time. Come now, take your pills.'

She sat on the edge of the bed and drew me into her arms. The comfort was immediate. She rocked me and crooned a song in her native tongue and I slipped, willingly, into deep, uncluttered sleep.

Chapter Ten

I awoke to the sound of my curtains being drawn back.

'Good morning Polly.' I watched her tie back the curtains and then turn to look at me.

'How are you this morning, Angelica?'

'I think I'm fine at this moment. Did you hear the storm last night? It was quite spectacular.'

'Yes, we lost our electricity for three hours. Luckily this place has its own generators.'

She walked towards the door on her way to leaving when she had second thoughts.

'I think you should have some exercise this morning. The weather is not so good, but a brisk jog through the woods will give you more energy for the day ahead.'

'It's OK, Polly, you can talk about the family visit. I'm not paranoid about it, I just want it to be over so that I know I have been able to do it.'

'Well done, that's the way. I still want you to have a jog though. See if you can include some of the others. I'll see you down there.'

She closed the door and reluctantly I got out of bed. The storm had left an incredibly clean smell in the air, but the temperature had plummeted. I chose a gold tracksuit emblazoned with the slogan, *I've got the cream*, and on the reverse was a cat licking his paws. It always caused a reaction, so let's see what it would accomplish today.

As I stepped into the corridor, Petra emerged from her room. She looked zapped.

'You coming down to breakfast, Petra?' I asked, tentatively.

'Yes, if you like!' She would not look directly at me. Her mood was flat, so I thought it wise to walk but not talk.

Halfway down she began.

'I had a bad turn on Friday and my brother had to bring me

back in. It was in the middle of the night, I can't remember much except that they banged me up in ICU for most of Saturday.'

I nodded, not knowing what to say, so I smiled and said nothing. She continued.

'I have an addictive personality disorder. Sounds grand, doesn't it?' She shrugged her shoulders, sighing deeply.

'I think I know what that is. You see, my eldest son had problems with booze and drugs last year and the doctors used that term at least once.'

'Well, to cut a colourful story short. I eat and throw it all back or I starve myself or I drink until I pass out. On good days, I am the life and soul and on bad days I try to kill myself.'

She looked relieved that she had told me and managed a shy smile. 'I hope today is a *good* day,' I said, showing some humour.

'Yeah! Don't you worry. Today I'll be good, it's Sunday!'

'I've heard you playing Vivaldi. My favourite is "Spring", it gives me a spiritual kick up the bum.'

We had reached the corridor leading to the dining room. I pushed my hand into Petra's and gave it a squeeze. She kept her eyes to the front and returned the grip, painfully.

'Hey, I need that hand!'

We both laughed and headed for the table by the French doors. The room was totally empty. I looked at my watch. It was 9 a.m.

'Do you think we are the last survivors? Perhaps the chef has poisoned the rest.' She poured herself a glass of water and ambled over to the hatch.

'Petra, is anyone in the kitchen? Ask him for some scrambled egg, please.'

I sat at the table, waiting for her to make some smart remark. She was chatting to someone in the kitchen and looked quite angry. Like a petulant child she banged the table and threw herself down onto the chair.

'What's up, problems?'

'That dolt of a chef said he is short-staffed and won't make an omelette for me – the prat – it isn't exactly heaving with people!'

'Did you ask him for scrambled egg, too?' My attempt at humour bombed.

'He said, "Look under the covers – 'cos that's all you're gonna get."'

She was so sulky that conversation was at an end so I thought it best to investigate under the covers.

'Eeee! You made me jump, Iain. You are my saviour!' He snuck up behind me and squeezed my waist.

'Why so, Milady?' He looked puzzled, then followed my eyes to where Petra was sitting, slowly pulling the flower heads to pieces.

'Oh, I see! She has joined us today, but is still struggling.' He jumped in, head first. 'Petra, I'm gonna have a full English. Shall I bring you the same?'

'Whatever!' she threw back at him.

We stacked the plates and returned to the table.

One by one and two by two, the inmates ventured into the dining room. Harvey and Alex arrived, so the Four Musketeers became the Famous Five.

'When did you get back Alex, last night?' I asked to start a conversation.

'Yes, quite late though, after the storm had moved on. That was a real humdinger. It actually put the whole station out of action.'

'I haven't seen forked lightning as intense as that for years, it was incredible.' He was still absorbed in the memory of it.

Harvey fidgeted and looked directly at me.

'You disappeared suddenly last night, was everything OK? I was worried that I had damaged you when I fell on top of you.'

'You did what!' Petra had come alive and was firing on all cylinders.

'It was nothing, honestly. The lights fused as the storm accelerated and Harvey missed his footing and fell over me. It was completely innocent!'

'Yeah! Yeah! We believe you. Harvey, you sly old dog. I didn't know you had it in you!' Petra had regained her spirit and was thriving on this frivolity.

I decided to change the subject to save any further embarrassment.

'How's the head this morning, Iain? Are you game for a jog through the woods?'

'I think I can cope with that, it'll probably blow the bells away. Are we all going?'

Petra was keen, but Alex and Harvey gave it a miss. Chris had joined us, so if the doc said it was OK, we would all meet up in half an hour. We changed into suitable togs and met in the lower lounge. Harvey was having coffee with a very elegant woman of about sixty. He raised his hand and she followed his gaze and smiled. I wondered, briefly, who she was.

'Petra, who is that woman with Harvey?'

'I'll fill you in while we jog. Shall we go?' She was hyper again, so much pent-up energy.

We booked ourselves out at reception and were joined by some others from the alcoholic rehab unit. I wasn't going to get involved with them, as keeping on the same wavelength as Petra was hard enough.

The courtyard glistened like a newly polished floor, but was slippery from the overnight rain, so we trod carefully. Once out onto the woodland tracks we were primed and ready to run. Polly was waiting for us at the entrance. Our outings had to be supervised as we were designated as people under care.

'Oh look! We have our babysitter waiting.'

'Petra, if anything happened to us our health insurers wouldn't pay out. Anyway, Polly is a superb athlete, she'll give you a run for your money.'

I didn't mean it to sound like a challenge, but the irrepressible Petra took control. She charged on ahead, with Polly close on her heels.

'Milady, may I join you for a genteel jog?'

'Parker, you are my right hand and I should be delighted to have you along.'

Even though it had rained copiously during the night, the land was so deprived of water that it had totally dispersed, leaving the ground slightly more giving underfoot.

'Are you coping, Iain? I know we have this play on words which conceals our true feelings, but if you need to come clean, you can!'

'The truth is, Angelica, I'm falling apart! If you are in the mood to listen, I do want to talk but I don't want to overstep any boundaries. We're not here to be shrinks, but to be shrunk!'

We both laughed, which broke the embarrassment and our jog became an amble. I linked arms with him and waited for his tale to begin. He was twenty-eight years old and had been married to Julie for two years. During that time he had risen from head of sales to store manager for a national chain of stores. He was a dynamic salesman and an astute manager, a real high-flyer.

As he talked I could feel his pride in his achievements and genuine love of his job. He expected his staff to be dedicated to which end he was a perfect role model.

The tinnitus began roughly a year ago and he had undergone various treatments, all to no avail. Then came the dreadful day when he attempted to take his life because he could no longer listen to the noises in his head. His doctor referred him to a psychiatrist, who eventually sent him to the Abbey. He was now convinced that he would lose his job, his wife and he really didn't care any more.

'All I want now, right now, is for this bloody noise to stop because it's *fucking crucifying me!*'

Tears of anger and desperation clouded his eyes as he held on to my arm.

'I'm so sorry, Angelica. I shouldn't have sworn. Why am I telling you all of this? I don't know. You just have the face of an angel.'

He broke free, turned and started to run back along the path, colliding with Chris who was walking with the two alco busters.

I shouted, 'Hang on, Iain. I'm coming back too.'

As I passed Chris, he muttered something about ignorance and bad manners, but I took no notice. I had lost sight of Iain and assumed he was too far in front to catch so I slowed down. By the fork in the path was on old derelict bench and there he sat, crumpled and out of breath.

'I got a stitch and had to sit down.' He rewarded me with a soppy grin. I gently touched my fingertips to his lips to stop any more apologies spilling out.

'Look here, Parker! I don't expect to be deserted in the middle of the forest, where there could be dangerous trolls or dragons, so kindly escort me back to the castle.'

I escaped back into fantasy speak. It was the only way I knew how to survive, it also relieved the tension that was so apparent in Iain's eyes. We were both on the edge of a precipice.

'Hey, Milady, have you ever thought of becoming a shrink? I could be your first disciple.'

Again, we linked arms and walked.

'Anyone would think that you are crazy,' I countered.

'Isn't that why we are here?'

'Absolutely not! It's all of those out there that are insane, they just haven't realised it.'

Strangely, I think Iain's outburst and my empathetic role had cleared my head. I was feeling stronger and more resolute about the lunchtime meeting being a success.

We had reached the lobby and the lady with the tea trolley was aimlessly wandering down the corridor, silently singing to the Walkman plugged into her ears.

I pointed to the trolley and cheekily hopped through the doors on to the patio.

'Thank you, Parker. Mine's a tea, please.'

'At once, Milady.' Dutifully, he flagged down the wayward trolley-pusher and secured tea and biscuits for us. Now was time for reflection as we supped our drinks and let the swing seat take the strain.

I closed my eyes and tried to visualise the faces of Rebecca and Sean. Rebecca had long, blonde hair, which she usually tied back in a ponytail or a thick plait. She was slightly taller than I was and as cute as a button.

Sean was an inch taller, with unruly blond curls, which I harvested for him occasionally. He was vertically challenged in comparison to his peers and had the hugest of thighs, so was nicknamed 'Thunder Thighs'.

They were fifteen and still fought for superiority. Becca battled like a boy and poor Sean often had to take a beating for fear of injuring his twin. Their love was a tangible masterpiece.

I tried to let their faces dissolve to be replaced by John's. His face was grey, cold and hollow-eyed. I shuddered involuntarily. I used to love that face, but now all I remembered was fear, loneliness and disbelief at what had happened.

'Angelica, open your eyes and drink your tea before it goes

cold! I saw you shiver. Ghosts? Do you want to talk?'

Bless him, he was offering a reciprocal ear.

'Thanks, but no thanks, not yet anyway. I must get through this lunchtime for the sake of the twins. If I begin to disturb the thoughts and memories, I think the turmoil will overwhelm me and I'll fall through the crack and disappear for ever.' My hands began the journey from lap to knees, so with every ounce of effort I stopped the motion.

'Look, the sun is beginning to break through. Shall we have a stroll through the grounds before you have to go up and change for lunch?'

'Great idea, Parker. Let's stroll.'

As we stood, the jogging party returned with lots of noise and commotion. Polly was trying to calm things and Petra was sparking off Chris. Two volcanoes spitting fire.

'Quick, let's get out of the way. It's not our problem.' Iain almost dragged me around the corner and we hastened towards the shrubbery.

'I wonder what happened to all the strawberries? Do you think they are lurking in the freezer?'

'Well, Milady, I think it's a fact that we'll have strawberry fool for ever!'

We had arrived at the gate to the allotments and hesitated, facing each other. Iain placed his hands on my shoulders.

'This is the "Kissing Gate", so as you go through you have to turn and kiss me over the gate.'

I stood very still, looking at his violet-blue eyes, almost level with mine, and two very soft, full lips and the adorable dimple in the centre of his chin. He was a handsome twenty-eight-year-old man, asking to be kissed by a passionate, forty-three-year-old woman. We were both vulnerable and at risk of doing something really stupid. Two beings lost in our separate nightmares. I sighed, deeply.

'Iain, it's probably wiser that we don't go there, so let's not cross the line, not today anyway.'

'Milady, you are something else! One day I'll tell you about this dream I keep having, hot or what!'

We turned back towards the rear patio and had to keep checking the look on our faces – *don't touch, 'cos I might like it.*

'This dream doesn't involve me, by any chance?' I knew the reply I was hoping for.

'Well, if it's not you then you have an identical doppelgänger!'

'Don't say any more, Iain.'

'You didn't say *no* in my dream, Milady.'

I went to swing a punch at his arm but he dodged to one side, putting both hands up in a sparring jest. Automatically, I did the same and we pranced our way to the patio, eventually falling on the hammock, laughing.

'Parker, I am now going to my apartment to change for luncheon. Be a good man and hose down your *mind* while I am away.' I shot away from his grasp and regained my composure.

'Milady, I wasn't joking. You are one *hot momma*. Enjoy your lunch.'

He closed his eyes and began to swing. I couldn't deny the sexual awakening that was occurring, my groin was overheating and my tongue was too full for my mouth. To make love was something I only did in dreams and desire, something I hadn't experienced for an eternity.

I pushed open my door, still having this conversation in my head. Autopilot kicked in and when I finally looked in the mirror I was pleased at my reflection. Time to go and meet my family, all except Jason, who I hope was still oblivious to my downfall and having fun with Toby in New York. Thank heaven for Uncle Toby, he'll be safe there.

Iain had left a message pinned to the door.

'Chin up, best foot forward. They *all* love you.'

I took a deep breath and shook my shoulders. There was a gremlin in the pit of my stomach. It started to growl and throw itself against my ribs.

OK, lady, take control and move. My hand was wet and slid on the handrail. Come on, Angelica, don't make a drama out of this. Now is when you have to be a grown-up and start building bridges. In an hour or so you can run and hide, but now they need you to be strong.

Tears sprang to my eyes. They were there by the reception, all three, looking uncomfortable and expectant.

'Mum, you look gorgeous!'

Sean covered the ground between us in one leap and swept me off my feet. Rebecca was behind him, trying not to cry. She had the habit from a small child of sucking her tongue between her lips and twiddling a strand of hair at the same time. I gathered her into my arms and breathed her smell into my nostrils. She relaxed and peeled away from me, leaving me face to face with John.

I wanted to hold him too, he was defeated and so alone, it made my heart break. He had lost so much weight and was trembling with nerves, unable to find the words to bridge the gap between us.

'Hello, John, how are you?' He was too full to speak so I took his hand and led him towards the dining room. The four of us together seemed a miracle.

'Angie, you look fantastic. When you've done with this place perhaps we should swap, because I am only barely holding it together.' His lips quivered, he was exhausted.

Sean playfully grappled with his dad, throwing his arm across his shoulder, while whispering into his ear. In my absence they had swapped roles, Sean was now the protector, the parent, and John had become the child.

The numbness was trying to invade me. Unwillingly, my senses were shutting down as the rush of the sea invaded my head. Focus on something, anything to stop this happening. I walked towards my usual table and, there they were, my Musketeers – it was all the encouragement that I needed.

Slowly, the embarrassment melted and a tiny explosion in my head triggered a 'resume normal mode' button. We deposited ourselves on the next table.

'You OK, Mum? You sort of drifted off for a while. Are you back with us now?' Again, Sean to the rescue. I was so proud of him.

'Sorry, I'm fine. I seem to have mastered the trick of switching off, you know, the thing you all do to me from time to time.' I directed this at John, he knew what I meant. He had cultivated the art of secrecy and deceit for years.

His hand covered mine on the table and squeezed so hard it made me wince.

'Don't worry, sweet, we'll get over this together. Won't we kids?' His voice trembled, but the resolve was there.

I couldn't remember any of the conversation, what we ate or how long we were together. Rebecca stuck to me like a limpet. We had become Siamese twins, knee against knee, hip by hip and the bare flesh of our arms brushing so closely to make the small hairs stand erect. What psychedelic demons were torturing our minds and how soon could we all break free?

'Mum, can we go and check out your room?' Sean was itching to leave the dining room. He was uncomfortable sitting among loonies.

'OK, best foot forward.' I smiled at the others as we passed their table but no one spoke.

We four climbed the stairs and entered my private world. I felt strangely protective towards my room and was relieved when they had seen enough.

John was unusually attentive, which was suffocating. Everywhere I happened to be, so was he, or his eyes were inspecting me. I had kept myself calm for too long and was beginning to recognise the signs of impending doom. How could I ask them to go?

'Shall we have a quick look around the grounds before we go? Will you give us a guided tour?' Rebecca had picked up my vibes, so a disaster was prevented.

'That's a great idea. Angie, shall we go?' John took my hand and led the way outside.

He had found confidence from somewhere and resumed his role as head of the family. I was baffled and confused, but now so tired that I could hardly speak.

There was a small gathering of inmates, lounging on the patio and we all offered a casual greeting. I had brief eye contact with Iain and took courage from the wink and grin.

'Mum, this is incredible, it's more like a leisure complex. Is there a pool, too?' Sean had found a badminton racquet and was searching for a flight.

'Put it down, son, you don't want to be challenged by a half-wit!' That's more like the old John, I thought.

'Did you eat a viper for lunch, you cretin!' I couldn't believe I had retaliated.

Becca grabbed my hand. 'Daddy didn't mean anything by it. Did you, Dad?'

'No, sorry honey, just a stupid, flippant remark. I am really sorry!'

He took my other hand and stroked it. *Who* was this stranger? My John would never have tried to apologise. He would have stalked off in a huff.

'Do you think that you can come home soon?' Poor Rebecca was so unhappy.

'Yes please, mum! Nanna is OK but she really gets on your nerves. She goes on and on about everything and keeps telling us not to mention to anyone where you are.' He put his hand over his mouth and sighed. Too much information! I had always taught my kids to tell the truth.

'Sean, keep your childish comments to yourself. Your nan has been the only person to hold this family together!' John was now angry and fighting to contain his emotions.

The tingling began and the march of the ants plundered my spine. No, please, not now! Rebecca's face was crumbling and the tears were clinging on to her lashes and I so wanted to smash the world into a million pieces. The *scream* was approaching.

'It's OK, Becca.' I pulled her hard against me.

'I shall be home soon, I promise.' We had reached the car park.

John looked at me with pleading eyes, but I couldn't give him any reassurance. He had killed my love for him and a resurrection was not a possibility.

'Would you like me to contact Jason? He should be told where you are or he will never forgive me.' He had controlled his feelings and broke the silence with a question I didn't want to tackle.

'Yes, I know you're right, but please be brief with the details. I don't want him to be too upset and do something silly, like catching the first plane home. That would crucify me.'

I was exhausted and wanted to be alone. We all hugged good-bye and they piled into the car. The tyres spun and kicked up the gravel as the 911 took off. Rebecca was squashed into the rear seat, desperately trying to be jovial. Sean was waving and grinning and John was a face in torment.

Realisation then hit me. John, the assassin in the balaclava, had become a killing machine in my nightmare. He was so caught up in his deals and self-destruction that he was poisoning the pond. Jason was banished to America. I was here in sanctuary. Rebecca was clinging on to hope and Sean was learning, all too soon, to be a parent. We were all victims of a stupid sin, *avarice*.

Something inside my head had exploded. I stumbled, blindly, onto the patio and knew that I had to *hit* something, very hard, to release this horrendous pain in my body.

The gang was all in conversation.

'Angelica, you look fit to burst!' Iain had taken my arm and led me past the inquisitive stares.

'Iain, I am so *angry*! I can't keep it all inside. My head, my chest, my hands are all stretched over this *shitting mess*.'

We had reached the stairs and he had the face of a child who had discovered the best secret ever.

'I'm going to get Polly. Follow me upstairs, but go to the fitness room, *now*!'

Onwards and upwards he jumped and the rage burning inside me kept me close on his heels. As I reached the top, he and Polly were running towards the fitness room. I was beside her as Polly unlocked the door. Iain wanted to stay, but was told, very playfully, to get lost. He was brimming over with excitement at the anticipation of *what*?

'Knock him to Hell and back!' he called over his shoulder as he disappeared.

'Push your hands inside these gloves and hit that punchbag with everything you've got!'

Polly almost shoved me against the wall and I had to balance myself before I could turn and face the red bag, locked onto the centre of the floor.

I stood, dumbstruck, looking at this innocuous blob, thinking, what am I doing here? The hurt and anger began to dissipate until I lurched forward, having been dealt a huge blow on my backside. I spun around, furious.

'What in God's name has got into you, Polly?'

She ducked behind the bag, taunting me. That was all I needed. I let fly a punch with every evil thought I could muster.

Polly took the full force of it and fell. The red ball hurtled back at me. I didn't connect that time as it took me by surprise, but I soon got the hang of it.

I screeched and wailed like a banshee, hitting it with all the passion and anger that had fermented within me. I had to punish it for the years of sadness and apathy until I felt cleansed.

Suddenly, I realised I was not alone. The red-hot anger had blinded me and as I cooled I saw Polly slouched against the wall, holding her stomach. I wrenched off the gloves and sat beside her.

'Did I do that to you, Polly? I am so sorry!'

Her grin was slow to happen and her pale-blue eyes were leaking water, but she found her voice.

'I think you would have given Tyson a run for his money!' She paused to draw breath and sat up. 'You are a woman of many talents, Angelica, and have thankfully proved that the spunkiness has survived. That was true, volatile *anger!*'

We both laughed, slowly at first and then with gusto.

'I wasn't aware of anything and didn't expect such an explosion of venom. The room was crammed with demons and voices and faces that I wanted to exterminate. It was so exhilarating, but I shouldn't have hurt you.'

'Don't apologise. I was in the wrong place. My reactions were slow. You looked like an avenging angel. You don't do kick-boxing too, do you?' she asked sheepishly as she pulled herself up.

I shook my head.

'Thank goodness for that – you would be a lethal weapon!'

Polly locked the door as we left.

'Do you see now, why we keep this door locked?'

'Yes, I do. I hope I don't have to revisit it too often, but I really quite enjoyed myself.'

I followed Polly to the nurses' station. The room was empty of people just the desk, chairs and filing cabinet, which were linked together by an ancient settee under the window. I felt lost. My thought processes had gone on strike. I was in the sixth dimension, aware but not part of what was going on.

Polly busied around. She put on the kettle and produced a couple of clean mugs and some ginger biscuits.

'How are you feeling now, Angelica, a bit shell-shocked?' She perched on the corner of the desk, facing me, waiting for my reaction.

It was the strangest feeling of nothingness. All I could do was sit, watching the steam escaping from my cup. I tried to form words, but I couldn't think of anything to say. What happened next had an instant reaction – *crack* – Polly slapped me across the face.

'Ouch! What was that for?' I had spilt my coffee and my face smarted.

Polly took my mug from me and wiped my top where the coffee hit.

'Sorry, Angelica, that was a bit unconventional, but I had to bring you back. You are in delayed shock, so drink your coffee and eat your ginger biscuit, or I shall have it and mine too.'

'I'm tired now. I think I should lie down.' I was beginning to feel really zapped.

'You have had a difficult day, which has released lots of pent-up emotions, but you are confronting them and I'm proud of you.'

Carmel came into the room and looked surprised to see me there. I had invaded her space.

'Hello, Angelica, you look comfortable there. Perhaps I should walk you back to your room.' It was a soft dismissal.

'No, that's OK Carmel. I can manage. Thanks for the coffee, Polly, and the sparring match.'

I left them to talk about me in my absence. My window was open and the slight breeze was spinning the window crystal, producing a myriad of tiny angel fairies throughout the room.

I pulled the curtains half-closed and sank onto my bed and was instantly asleep. How long I slept I had no idea.

On waking, the room was in shadow, but not so dark that I couldn't see the clock. It was exactly 6 p.m., so I had been sleeping for three hours. Gosh, my arms were aching, then I remembered the saga of the red punchbag and had a little chuckle.

If I turned over I could go back to sleep, but then I would wake later and be ravenous. The decision made, I stood and drew back the curtains. How beautiful the evening was. The grounds were breathing in the last of the rains, with the trees swaying and reaching towards the warmth of the dying sun. Some squirrels were prancing from branch to branch, playing tag. My gentle mood was interrupted by the telephone.

'Hello?' I held my breath and waited.

'Angel, it's me, how are you?' His voice caressed me as it always did.

'Simon, what a lovely surprise! I'm doing fine, how are you?' I sat down with a bump. Why now, Simon? I thought.

'Oh, Angel, I am so ashamed that I didn't keep in touch. It was like breaking into Fort Knox trying to persuade them to let me speak to you. I said I was your cousin.' He really did sound concerned.

'Don't beat yourself up, I was an accident waiting to happen. There was nothing you could have done to prevent it. It was inevitable.'

'Look, honey, we can't talk over the phone. When can I come up to see you?'

My heart was thumping and my body responding to his voice. Foreplay was totally unnecessary where Sexy Si was concerned. I was picturing his face and tasting his lips.

'Simon, I'd love to see you but it's too soon. I have a mountain to climb and monsters to fight before I am able to socialise sensibly.'

'Angelica, my angel, I didn't realise how low you had become. Why didn't you make me see? I would have come, you know I would, I love you.'

These were the words I had wanted to hear for so long. Were they too late? What made this man suddenly pick up the phone and decide he was ready to be Sir Galahad? Had his latest love become too demanding and been rejected?

'Darling, can I have a rain check. Phone me next week when I shall know how well my rehabilitation is going.'

I could sense his confusion and it was inevitable that the delay might cause a change of heart. He needed an escape clause.

'Angelica, I don't understand, you're not a prisoner, are you? Why can't you come out to play?' He was being flippant to cover his lack of understanding.

'Simon, it's hard to describe but this is my sanctuary. I am afraid to go outside. In here I am safe and if I am nervous then there are trained people to help me.'

'Sweetheart, I'll be there. Nothing will harm you again, I promise.'

The unease was beginning to creep around me. I no longer wanted to talk. Why couldn't he accept what I said and say goodbye.

'Simon, I have to go now. Please, phone me next week. Bye.'

I hung up, pressing the receiver into its cradle, almost suffocating it. Why did I have to have all this confusion? I don't want to think any more.

I jumped into the shower, turning it on at full pelt, first hot and then cold. Excellent! It's time to be *me*. I am a *lioness* in waiting. I am *alive*!

The evening temperature was marginally cooler that night, so I dressed in a jersey catsuit and fluffed my hair to resemble a poodle in need of hair management. It was 6.30 p.m. and I was starving.

I followed the two elderly ladies into the dining room and saw that my table was quite full. Iain saw me and patted the empty seat next to him. Alex had the head of the table and appeared to be holding court.

'May I enquire, how you are this evening, Milady?'

'Absolutely spiffing, Parker, and how are you?'

'I am very moderate to fair and very glad to have been of service to you this afternoon.' He looked at me, expectantly, and I blushed.

'Tsh! Tsh! Parker, I'll tell you later, first I must eat.'

I escaped to the service counter and piled my plate high with Waldorf salad and eggs in mayonnaise. Immediately, I thought of Jeannie at the hydro and her farting jokes and bottom burping. We did have a laugh.

The people sitting around the table were already eating their dessert, so I had to play catch-up. Petra and Chris were still sparking off one another, but neither looked hostile, it was more a verbal game of chess. Alex and Harvey were in deep discussion about the price of fuel and the role of the Monopolies Commission, which left Iain and me, and he was watching me like a dutiful retainer.

'How about some delicious strawberry trifle after your salad? I could procure a portion for us both.' He had risen from the table awaiting my reply.

'Sounds scrummy! Just a little for me, thanks.'

To an onlooker, we probably resembled a normal group of friends, having a meal together. It was amazing, looking from one to the other, where four out of six had attempted suicide – how macabre. In fact, I wasn't sure whether or not Chris would have made it five and I was the only non-contender.

Chris challenged Petra to a game of backgammon and Harvey appointed himself as referee and they left the table. Alex was in a mellow mood and kept giving me a sideways, soppy grin.

'What's up, Alex? You are looking terribly smug and bushy-tailed.' I leaned on my elbows and stared at his warm, green eyes.

'Well, Angelica, someone told me, in confidence of course, that you assaulted the punchbag this afternoon and were victorious.'

He now returned the stare, with face in hands, leaning towards me, and Iain mimicked us too.

'Oh, that, it was nothing, just a vociferous workout. Actually, it could have been disastrous as I knocked Polly off her feet, when the bag flew out too fast.'

With the interjections of gasps and giggles, I recounted the tale and they were suitably impressed.

'I've got my first rehab session with Dr Michael tomorrow, after the art therapy class. Have either of you been to art therapy?' I looked from one to the other and both were in the negative category.

Iain admitted that he had been so pissed off with Ann Amery that he had fought shy of attending anything to do with her, in fact, he hadn't cooperated very much at all.

Alex was on a one-to-one with his personal therapist, Tom, and had not been pressured to attend any other classes but he hadn't heard of any horror stories linked to the art class.

'I have to admit that the assessment I had with Dr Michael freaked me out. Dredging up all the sordid stuff is like walking back into Hell.' I shuddered and both men took a hand each, which made us all laugh.

'We are, yet again, the Three Musketeers.'

'I have a suggestion! Your consultant's room is next to mine, so why don't we three go and have a sneaky peek inside so that you will feel more at ease tomorrow! That's if the door is open.' Iain was triumphant at offering such a coup de grâce.

I wasn't sure it was a great idea, but Alex thought it was a gas.

'It'll be a breeze as there is only a skeleton staff on tonight. We used to get up to far worse at school.' Alex was in his element.

'Were you a public schoolboy, then?' Iain was curious.

'Not something I care to be reminded of, but yes, I was.' He stood up and we followed.

We were as conspicuous as doves among the ravens, but fortunately there was not a soul to be seen. Dr Michael's room was directly opposite Chris's room, so we knew we wouldn't be overlooked from that direction.

I twisted the handle and the door gave way. The room smelled of leather and polished wood – it was so comfortable. I hoped I felt the same when I entered tomorrow.

'So this is where you lie when Dr Michael psychoanalyses you.' Iain threw himself down onto the chaise, mimicking a damsel in distress with his hand draped across his forehead.

Not to be outdone, Alex assumed the meditating position of the venerable doctor, seated at the desk, looking into space for divine intervention. I wandered over to another pair of doors just behind the desk and turned the handle. It led into another room, which appeared to be an aromatherapy studio. The couch was in the centre of the room and to one side was a stand with a fantastic array of oils and monogrammed towels. I was in seventh heaven, this was my forte, my passion in life.

My eyes focused on a superb, six-foot statue of a Roman god, with long curling locks and full, sensuous lips and a very small willy. They always seemed to have just a small acorn for a penis. He stood in front of the French doors, which overlooked the gardens. Then, against the one remaining wall, was a set of cupboards with louver doors.

I was debating whether I should look in the cupboard when I heard a click of a door handle. As I turned around I saw the handle to the door, which led into the hallway, moving up and down. It was locked, thankfully.

Alex and Iain had heard too and were instantly by my side.

'We are either going to get caught or we have to hide,' Alex whispered.

'In the cupboard.' I opened the door and mercifully there was enough room to wedge ourselves in. We were like a row of toy soldiers, with Alex in front and Iain behind me, amid boxes and papers, but fortunately the doors held shut.

Two people entered the room via the communicating doors and it must have been a clandestine meeting because they too were whispering and had not put the light on. I could only see their feet through the lower slats of the door, so I knew it was a man and a woman.

Although the voices were hushed, the man's was foreign, with a deep, melodic tone, and the woman was breathless and excited, her few words punctuated by sighs and giggles.

She was wearing white leather pumps with a fringe across the top, which were hastily discarded and her bare legs and feet were soon dangling in the air and then disappeared. By the position of the man's feet, she had been lifted onto the couch and he was about to massage or manipulate her body.

He was wearing unusual, plaited leather sandals, the type you would find in the Far East, and green trousers. The couch began to move and shudder and the female was purring and making guttural noises.

We dare not move or hardly breathe, for fear of discovery.

Poor Alex had to hang his head to one side because of his height. I could see his teeth shining in the growing darkness, so I knew he was grinning. His hands were flat against the side wall to give him support and I had my hands against his back.

Iain had nestled his back against the other wall and had cunningly glued his hands to either side of my hips. And so we stayed, for however long, witnessing an erotic performance, by sound if not by sight. Every noise was accentuated by our imagination, as we became accidental voyeurs.

I was an holistic aromatherapist, so would have been prepared for at least a half-hour session. What I wasn't prepared for was sexual therapy after dark. I was trying to visualise a normal effleurage as the oil was smoothed over the body; instead I heard the hiss and sigh as the manipulator caressed the body, encouraging the woman to accept his exploring fingers and then cry with satisfaction. The sounds of erotic wetness were unmistakable as she purred like a cat, urging the predator to go on and on.

Through the small vent in the louvers, the green trousers were now in a heap, covering the leather sandals, and the lovers united. The groan that followed, I thought, was mine as I seemed to be part of this sexual pantomime, but it came from the woman on the massage couch.

The muscles on Alex's back had become hard and raised and I needed to remove my hands but couldn't. Behind me, Iain had become so aroused that his willy was trying to bore a tunnel in the valley between my buttocks, while his hands, against my thighs, pulsed with every movement of the couch.

Inside my head I had two thoughts, one cried out for this drama to be over as I was becoming claustrophobic and the other voice was crying – how I wish it were me being ravished.

It had stopped! There were two pairs of feet, one in plaited leather and one in white pumps and together they left the room.

We fell out of the cupboard in total disbelief. We all knew, without a shadow of doubt, what we had just witnessed. I think we were all too embarrassed to make even the smallest comment. Instead, we silently, tiptoed past the offending couch, through the connecting doors, across the consulting room and into the corridor.

In single file we walked past Iain's room and into the downstairs lounge. We still hadn't spoken. There wasn't a soul to be seen, not even low conversation coming from the nurses' station. It was only just after 8 p.m. Perhaps everyone was upstairs.

Alex was standing, in the half-light, looking out across the lawns, and began to chuckle to himself.

'Do you think that happens every night, with different women? Good grief, those squirrels out there must have a few ripping yarns to tell!'

By now, we were all nervously laughing, which grew into belly-holding guffaws.

'What did happen in there? *Really*! Did we all have the same limited view?' I managed to ask the question before my laughter turned into hiccups.

'Well, Milady!' Iain was coughing and spluttering between words. 'My interpretation is this!' Again he choked with laughter.

'I think it was either number seventeen or thirty-four, if I remember the pages correctly, but whichever it was, it worked for her and it worked for *me*!'

That revelation was too much information and we became an uncontrollable heap of bodies on one of the sofas.

'Shush! Shush! Shush! Whatever is going on in here?' It was the miserable night sister, who rarely visited the second floor lounge, so this was her territory.

'Anyone would think it was carnival time!' She wagged her finger and said she would get some water for my hiccups.

I had tears streaming down my face and the boys were unrepentant. Suddenly, Alex pointed to her shoes – they were white moccasins – and the crescendo of laughter peaked.

'That is *enough*! Stop this immediately and retire to your rooms. Do you *hear* me! Stop this nonsense at once!'

We exited as quickly and orderly as we could and headed for the patio, like naughty children. The hammock swallowed us among the cushions and slowly we calmed, escaping into our own space to review the events of room 12.

During our time of incarceration, Petra had thrashed Chris at backgammon and royally annihilated Harvey, too. The upstairs lounge was settling down, nicely, into groups of TV watchers, readers and game players.

Petra had lapsed into melancholia and disappeared to her room with the attending night sister. Harvey and Chris were bored and decided to track down the elusive Musketeers.

It was uncanny how the majority of incumbents could cope quite pleasantly with life within these walls, but put them on the outside and they would revert to being victims.

They approached us, stealthily, as we silently swung in the hammock.

Harvey, who was often jealous, exclaimed loudly, 'What's this, a cosy evening at Squirrels Farm?'

Three pairs of eyes opened at the same time and saw the same thing. Harvey was wearing *white leather shoes*. We couldn't contain ourselves, as our laughter almost became hysteria.

'What's the joke, then, have you gone completely mad?'

Poor Harvey, he always seemed to be the butt of the joke and it wasn't fair. Try as I might, I could not speak, so he sat down in a huff and Chris regarded us with disdain.

'You lot are as crazy as those squirrels.' He just stared at us, longing to be part of the fun. I had regained my composure and reached out for his hand.

'Sorry, Harvey, from this day forward, let's call ourselves the Screwed-Up Squirrels Club.' We all piled our hands one on top of the other, even Chris, who usually hated to be touched.

'So, come on then, what was the wheeze all about?' Chris sat with his elbows on his knees and chin in his hands, waiting for someone to enlighten him.

Finally, Alex elected himself to tell the tale of room 12. When the tale was complete, Harvey looked down at his feet and collapsed in laughter.

'Well, who was it then? Was he a doctor?' I could tell that he would recount the story in the future, only he would be one of the characters in the cupboard.

'The only definite possibility is that, as he was wearing 'greens' he could have something to do with ICU. He had a foreign accent and wore strange sandals. As for the woman, she could have been anyone, but probably a nurse as she was wearing white pumps.' I wondered whether the secret would ever unfold.

We left the patio area and headed upstairs for a bedtime drink. There wasn't one of us who would forget that night: we didn't imagine it, we didn't dream it, it happened.

It was now quite late, so the lounge was totally empty except for us. With our drinks, we nestled in front of the TV to view the latest news. In reality we were all thinking of the sex act. Iain wriggled beside me.

'Did you feel me? I could hardly contain myself,' he whispered, softly.

'Parker! I am shocked,' I whispered back.

'It was the best orgasm I have had in months. Can we do it again, soon?' He was still very aroused.

'Well, in reality, your room is within close proximity to room 12 – The Pleasure Dome – so you could pop back into the cupboard whenever you had the urge.' I could not resist the tease.

'What are you two whispering about, as if I didn't know? Do you think there will be a replay? Perhaps it's always on a Sunday!' Chris swivelled in his seat and regarded Iain.

'You do realise that we have the best advantage, my room being opposite and yours next door but one.' He was planning a rerun.

'What do you propose, Chris, shall we keep vigil on Sunday evenings?' They were acting like two adolescents.

'Time for me to go to my bed. Night, night.' I rose to leave with goodnights from the newly formed Screwed-Up Squirrels Club.

Actually, I was desperate to get to my notebook and pen some more saucy poetry before it dried up. Carmel handed me my little pot of pills and wished me sweet dreams.

'I shall tuck you in later, so I will, my little Cassius Clay!' She gave a wink and slapped my bottom. So, my boxing prowess was now legendary.

Françoise and her David were in front of me, closed in an embrace. She looked towards me, enveloped in an aura of love.

'Angelica, my friend, we have had such a wonderful day. I am so – how you say? – overfilled with passion!'

I smiled indulgently.

'Well, you understand, I know it!'

I was turning the handle of my door, when she added, 'It is good news, too, ma cherie. Tomorrow, I shall be discharged to see how I go for a while. It is great, yes?' Her joy was intoxicating, I was so pleased for them.

They passed by and I closed the door, this time not feeling any envy. Some day I would have what I searched for.

I put pen to paper and began the 'Ode to the Abbey Lover', but no sooner had I penned the first line, when there was a light tap at the door. I opened my door and there was Françoise.

'Do not ask me to enter, ma cherie. I needed for you to know about my picture for you. It is almost complete and I shall send it to you next week. A masterpiece, yes!' She turned on her heel and ran back to her room. I was in awe of this spectacular female. Had she found her peace of mind, this time?

I resumed my writing, revelling in the memory of room 12, when there was another knock and Carmel entered.

'Aw, come on you little rascal, 'tis bed for you so it is. Enough of this prosing, it'll wait till tomorrow as sure as the sun will shine.'

Today had been revolutionary and I dreamed of myself as a squirrel, peering in at a window, slightly obscured by a Roman statue. What fun!

Chapter Eleven

Monday was probably the real beginning of my rehabilitation. The day when I began to understand why I had become dislocated from reality. I awoke early and scribbled down the words of my latest ode into the book and tumbled down to breakfast.

Without realising, I had begun the day without apprehension. The soldier ants were not attacking my nervous system. I was tingle-free for once.

The lads with striped legs were slightly uncomfortable at my early appearance, as the tables hadn't been fully prepared for breakfast. I apologised and waited by the windows, watching the world waking up.

Daydreams of things yet to come took my eyes to the huge doors of the art studio, where I would be in a few hours from now. A gentle touch on my arm brought me back. Françoise stood beside me, looking like a model from the front page of *Vogue* magazine. Her golden hair was twisted into ropes with a chiffon scarf of vibrant ginger, complimented by an elegant crêpe trouser suit in the same muted colour and a cream camisole. My memory of her then would be a 'Ginger Cream Biscuit'.

'Ma cherie, Angelica. David is here to collect me and I am so content that you are awake early enough to wave me goodbye.'

We did the usual things, hugged, hoped we would meet again and then I had inspiration.

'I have a superb idea, Françoise. When you have finished my portrait why don't we meet under the Arc de Triomphe at a selected time. We shall seal our friendship and I can have a holiday too.'

She gave me her address, kissed both cheeks and flew through the doors to her David. It was a fantastic thought, if not a little fanciful but I would endeavour to make this dream a reality. I secreted the piece of paper in my pocket.

One by one, the group arrived. We munched through breakfast, jogged through till about 11 a.m. and reviewed our morning, sitting at the same table, looking at the same pair of doors.

Promptly, at 11.30 a.m., Petra, two other ladies and I crossed the courtyard and entered the domain of painters, potters and medics. As the doors opened we were almost suffocated by the smell of clay, paint, linseed oil and glue. It was more like a baronial hall than an old fusty carriage barn. Some of the original, huge oak posts were still supporting the roof and the floor was made of ancient, dark-brown brick tiles.

Well-polished refectory tables with saddle-backed chairs were placed at random and there were two potter's wheels against the far wall. Half of one wall was an opening to a smaller area where I could see a butler's sink and stacks of bottles, buckets, pots of paint, brushes and tubs of glue. The sights and smells made me come alive.

Ann Amery was seated next to a dilapidated wardrobe, whose doors were wide open, displaying piles of newspapers and magazines, spilling off the shelves.

'Good morning, ladies,' she said, with transparent apathy.

'Sit wherever you feel comfortable and I shall endeavour to explain a little about art therapy.' She stood erect and started to handle a pair of long-bladed scissors, as she spoke.

Basically, we were to have three sessions of one hour each. The first session was dedicated to selecting and cutting out pictures from periodicals and keeping them in an envelope. The second session was for finding and cutting out text that seemed special to us and putting these pieces in another envelope. In the final session the pictures and text would be joined together and glued onto large sheets of paper, forming a collage of our inner thoughts.

There was something decidedly unfriendly in the way she caressed the blades of the scissors as she spoke. She had the power to make or break minds, or perhaps become a mind-bender!

The door crashed shut behind us, which startled me. Some people had entered the room. They were obvious outsiders.

'Ah, good! I expect you would like to finish the tapestry and the pots for the fete. Just go through, I'll join you soon.' Ann smiled and became quite animated for a second.

The people moved through without any sign of recognition to us and Ann proceeded to select four pairs of scissors. She walked towards Petra and I; we were sitting together at one of the tables. The other two ladies had chosen separate tables.

'Before we begin, would you two ladies please sit at different tables.' She pointed at Petra and then at a table in the corner.

'What's the problem, Doc, do you think we are going to cheat? Huh?' Petra hated authority and couldn't help but retaliate.

'Don't be stupid, Mrs Edwards, you are all going to need an entire table and it will also help you to concentrate. By the way, there will be no talking, either!' She was really enjoying the power. I had a sudden vision of her dissecting live insects, and relishing it.

Ann kicked the leg of my table and handed a pair of rounded scissors to me, directing the next statement at me.

'Shall we begin, ladies? As you can see, a very full cupboard is waiting. Take as many books as you wish and start cutting.'

I was nearest so took a huge pile from the bottom shelf, leaving a gaping hole. We had each been given our manila envelope and Ann left us alone.

We four sat quietly and attacked our separate piles of papers. Petra coughed, loudly, so I would look and was mimicking self-abuse with her scissors. I yelled, 'Don't do that!' without thinking, and Ann pounced back into the room.

'Just get on with the job quietly, please. You can do that, can't you?' She returned to the outsiders in the next room.

I could hear them laughing and naturally thought that we were the topic of hilarity and felt ashamed.

For an hour I flicked the pages and cut the pictures, discarding one magazine after another, totally oblivious of my surroundings or how large my selection had grown.

BRRRING! Ann's hand slammed shut the hammer on her alarm clock. I wasn't even aware of her presence in the room.

'Time's up! Gather together all the mutilated books and put them in that sack in the corner.' She pointed to a sack that was already overflowing.

It was incredible to find that my envelope contained dozens of clippings and for some peculiar reason, I felt I had achieved something. The four pairs of scissors were spirited away and the envelopes collected without a word from Ann. She resumed her stance behind the table and stared at the main doors.

'You may go now. Please be prompt tomorrow!' We were dismissed.

Petra was first out and grabbed my arm as I stepped into the yard. 'That woman is a witch! There is something seriously wrong with her!' She pushed me towards the open French doors of the dining room.

'Perhaps she's been around deranged people too long!' I was trying to make light of Petra's observation.

'Oh! Let's eat! I'm famished! You took that seriously, didn't you? You must have collected a hundred photos. I watched you, snip, snip, ssssnnnippp!'

She hurried to the counter to fill her plate, and before I had selected mine she was already cramming food into her mouth like a starving refugee.

Iain was sitting waiting and watching, watching me, watching Petra. We were becoming interdependent, for better or for worse. Like pieces in a puzzle we were choosing characters to adhere to, using their strengths and weaknesses to enhance our own.

'How did it go with Boadicea?' Iain laughed and beat his chest.

'She's quite formidable, but I wouldn't fight her. There is a fundamental truth in what she says and there is an undercurrent of venom that seeps out which she has no control over. I find that frightening.' I couldn't help frowning.

'Milady, you are getting too deep for me. All I see is one hell of a bitch who enjoys taunting desperate people who have already been tortured in some way, out there!' He pointed to the outside world, shrugged his shoulders and returned to his lunch.

Perhaps he was right. Why should I defend her actions? She gave me the creeps, but there was something else, something that I couldn't put my finger on. Did she play mind games? Was that part of the healing agenda?

Too much thought and not enough eating. Day by day my appetite was improving, my nightmares seemed to have abated, but unfortunately so had my hedonistic dreams of the health hydro.

Lunch passed quickly, Petra being the first to vacate her place, as usual. 'If anyone fancies beating me on the badminton court, the net will be in place in twenty minutes!' She was gone, probably running to her private loo for an up-chuck session followed by the rapid consumption of a packet of biscuits, depending on her mood.

My gaze drifted around the table and rested on Alex. He looked more serious than normal and hesitated in returning my smile. Again I was aware of someone watching me, watching someone else and I turned to confront his eyes. The pain within was transparent.

'Iain, are you ill? Quick, Alex, catch him before he falls!'

We all jumped up as Iain's inert body hit the floor. Alex was too late to collect his weight, but was trying to cradle his head. The woman who cleared the tables pushed the alarm button on the wall. Within seconds a doctor and nurse appeared from ICU.

Iain's face was grey and sweaty and his pulse was bouncing against his temple. We watched as the doctor picked him up, with Harvey's help, and carried his limp body to the medical unit. As the doors sucked together Petra appeared.

'What's going on, someone died?'

Between us we ushered her outside and explained what had just happened to Iain.

'So if you don't mind, Petra, I am going to sit on the patio to wait for some news.' I sat down at a table and everyone followed suit. Petra looked downcast, throwing herself onto the hammock and ramming the racquet between her knees.

It wasn't long before good news arrived with Archie. He came straight to my side and whispered, conspiratorially.

'He's OK! He has regained consciousness and is expected to be as right as rain!' He squeezed his face into a grin and shuffled back to his desk.

It was about 2 p.m., when the sun was at its zenith, much too warm to run around. Luckily for Petra, another younger lady, with extremely long legs, came over and asked if she could have a game. They bounded off and we watched their antics in silence for a while. A blanket surrounded us, while we kept our vigil, invisibly hugging ourselves until Alex spoke.

'Anyone fancy a stroll?' He looked from one face to another.

Harvey declined, he wanted to sit and read. Chris also declined as he was engrossed in watching the girls play badminton, which just left me. I stood and pulled him to his feet.

'Shall we amble, or do you have a pre-selected direction, Alex?'

'Let's amble.' He tucked his arm through mine.

After a while we found a bench in the shade, beckoning for us to sit down. I was grateful to be out of the heat. Alex was battling with his thoughts and had finally reached his decision. He took a small packet from his pocket and handed it to me.

'I was in the town this morning and saw this and immediately thought of you. I hope you're not offended.' He looked embarrassed.

I opened the paper parcel and inside was a fridge magnet in the guise of a coral-coloured, fluffy cat with amber eyes. Under the front paws were the words – *Love lives here*.

'Oh, Alex, it is beautiful.' I was touched.

Alex beamed with delight.

'I wasn't sure whether you would like it, I'm so glad you do.'

He was like a puppy, which had been rewarded with a pat on the head. 'It is so sweet of you, Alex. What is the reason behind it?'

He held both my hands, like a lover about to declare his feelings. I was beginning to prickle and tried desperately to keep calm.

'I don't know why you are here and I find the thought unbearable that anyone could hurt you. When I watch you with others, you radiate, you make everyone feel special. I have a tide of emotions, which overwhelm me when I am near you. I want to protect you.' He had exhausted himself and was sweating.

'Crumbs! That was a speech and a half. Don't you think it is because our emotions are raw that we cling to each other; we are searching for a lifeline.' I gently eased my hands from his grip.

'To be honest, Angelica, I haven't a clue who I am or when I closed off from reality. I cannot accept any form of responsibility, even for my wife and baby. I am devoid of any normal response and it's frightening.'

For the next hour, I sat in silence, while this rugged man

emptied his soul into my lap. I knew I shouldn't have listened, I should have pushed him away or shut my ears, but I was trapped. Clutching my tiny, ceramic cat, I listened to the most horrific and tragic story of a tormented child who was abused through to adulthood.

Alex was born to a Methodist minister and his wife. His older brother was destined for the church, but Alex was a quiet boy who loved reading and played with imaginary friends. He was a misfit, or so he was led to believe.

He was not an academic or a fine athlete, just ordinary. His father pushed him, trying to make him aspire to greater achievements and finally enrolled him in a boarding school. Alex was relieved, as the beatings were becoming too regular. The thought of this made him shudder.

He told me he was quite sad in one way, because at thirteen he had become quite muscular and considered to be good-looking and some of the local girls were keen on him. Anyway, he had no choice but to be sent away as his father had very important work to do with his brother's future.

Alex then lived in a waking nightmare for five years. There was no one to protect him, no best friend to confide in and nowhere to run to. He was the New Boy, so had to endure the rituals of initiation and humiliation from the Seniors, which culminated in bed-wetting and more humiliation.

Eventually, he settled down and made a few friends until the advent of Daniel. This was the new head boy, Daniel the Destroyer, who had a clique of minions who obeyed his every command.

Alex was elected, by 'private council', to be the lower school fag. Daniel was evil and sadistic to the core and he wanted Alex.

I wasn't sure that I could listen any more to this macabre tale, but I couldn't stop the flow. With his head bowed, Alex spoke, pulling at his clothes as he remembered.

The ordeal began when he was summoned to Daniel's Kingdom, over in the north wing. It was late and he had been asleep, when the goons arrived and dragged him from his bed. They gagged him and frogmarched him to meet Daniel. He was honoured, yet terrified, fearful of falling short of what was expected of him. He had no idea of what was to come: that was why he was chosen, because he was an innocent.

Once in the Chamber of Horrors, he was blindfolded, stripped, tied to a table, flogged and raped, in that order. By the time the final abuse took place, by Daniel himself, he was feeling no pain as his conscious self had left his body.

He remembered, vividly, how Daniel crooned in his ear as he thrust himself against him and finally groaned when he climaxed. The homosexual act had not been witnessed, as Daniel had dismissed his goons. He told him it was the highest accolade and gift of love to be the 'Chosen One'. Alex was the most splendid of the entire new intake.

'Alex, stop! I can't hear any more. It's too disgusting! It's just too much information. My head is full of these awful scenes. You poor, poor soul! How on earth did you survive?'

I wanted to comfort him, but I could do no more than hold his hands. At that specific point in time I wanted divine intervention and retribution. A stake through the heart of the wicked Daniel would suffice.

'I have never told anyone the full truth, in all these years – you must be an angel. It was so easy to talk, once I got going. Thank you so much for listening.' His smile took over his entire face and the haunted look seemed to vanish.

'Would you mind if I was alone for a while, Alex? I need to collect my thoughts before I go in to see Dr Michael. Will you be OK?' I was hurtling round in a kaleidoscope of horror pictures and I wanted solitude. 'Sorry, sorry, sorry! I am so selfish. Having you to myself was an opportunity I couldn't miss. I didn't intend to abuse your kindness, it just happened. I'll see you later.' He shambled off towards the patio, turning to give me a wave.

I sat, musing to myself: here I am trying to make sense of my own dilemma and becoming the Mother Teresa for waifs and strays. I closed my eyes, trying to blank out the last twenty minutes and was overcome by a wonderful feeling of tranquillity. Meditation wasn't an art I had adopted before, so what I was experiencing was uplifting.

Concentrating on my breathing, I visualised myself drifting on clouds of marshmallows tied with pink ribbons. I had become a translucent butterfly, with the body of a fairy and was wafting on the currents of air, in and out of the pink and white. If this was a glimpse of Heaven, then I wasn't afraid to go there.

Not a soul disturbed my peace. I placed the revelations made by Alex into a compartment and closed the door. I reviewed my meeting with John and the kids and congratulated myself on getting through it. I had to concentrate my energy on feeling good and not on feeling guilty.

I could hear my name being called, somewhere in the distance. It was Sam. She was standing outside the consulting room doors, curling her finger at me and speaking my name. I mouthed – OK I'm coming, and strolled across the lawn. Dr Michael was sitting in an easy chair, watching my approach.

'Isn't it good to be alive on such a balmy day, Angelica? Please relax on the chaise and we will reminisce!'

As I lay back he closed one of the doors and motioned for Sam to start the recording tape for this session. He pulled his chair nearer to me and took my hand.

'Today we are to build a verbal scrapbook of your life, from as early as you can remember, to perhaps your teenage years. Close your eyes and listen to the metronome and take me back to when you were five years old.'

An invisible breeze blew the pages of time further and further back to experiences only a child remembers. There was a brown, fluffy rabbit with large blue eyes, which lived in a hutch outside the kitchen door. I squealed with delight when I discovered that the two white mice that lived in an old battered shoe box in the garden shed had suddenly become fifty mice, most of them were pink, skinny things without any hair. I was ten years old and in fear of being stripped naked and tied to a tree in the woods outside my school. I remember standing beside my dad and waiting to see Mr Ford, the headmaster. Roger was flogged and sent home, I couldn't believe he would have done it, as I loved him, my first love. His co-conspirators at the high school were also flogged and the ringleader was expelled.

My hair was so very long and had to be tied in rags at night so that I could have ringlets for the dancing exhibition the next day. I dreamed of becoming a famous dancer, but we moved house and

I was never enrolled for dancing again, but nobody explained why – perhaps I had done something bad and was being punished.

I won a place at a very prestigious school, my dad was so proud but I don't think my mum had any thoughts on it. The school was far away and I missed my friends, they called me a snob. I tried to explain how lonely I was, to no avail. That wicked teacher, Miss. Bainbridge, would tie my hair with string to humiliate me. She hated the fact that I would not conform even though I quaked with fear in her classes. For five years I was in purgatory and in all that time my parents visited the school only once. There was always a justifiable reason for not attending functions, but it made me feel insignificant.

The good times were great! I could roller-skate as well as any boy and fire a pellet gun while cycling with no hands and hit the target. We used to go over the Dell and slide down into the pit on a sheet of tin or go scrumping for apples in the orchard next door to the vicarage. Sometimes we would climb the trees and find cold bird's eggs. You had to put them in your mouth on the way down so they wouldn't break. My friend, Paul, showed me how to blow the dead baby through a pinhole. Of course, there had to be a hole on both sides, or it wouldn't work.

The best of all was becoming a teenager and being kissed by boys and dancing. How I loved to dance. Wherever there was a hall, there was a dance, at least three times a week. We learned to rock and roll and jive and I never sat down all night. Dancing was my passion and I was recognised for it. I had free entrance to some of the local discos, as I had become a special friend of Colin, the drummer in the Condors. Then I dated Crissie Andrews for a while, he was a popular singer, so wherever he went, I went too. Dancing was being carefree and alive.

Something had disturbed my memories and I was returning to the present. There was someone else in the room. I focused on the hand holding mine and heard the irritation in his voice. The interloper had broken the spell.

The person was standing close to me but out of my line of vision. He was quietly speaking to Dr Michael in apologetic tones. I moved my head and saw, first, the green trousers from ICU and then the peculiar leather sandals. Slowly, my eyes travelled upwards until I met the face belonging to the 'Mysterious Masseur' from the adjacent room. Without any thought, I said, 'Oh, it was you!'

Dr Michael looked at me in wonder, while the stranger just smiled. I had seen that smile before and realised I had seen him coming from the ICU recently.

'I am so sorry for the interruption, madam.'

'He gave a short bow and passed through to the therapy room, silently closing the door.

I was now sitting upright and fully awake, waiting for Dr Michael to say something. A few skeletons had been discarded, without tears, and my mood was mellow.

'Well, Angelica, we are definitely progressing. I shall look forward to seeing you the day after tomorrow.' He walked me to the French windows and pushed the door open wider, for me to go through. He was totally distracted and as I brushed past him he said, 'Have you been in the company of Dr Raschid before?'

I think I blushed, remembering the erotic happenings of the night before, but as calmly as I could, replied, 'No. I believe I saw him in the corridor and he said hello. That's all. See you Wednesday. Bye!'

How I managed to keep a straight face, I don't know. He was watching me walking away and I had a terrible urge to turn and wink, but the mischief within me would dance another day – not right now.

Approaching the patio, I was overjoyed to see Iain, lying on some pillows on one of the loungers. He appeared to be sleeping so I decided to leave him in peace. I tiptoed towards the door, but heard a soft moaning.

'Iain, are you feeling bad? Can I do something for you?' I leaned across him and lightly touched his forehead.

That was too much temptation for the invalid, so he pulled me down and parted my lips with his tongue. Such a succulent kiss I hadn't tasted for aeons and reluctantly took my face away. His grin was wild as he rolled his tongue over his mouth, savouring the sensation.

'Parker, you are a disreputable bounder and should be flogged!' I wouldn't tell him how much I enjoyed it.

The grin became more lascivious.

'Did you feel the earth move, Milady, or was it heaven knocking on my drawbridge?' He moved up on his pillows and studied my face.

'Iain, you are stupid. Anyone could have seen. You know what Harvey is like – he would have sulked for a week *and* reported us to matron!'

I sat beside him, attempting to look annoyed, and he tried, very badly, to look repentant.

'You gave us an awful fright at lunch. Explain to me what tinnitus is like. Can you describe what goes on in your head?'

He stared into space as he tried to picture the vibration.

'It changes, that's the dreadful part. If I could depend upon the same repetitive tone and decibel I think I could almost bear it. Sometimes it is like the hush of the sea from a conch shell and other times it is as shrill as an orchestra of kettles. It never goes away.'

'How do you sleep if it is constant?' I couldn't begin to understand. 'They give me very strong sedatives that knock me out, but if I take too many, the side effects are even worse, so I forget to take them.'

'What are you hearing now?' I was trying to comprehend and ended up frowning.

'Don't look so concerned, Milady, today I only have the sea and your dulcet voice. I can cope with that.'

Alex, Petra and her badminton partner emerged from the gardener's shed, all three looking hot, flustered and chatting gaily. As they bustled towards us it was obvious that there was a new development. Petra was first with the news.

'Old Tom, the gardener, is going to mark out a proper court for us. Isn't that great?'

I tried to look enthusiastic.

'You must have charmed him with your talent, Petra!' I grinned and she stung me with a sarcastic smile.

'Well, I'm going up to wash off this sweat. Are we meeting at 6.30 p.m. for dinner?'

We all said aye and she and the other young lady left us. I still had no idea of her name, but it was of no consequence.

'Now there are just the three of us, I have to tell you that I have solved the mystery of the Abbey lover. I have met him!'

'Well, come on, who is it then?' They were both intrigued.

'It is the dark and dangerous Doctor Raschid from ICU, unless there is more than one wearer of Indian plaited sandals and green trousers.'

'How did you meet him?' Iain couldn't hold back.

'He came into Dr Michael's room when I was having a session. I was so shocked I actually blurted out something like – Oh, it was you – but luckily no one took any notice.'

'Great, so all we have to do now is locate the small white shoes worn by a very slim ankle, possibly a nurse, then we have them!' Alex was now emerging as the Abbey sleuth.

'What do you suggest we do, Holmes, sit in the cupboard and wait for the next episode?' I studied his face.

'No! I suggest we track down the white shoes, to identify his prey and then sit in the cupboard every night until the performance is repeated!'

We degenerated into gutter thoughts and raucous laughter. I caught sight of Dr Michael, studying me through the corridor window. He raised his hand in a mock salute and turned to speak to someone. I was totally embarrassed seeing him there, while I had these lurid pictures going through my mind. It was as if he saw my thoughts and was judging me. Paranoia, or what!

'Time to change, fellas! I think I'll be a butterfly next.'

I blew them a kiss. It was surprising how we had nestled into a routine. Here, we had no peer pressure or conflict, nothing to do but heal. If everyone wrote in a diary I feel sure that the word 'sanctuary' would be written most often.

After such an enormous day of happenings the evening paled into insignificance. The white shoes were nowhere to be seen.

Chapter Twelve

I slept uneventfully and Tuesday arrived at about 8 a.m. without fear or marauding ants clouding the issue. I went to breakfast, as usual, and on the morning jog; then, with Petra and the two quiet ladies, I entered 'Boadicea's Kingdom' for an hour of paper cutting.

Petra was less intense since the arrival of Claire, her badminton partner. They were forming a real bond, which was noticeably improving her disposition.

Obediently, we sat at the same tables and in turn selected our pile of papers and received our scissors and manila envelope. The five craft interlopers did not materialise, so Ann sat like a statue watching us. Not a word was spoken, which was a relief, as I wanted to examine my thoughts quietly.

Strangely, it wasn't as easy choosing words as it was choosing pictures. I found myself turning pages and finding nothing and having to reread pieces in order to select something that had a meaning. The hour flew by until the bell shrieked on the alarm clock and brought the session to a close.

I knew Ann had been watching me for some time and as we silently packed the discarded papers into the black sack and handed in our scissors and envelopes, she touched my arm.

'You really do love words, don't you, Angelica? Perhaps that is your forte. Have you ever considered writing for a living?'

The others had gone and we were facing each other across her table.

'Actually, I have written some poetry, I know you have read one of them. I don't know whether I am any good, but it releases frustrated emotions, so that's productive, isn't it?' She still gave me the creeps so I had to protect myself from her and her bullying tactics. Why was I so suspicious of her? What was it in her attitude that made me defensive?

She shrugged her shoulders and pulled down the corners of

her mouth. 'Just a thought, Angelica, not a challenge! I'll see you in the awareness class tomorrow. I think you are ready to face yourself.'

I was dismissed and turned to leave, when something caught my eye. There, by the door, was a picture of a small child in silhouette. She stood by a door that was slightly ajar and she was crying. I walked closer to examine it.

'Françoise painted that for me before she left.' Ann was standing behind me and placed her hands lightly on my shoulders.

'I thought it was her work. Isn't it beautiful, in a sad way? I wonder who the child is?'

I turned and saw such a haunted look in her eyes that I wanted to comfort her. She recovered instantly, coughed and moved to the safety of her desk, resuming the blank stare.

'There is a lost child in all of us. It could be anyone. It is just a black and white sketch. That's all!' I had stumbled on a chink in her armour. Or had I discovered her soft underbelly?

'See you tomorrow, then, bye.'

I crossed the courtyard, reflecting on the conversation and that poignant picture of a lost child.

The dining room resembled a mess hall, mouths opening and closing to consume fodder and make the occasional remark. My chair was vacant, waiting for my bottom to lay claim.

'Last but by no means least, Angelica. Have you had an industrious morning? Petra informs us that you are a diligent student.' Harvey could be so pompous and so *real*.

Everyone roared – even Harvey!

'Oh, well. Once a gentleman always a gentleman.' He was profound.

'Hear! Hear! Harvey. You certainly are that!' Iain slapped him on the back and grinned.

It seemed that we all had a free afternoon and there was much discussion on how to pass the time. Our merry band had grown: there were now seven of us, three women and four men, and, naturally, we wanted to do different things.

Chris had taken quite a fancy to Claire, but so had Petra. The three had decided to go on a shopping spree and Chris would be the 'bag carrier'. I wasn't in the mood for shopping, being uncertain about visiting the outside world, so we remaining four decided to go horse riding. The local stable provided tuition, ponies and hard hats, all our needs.

We parted at the gates to find our way across the common to the livery stables. Iain and I were seasoned riders, but Harvey and Alex were novices. With much ceremony, Harvey was seated on a dowager mare and a plump cousin was chosen for Alex, both horses wouldn't go above a trot.

Iain was given a frisky gelding called Tom and I chose a stunning piebald called Firefly. The stable-girl, Ginny, took the lead on her own pony and so we walked out of the yard. The lane meandered through dense woodland and onto the common.

After ten minutes or so, Ginny reigned back to let Iain and me pass, so that she could supervise the plodders at the rear.

'If you keep to this path it eventually opens out to a small paddock, where you can use the jumps, if you wish. Don't go above a canter through the woodland! We'll see you in the paddock.'

Iain was off, in his element – the man astride the saddle of leather – and my little filly didn't need much encouragement either. I hardly touched her sides and she was in pursuit.

'Yahoo! Yahoo! Catch me if you can!' he shouted over his shoulder.

The lower branches whizzed and bounced off our hats and the sun dappled the path. All at once the trees fell behind us. We were in the paddock, which had half a dozen small exercise jumps in the centre.

Firefly whinnied to Tom as he pounded the ground with his front hooves. He danced sideways, with ears pricked and nostrils flared, making his approach to the first fence. It was only about two feet high, but he was showing us his mastery. At one with his rider, he flew through the air and kicked up his hind legs on landing.

'What a showman!' I called across to Iain as I allowed Firefly to trot, gracefully, around the paddock.

Tom popped over the remaining jumps and came alongside my filly. The two horses blew down their noses at each other, which made us laugh.

'Are you going over the sticks, Milady?'

'We are contemplating, Parker! If Firefly decides to jump, then jump we will!'

She heard me and took the fences in reverse order. She was in control and loving it. At the far end of the paddock Ginny arrived with Alex and Harvey in tow. They were smiling and chatting and obviously having a genteel country walk.

'How have you two got on?' Ginny was delighted at our replies and watched us as we both performed a round of honour.

'This is the life! Hey, what? I think I could make a country squire. What do you say!' Harvey pushed his mount into a trot and bounced around on her back, grinning from ear to ear.

What a fabulous afternoon! I tried not to think about how dysfunctional my life had become but the invaders were back, creeping into the corners, taunting and unnerving me. The ants began their march from knee to head and I couldn't stop them.

The voice was saying – one day you are going to have to go home and face your demons, this is only make-believe, where weaklings allow their health insurers to pander to their 'illness' and indulge their fantasies.

The peace had disappeared and the faces were all strangers. I had to get back to my sanctuary. I didn't wait for Ginny to suggest the return walk; instead I took the lead and headed for the bridle path.

Firefly sensed the urgency and with deft manoeuvring we glided over the hardened soil, two as one. I could hear Iain yelping in the distance, like a downtown cowboy, urging Tom to lessen the gap between us, but this was one race I was going to win. Firefly was flying!

As the wind touched my face the tension began to ease from my neck and the disturbing thoughts were rejected. I forced myself to relish the freedom and lose the guilt trip.

We arrived in the yard almost in tandem, dismounted, tethered our horses and still there was no sight of the others.

'That was amazing! Do you know I wasn't aware of the tinnitus the whole time? That's the cure! I must wear a hard hat at all times.'

He yanked off his hat and hung it beside mine in the tack

room. I was finding it difficult to speak as I was still spiralling within the panic attack. I needed to sit on the floor, so I did. It would prevent me from falling over. Iain looked at my face and luckily recognised the signs.

'Stay there! I'm going to fetch you a glass of water. Don't move!'

I watched him push open the door marked 'Office' and disappear. There were agitated voices and he reappeared with a cracked mug and a dishevelled, whiskery man of indeterminable years.

'Done a bit too much today, 'ave you, luv? Not to worry, 'cos we'll drive you back in the truck.'

I think I smiled, took the mug and drank its contents without even thinking of being poisoned. Whatever it contained, it did the trick. Somehow the 'resume normal mode' button clicked into place and I was back.

'P'aps the 'at was too tight, luv!' He shuffled back to his den and Iain crouched in front of me.

'I don't know, Milady. The 'at was OK for me, but obviously squeezed the juice from your brain.'

My laugh was more a rasp as I watched Iain imitating the old man.

The others had finally arrived in the yard. Both men were trying to impress Ginny, which I'm sure she was quite used to.

'Don't mention my blip to anyone, will you, Iain! I can manage a slow walk back, I don't need to be driven.'

He pulled me to my feet and gently pressed his lips against mine, nothing sensuous or invasive, just loving.

'Milady, I am your servant and will do your bidding.' He swept the floor with his hand, then shuffled like the old retainer. He was my clown.

I would have given anything, at that moment, for time to stop while his mouth was on mine. I was a dry husk, needing an infusion of warmth and love and – what the hell – *sex*! This dynamic urge for flesh, lust, tongues entwined and the heat of passion was ever present. Just the thought of making love was electrifying my loins and I remembered Sexy Simon.

The walk back was peaceful. We playfully discussed our respective mounts and how considerate they had been not to dislodge us. Iain guarded me, fending off any comments, which he thought would evoke a return of the anxiety attack.

It was uncanny that each day we seemed to exchange our role play: whoever was the most confident took the lead.

The Abbey loomed at the head of the avenue and I was relieved to see it.

It was very necessary to close my eyes, soon. The clock tower chimed four times as we strolled onto the rear lawns, littered with recumbent bodies. Thankfully, Petra, Chris and Claire were nowhere to be seen. I wasn't in the mood to be bombarded with questions.

I left the boys and went upstairs. The curtains were closed, the duvet wrapped around me and I was asleep. Memories returned from my childhood. I had inadvertently resumed my place on the couch with Dr Michael and the years passed like turning the pages of a photo album.

I was four or five, with waist-length hair in brushed curls and apart from flowers, made from crêpe paper, in my hair and a grass skirt, I was naked. It was a fancy-dress pageant at Hilly Fields Park and I was Man Friday's girlfriend, the only costume my Mum could rustle up on the spur of the moment, as I had been overlooked.

My older sister, Miriam, was dressed in a pale-blue satin outfit with white silk socks and her thick curly hair had been powdered and tied back in a silk bow – she was Prince Charming. Her friend, Sylvia, whose mum was a seamstress, was Cinderella, dressed in a beautiful flouncy ball gown. Sylvia was not a pretty child, so the picture created was rather grotesque. She resembled one of the ugly sisters, but as her mother made the costumes everyone said she looked like the belle of the ball. Needless to say, they won the contest and I received a tube of Smarties.

The next page turned and I was on the stage, somewhere in London, tap-dancing in a troupe of six girls. I swung my head and my burnished curls bounced against my cheeks while my little tap shoes clattered on the floorboards to the music of 'Animal Crackers in my Soup'. The applause rang throughout the auditorium as we curtseyed in unison to the appreciation of the spectators. My dance teacher thought I could be the next Shirley Temple – it was a nice thought.

Over the page and I had transformed into 'Tomboy Angelica'. I could shin up trees and would collect the eggs, blowing gently as all the contents escaped. Ugh! How I hated it when the egg was addled and it collapsed in my hand, leaving behind that awful stinky smell. Oh! What adventures! I was the only girl in a gang of boys. My bike was called 'Black Bess', it was very old and had no gears, but I was granted no leeway with the boys, if I wanted to tag along I had to keep up.

Then there was jive dancing at the British Legion hall. This was the Beatnik era, mohair floppy sweaters, ethnic beads and bangles and unruly hair were imperative. We were the non-conformists, who would dance the night away, then find a beach where we would watch the sunrise, sitting next to an open fire.

The Swinging Sixties, when we tried to taste everything. Over-indulgent parents allowed us to sow our wild oats, uninterrupted. My parents were fairly lenient. I was the middle child of three girls. My older sister towed the line because it worked for her, where my younger sister had the gift of endurance and getting her own way. I had no idea who I was or where I was going, but I usually felt overlooked. Strange how life repeats itself!

Now was the time to discover the difference between illusion and fact, between reality and fantasy, the real me. I had to kick out old habits and deal with life head-on.

These last thoughts were gelling as I stretched and woke. I lay there with my hands on my belly, trying to imagine it so huge as my babies grew. Jason, soon to be seventeen, was eight pounds and so hard to deliver. I remembered the doctor saying, 'What a whopper,' and immediately thought he was referring to his willy and chided myself to have more respect for my newborn.

Rebecca and Sean, the twins, were tiny in comparison, only four pounds and five pounds respectively. Becca was long and slender and Sean was shorter and chubby, but both so wonderfully perfect.

I opened my eyes, still holding the small swell of belly and prayed that they would forgive me and understand my 'falling off'. One day we would all laugh about it and refer to it as, 'Oh, that was when Mummy went mad' – except John, who said it was when I was 'brainwashed by idiots', when the real 'me' died and a stranger stole my life.

Who knows, perhaps both descriptions were true. I rolled off the bed, stretched like a well-rested cat and prepared myself for the evening ahead.

We band of merry lunatics – just joking – converged on the dining room. Petra was looking spectacular in a glamorous, clinging, sheath dress and her eyes shone like a turquoise sea. As she approached the table, I followed her gaze. There was the reason for her metamorphosis – Claire the long-legged blonde. Oh! La! Petra was in love.

Unfortunately, Chris was also infatuated with her. Ha! Ménage à trois, I thought. If Claire was aware of the complicated scenario, it didn't show, and the modification it made on Petra was worth it. Chris was softening too, far less abrasive.

So tonight we were the Four Musketeers plus three. Harvey took the head of the table and revelled in his prowess as an equestrian. Petra was behaving coquettishly, fluttering her mascara-laden lashes and giggling at everything. Iain and I sat, knee to knee, occasionally allowing a hand to wander along a responsive thigh. Petra's antics were nicely diverting, which meant we could play our game, unnoticed.

'Do you see what I see, Iain, and if so, are the others blind to it?' I whispered behind my hand as I looked at Petra and Claire.

'Well, Milady! It takes two to tango and I think the odds are on three!' He raised his eyebrows and looked at Chris.

'Someone is going to get hurt. Can't you warn him, first!'

Did she understand our suspicions? Petra looked at me with a satisfied grin. She had discovered herself and was happy.

Later, in the lounge, Mrs Dighton revealed the story of the two elderly ladies, who sat in front of the TV, while she gave us our evening drink.

The ladies were spinster sisters, who could not survive without each other, so when one became seriously ill and needed to recuperate at the Abbey, the other came too. Punctually, at 9 p.m. they toddled off to bed, like two little hamsters.

The film showing on TV was a real classic, *Charade*, with Cary Grant and Audrey Hepburn, a film to cuddle up to. Alex swivelled in his armchair. 'Do you know, you could be taken for Hepburn, if you piled your hair on top of your head, Angelica!'

'Wowee, Milady! You, a film star!' Iain started to twirl my hair.

'Very funny, Alex! Let's just watch the movie!' Iain moved closer to me in the growing darkness of the room.

'I want to be face to face with you in that cupboard, sucking your lips into my mouth, holding your body and entering your—'

'Who's for another cuppa?' What a timely interruption.

'That'll be lovely, Harvey. You being mum tonight?' I stood up and followed Harvey to the trolley, throwing a cushion in Iain's lap to conceal his expanding pleasuring stick.

'Iain, would you like something hot or cold?' We were conducting our own play on words. I was so lovesick, or lust-sick, that I could have torn off his clothes and mounted him there and then, but, a hot chocolate drink would have to suffice.

This time, I broke the silence, as I sat cosily beside him.

'Do you think the pills they give us make us randy?'

'Could be! All I know is my groin is aching and my cock is about to explode!' He pulled my finger into his mouth, which made me squeak. 'Eee! You bugger!'

'What's going on you two? You're like a couple of kids. I thought you wanted to watch this, Angelica?' Harvey was really ticked off.

'Sorry, mate! I mistook Angel's finger for a chocolate biscuit.' Iain's humour made everyone tut, then silence reigned and we restrained ourselves.

The film was finished and we retired to our rooms. I watched the stars in the night sky and sighed. Strange day, mixed up with turbulent memories and erotic urges. My bed wanted me and I would not disappoint it. Sleep was a perfect partner. It gave all and wanted nothing. As Shakespeare said, *To sleep, perchance to dream.* Well, Will, I'm with you. The ride into dreamscape was instant.

It was snowing hard and we found it difficult to pull the sledge back up the hill. The dogs were yelping and barking, trying to eat the flakes as they drifted around them. Rosco and Dino, the Dalmatians, were constantly at war with each other. It was canine, sibling rivalry.

John was already by the jeep and had stowed his toboggan in the back and was shouting at us to hurry as the snow was getting worse. The twins were above us, almost at the top, both clowning around like monkeys. While Jason and I struggled to haul our sledge the last hundred yards, it happened.

I fell face down in the snow and Jason lurched backwards with the sledge on top of him. He slid away from me so fast that I couldn't hold on to him. I searched for him in the falling snow but all I could see was the blizzard. I was screaming, 'Jason, Jason, where are you? Where are you?' The light went on and the night sister was looming over me.

'Do you see what happens when you overdo things! Now, settle down! You were screaming in your sleep! Just drink this and go back to sleep!'

She was really pissed off. I haven't had those pills before. What a horrible dream!

Chapter Thirteen

I was cocooned in my drug-induced sleep, hoping that Wednesday would eventually appear. Breakfast passed without me and I woke to find Sam administering a cold compress to my forehead.

'Wakey! Wakey! Angelica! Do you feel able to sit up?' Her little face tilted from side to side, examining my face. She was relieved as I spoke. 'What's the time, Sam? I've missed breakfast, haven't I? Can I have it here? Oh, my head!' I pulled myself up but my hands ached.

'You seem to have gripped tightly onto the duvet and it has cramped your hands. Perhaps it was something to do with your dream?' She massaged my fingers.

'I don't know, I can't remember much. It was cold, snowing, I was clawing at the snow and there was an accident – Jason – it has something to do with Jason! There is imminent danger and it's imperative that I phone Jason.'

'Don't panic, it was only a dream. I am going to get you some breakfast.' She slipped out of the door as I started to get out of bed, slowly.

Growing urgency and apprehension was overwhelming me. What was happening? I was sweating and couldn't focus properly. I sat on the floor, resting my head against the bed. What had they given me?

I saw the shoes then the trousers and I lifted my face to see Dr Raschid, with Sam behind him.

'Madam Reeves, if I give you my hands, can you come to your feet? Yes!'

Everything was happening in slow motion. I seemed weightless.

'Yes! I am standing! Why are you here, Dr Raschid? Where is Dr Michael? Oh! My poor head!' My voice sounded surprised.

'Dr Michael is not here today so you have to put up with me. You are a little disorientated so we will sit you here.' He sat me on my chair and proceeded to check my vital signs and shone a light across my eyes.

Very quietly he spoke to Sam and she wrote something on my notes. Sam knelt beside me and Dr Raschid left the room.

'The doctor has gone to fetch a remedy for your headache. You shall then have some breakfast and we can go for a walk afterwards.' Sam looked pale and nervous and my dull brain was attempting to work out why.

She kept patting my hand and smoothing my hair, with agitated movements. My thinking was clearing with every second. She got to her feet as Dr Raschid re-entered the room.

'Here I am, Mrs Reeves, with an elixir that will improve your headache.' He poured some liquid into a cup and handed it to me.

He was so smooth. No wonder he was the Abbey gigolo, enticing vulnerable women into his massage room and seducing them. Angelica, what are you like! That person was in my head again, maligning this poor doctor who was in the process of rectifying an overdose that was accidentally given to me last night. Perhaps I was schizophrenic?

The pause button in my head released itself. I was back in control and the trump card was mine to use or not to use.

'Dr Raschid,' I said very quietly, 'did the sister give me a wrong prescription last night?'

He was directing the measuring cup of liquid towards my hand and hesitated for a second. I could almost hear the thoughts crunch in his brain. Which way would he jump? Luckily for all concerned, he chose the right answer.

'Unfortunately, there was a reaction with your usual tablets and the sedative, which has taken a while to pass through your system and was too strong. This liquid will rectify the error and establish normal functions with no harmful effects.' He swallowed *hard*! Good speech!

I turned to Sam and asked her, politely.

'Should I believe him, Sam? I'm not going to puke all day, am I?'

'Angelica, trust me, you will be fine but you might have to visit the loo more often than usual.' She was firm and direct and I trusted her.

'One thing I do insist on, if you don't object, Dr Raschid, I want to read what you have written in my notes.' He didn't object, but smiled and handed the papers to me.

After he had gone, Sam brought me a boiled egg with soldiers and half a grapefruit. She laid out my clothes on the bed and stood behind me, I thought to look out of the window. Very gently, she pressed her fingers into the nape of my neck and across my shoulders. I was glued to my seat as, surreptitiously, her healing Chinese fingers travelled through my hair, teasing, tugging and circling until my head felt as clear as crystal.

'You like Chinese head massage, lovely lady?' Sam had reverted to Chinese-speak and we both fell about, laughing.

'How about this walk, now? I need to talk about some weird dreams I am having and I *must* contact Jason.'

'OK, we need jackets today as there is no sun. I'll be back in ten minutes or so.'

She left me to get dressed, so that she could collect the tape recorder and establish our whereabouts for the next hour.

My head was now completely clear, but I needed to release some pent-up energy.

As Sam predicted, I had to dive behind the shrubs a few times. I had no idea where the water was coming from. We walked arm in arm along the trail towards the Woodland Convent as I recounted my most recent dreams for the benefit of the tape.

I explained that I was a little afraid of nuns in their habits; they reminded me of huge black ravens, swooping and pecking, and gave me the creeps. We stood by the railings and I took a deep breath.

'Do you see? There is nothing to fear! This place is in fact used as a retreat for all religious orders. The grounds, unfortunately, have been allowed to become overgrown, but I am told that it is still in use.' Sam tucked her arm back through mine and steered us back along the path.

'I have ice in my spine. Don't ask me why. It is an unsolved mystery.' I shivered and needed to be out in the sunshine or just somewhere warm.

The self-awareness class was about to start in the upstairs lounge and Sam walked with me as far as the doors. It was my initiation session and I admitted that I was nervous.

'Remember, if it is too intense you can walk out at any time. Best of luck! I'm only next door.'

Gingerly, I pushed the glass door open. The chairs had been arranged in a circle and there was a white pillow on each seat. All the sofas had been pushed against the walls. Some people I did not know were sitting on easy chairs under the far windows and Ann was sitting at a table in the corner with a display board by her side.

'Angelica, don't be shy, come in and choose a chair!' She almost smiled, except her eyes, those blank, pale eyes.

There was a commotion behind me and Harvey, Alex, Chris and Iain tumbled into the room.

'Well, well, well, gentlemen! What an entrance! Let's hope you are just as expressive in the session!' Even her venom was diluted.

'We missed you this morning, Milady. Where were you?' The faces of the Four Musketeers were waiting for an answer.

'I'll tell you later.'

Boadicea stood with her feet planted apart and tapped a small cane against her display board. When she was satisfied that her audience was alert and attentive, she told us to choose a chair and sit with the pillow in our lap.

There were eleven of us in the group, seated and waiting. All eyes were focused on Ann, who looked perilously like a Gestapo executioner. I seemed to have formed the habit of linking my hands across my rib cage and very gently massaging them and I was now aware of this. Still, it was far better than massaging my legs. At least I had progressed a little and wasn't making it so obvious that I was uncomfortable.

'Some of you are regulars at my awareness class, a few are initiates and I see one or two who have elected to come even though they have not been invited!' She stared directly at Iain, who immediately blushed scarlet and was about to defend himself, when Boadicea stopped him.

'But, we shall see how things go today, so welcome one and all!' She swivelled on her low-heeled shoes and again tapped her board.

'Read this and I shall explain the process of turning negative to positive. It is all about re-educating your thought patterns.'

The lecture progressed as she took us around the points of

instruction, noted in a circle on her board. Two or three people began to fidget, first coughing then adjusting their sitting position. A very large lady took out a handkerchief and blew her nose so violently that it made me giggle. She gave me an apologetic smile and began to play with the hanky.

'Well, I can see that your concentration levels are pathetically low, so I shall pause here and ask for some comments, in turn, going anticlockwise around the group. As you begin, please introduce yourself to the others and tell us how you will achieve *one* of the positive aspects on this board.'

Her power was mesmerising. She truly was Boadicea reincarnated. I had to admit she was excellent. After twenty minutes or so, we had all attempted to grapple with the science of self-destruction and how we could achieve a more positive attitude and she seemed quite pleased.

'OK! Now, we shall put this into practice. You have a pillow on your lap and it is your *pain*, your *agony* and your *anger*. Focus on your worst memory and embrace the pillow. You will accept the *pain* and put it with your pillow – *behind you!*'

The reaction in the room was extraordinary.

The large lady wouldn't let go of her pillow, but rocked forwards and backwards, sucking her thumb.

Harvey, quietly, placed the pillow behind his head, extended his legs, folded his arms and closed his eyes.

Alex put his pillow under his chair, clasped his hands as if in prayer and sat motionless, staring into space. He had totally closed down.

Chris was agitated and dropped his pillow in front of him, looking around the room for an escape route.

But the most violent reaction came from Iain.

'You're a *fucking lunatic!*' He just exploded. His pillow hurtled across the room, colliding with a lamp, which hit the floor, and in blind anger he crashed out of the room.

And then there was me. I completely fell apart. I hugged my pillow to my face and cried and cried and cried – oceans of tears silently saturated the pillow. I was crying for the *world*.

Harvey couldn't stand to see my sorrow and got to his feet to comfort me, as did another lady, but Ann intervened sharply.

'Don't! Leave her alone! It is her pain, she has made it and will wallow in it until she rejects it and gets – *angry*!'

She shouted the last word and it shocked me. I could see white spittle in the corners of her mouth. I couldn't take my eyes from her contorted face. The entire room was in extended animation. Waiting!

Time was irrelevant, no noise, no movement, nothing. The room became the lungs of Boadicea. We were inhaling her dynamic persona, breathing in a transfusion of *positive anger*. She had controlled her emotional outburst and was calm, retreating into her armour and viewing us through those blank eyes.

'Well! I think we should take five minutes to reflect and then we shall spend some fifteen minutes of bonding.' Everyone, instinctively, retrieved their pillows and we became a passive group of people again. There was a knock at the door and Iain re-entered. Before Ann had time to react, he spoke.

'Ann, I sincerely apologise for my disgusting language and would like to rejoin the group.' Ann nodded, I think in disbelief at his return and he sat down in his vacant chair.

'I now want you to select any person in the room, go over to them and give them a hug. Put your pillow on your chair and be friendly!' She stood and watched like a bird of prey, waiting for our reactions and any sign of rebellion.

Eyes went from one to another. Who would take the lead? Iain leapt to his feet and hurled himself in my direction and we hugged, the tension was broken.

A young woman, of about twenty-five, made a tentative approach towards Chris, who stood like a statue, extending his pillow in front of him to halt her advance.

'I can't do this! Please go away!' Chris was grey with fear.

As she turned from him, Harvey took control by taking her hand and sort of dancing rather than hugging.

Alex and I embraced, warmly, and he sighed into my neck.

'Angelica, what is all this about? Don't you just wanna get out of here?'

Iain was trying to make contact with Chris, but his eyes had dilated and was terrified. Ann didn't intervene; her role was only to observe. How long would she let this go on?

I had time to sneak up on him and manoeuvre my way past his defence. The top of my head was wedged under his chin and I locked my hands behind his back. He was frozen to the spot with his arms outstretched, leaving a gap where the pillow had dropped from his grasp. His heart was booming in my head.

'Angelica, please let me go or I shall be sick!'

'No, Chris! You won't be sick! You don't have to hug me back but I am not going to hurt you or take anything from you. I am now stepping away from you, so don't be afraid.'

I stood back one step and visibly saw the blood flooding back into his face. The *iceman* was melting.

'Good, good, good! That's enough for today. Go and have your lunch. You have done well!'

There was, suddenly, almost a frenzy of rearranging the furniture. People needed to expend some energy on something mundane and practical.

Another strange occurrence was taking place. Iain had strolled over to talk with Ann and they were actually chatting and laughing. The wonders of human nature were amazing.

'Angelica!' Ann was beckoning for me to join her. What was I in for now?

'I have a free hour this afternoon, could you come to the art room to discuss your artwork?'

No, this wasn't fair. How could I get out of it?

'As it happens, I have an appointment with Dr Michael.'

'Yes, I know, but it isn't until 4 p.m., so you could be there at about 2.30 p.m., OK?'

'Oh, all right!'

'I won't bite you know. Just a little extra therapy.' She looked down at her diary and dismissed me with a wave of her fingers.

The gang was waiting for me in the corridor and full of questions.

'Don't ask! I have been summoned for an extraordinary therapy session after lunch, which has almost taken away my appetite. Why *me*?'

Chris was giving me very peculiar looks so I kept out of his way. The irrepressible Iain couldn't wait to have my undivided attention and linked arms with me on our way to the dining room.

'What in God's name got into you, Parker. I thought you were going to chop off her head?'

'I had a naughty boy tantrum. It happens when I am confused. I suppose it's like being caught on a hook and my natural instinct is to fight to be free.' He gave me a sheepish grin and put it all behind us.

We sat, just us five, at our usual table by the open windows. I don't think anyone dared to sit there. There was an invisible *reserved* sign in place. I studied the huge doors of the art room. It was a studio full of pots of paint and haberdashery, but for me it had taken on a different guise. It was The Temple of Boadicea.

'A penny for them.' Alex placed his hands over mine on the table.

'I suppose I am trying to make sense of that strange session. It has left me feeling flat, sort of disjointed. Do you know what I mean?'

Within his macho exterior he was such a gentle man. His 'in denial' mode was his security blanket and he was well practised at using it. Some days he avoided contact by staying closeted in his room or walking out at times when he knew he would be undetected. Today he was affable yet quiet, approachable yet not demonstrative, but he wanted to be a friend to me.

'Believe it or not, that was the first group session I have ever had. A sort of a milestone. I have never had the confidence to attend before. I was there today as an uninvited guest – one of the "unwashed".'

'I am always so tired after a session. It should be a piece of cake but they annihilate me and I've got two more this afternoon.'

Iain was listening and decided to make a suggestion. 'Milady, don't go! Play truant, just like me!'

'Parker, you are a disruptive influence. You must be punished!'

'Ooh, yes please! I can't wait.'

That was the end of sensible conversation, which was what the doctor ordered.

We all chatted our way through lunch and finished by having a cuppa on the patio.

It was bliss to let the hammock take the strain and take me to a quiet place where there were no questions and no replies, swinging me into a comfortable, passive mood.

Petra and Claire had been out in the town all morning and had eaten lunch at The George. They had adopted each other and seemed as close as Siamese twins. One of the boys remarked that Petra should have been at the awareness class, to which she made a caustic comment and a very flamboyant hand gesture. The two buddies flounced off to play tennis. They were both avoiding their problems, but sooner or later their respective psychiatrists would tire of the game and withdraw the support. Not my problem, but it seemed such a shame that one or both would be at the bottom of the well, trying to climb back up again.

2.30 p.m. was fast approaching and I was loath to leave the safety of my Musketeers. Alex and Harvey were going to check out the local gym and Iain decided he would give them a challenge on the apparatus.

'Enjoy your interrogation, Milady,' was his parting remark.

'Thanks a bunch for your uplifting wit, Parker. See you all at dinner.'

I drank two cups of water from the dispenser and crossed the courtyard to the studio. The doors were wide open and it was quite cool inside. Ann was sitting, waiting, with each of her hands covering my manila envelopes.

She looked up and smiled, nothing intimidating, just a regular smile. 'I didn't mean to interrupt your leisure time, Angelica, but I thought you would benefit from continuity. You were uncompromising and really got stuck in, so I feel we could wrap this up today.'

I was trying to find an underlying meaning in what she was saying, but came up empty.

'What do you want me to do then?' I stood to one side as she stepped around the table and guided me towards a table with large sheets of white paper covering it.

'I want you to make a collage of all your picture cuttings and when you are satisfied that they are in the correct order, glue them into place. Next, take out the text and match the titles with the pictures and glue them too. Then, we shall have a story, your story.' She looked triumphant.

Now I knew what was to happen I relaxed. Energetically, I shuffled the pictures around like a deck of Tarot cards. Finally, when the most pleasing order was selected I pasted them to the backing paper.

Ann was occupying herself clearing out one of the cupboards.

'Would you like some background music? I have found this old tape deck and some antiquated cassettes.'

'If there are any classic soul singers or blues, that's my preference.' I was quite elated that she was so friendly.

'How about *The Best of Frank Sinatra*? It's a very old tape but it might work.'

'Yes, he'll do fine!'

It was a touch of nostalgia, but crackled more than he would have liked.

I opened the second envelope and was overwhelmed at so many pieces of paper. Not to be daunted at the task I used another table and spread the pieces out until I could read every one. Those that fell on the floor elected rejection and methodically I discarded even more.

The music played on and the time flew. A pattern was emerging as the words chose their own pictures and I fixed them into place.

'Jees! You made me jump.' Ann had crept up behind me and I was only aware when I felt her breath on my neck.

'Sorry, you were so rapt in what you were building that I didn't want to stop the creative flow. In twenty minutes you have to see Dr Michael.'

'I've finished, all but two pictures and I don't seem to have the right words.'

'Have you looked on the floor? Something may have escaped your notice.' She stepped away, leaving me to look and there they were. It was complete. I was satisfied and exhausted and I liked what I had achieved.

'Excellent! When it is dry, I shall fold it, carefully, and we shall evaluate it at our next meeting. Go now, goodbye!' The smile had disappeared.

That was OK! I was off to see my honey-coloured teddy bear, Dr Michael. On my way to the consulting room, I fairly bounced by Archie, who jumped to his feet and gave me an encouraging smile. He was exactly the right man to have on reception, friendly, courteous and totally unassuming.

The door was open and I could see my doctor in heated conversation with the one and only Dr Raschid. He was lounging against the desk, looking nonplussed and unaffected by their conversation, whereas Dr Michael was furious about something.

I hovered on the outskirts, not wishing to intrude, when Sam saw me and closed the door to avoid my witnessing the altercation within.

'Would you care to wait in the lounge and I shall fetch you shortly.' She was embarrassed and stepped back inside.

No sooner had I reached the lounge than she was back at my side. 'Sorry about the delay. Dr Michael is ready for you now, Angelica.'

We walked the few paces back and I was soon to be ensconced on the chaise looking into his deep, mystic eyes.

'Angelica, you are as radiant as any star. There is such a transformation over this past week, which is all due to your hard work. *But*, and I have to say it is a big *but*, it has been noticed that you are becoming too involved in the problems of other patients and this is a habit you must *stop!*'

In one breath I had been given an accolade, which had been extracted from my grasp as I inhaled. I knew, without hesitation that he was right. My silence was his answer, so he continued.

'You are here for self-healing and must allow the professional counsellors to attend to the other patients. Do *not* open your heart or your ears to them because you will only harm your own progress and probably impede theirs too.' He leaned over so that his face was almost level with mine in order to confront my down-turned eyes.

'Angelica, you do agree, don't you?'

'Yes, yes I agree. I know I am doing it. It is so easy to have empathy because I can then avoid my own pain and substitute theirs.'

This wasn't going to my plan. Today was a plus in the scheme of things and it was slowly being flushed down the toilet. How dare *he* spoil my Karma. I think I shall get up and go. That'll teach him.

I swung my legs round, with my feet almost touching his, which surprised him, and I prepared to stand.

'Running away is not going to help, Angelica. You have to face your fears and I shall help you. Settle back on the chaise and we shall begin again.' He pushed me down, gently but firmly, and indicated for the metronome and tape to be started.

'How are you coping with your therapy classes with Ann? Any comments?' He had diffused the situation, elegantly.

'I am not totally at ease with her and I still find her quite unpredictable. There is an open hostility, at times, which is unbridled, but I no longer fear her.'

I was calm and floating behind closed eyelids, surrounded by the most wondrous explosions of light and colour. I was within my own kaleidoscope.

'What happened when your husband was arrested? Try to take us back to that day and how it affected you. How did you cope and what repercussions affected you, your family and your friends? Let me hear the whole story!'

Chapter Fourteen

It was snowing and I was looking forward to dining with my friends at the health hydro. It was the only week in the year when I could be myself, my chosen theatre where I performed a role of self-indulgence and acted out my fantasies. I was a lotus flower, completely abandoned and yet innocent.

Then my life stopped. Someone pulled the plug. I was so happy when the phone rang but my heart stopped when I heard the voices of my twins. Mum, come home! Dad has been arrested!

I drove home, terrified of what I would find. All I could see through the wipers in the car were the tear-stained faces of my kids. My guilt, at not being there, was suffocating me, but if I didn't breathe I couldn't drive, so I ploughed on through the snow. Driving into the grounds of the house and seeing the lights in the windows and the Porsche nestled under the eaves of the garage made it all seem surreal.

I remember switching off the engine and thanking Orgasma for finding the way home. The front door opened and they all fell through it, the kids, the dogs, but thankfully not my mother-in-law, she was not there.

Sean had built a spectacular log fire which was roaring in the hearth, so we pulled all the cushions on the floor and with the duvets from the beds we camped there; even the dogs and cats lay with us, not wanting to be left out.

Between them they told me how the men had come with their father, who looked grey and sickly, and he tried to convince them that it was all a mistake. Methodically, this man machine turned over the entire house, totally ignoring the fear and confusion of my children. Eventually, they left, taking John with them and leaving a telephone number for Mrs Reeves to call on her return.

Once the story was told, two ashen-faced teenagers looked to me for comfort and the certainty that I would perform a miracle and return their lives to normal. How could they have been so brutal to my kids, showing no concern for their welfare? What animals were these men? Where did the police think I had been? It was already a day since they had taken John away. Was it too late to phone the station at 10 p.m.? Sean handed me the phone and the piece of paper with the London number written on it, imploring me to get his dad back home.

It was only their faces that gave me the courage to do it. Absolving myself of any responsibility was not an option. The police were non-committal and succinct. Commander Johnson, who was heading the enquiry, was not available until the next day. Mr Reeves was cooperating, helping them with their enquiries and I could visit him at 10 a.m. the following day. Only then would I be appraised of the situation and the procedures that would follow. He would be held in custody for at least another twenty-four hours.

The phone sat in my lap as I watched the flames in the fire. I had a thousand questions, knowing there would be a silent answer. Tentatively, I outlined what tomorrow might bring and how we would tackle it together. So far, we weren't public knowledge and we must try to keep it that way.

The house was beautifully tidy, as I had left it. The brass scuttle gleamed in the light of the fire, the jardinière was overflowing with newly glistened foliage and everything that could be polished shone. Then they dragged me to the den, the only room that had been left untouched after the police ransacked it. It was a disaster zone! Papers, files, upturned drawers were strewn all over the floor. Bastards! Bastards! Cretins!

I remember we snuggled into the duvets, clinging to each other, not daring to let go, then gradually they softened against me and sank into the warmth of sleep. My bottom ached and my legs cramped, but I had to keep vigilant. Fear of the unknown was engulfing me. Who could I tell? Who would be there to protect us? Eventually, I slept among the human bundle of bodies and canine snoring.

'What happened next, Angelica? Can you go on?'

The morning arrived and both Rebecca and Sean refused to go to school. How could they face their friends knowing what had happened? What excuse would they give for being away? On that day I couldn't argue. I wanted them to feel safe, so I let them be. So I phoned the schools and began the series of lies. Funny isn't it! I never used to swear or tell lies.

Where was John's business partner? Why hadn't he phoned? Had he been arrested too? I phoned his number – nothing! I phoned the office number – nothing! I was trying not to panic, but my head was becoming very hot.

I was supposed to be at the hydro so I could lay low for a week. The next job was to phone John's mother and tell her that I hadn't gone to the Health Farm after all. She made some acid comments, but accepted the lie. Then I drove to London with the children sitting quietly in the back seat. I managed to find my way to the police station and was allowed to park in the station car park. Two frightened faces stared at me as I left them in the car and entered the building. I blew them a kiss and tried to smile.

The officer leading the investigation, Commander Johnson, was courteous, almost friendly, in fact I was treated like a VIP. He introduced himself and walked me downstairs. I hardly took any notice of him but I think he was of medium height and very much in control. The officers stood aside as we approached and he said goodbye at the door to the cells and turned away.

John was confined to a dimly lit cell. He looked so old, grey and dishevelled, wearing the same suit he had worn for two days, but his tie and belt had been confiscated. The duty officer took the change of clothes I had taken for him and offered me a cup of tea. I declined, but asked if someone could please go and check on the kids in the car.

John's cold hands held onto mine and he pleaded with me to forgive him. He was so afraid and inside I was already *screaming*. Gone was the confident peacock: he had shrunk into a shivering, helpless child whose lies had caught up with him. He talked and talked and talked and I tried to listen, I really tried, but my mind had started to close down and my responses were robotic. I had gone somewhere else. This *me* was someone else. My comforting words were as futile as a cup of water on a forest fire. How could I offer him any solace? What did I know of the criminal justice system? The only solicitor I knew dealt with births, deaths and conveyancing. He wasn't a QC or a barrister.

The time was up and I was ushered from the cell. John was about to go before a magistrate to be remanded for another twenty-four hours, when he would be charged or released. He had been swallowed into a maze of interrogation rooms, hushed voices and conspiracy. I didn't even know how serious the offence was or whether he had committed an offence. I just wanted to get out, for it all to stop! I wanted to clutch my children to me and run, run far away. Go anywhere! Just leave this crap behind!

'Angelica, would you like to stop for a while?'

'No, I want to get this out of my head!'

What was I expected to do next? I hadn't been in a police station before. The same duty officer took my elbow and guided me to the front desk and left me there, saying someone would explain the procedure. Phones were ringing, people were laughing, buzzers were buzzing and I felt naked, with this *scream* building up in the pit of my stomach, but I had to suppress it. I was standing by the front desk, waiting to ask when I should phone or to be told when I would be receiving a call from them, when I sensed someone was watching me. I turned slowly to challenge the intruder.

A middle-aged man in a shabby pinstripe suit, which was definitely past its sell-by date, coughed to gain my attention. He pushed his hand into mine, pumping it up and down. I shall always remember that touch. His hand was dry and callused, like his voice and his smile. His legal patter was well practised and colourful. He said his name was Cohen and he would be representing John in court. The man was a reptile, sneaky and vicious. I took an instant dislike to this predator and was proven right. At the time, who else was I to engage?

This apology for a brief had lived in the world of fabricators for so long that the truth was immaterial. The only important criteria was money. He pushed a card into my hand and with a nod disappeared into the lower regions of the station. From that day forward everything went downhill.

Eventually, an officer apologised for the delay, telling me that the Commander was tied up and would contact me later at home. I waited for the call, but it didn't come that day.

John was remanded twice more on technicalities, charged and

taken to the Scrubs to await trial. His so-called brief convinced him that the more time he spent on remand, the less time he would serve if or when he was sentenced. He could have had bail and not suffered the months in purgatory on remand. Instead, he chose to suffer in silence. He was too frightened to talk, as the consequences were lethal.

I was interviewed a dozen times by different policemen wearing different badges asking similar questions. Eventually, Commander Johnson of the Flying Squad called to see me. He was so cool and efficient, like the blade of a knife, so sharp that you don't feel the cut. His main question was: how could I not know what was happening in my life? I must know something of John's dealings! I spoke for a while and I think he realised that John and I were running on two different tracks, in different worlds and I really was in the dark. His attitude changed and he actually smiled, saying he would help me through this difficult time if he was able to.

There had been a small caption on the front page of the national papers, stating when and where John had been arrested. I prayed that the locals would not see it. Thankfully, some didn't.

After a week of notoriety, the kids had settled back into school. Rebecca was mortified for a while; her sensibilities had been bruised, but a few decent friends pulled her through. Sean, on the other hand, became a junior James Bond. He milked the interest and I'm sure embellished the tales that he told and the head teacher hated him for it. He learned to survive the only way he could. Having John as his father had taught him how to fabricate stories.

The repercussions for me, in the adult world, were too complex for me to adjust to. My own family didn't talk about it – it never happened – so their support was non-existent. John's mum became the Wailing Wall, pious for one minute and crying the next. His family said he was cursed, an accident waiting to happen. The company, his partnership, had ceased trading, disappearing overnight. There was nothing left. If anyone else was involved, they had melted into the crowd. Thankfully, my bank account wasn't frozen, so I still had money.

Some friends stayed and some found it too difficult to pick up the phone. I organised a roster of prison visiting and pleaded with people to go and see him. I played the part of a dutiful wife but I was dying inside. I lost *me* on the walk to the Scrubs. The indignity of body searches, of bags and belongings being scanned, of strangers watching your face, your hands, the way you sat, became an integral part of our lives.

I walked the walk of a dead person on my weekly visit to the Scrubs, pretending to be confident and in control to give courage to Rebecca and Sean. But I was quaking inside. We queued at the entrance with anonymous people alongside us. The door opened and one by one we entered the inspection area. It was so degrading; having men's hands searching you while others leered and made banal comments.

As our name was called we sat at our allocated table, waiting to be joined by John. He was pale, tired and always looked as if he was about to cry. I would hold his hands and try to comfort him but I could never shut out the sights and the smell of that awful place. People were laughing and chatting, seeming to enjoy the outing. I could only sense the vigilant eyes of the screws, monitoring every movement. We were being exposed to the virus of corruption that insinuated itself through the walls of the Scrubs. I didn't want my children to be infected by the malevolence that was there. My prison had no bars, it was in my mind, but after an hour I could walk away to fresh air and freedom. John could no longer do that.

There was a huge maggot growing inside me that forced itself into my stomach. It took my breath away and gorged on my food until the weight dropped off me, leaving me hollow. I had become a non-person.

The school governing body suggested that I should resign, so I did. The beauty shop, where I worked as a therapist, no longer had sufficient trade, so I was asked to leave. I left with a small bonus payment and the promise of reinstatement, but I knew it would never happen.

Jason was safe in New York with Uncle Toby, his diligent protector. He wanted to come home, but I convinced him to stay out of the limelight. How much I missed him, he will never know!

The twins were my anchors. They were healthy, happy and we

were together. Within the boundaries of our land we were secure, or so I thought.

I don't recall exactly when it began but the ultimate horror crept upon us in the dark. We seemed to be adjusting to our life. John was seeing us at weekends. The police had finally stopped harassing me, believing I had no information, and the journalists and gossips had found more interesting news.

On the advice of an inmate, John had instructed another firm of barristers from Lincoln's Inn to represent him. A meeting had been arranged with his new man, J Bowles-Smith, a highly respected QC. We had paid thousands already to the scaly little man and this firm would cost twice as much. If it meant he would be released it was worth it. Whether it was a coincidence, or not, the 'Organisation' began their terror campaign against the Reeves family at the same time.

It happened when Rebecca and Sean were away at Auntie Betty's. It was half-term and they had taken some friends with them. She lived on her own in this lovely old fisherman's cottage, at a place called Orford in Suffolk. They were having a great time, doing what healthy teenagers do.

Jeannie and Mike had given me some hours at the pub, which was a blessing. I needed the company and the money and they were short of staff. I finished quite late that night. It must have been about midnight as I approached my house.

I drove down my lane, past the Greens and the Lowrys and the old derelict cottage on the opposite side. The cottage had been empty for ages, since the owner had died. Our house was at the end of the lane, where it became dense woodland and the lane ended. It was eerie at night, as there were no lights, so I put my headlights on main beam. I had to stop the car to open the gates. Why hadn't the house lights gone on? It should happen automatically. I was nervous of the dark.

A pair of white lights appeared in my rear-view mirror and were slowly approaching. They had come from the grounds of the empty cottage. I swung the car into the drive and still the security lights had failed to come on. Was that someone by the side of the house? No, it was just the bay tree. Where had the car lights gone? Behind me the darkness was overwhelming.

The dogs were barking and throwing themselves against the front door. I slammed the car door shut. A stupid thing to do as I could no longer see. It was pitch black and I fumbled for my keys.

I pushed the key into the lock and I knew someone was watching me. The rush of cold air on my stocking-clad legs made me turn around. Fight or flight kept going through my brain.

No one! No car lights! 'Come out! Who's there?' I shouted to the darkness.

The only noise was the rustling of the trees and the click...click...click as the engine grew cool. But someone was there... I was positive!

I threw the front door open and Dino, one of my Dalmatians almost knocked me over. Snoopy, my scruffy Schitzu was biting my ankles, but where was Rosco? Dino charged at all the closed doors. His brother must have got locked in!

The lights were now on. Where was Rosco, my beautiful soul mate? There were dark stains on the floor tiles and splashes up the wall. I could hear him barking and a noise like a drum banging and Dino growling. He was so angry at being left out. He wanted to share whatever was happening to Rosco and started to bark.

Why were all the doors shut? Frantically, I opened each door. Not in the lounge! Not in the kitchen! Not in the dining room! My mind was going crazy! Please don't be dying! Finally, the shower room and the banging was getting louder. Oh! My poor baby! I'm coming! I'm coming!

Rosco was there, hobbled to the radiator and he was beating his tail against the shower cubicle. Where was the blood coming from? Had someone cut him? There! A small bag had been fastened to his collar, dripping blood down his white coat. I tore it off in disgust and threw it into the sink. What sick creature had done this? Oh, my God! Was someone there waiting for me? I screamed aloud, 'Come out, you *bastard*! Come out, you *coward*!'

There was now pandemonium as all the dogs tried to lick the blood from his coat and he started to retaliate and growled fiercely. I opened the back door to the dog enclosure and turfed them out, letting them run off some steam. There was no sound in the house. Should I phone Mike?

It was then I noticed the light flashing on the answerphone. I rewound the tape and listened to the message.

'This is just a warning, Mrs Reeves! I hope your Dalmatians are not too stained. Such pretty dogs. Next time they won't be so *alive*! Imagine them impaled on your walls. What adorable trophies! I know where your Jason is – I know where the twins are – and of course I know where you are. What a lovely body, especially naked, too beautiful to be razored, but perfect to be *fucked*! Tell your husband to keep his mouth shut or…' It stopped. I screamed at the phone… What! What else!

Tell me! Then a second message began.

'Just one more thing, Mrs Reeves, don't inform the police. They couldn't help you anyway – far too stupid. Remember I am always by your side, in the shadows, here for *you*!'

The voice had stopped and I threw up all over myself and I cried and cried and cried. I was useless. I didn't even manage to get to the bathroom. I looked at the vomit in the mirror but didn't really see it. There was a shushing noise way back in my head, like a distant train ploughing through the snow. I felt so alone and so helpless.

Who was this Voice? What did he want? Where was he? How am I going to be here alone in the dark? Should I phone Mike? Should I? I stood with my back against the door, shuddering. There was blood all over the floor tiles and vomit all down my clothes.

I remember pulling off my jumper and throwing it in the sink. Methodically, I filled a bucket with bleach and water and scrubbed the floor in the hallway and the paintwork and the tiles in the shower room and then another bucket and did it all again. The kitchen was next, I cleaned until everything shone and all I could smell was bleach. Then I let the dogs come back in. They hurtled upstairs, yelping and barking but there was no one there.

I was exhausted. It was 2 a.m. The phone rang. I knew it would be him before I picked up the receiver. The voice was disguised but the accent was guttural, German or South African.

'Mrs Reeves, why don't you go to bed now? I want to see your body! I want to lick your body! I'm hungry for you! I can do it *hard* or *slow* but I *will* hurt you!'

'*Fuck off*, you pervert! *Piss off!*' I screamed. Was that *me*? I slammed the phone against the wall and pulled out the plug. What the hell was happening to me? He won't do it! He won't touch my kids or I'll *kill* him!

That sick moron wasn't going to get me! I emptied the contents of my handbag on the floor and found the card. The special officer from the Flying Squad had given me a private number to call. I couldn't do it then because *he* would know so I would do it the next day. I would phone my Auntie the next day and speak to my babies. This was just fear tactics to frighten me and, guess what, it was working!

'Is that what you did, Angelica? Did you phone the police?' Dr Michael was there. He was sitting on the chaise with me.

'Yes, I did. The next day I drove to the pub and told Jeannie what had happened. Mike said I should phone the private number to ask for their help. I still didn't believe it was actually happening to us. It didn't make any sense. Oh! I phoned the kids and they were fine.'

The story continued.

I didn't meet the detective, I had to leave messages and he called me at the pub. It was not a good idea to use the pub because I didn't want to involve Jeannie's family, so I would contact the number from a public phone. My home telephone was tapped, so couldn't be used and John was interviewed on some pretext to make him aware of what was happening.

Auntie was fantastic. I tried to be as light-hearted as I could with the kids and said I would be up to collect them in a couple of days. I explained what had happened to Auntie, and confidently, she took on the role of Miss Marple. She even confessed to me that she had a twin-barrelled shotgun in the shed, but hadn't fired it for years. Believe it or not, I think she would have used it, but I convinced her to leave it where it was and not to tell a soul.

The nightmare wouldn't go away. Where could I go to find refuge? When would the thoughts stop crowding me? John got us into this mess, stupid, stupid fool, and I vowed I would never forgive him, not if I lived to be a hundred years old.

I left the pub after lunch and drove straight home. The drive down the lane in daylight was not a problem; it was at night that I became unhinged. My first thought was to phone the kids.

The van outside the garage had BT emblazoned on the side and a young man was waiting for me. Someone had reported a fault on the line and he was there to repair it for me. His credentials were in order, so I let him proceed. I had no reason to doubt him, as his identity card looked correct.

I had forgotten to plug the lead back into the socket and said that was possibly the reason but he stayed for about an hour checking the wires inside and out. He had a cup of tea, then left. He seemed a nice guy.

The telephone rang. It was the Voice again.

'Don't test my patience, Mrs Reeves,' he said very quietly. 'Your husband is aware of my presence. We don't want any accidents, do we?' He was gone.

I phoned BT and asked the fault department if they were satisfied with the repair. They hadn't any record of a fault and no engineer had been to my house. I dialled the pub and asked Jeannie to phone me back. She dialled my usual number and it worked. I phoned the special number from my mobile and arranged to meet someone at Liverpool Street Station. I was totally unhinged and thought I saw assassins in every carriage. Surely, whoever was watching me wouldn't follow me to London.

We met a couple of hours later at the Station Cafe. It was obvious, even to me, that we were being shadowed. He admitted he had a surveillance team in the vicinity. The engineer was nothing to do with the police or BT, so it had to be the 'Network' behind it. 'Network', 'Organisation', they were all words out of an Al Capone movie, not in my world!

Very briefly, he described the 'Network' and their unlawful trade throughout the world. John had been manipulated over many years by a pawn in their set up and was probably totally unaware of how vast and corrupt this organisation was. Someone had triggered a sensitive connection, identifying names and locations that should never have been uncovered, like a navigation screen of underworld crime and John was trapped in the middle of it. No! Not just John! My family was drowning in the cesspool too!

They were using scare tactics to keep John silent. It was working. I was terrified. They, the police, were trying to place a virus on the line to monitor all incoming calls but then this Special Branch officer dropped the bombshell. If all else failed we would be taken to a safe house and given new identities until it all blew over. We would probably be taken abroad.

Up until then I had been brave and able to comprehend what was happening. I looked at this man of thirty-something with the boy-next-door looks and laid-back charm, talking to me as if we were having a casual meeting, when my calm evaporated. I gripped his hands across the table, digging my fingernails into his skin and through tears and clenched teeth I was yelling.

'Who do you think you are? You can't play with our lives as if they are expendable! We're *real* people, we are *real*.' I was hysterical, so they bundled me in a car and we lost ourselves in the traffic.

Dr Michael was rocking me to and fro in his arms. Had he let me go too far? Again I was crying, but this time it was rock bottom, gut-wrenching, Niagara Falls. I wouldn't go this way again. Perhaps I had finally confronted my nemesis head on and now I would recover. The Devil had been laid to rest. But if I ever met him, I would cut off his balls!

I could still hear the tick-tock of the metronome and saw Sam reach for the pendulum to stop it. Her face was very sad; she too looked as if she had cried. The strong arms of Dr Michael encircled me and he whispered in my hair, speaking in his native tongue. He was my hero.

The burden of fear and guilt had lessened and I felt strangely relieved and lighter. Would I still have to resort to my Dream-scape and Fantasies to survive? The only way now was to make my role-play the real thing. The flight of the butterfly was soon to end as the Age of the Lioness was emerging.

I was enjoying the warmth and protection of this man's embrace probably even more because there were no hidden agendas. Calm had returned and Sam walked me to the door, both anticipating a more proactive session next time.

Dr Michael looked stunned as I left. I forgot to ask him if he would contact Jason and I didn't want to ask John. Whenever I thought of my husband I wanted to crawl into a corner and sleep, close my eyes on the person who had inadvertently shattered our lives. My forgiveness for the mistake was given, but coming to terms with the loss of my life as I knew it and the bereavement of lost friends was much more difficult. Slowly I walked the familiar route to room 36.

Heavy clouds were spoiling the blue of the sky. Another summer storm was approaching and it grew black as the temperature cooled. It was nearly 6 p.m., as I was climbing the stairs. I pictured the squirrels gathering the last of their trophies and swinging from branch to branch to reach the safety of their hiding place.

By the time I reached my room the thunderclaps had begun and the rain poured in waves. Huge spots hit the ground like exploding water bombs. I was fascinated with how the earth changed after snow or rain and how much more energy we had.

The rain was relentless and had set in for the night. Was I in the mood to socialise? I had to eat, but I could do it alone, or I could eat and run. Wise thoughts, but how contrary the evening would prove to be while dining with my friends.

Calamity had struck in the guise of another rival for the affections of Claire. Both Petra and Chris were sulking because Claire was escorted into dinner by a stranger. He was tall, elegant and, at a guess, in his forties, about ten years her senior.

We sat at the table taking turns in giving him a title. Was he her brother, her lover, a friend, her doctor or perhaps her boss?

Petra was not amused and slunk off to lick her wounds as soon as her plate was empty. Chris concealed his hurt pride by feigning disinterest. I found the whole thing amusing and said we would find out soon enough. This friendly banter was a perfect antidote to the manic session I had undergone with Dr Michael.

The Musketeers had a great afternoon in town. Although it was frowned upon to partake of alcohol, they had consumed a pint or two after viewing the fantastic equipment in the local gym. There was every training device imaginable and a resident Roman gladiator. He offered them a temporary membership at a minimal fee and his personal attendance. They said they would think about it and went straight to The George to discuss it.

'What about you, Milady? Do you fancy a workout with a muscle man?'

Whose muscles was he referring to? I wondered. 'Sounds good to me, Parker! You name the time and we'll go find the place. I could do with a thorough toning session!'

I looked at Chris, his face was so hard and his lips so tight, they looked as if they had been glued together.

'What about you, Chris? You're young and fit, it might do you some good!'

'I don't know, I might. It wasn't much of a gym, not as good as the one I go to.' Was he suffering from 'Claire's new friend' phobia?

He fidgeted in his seat and was a hostile participant in the conversation. 'It's not a competition, Chris! It's just a bit of light relief. Well, I'm going to give it a whirl, I need to lose a few pounds.' Alex was game.

'A few pounds! More like a stone, old boy!' Not a tactful remark from Harvey but he winked at Alex proving he was only funning.

'OK, you over-age Adonis! Let's have a wager to see who is in the best shape after, let's say, five visits.'

Everyone was now enjoying the challenge, even Chris. He definitely had a problem communicating with people, taking everything too seriously. He seemed to assume that his competency was under threat so he had to emphasise his superiority. He was a sad specimen. I couldn't imagine him doing anything without analysing it, pulling the guts out and being left with nothing. Did he ever chill out? Did life make him this person or was he born pessimistic?

Here I was again! Trying to understand and evaluate other's dysfunctional attitudes, when I was screwed up myself. Physician, heal thyself! Isn't that true?

The rain was continuous, making the evening dark and moody.

Most of the inmates had left the dining room and the stripey-legged boys from the kitchen had moved some of the tables together to make a large table for a special gathering. At least a dozen members of the nursing staff had entered, found seats and were anticipating a fun evening.

There were a few cards and a huge parcel, festooned with

ribbons and bows in the centre of the table. It was somebody's birthday, perhaps! Dr Raschid walked in flourishing a magnum of champagne and proceeded to pop the cork with great gusto. We watched as all the glasses were filled and waited for someone to make a toast. Who, I wondered?

It was Joanna! To much jeering and cheering and applause, Dr Raschid rushed round the table and scooped her into his arms to stand her on her chair to receive her present. She looked pink and flushed and very feminine, with her blonde hair long and around her shoulders. She was in her white nurse's uniform, instead of the usual running gear and white shoes.

Did the Musketeers make the discovery at the same time? Was there instant recognition and realisation? How many pairs of white leather pumps, with a dainty fringed instep flap, could there be?

I swallowed and put my hand over my mouth, swivelling around to look at Iain. He followed my gaze and twigged immediately. He pulled Alex's attention away from his dessert, gave a throaty cough and nodded in the direction of the shoes.

'Well, well, well, what a surprise! I wouldn't have guessed it was her in a million years.' Alex couldn't restrain himself and almost fell of his chair in giggles.

'Come on, laddie! What's the wag? Must have been a good one! Come on, Iain. Tell it again, I didn't hear the punchline.' Harvey had misconstrued the plot and as subtly and quietly as he could, Iain told him. 'We have solved the identity of the mystery shoes!'

'When, where, how?' Poor Harvey was so excited and also crestfallen that he was the last to know.

'Oh, come on then. Don't keep me in suspenders!'

Iain kicked him under the table, indicating with his eyebrows to be less vociferous and more discreet.

'OK! Mum's the word!'

His mop of grey hair turned in all directions, trying to get a glimpse of the nurses' shoes. Chris viewed the comic relief with derision, either because he wasn't there at the original sighting or just because he was Chris.

I ventured back to Sunday night and my hormones went into orbit. What would I have given to have laid on that table with

Sexy Simon? I was having a miniature orgasm, reliving the cupboard scenario, a self-gratification without moving any external body parts. I wondered what the others were thinking?

I kept looking at Dr Raschid, whom I didn't fancy at all, and then at Joanna, a soft, English rose. She was flushed with anticipation, not alcohol. The signs were there, the glances, the lowering of the lashes, the tongue flicking across the lips and most erotically of all, the occasional sucking of the fingertips. Believe me, her digits couldn't have been that sticky if she had eaten the entire cake.

An emergency exit was necessary for me. My sexual appetite was overflowing and I was in need of relief, in private.

'I'm going to my room, folks, so I'll meet you in the lounge for the verdict.'

As I rose from the table, Iain rose with me and said very quietly.

'Can I give you a hand or can you manage yourself?' He smiled ruefully – was it telepathy or just wishful thinking?

'Parker! I am not amused, just astounded!'

I raced up the stairs, trying to expend as much frustrated energy as I could. No one saw the going of Claire and her companion and as I reached the second floor I could hear the familiar strains of Vivaldi. Petra was incommunicado.

After my necessary self-adjustment, I entered the crowded lounge. I took in the scene and realised that the two elderly ladies were missing from their front-row seats. Lady Shirley and a gentleman of advanced years were there instead.

Chris was sitting in a corner with Claire and her friend and looking very relaxed and the Three Musketeers were huddled together in animated conversation. Mrs Dighton beckoned me to her trolley and gave me a specially prepared mug of frothy chocolate.

Harvey patted the space next to him, so I plonked myself down and curled my legs up beside me.

'While we were waiting we have decided, if you agree, that we should settle this intrigue once and for all! We should secrete ourselves in the cupboard, immediately, 'cos we think the re-enactment will be tonight! What do you say?' *All* eyes were focused on me.

'I don't know, Harvey, it seems a bit crass! I don't think I can go along with being a *premeditated* voyeur!'

The thought of sneaking down, hiding and possibly witnessing an intimate love scene suddenly made me feel cheap and nasty.

'Scaredy-cat! What harm can it do? We can't actually see anything, so why should the squirrels get all the juicy fun!' Iain was determined to get off on it. Did he have an ulterior motive? Did he want to satisfy his primeval urges by holding himself next to my body? Had he programmed his own sexual therapy after dark?

'We can't all get into the cupboard for a start! You remember that three of us were crammed like sardines.' I had thrown a spanner into the works.

Harvey frowned in concentration then raised his finger.

'Got it! We'll draw straws and the longest doesn't get in.'

'Great, mate! Where do we get the straws from? We're just wasting time!' Iain was getting tetchy.

'We'll improvise. Who smokes?' Alex had thought of a plan.

Chris was walking over to see how the escapade was going and funnily enough, he was smoking.

'Hey, Chris, have you any matches?' He felt in his pocket and produced a lighter and held it out to Alex.

'Sorry, Chris, we really need matches!' Alex explained why he wanted them and outlined the imminent adventure. Chris declined to take part as he was claustrophobic, but gave Alex four cigarettes to mutilate at will. As Alex was shortening the lengths, Iain had a surprise realisation.

'Hold on a minute, that cupboard wasn't very high. How on earth is Harvey going to fit inside? He's too tall.'

The deflated look on Harvey's face was too comical to describe.

'Oh! Buggeration! That takes the biscuit! Rejected before we begin! Why is it always me?'

'If it's any consolation, I won't go either!' I gave him a hug.

'Yes, you bloody well will! I insist! If I can't then you must go in my stead!' He was pontificating like a major general.

I was trapped in the tunnel like Charles Bronson in *The Great Escape*.

Iain slapped his knees and proclaimed, 'That's it! Let's do it, or we'll miss the show.' It was about 8.30 p.m. as we casually sauntered past the nurses' station. The miserable night sister was on duty, sorting out the pots of tablets, and didn't see us pass by. On tiptoes we rounded the stairs before we spoke. The plan was unfolding. Harvey and Chris were going outside, via the fire exit, to have an evening stroll. Thankfully, the rain had stopped. There were a few stars out but no moon. They were going to stand outside the French windows of room 12, hoping for a surreptitious viewing. Their mission was The Secret Squirrel Sex Odyssey (Part Two).

Alex and I would nonchalantly chat by the foot of the stairs, while Iain called out good night and casually rapped on all the doors on the left-hand side on his way down to his room. He would look into the lounge and lower nurses' station and make his way back. Not only was he knocking, but also turning the handles to see if the door opened. From where we were standing, all the doors appeared to be locked.

Joanna's party had finished and all was in darkness. The reception desk was unmanned at night, so all we had to do was keep an eye on the ICU doors. We got the thumbs-up from Iain and he started his way back. Opposite his room was the lower refreshment area and as he passed it he disappeared. We could hear voices and Iain emerged with the very large lady, whom we met at the awareness class.

She waved a greeting and, as she had both hands full of bars of chocolate, Iain opened her door and closed it behind her. That was room 13 and the next was room 11, which we knew was empty, because it was Chris's room.

He looked both ways, then beckoned to us as he entered The Lothario's Lair. Alex and I hurtled down the corridor, jumped inside and closed the door. Something had changed. I scanned the room and realised that vertical blinds had been put over the French windows. I had a little chuckle. The boys outside wouldn't see a thing, so I opened them, just a touch.

Alex checked the interconnecting doors to the consulting room and found them locked, so I went to the windows and pulled the bolt up in case we became trapped. There was still time to escape, but I hesitated.

This room's door to the corridor was the only one that was

unlocked, which seemed curious. I looked inside the cupboard: nothing had altered, and there was plenty of hiding room. Harvey gave three gentle taps on the window to say he was there, when it was too late to go, as the door handle turned.

We crammed ourselves into the cupboard, closing the door as the main door opened. It was Joanna. She was standing, talking to someone.

'I won't be long – hiccup – ooh – hiccup. I'm a bit fuzzy! Too much bubbly! Just gonna collect a few things and I'll join you all down the pub. See ya!'

Our entrance into the cupboard was so swift that I found myself facing the sidewall. Craning my neck around, I saw that Alex was facing the other side and Iain was facing outwards, holding the doors together. There was a narrow gap between the wall and the door by the hinges, so I had a continuous strip of vision.

Joanna was reeling a bit and swerved towards the couch. She kicked her shoes off and was instantly naked. She hadn't put any lights on but I could see her clearly, may I be forgiven. Why was I here? I felt sick! What we were doing was *sick*!

There was movement outside in the grounds and I heard raised voices. Almost simultaneously, the door to the corridor opened and Dr Raschid slipped in. Were we about to be discovered?

I closed my eyes and held my breath, waiting for the lights to go on and the cupboard doors to be opened. Dr Raschid was frantically helping Joanna to put her clothes on, as she protested and they were gone.

Iain flung open the doors and we all fell out. We looked from one to the other in disbelief.

'What the hell happened there?'

'No time to talk! Let's get out of here!'

Alex was peeping out of the windows and gestured for us to follow him.

There was someone nearing the patio, who was shining a beam of light. We hugged our bodies to the wall and waited. I thought back to the cupboard and made myself a solemn promise – I'm never going back in there.

The gardens were in darkness as we crept along the side of the building, praying that the doors onto the patio had been left open.

'Where in God's name are Harvey and Chris?' Alex was first to try the patio doors and they were locked.

'*Fuck!* What are we going to do now?'

He really looked anxious. I had never heard him swear before. Iain burst out laughing and fell about, holding his belly.

'Look at your face! You girl's blouse! I can't cope with such a softie!'

'It's all right for you! You reduce everything to a banal level.' Alex had hit below the belt and he knew it.

'Hey, come on you two, don't get serious over this. Harvey's room is next door but one to mine, so we could toss a stone up to his window.'

Alex shrugged and held out his hand to Iain, who chose to ignore it. Silly boys' playground games.

We retraced our steps back to the consulting room and threw a stone up to the window next door to Petra. Success! As luck would have it, Harvey must have been there, waiting. He pushed the window out as far as it would go and suggested we walk along further to the ground-floor lounge windows and he would come down to let us in.

Mercifully, all other inmates conformed to the rules and were tucked up in their beds or having their bedtime drink in the top lounge. The lower nurses' station was in darkness, as was the lounge. Harvey was triumphant. He had saved the day and it was only 9.15 p.m.

'Let's go up for a drink and I'll explain what happened. Why did you lot end up outside? What happened with Dr Raschid and Joanna?' Harvey could hardly wait for the explanation.

'Shall we go upstairs and we can swap stories.' It was all an anticlimax. 'Sorry, the doors were locked, but there was no alternative. It was the nightwatchman.'

This was all too ridiculous to be believed. It could have been an episode of the *Famous Five* series. Alex said goodnight as we reached his landing on the first floor. He had completely lost it earlier and needed the solace of his room. No one tried to persuade him otherwise.

'And then there were three!' Iain linked arms with me, giving me a chummy squeeze. There was a low light coming from the nurses' station and only a handful of patients still in the lounge. We each took a hot drink from the trolley and sat as far as we could from the TV.

'What happened outside, Harvey? Who spotted you?' We huddled together to listen to the explanation. He and Chris had been found by the nightwatchman on his rounds. He was quite irate and lectured them for the entire walk back to the patio area. On the pretext of having a cigarette, Chris tried to lose him and stall their lock-in, but he insisted on sitting with them until he could escort them inside and secure the doors. In a fit of pique, Chris had a couple of drags and stormed off inside and went straight to his room. Harvey had no alternative but to do the same and so the door was bolted.

'Why did your escapade terminate so quickly?'

I left it for Iain to tell our brief tale and we agreed that we had conclusive proof that Dr Raschid was the Abbey gigolo. Joanna was obviously one of his conquests and there was absolutely no reason to go there again. I said I would rather blank the entire episode. It was not an adventure I was proud of.

What a day! We were supposed to be recuperating and instead we were developing the science of becoming super sleuths. I was so tired and needed to go to my bed.

Like obedient children we queued at the door to receive our evening tablets and to be rebuked by the miserable one. Evidently, the nightwatchman had informed the sister that some patients were wandering in the grounds and she, rightly, assumed it was us.

The evening had ended very flat and I still hadn't spoken to Jason.

Chapter Fifteen

The morning jog brought a full compliment of inmates. I think we all wanted to view Joanna in a different light. The rains had completely cleared and it was going to be a scorcher. There wasn't a cloud in the sky and it was so calm, not even a faint breeze to fan the leaves.

I must have been exhausted from yesterday's intrigues because I had a dreamless sleep and awoke still feeling lethargic. In fact, we were all subdued and preoccupied. The precocious banter that normally accompanied our morning walks was missing.

Iain, my little buddy, was especially pensive. I needed to assure myself that he was OK.

'Have you got an orchestra of kettles today? You look very gloomy!'

He gave me a lopsided, soppy grin.

'Nothing changes, in fact, it is quieter at the moment. They haven't a clue what triggers off the excruciating noise. Anyway, it doesn't matter any longer because they are kicking me out tomorrow. My insurance company won't pay any more, so I'll have to go back to being an outpatient when it gets really bad.' He was so forlorn and had to find a way of dealing with the news.

I was struggling to find words of comfort.

'Well, Parker, I think we should have a picnic today, to celebrate our friendship. What say you?' I resumed fantasy-speak to cover up my disappointment at losing my best pal.

'I think that will be splendiferous, Milady!'

Both now smiling, we jogged on, occasionally making idle chitchat. Petra and Claire were in harmony, jogging in the leading group with Joanna, who looked full of beans. Chris and Harvey were tagging along behind them. Harvey was as inquisitive as any female curtain-twitcher and would most definitely be interrogating her at the earliest opportunity.

Chris, on the other hand, liked to be wherever Claire was. He had become obsessed with her. She realised this fact and used it to her advantage. He was her lapdog, fetching and carrying whenever it suited her. Oh, well, that's life!

On arriving back at the Abbey, we looked at the bulletin board to see what was happening today. Nobody fancied meditation or yoga, so we decided to do our own thing.

'Come on, Iain! Let's order a picnic basket from the kitchen and take it onto the common. If this is going to be your last day, you don't want to be stuck in here.'

Iain was instantly relaxed. 'Milady, you are always an inspiration. I shall carry your basket and be your clown for the day.'

'What's all this then, a private party?' Harvey, Chris and Alex had overheard and wanted to be included in the lunch party.

We made our way to the kitchen, bumping into Petra and Claire on the way. They wanted to come too, so now we were seven. Not quite an intimate twosome, but perhaps that was a blessing.

The chef wasn't amused, in fact decidedly grumpy at our request, but acquiesced. Half an hour later we assembled at his kitchen door and collected seven white cake boxes, containing our preferred selections. One of the stripey-legged boys, or souschefs, had printed names on each box and tied them with a carrying handle.

To the tune of 'Hi-Ho, Hi-Ho' we tramped along the woodland path towards the common, making for the royal oak and its canopy. It was already sweltering, possibly the hottest day of the year. There hadn't been a summer like this for years. We were determined to make the best of it, as the weekend was approaching when we had to face our families.

The lovable Harvey produced a blanket, which was spread by the tree trunk. The picnic boxes were piled on top of each other and we lay under the protection of the tree. Petra and Claire preferred the full sun, rolling around on the grass. They chatted over the possibility of using the gym in the afternoon and, without invitation, Chris said he would go too.

I fancied another trip to the stables and my Musketeers wanted the chance of a walk on the wild side. So our entertainment was decided. We ate and chatted and mellowed.

Tomorrow was a major consultation day for some of us. I lay, looking up through the leaves of the majestic tree and admitted to myself that I was overcoming my fears. I had to be *me*. I didn't have to pretend any more. If I could accept who I was and do the best I could, then that was enough. Slowly, I was making sense of why I had fallen off the world for a while. I had to find *me*. I grabbed my notebook and hastily wrote down some choices.

If there were a choice of being, what would fate choose for me? A feline independent queen with strong poise and dignity! A canine having strength and grace, with shiny coat and running free! An iridescent butterfly, with wings adorned in symmetry! A golden eagle on the wing, surveying his world with majesty! The die is cast, the choice is made, the mirror of life reveals *me*!

My friends watched me scribbling away and enjoyed my quirkiness. Who knows, one day I may see my poems in print, but for the time being it was my way of releasing my energy and my emotions. The picnic was a great success and we all sprawled over the blanket, telling stories.

Before my meal had time to digest I was asleep, flying through the clouds with a handsome young man holding my hand. I had transformed into a silver-winged butterfly and was transporting this youth into the magic land of fantasy and light. Not my usual erotic dream, but one of breathtaking vision and exotic colours. The simplest of clouds became our own cotton-wool carpet, whisking us across the world, higher and higher. I couldn't keep him for ever, only when my eyes were closed, and I knew him instinctively.

Something was tickling my nose and I really didn't want to open my eyes because my dream would fade.

'She's awake! She's just feigning sleep!' Alex grabbed hold of my nose and tweaked it hard.

'You wicked monkey. I was having such a delicious dream.' I rolled over him and pummelled his chest, which he enjoyed immensely.

'Milady, enough of this body boxing, we definitely need to go riding.' Iain jostled me to my feet and within minutes we were gambolling across the common towards the stable yard.

'What happened to Chris and the girls? Did they go to the gym?'

'Yes, Milady!' The Three Musketeers bellowed in chorus.

Then Harvey tripped Iain and he in turn pushed Alex and so we travelled to the stables, baffooning around like friends do. A few cirrus clouds puffed overhead, which gave the sky a softer hue.

By 3.30 p.m. we were saddled and ready to go. The old codger shuffled out from the back office and raised his cap to me.

"Ow you doin' today, lass, good yeah? Now don' go racin' aroun' 'cos it'll do you no good in this 'eat!'

I grinned at him in agreement and reigned in Firefly to make a circle in the yard and approach the exit head on. Iain was lucky enough to get Tom again and Harvey was mounted on a huge dappled grey called Windsor. They suited each other, two big boys with pale-silver manes. On this occasion, Alex rode an elegant palomino called Gretchen and she had recently been clipped for competition. She was a real beauty.

We trotted into the shade of the woodland, with Ginny bringing up the rear. Today, as it was so hot, we elected to keep to the forest trails. There would be one chance of a decent canter between two copses that marked the corners of the common.

Iain had taken the lead, as before, weaving his way through the overhanging branches. I hugged close to Firefly's neck, laying low across the saddle, feeling her power under my thighs, my knees barely touching her sides. Since I had begun my metamorphosis, every experience was heightened. It was as if my senses had been finely tuned.

We reached the open land and this time I decided to give Iain a riding lesson. I wasn't as rusty as last time. Firefly didn't hesitate; with one initial suggestion from me, she was in the wind. With the opposite copse fast approaching we were alongside Tom and then past.

Iain was mortified and tried desperately to accelerate, but we were too far in front. I halted Firefly, just under cover of the trees and pulled off the track. Tom's hooves thundered past and I could hear Iain urging him on. I couldn't believe that he hadn't seen me, perhaps the darkness of the wood had obscured his vision.

I guided Firefly back onto the path and we went in search of Iain and Tom. This copse was denser and darker than the previous one, making the pathway tighter, so we kept to a slow trot.

We heard the whinnying before we saw the body. Tom was restless, but Iain still had the reins caught under his body as he lay on the edge of the path.

I wrenched off my hard hat and vaulted out of the saddle, my heart pounding in my ears, please don't be dead. Firefly nuzzled Tom as I gently eased the strap away from Iain's chin and loosened his hat. There didn't seem to be any lacerations on his face or neck and he was breathing.

He appeared to be sleeping and his pulse was strong, but I decided not to move him. I would have to wait for the others to catch up or perhaps I should go and find them. No, I couldn't leave him. If I took his hat off I could make him more comfortable. I leaned closer to see his face.

'I've got you, my lovely, grr!' He pushed me down and straddled me, grinning all over his cheeky face.

'Iain, you bastard! You could have given me a heart attack.'

'Well, I so wanted to know what it felt like being on top of you that my adrenaline got the better of me.'

Very deliberately he covered my mouth with his and I offered no resistance. Our kiss was long and succulent and did us no harm. Did I feel guilty? Possibly, a little, but it wasn't going to go anywhere and the delicious awakening in the depths of my female organs was excellent. An erotic, exploring kiss sends electric impulses to the very root of my soul, dampening my valley and turning my nipples into chocolate mountains. On a score of one to ten, this was climbing the pyramid.

'Oh! Parker! You have titillated my taste buds and sent my fantasy channel into overdrive. I shall relive this for days.' His mouth was so soft and his tongue so demanding, but to continue would be foolish.

It would have been so easy to go to the next level, as we were both primed, but we pulled apart and reluctantly remounted our waiting horses. Conscience must have played a part.

We trotted out into the field and slowed to a walk to go side by side.

'Angelica, do you know, sometimes when I am near you and definitely then, when we were kissing, my tinnitus almost disappears. I would like to think that I am imagining it, but I'm not, it's true!' He was so rarely serious, as he fooled around to cover his discomfort, so what could I say? There was no answer, no perfect solution.

'I wish I could make it right for you, Iain, but I am not your solution. We have difficult decisions to make and so many mistakes to face up to before our demons fade. Let's hope we keep our sanity and are strong enough to accept our faults and learn to trust again. I am going to do it and I pray that you do too.'

We smiled and briefly touched hands, knowing we had also touched hearts. Tom's ears pricked. He had seen the others at the edge of the first copse. We encouraged the pair into a canter and raced each other across the divide. This time we finished together.

Harvey was resting in his saddle, puffing on a cigar, looking every inch an English gentleman at leisure.

'Far too much exercise for me, dear lady!' was his greeting as we approached. Alex looked uncomfortably warm.

Nestling in behind them, we walked Indian file back to the stables after another successful outing. The Four Musketeers strolled back to the Abbey, enjoying the afternoon sunshine and taking respite from their individual war zones.

Drinks all round on the patio was the next order, organised by Alex. I found I had three telephone messages awaiting me. Archie called me over to his desk to hand me the call list.

'This is something new, Archie. Am I now allowed to receive incoming calls that haven't been vetted?'

'It seems so, Miss Angelica. As you can see, you are now on the direct line system.'

He handed me the schedule, pointing to my name.

'Good heavens, I feel like I have graduated.'

I left the others on the patio and climbed the stairs to my room, studying the names and numbers as I went. One was from home, one from my parents and the other from Simon. The butterflies were bouncing around my stomach, as I was a little apprehensive at making my first outside calls.

The telephone sat, proudly, on my table beside the wilting flowers and abundance of cards. I reread the list and took the receiver in my hand. Ready or not, I dialled.

'Hello? Oh, hello, Angelica, I'll get your dad,' and she was gone. Why couldn't my own mother deal with this? No wonder I felt so alone, so empty.

'Hello, Angelica, how are you now? Sorry that we haven't been over, but it is a long drive.'

In fact it wasn't more than an hour in the car, but I knew it was because Mum couldn't face coming. Dad did come when I fell off the edge, in fact he cried like a child, I remember that. Even then, Mum wasn't there. She was never there when I needed her; it was always Dad.

'Hi, Dad, I am doing OK. How is the garden? I bet it looks a picture.'

'When are you going home, Angelica? I have spoken to John and the twins and they need you at home, but only when you are ready.'

'Thanks, Dad, I still have a few things to work out, but I'm improving every day. Got to go now! I have to go to dinner. Love you both, bye.'

I couldn't speak any more. My sorrow and loneliness engulfed me. I wasn't as strong as I thought. Why didn't they see? Why didn't they understand how much I was hurting? Just for once, why wasn't I first?

OK! That's enough self-pity. I'm a big girl now and if I felt overlooked when I was a child at least I wouldn't do it to my children. My eyes were pulled back to my home number and I dialled. As I waited for the connection, strength flowed into my thoughts. I am as strong as the fiercest Siberian tiger.

The shock that followed sent my head and heart reeling. Whose was the voice that answered the phone?

'Hello, this is the Reeves house!'

'I can't believe it's you! Jason, it's Mum, what are you doing there?' I could see his gorgeous face, smiling as he heard my voice and desperately trying not to cry.

'Mum, oh, Mum! I've missed you so much. I came straight home when Dad phoned Uncle Toby. You've got me now, Mum. Please come home. Let's you and me go to Uncle Toby's. It's fab out there, you'd love it! Dad's a bastard! Uncle Toby is terrific; he even paid for my flight home.'

He was talking at 100 mph to cover his embarrassment and his impatience.

'Darling, slow down!' I had to sit down, quickly, as my legs had disappeared from under me. It was such a shock.

'Christ, Mum! Why has all this crap happened to us? I don't know why you stayed with him. He is such a selfish bastard!'

'Don't swear, Jason! I love you and need you to be calm. I am so sorry that I am not very well at the moment, I've let you down.'

He tried to butt in. He was so uptight and I had to fight to keep control of my emotions.

'Darling, what's happened is history, we can't change any of it and I'm sure, with hindsight, your father would.'

His voice exploded in my ear.

'He would have done exactly the same. Mum, get real, he's up his own backside. I just want to *hit* him, so badly. I hope he goes down for a long time. Do you know how hard it is to be in the same space as him!'

'*Stop it*, Jason! He is your dad. You don't understand all the implications. Jason, just stop for a minute!'

We both went quiet and then kept saying, sorry – sorry – sorry, again and again.

'You are obviously alone, Jason, to speak so angrily!'

'Yes, the others have gone with him to get a Chinese.'

'When did you arrive, today?'

'Yeah, about 2 a.m. Mum, does everyone know about us? I can't go out. Can I come and stay with you? All this is really shitty!'

He had reverted to my little boy. The anger had subsided and he needed a cuddle. The twins were a powerful force, strong and independent, as long as they were in tandem, but Jason was a sensitive romantic – like me.

'Sweetheart, listen to me. I am coming home for the weekend as it is part of the "getting back to reality" process. We'll try to fill in some of the cracks. Unfortunately, it's not an instant fix, just a little at a time, but if we all work hard we shall get there, together.'

I could hear the cogs in his brain working and visualised him biting his lower lip as he chewed over his thoughts.

'Mum, am I still on your car insurance?'

'Yes, I haven't altered it. Why?'

'I'm gonna come and get you on Saturday morning, on my own. Can I come early?'

'Yes, yes, of course you can. I'll be in the car park, waiting for you. Is 9.30 a.m. early enough? Jason, you don't know where it is!' I was breathless with joy, my big boy, my little soldier, was coming for me and I couldn't have asked for more.

'Don't worry, Mum, I'll find it. I'll have to ask, won't I? I love you and I'm going now – bye – see ya!'

The line went dead. I knew he was full up with emotion, as I was. The handset sat lifeless in my lap, catching the tears as they dripped off the end of my nose.

I jumped, danced around, laughed, shouted at the walls. I was so excited, I wanted the world to know. My body was so alive that I couldn't stand still. *Shower*! That's what I'll do. *Sing* in the shower, all the oldies.

How I managed to dress, I can't remember. I was running down the corridor to the nurses' station because I had to tell someone. It couldn't have been better. Tania was back.

I flew at her like a homing pigeon, almost knocking her off her feet.

'Wow! What a beautiful welcome!' She held me away from her and her dark eyes took in everything.

'So, my little coffee-coloured angel, you tryin' to be as black as me?'

I blurted out my news.

'Tania, he's home, my Jason is home from America!'

'Well, an' there's me thinkin' you was jus' pleased to see me!' She had reverted to her Caribbean tongue.

I gabbled away and she listened. Once the news was told, I felt relieved and a bit stupid. She disentangled herself from me and sent me off to dinner.

There she stood, clucking her tongue and sighing with pleasure for me. The huge momma, wearing the wholesome smell of vanilla, was back.

My euphoria lasted through dinner. I can't recollect how many times I retold the story of the phone call, but I was flying high. It was obvious that I had withdrawn into myself and no one intruded or tried to break the spell.

The evening was a total blur and I needed tablets to help me to sleep that night.

Chapter Sixteen

Friday arrived with a shrill, unrelenting tone. I rubbed my eyes and fumbled for the phone.

'I have a spare hour this morning, Angelica, and would like you to be in my office at 10 a.m. Please be prompt!'

That was Boadicea at her best, no please, thank you, how are you, just a command. Nobody could hurt me today, not even Ann.

Sleepily, I focused on the clock, it was already gone 9 a.m. I would have to rush through breakfast to make the appointment on time. Punctuality, was a priority, like clean shoes and coordinated clothes – it was part of who I was.

Iain was disappointed that we weren't walking together, as he was dreading his discharge and already felt that he had become part of my past. I understood his need for continuity and his fear of tomorrow. We were all awaiting consultations with our respective shrinks and promised to compare dilemmas at lunch. I was still floating on my cloud of expectation.

I knocked, stared at her name carved on the brass plate and waited. She commanded me to enter, so I did.

On this occasion she was studying me from the moment that I stepped inside the door. Those palest of pale, unblinking eyes, framed by the regimental haircut, watched me approach.

Spread across her desk was some of my artwork; the rest was on the floor. She asked me to sit beside her and together we would interpret the story of my life as I had described it on this collage.

'Angelica, I admire your courage and have given you a premature slot in my busy schedule because you have earned it.'

I was speechless. I was receiving special attention and didn't have a clue why.

Our close proximity was without intimidation; in fact, it was quite comfortable, which surprised me. She smelled of coal-tar soap and her ringless hands were neatly manicured.

As the story unfolded I was amazed how words and pictures,

selected at random, had such a bearing on my character. With minimal help, she allowed me to tell my own story, putting so many life experiences into perspective.

The canary in the gilded cage was the remoteness of my mother and lack of closeness and communication. There was a predominance of black and white, which I saw as the blinkered view I had on life – no softness – no curves – no middle ground, unloved and colourless, almost hopeless.

There was an army scene, with tanks and guns and soldiers, denoting turmoil and struggle, flanked by a pair of white doves in flight, promising freedom and love.

Two pictures on this page stood out the most. The first was a striking picture of Audrey Hepburn, looking austere and rigid and very frail. The other was of Princess Diana and Charles, she looking over her shoulder, poignant and afraid and he striding forward, already having deserted her. Again, it reflected my feelings of desertion and neglect.

The final page seemed to show hope for the future. These pictures were dedicated to couples, smiling at each other, especially a wonderful photo of James Coburn and his new, young wife looking radiant and happy. The caption beneath was *Cherish is more than a word*.

Lastly, was a photo of a thatched cottage. The words for this one were, *Someday – Somehow – Somewhere*, followed by *Will this ever be me?*

We both sat back and sighed. The hour had flown by and we had almost become friendly, in a reserved kind of way.

'You have weathered an extremely agonising ordeal, Angelica. Do you see how you have chosen to survive in your artwork? I am truly relieved. I thought you would have gone through at least half a box of tissues!'

'I have to admit that I am relieved that it is all done. Telling the story didn't seem to have anything to do with me, it was as if I was narrating someone else's life, but it did make sense.'

'Composure is a talent, Angelica, but never lose your passion or your ebullience. It is a most endearing quality, usually found in children and very rarely in adults.'

She was smiling at me. I was uncomfortable in the presence of this different Ann. She folded the sheets of paper and handed them to me.

'If ever you are feeling insecure, refer to these papers, they will give you courage. Go now and have a cup of tea. We'll meet again in the awareness class.'

I walked to the door and turned. 'Thank you.'

She was standing, watching me go, and looking quite soft, almost doting. I closed the door behind me, in total confusion. That person wasn't Boadicea; it must have been her twin. The corridor to the ICU was not the place to linger, so I pushed the suction doors forward, coming face to face with Dr Raschid.

'Good morning, Mrs Reeves, you are blossoming more each day.' He smiled and was swallowed into the ICU.

'Hello! Miss Angelica! I have some more messages for you. What a popular lady you are!' Archie handed the slip of paper to me and I made my way to the lounge.

I was sorely in need of a cup of something. Tania wolf-whistled me as I passed her, which made me grin. Life was certainly improving.

None of the crowd was in the lounge, so I took my drink to a seat by the window and curled my legs under me, closed my eyes and dozed. I was pleasantly tired. Tomorrow I would attempt to reconcile Jason and John and try to be a regular mum.

The slip of paper was still in my hand. A call from Simon, marked *urgent*, another from John and one from my cousin, Karl, on a London number. That woke me up! I didn't have a cousin called Karl. I racked my brain to think of who it could be. The ants came walking and I shivered. Who was Karl?

People began to move in and out. Ann entered the lounge, walking straight towards me, no longer showing the fierce look of intolerance, but one of concern.

'Another change of plans, Angelica. Dr Michael would like to see you earlier, at 2 p.m., and you must expect a longer consultation. Don't look so worried, it'll be fine!' She patted my hand and then left to organise her class.

All I could think of was: who was Karl?

Harvey was the first with his news. He stood before me, doleful and resigned.

'I'm going home tomorrow! Dr Hughes said I've got to start rebuilding my life. He said no more self-indulgence! What does he know, eh?' Poor Harvey, he was so deflated.

'I am sorry, Harvey, but all things have to come to an end, eventually.'

'Yes, I know, but I don't think I can do it! How does anyone know when the time is right?' He sat beside me with his head in his hands.

Iain and Alex strolled over and told their news. Iain had it confirmed that he would be leaving after lunch today and was resigned to his future with the 'Saga of the Whistling Kettles'. Julie was collecting him and said she had some good news to cheer him up. Something to look forward to.

Alex said he didn't know whether to be happy or not as he was to be moved from the 'long-term' first floor to the 'intermediate' second floor. He was going to be encouraged to participate in more classes, integrating himself into a more established role. In fact, he was taking over Harvey's room. Harvey was dumb-founded.

Ann had returned and tapped her board, indicating that conversation was at an end.

Only seven people turned up at this session. The rumour had it that Petra had overdosed again, due to a row with Chris over Claire. Chris was petrified at the consequence of the row and would not leave his room and Claire had been collected by her parents for a long weekend at the coast. Iain was the source of the information as his room was near the ICU.

One by one we were encouraged to tell a more intimate version of our 'illness', being as honest as we could. Ann interrupted at will, to explain alternative ways of improving our negative attitudes.

This time it wasn't my tears that flowed but Edna's, the large lady from room 13 who suffered from agoraphobia. For years she was locked in a cupboard at the whim of her violent mother. How could any human being torture a child in such a way, leaving her in total darkness for hours on end? What incident made her return to her childhood memories and trap her there? She was happily married, with two loving daughters, and had a very successful career as a teacher, then one day the lights went out and she reverted to the child in the cupboard. In two years she had gained five stone in weight and had not left her house. Would she ever regain a peaceful life?

Ann asked me to recite one of my poems that she thought was relevant.

> I want to be *me*, no compromise.
> I want to be *me*, no longer wise.
> I want to be *me*, not someone else.
> I want to be *me*, all by myself.
> I want to be *me*, not let's pretend.
> I want to be *me*, my own best friend.

It was received in silence, then everyone clapped and started to make comments on the sentiment I had expressed.

'Milady, you are indeed a poet and we did not know it!'

'Touché, Parker! I like your style!' He was back!

'That's it everyone! Time for lunch.'

We were dismissed, but the pale eyes followed me to the door.

Lunch was a 'happy-sad' affair. Petra was out of ICU and very subdued because of the loss of her friend. Claire's parents were Lord and Lady Something and would not acknowledge Petra's existence, which she couldn't understand.

Alex was nervously excited. He wasn't too sure if he was ready to jump the next hurdle, but he was going to give it a damn good try. Harvey was trying to be positive, as he had to live with his brother for a while.

Chris had calmed down, under medication, and was back to his irritating, chauvinistic self. If he ever played Russian roulette, he would be sure to kill himself: he was always on self-destruct mode. I preferred him when he was quieter and funny, but all too soon he sank into melancholy and denial.

And then there was my precious, mischievous Parker. He was hurting and desperately trying to be frivolous and Machiavellian. The clown, trying to deceive, but I knew how afraid he was.

'Friends, Romans and Musketeers, this is the Last Supper, so let us eat and be merry.' He was the court jester to the end.

Iain said his goodbyes and rose to leave the table. I explained that I had an extraordinary meeting with my doctor and would walk down with him. Arm in arm we left the dining room, walking, not talking, being there for each other.

I sat on his bed and watched him pack his suitcase and with a last act of defiance, he nicked a towel, ramming it into his case with a flourish.

'Just a memento with the logo to prove that I was actually here.'

'Look, you know the number, call me if you need a friend!'

Nothing more could be said. We hugged and I watched him walk towards the way out. Under my breath I whispered, 'May God go with you,' and then he was gone.

I thought, isn't it strange how the adorable things disappear and the evil lives on? I don't think I really believed that sentiment, but it was appropriate at the time.

The 2 p.m. appointment was here and I was standing outside room 10. I knocked and waited. The door opened and Ann Amery was standing there. Why was she there?

'Come in, Angelica.' The voice belonged to Dr Michael. He sidestepped Ann, took my arm and was leading me to the desk, beside which, two men were seated.

I knew these men and was startled to see them there. I had no control over my fear; again the ants were on the move, along my veins and to my stomach.

'Why are these men here, Dr Michael? What is going on?' My mouth was dry and I could feel the blood draining from my face.

Both men jumped to their feet and Commander Johnson was by my side in a second.

'I am so sorry to frighten you yet again, Mrs Reeves, but this meeting couldn't wait. I do apologise.' He shook my hand and helped me to a chair. Dr Michael resumed his position of authority and immediately took control.

'Gentlemen, please be seated. You have to be aware that this is a place of healing and you are here at my indulgence. If I am at all concerned for the health of my patient I shall insist that you leave. Is that clear?'

I wanted to cheer, 'Hear! Hear!' but instead I held on to the hand of my champion, Ann (Boadicea) Amery.

'I agree, Dr Michael, thank you.' The Commander was contrite.

'I shall allow you thirty minutes of conversation and then you must leave. Ms. Amery and myself shall attend.'

'All this is fine, Dr Michael. I am only here to help Mrs Reeves through a difficult time, not to upset her further.'

He looked at me with kindness and perhaps sympathy. It was now history that the police had been cavalier, to say the least, when they ransacked my home and interrogated me without mercy. They insinuated that my claims of receiving horrific, degrading phone calls were exaggerated until they tapped my phone line and heard for themselves. My family had become victims through neglect.

I sat listening to these two men, almost in total disbelief. The Organisation behind this money crime was involved in business throughout the world. Anyone who threatened to expose it would be terminated. It had no morality and no conscience. Unfortunately, John had become involved by mistake and couldn't get out. The holes in the net were so large that everyone fell through, except John. Sod's law!

His trial would begin next week and there would be an automatic prison sentence if he were convicted. The Special Branch had suggested that Toby send Jason home in order that the family would be together and more easily protected by the law. The Commander said that it might be advisable to book a holiday, immediately, and we would be taken to a secret location until the trial was over.

The sea was crashing over me, my ears could no longer hear. I was watching his lips move, but nothing was making any sense. It was like watching a movie with the sound turned down. Dr Michael stood up and raised his hand.

'That's quite enough! Mrs Reeves cannot take in any more. She needs to rest.' His voice was breaking through in waves. Did he see that I was swaying? Is that why he put a halt to this?

I looked down and saw Ann's hands covering mine and it became clear. That was why she had been so indulgent today, she knew this ordeal was to follow. The shock had dissipated and my senses were returning.

'Just before you go, Commander Johnson, I received a phone message today from a cousin that doesn't exist. Do you think it could be a warning? I haven't called the number yet. It's somewhere in London, I think.'

I showed him the piece of paper with the telephone number on it.

'If you will sanction it, Dr Michael, we could put a listening device on Mrs Reeves' phone and a tracer on the line? I wouldn't suggest it if I didn't think it was imperative.'

Dr Michael was out of his depth. He was the most senior consultant at the Abbey, but that was all he was, a doctor. To gain permission for this type of thing from the directors, on a Friday afternoon, was impossible.

'I don't have the authority. I cannot give you permission.'

The two men looked irritated and I appealed to Dr Michael with my eyes. Please let this happen! Can't you see how important it is?

'Would it be at all possible that we could erase this part of the meeting and you could turn a blind eye to the phone call? I believe it could be crucial.'

Both men were staring at Dr Michael. Was this a form of intimidation? Didn't they realise that you couldn't 'out-psyche' a psychiatrist? Not one as competent as my shrink.

Dr Michael asked Ann to join him and they went through the connecting doors into room 12. Commander Johnson turned to me.

'Mrs Reeves, please believe we will protect you and your family. I would not have come here unless I thought it was important.'

Good speech, I thought, but I was not an imbecile. They were here for their own gain and if there were a few casualties in the process, that was unfortunate. My family was a disposable asset.

Dr Michael and Ann returned. Ann resumed her hand-holding role, for which I was truly grateful, and Dr Michael paced the floor with his hands clenched in front of him, looking stern.

'I will acquiesce to your suggestion, only because I believe it will expedite matters and hopefully accelerate a positive conclusion to Mrs Reeves' dilemma.' He could just have said yes. He sat down and gave me one of his 'teddy bear' smiles.

'Thank you so much! We can put this into operation immediately. I'll send my colleague to fetch what we need from the car. May we use your office, Dr Michael?' He nodded in agreement.

'You have my permission. Please work quickly!'

While the Commander's sidekick was out of the room, he made various phone calls and seemed satisfied. The other policeman returned and they busied with a tiny machine and wire and headphones.

Dr Michael was calm, as I was, but Ann seemed strangely distressed. Had this brought back a bad experience from the past or was she only concerned for my welfare. She kept stroking my hands.

Everything was ready. I was about to dial the number when Dr Michael raised his hand.

'I need to say one thing more, Angelica. If, for any reason, you do not wish this to proceed, we can stop it now!' He had to affirm the importance of my health and I admired him for it.

'Thank you, Dr Michael. Unfortunately, like all the old clichés – it's life or death – I no longer have a choice.'

I dialled the number and waited. Both men were intent on their machines. Ann was passive and as white as a ghost. Dr Michael just stared at the phone in my hand.

It seemed an age before the call was answered. When it happened, it surprised me – the voice was Scottish.

'Och, at last, wee lassie, I thought ya didne love me.'

'I don't know who you are. Why are you calling me? You're not my cousin. If you are Karl, what do you want with me?' I tried not to sound too hysterical, but I had to stay on the line as long as possible.

The phone was being passed to someone else, so my questions could have disappeared into space. The next voice I knew and dreaded, it was harsh, guttural and disgusting. The porn and threats came fast and furious. I didn't want to listen, but I had to keep him talking.

'Now, do you understand, Angelica, we can find you anywhere. I am so sorry that you are not well, but you are alive, at the moment. I miss looking at your body! I could make you purr and Rebecca, too!'

'Don't do this to my family! What have we ever done to you?' My voice was almost a sob and my legs were trembling, but there was no way I could hang up.

'Listen, you silly bitch, and listen carefully! I know when Jason arrived and the hour he got home. I know where your other children are. Of course, I have your husband under constant surveillance and I can take anyone of you *out* just like that, poof!' He started to laugh, which made me angry.

'OK, you can do all of this, I believe you, but we can't hurt you, we don't know who you are.'

'We are your worst fucking nightmare! Tell your husband to keep his mouth shut and we shall let you live!'

Click – the line was dead.

I was shivering and helpless. The only people who heard the taunting remarks were the men who were now tidying away their gadgets. Ann took the phone from my hand and replaced it onto the cradle and pulled her chair closer to mine.

Johnson looked at me with pity.

'That was loathsome, Mrs Reeves, and I'm so sorry that you had to go through it. Was that what the other calls were like? Was it the same voice?' He had become very matter of fact and controlled.

'Yes, it was the same German voice. I will never forget that slimy voice.' All I could hear were those awful words in my ears.

'I don't think he was German, possibly Dutch or South African, but I'm no linguist.' They rose from their seats and were ready to leave.

'Mrs Reeves, the ordeal you have just been through was horrendous, but necessary if we are to have a chance of finding these animals. When you return here after the weekend there will be a list of instructions for you to follow. We have now become your shadow. Your son, Jason, will be collecting you – we know this and they know this. Most of what I tell you has to be for your eyes only in order to protect those around you, I am sorry!' He extended his hand to Dr Michael.

'Thank you, Sir, for your cooperation and please accept my personal apology for the intrusion into your hospital.' They were through the door and gone.

Dr Michael pulled me to my feet, enveloping me with his body and rocking me. We moved towards the chaise, where I lay, gratefully.

'Angelica, I have witnessed many tragic crimes in my long time on this earth. Although I couldn't hear what was said to you, I could see by the look on your face that the perpetrator was an animal not fit to be alive.'

'Dr Michael, I have to believe that I will be protected and trust these men. At least I am more prepared now that I have recuperated here for a while.'

We had forgotten that Ann was still in the room and she excused herself, leaving the room quietly. There was no need for the metronome or the recording tape. The following conversation was between my doctor and me. The responsibility he had accepted over the past hour could not be measured. He sat beside me and listened as I poured out my thoughts and fears.

The fear of relocating to a strange place, without family or friends, was very real, but I had no choice so I would be equal to it. I would have to encourage the kids to be strong and adaptable in their new role. John would have to face the trial and the outcome and deal with it, as I would have to protect my family, alone.

This was a time in my life that was being directed by others, but once back in my control I could take a new direction. Out of tragedy we could build a prosperous beginning. There were decisions to be made and paths to choose and I wasn't going to be on my own, I had my children too.

My confidence was rising with every breath I took. I left room 10 with determination walking by my side. There was no time for tears or recriminations. But I did feel very tired – no, I felt knackered!

How I wished Iain were here. From today he was just a memory, my mischievous playmate.

Dr Michael was loath to let me go, but he wasn't my keeper and was committed to his schedule and his other patients. I had to take in and digest the onslaught of gutter language from the criminal and then the wise words and instructions from the Commander.

Strangely, I no longer felt afraid of being alive. Instead I felt a new kind of fear, a fear of being murdered. This new emotion was heating up from within and I was getting stronger through anger. The lioness awakes!

Jason was back and together with the twins, we would escape. I had an ache in my heart for John, but we were destined for different lives. Last weekend, he told me I was being brainwashed and that he would change my attitude when I returned home. We both knew that wouldn't happen. I had no love for him, so we would be happier apart. How much did he really know about the 'Organisation'? I suppose I would never know.

It was past 4 p.m. and the grounds were dotted with patients and their families, some taking a stroll and others carrying bags to the car park. Harvey was nowhere to be seen, or Alex; hopefully they were enjoying a peaceful Friday afternoon.

I headed towards the avenue of trees that led to the common. It was that perfect time of day when the sun was subdued and the restlessness of the morning had tempered into a golden glow of acceptance.

'Where are you off to?' It was Alex and Harvey returning from a trip to town.

'Oh, hi! I was miles away. I want to commune with the "Spirit of the Oak Tree". It gives me answers without question.' I laughed at myself.

'That's just to let us know that you want to be alone.' Alex's intuition was spot on and he pushed Harvey towards the Abbey.

'See you both later!'

What a sweetheart, I thought, as I strolled onto the common, being drawn by the compelling power of the tree. Why was it always free of interlopers? Was it waiting for me?

I nestled back against the huge trunk, finding a flat bit between the ridges of the bark. For a while I watched the coming and going of men and women, using the common as a thoroughfare from house to town. Groups of teenagers were lying about, laughing, talking, smoking and impressing their friends. I couldn't see any dog-walkers, swinging their poop-scoop bags, but there was the occasional stray dog. The noise surrounding me was like the chewing of honeycomb, soft and bubbly.

The sun was directly in front of me, a vibrant orange ball hanging on invisible wires. Closing my eyes against the glare, I drifted into a state between sleeping and waking. It was time to review my thoughts.

The nightmares had ceased and I understood why they began and how I had expelled them from my sleep. I had confronted my fear and was stronger dealing with it rather than running away from it. I no longer felt the burden of guilt and was able to reject the way of life that was suffocating me and welcome the dawning of a new me.

The police visit was traumatic, but totally eclipsed by the voice of my firstborn, singing in my head and coursing through my veins. For the first time, in a very long time, Jason sounded confident and glad to be alive. The combination of New York and Uncle Toby was obviously helping him to come to terms with who he was and his erratic behaviour six months ago. I hadn't seen him since he was asked to leave school and the subsequent expulsion to America. I was aching to see his face.

I believed that I had drifted off because I could hear a voice calling my name, but it seemed very distant. Opening my eyes a little, I squinted through my lashes towards the sound and thought I saw a figure, blocking the sun, approaching me.

He was tall, agile and was waving to me. It couldn't be *him*. He wouldn't have come on spec, not without calling first. He didn't even know where or how to find me. Blinking, repeatedly, I tried to focus. This was a dream.

'Hello Angel! Surprise, surprise! The mountain had to come to Muhammad!'

'Is it really you? What are you doing here?'

'Don't ask silly questions! Move forward and I'll sneak in behind you. I am going to usurp the royal oak.'

If the most lyrical poet put words onto paper at that moment, he couldn't have described the wondrous tide of emotion that flooded my soul. This wasn't a dream. It wasn't even a thought I had conjured up. This was real flesh and blood.

He slid down behind me and fused his chest to my back. I could feel his muscles against my shoulders. His long legs were arched on either side of me, forming an armchair, while his arms wrapped around me, sliding across my chest and anchoring over each bosom.

I was Andromeda on the rock, waiting for the Craken to devour me and I was ready. My heart was in need of this magnificent man. He kissed my hair, drinking in the smell of me. I tingled as his tongue licked the hollows in my neck and his hands caressed me, slowly awakening the erotic memories of the health hydro.

No words were necessary as each heart beat in time with the other. My disjointed world had disappeared as I sat in the arms of my Sexy Si. 'How did you know where to find me?' I could hardly put two words together, I was in such rapture.

He cuddled me so gently and whispered against my head, 'It was a silver-headed gent, who was in desperate need of my scissor-hands. He looked like an albino golly. He said I would find you under the oak tree in the centre of the common and here you are.'

'But it's Friday, your busiest day of the week!'

He stopped further protest by covering my mouth with his. We kissed and talked for what seemed to be years under our leafy umbrella. I told him chapter and verse of my growing depression and eventual collapse. He listened to the dark tale of the notorious villain and the predictions of the police and my forthcoming departure from the Abbey and well-earned holiday. He could never know the actual truth of my next journey.

With rhythmic rocking and butterfly kisses he listened without interrupting while I recounted the story, just allowing the avalanche of words to fall. What made him come, I would never know, but his motive was unimportant. All I needed was to be loved, unconditionally, and of that I was in no doubt. It was a difficult lesson, but I was beginning to adhere to a criteria that some people lived by – live for today, for tomorrow may never come.

He yanked me to my feet and, with his arm around my waist, we walked towards the pub on the green.

'Mrs Reeves, I have never seen you looking quite so beautiful and would love to satisfy my primal urges; instead I shall buy you dinner.'

A deep giggle bubbled from my throat. 'Can I have dessert too? I know a sleepy hollow, not too far from here, where the bedclothes are leaves and the water-carriers are squirrels.'

'Mrs Reeves, you are a very naughty girl, but I like it!'

We sat like young lovers, oblivious to the throng of business folk and revellers, indulging our culinary appetite until it was time to retreat to the woods. For a short moment I could forget the pain and just be loved.

Under a canopy of trees, we reclaimed our lust, witnessed only by the wild creatures. No lovemaking could have been more altruistic, giving one another the ultimate satisfaction. If only it could have been for ever, but then that would have been me dreaming again.

Simon walked me to the entrance of the Abbey and I stayed there, watching his athletic swagger take him out of sight. There were no promises, no declarations of undying love. We saw, we conquered and we came – as loving friends. I wished him a silent farewell and blew him a kiss. It was nearly 7.30 p.m. and I realised that I had broken all the rules and played truant. As luck would have it, the main entrance door was open as some patients were leaving for the weekend, so I snuck inside undetected. If anyone questioned my whereabouts I would say that I had fallen asleep on the common.

Archie Dickens had long since vacated his desk, so I was able to go to my room unobserved. I had one more phone call to make, to John, and in my present state of euphoria now was the time to do it.

'The Reeves house, hello?'

'Hi, Jason, how are things?'

'How strange, Mum! We were watching some old videos and you were in some of them and here you are on the phone. You looked so different when we were little, much too young to have had us sprogs. You were quite cute, the bone structure was good too!'

'Funny boy! You know that sarcasm is the lowest form of wit!'

'No, I'm serious! Uncle Toby has taught me heaps. I am a budding David Bailey I'll have you know, not just a gofer. He's even let me take a few shots. Well, sometimes.'

'I am very proud of you and I'm sure you'll be better than Bailey, after all, look who made you.'

'OK, you win! Is this a prompt call about tomorrow? Dad wanted to come too, but eventually agreed to let me come alone, thank goodness!'

'It's your dad I wanted to speak to Jason. Is he there?'

'He was a minute ago. Hang on and I'll go and find him.'

I could hear Jason calling his name and then nothing. I took a couple of deep breaths and swallowed hard.

'Sorry, Mum, I don't know where he's gone, probably looking for more old movies in the loft. Can it wait until tomorrow?'

'Yes, no problem, I was only returning his call. Tell him I called, will you?'

'I can't wait till tomorrow. I love you, Mum! Bye.'

'I love you too. Bye for now.'

Well, that's another hurdle I had overcome, even though I hadn't actually spoken to John. I slid my chair into the tiny recess by the window and pushed the two windows open to their full extent, all of about six inches. With elbows on windowsill and chin in hands I gazed out over the fabulous grounds of this piece of English heritage.

Across the lawn, the gatehouse and office buildings were original eighteenth century, but the conference centre and main building were built after the Second World War. The architecture was sympathetic in construction to the original structures, down to the colour of the bricks.

The overall feeling here was one of peace, but not isolation, protecting the reawakening of self without external pressures.

For a brief moment I was savouring the mixture of Aramis on my skin and the clean, green freshness of the gardens. At this second in time I was in love with life.

The knock came to halt my daydream and Tania walked in. 'An' where have you been, young lady?' She stood in front of me with her hands on her voluptuous hips and her white teeth smiling.

'I sort of wandered off for a while. I didn't worry you, did I?' I couldn't look her in the eye, so she cupped my chin in her hands.

'What you been up to, you little minx? I know you had a *really*, *sexy* guy looking for you earlier. Is zat where you haz been, wiz zat *hunky* man?' She lapsed into Caribbean-speak to emphasise her approval. She wiggled her hips and shimmied her shoulders, making provocative gestures.

'Yes, ooh yes! He foun' me an' made me feel real good!' I mimicked her voice, which we both enjoyed.

'I think I'm gonna spank your bottom, girl!' She pulled me to my feet and we jigged around the room.

'Heavens above, you iz one funky lady and I'm really gonna miss you. I hear you are goin' home soon. Oh, I nearly forgot, Dr Michael left this letter for you before he left.'

She handed the envelope to me and turned down my bed, leaving me with my little cup of tablets by the water jug.

'You gonna have your cup of chocolate in here or in the lounge?'

'In here, if you don't mind, Tania. I'm quite tired.'

'I'll bet you are! That *hunky* man's not hidin' under the bed, is he?'

She left my room, chuckling to herself. I thought how funny it was that she slipped into Caribbean-speak when she was relaxed. I looked at the envelope in my hand and broke the seal. Inside was one sheet of white vellum paper. The message was handwritten and one of the most endearing I would ever receive.

My dear Angelica,

Today was a stern test for you, far earlier than I should have liked, but unfortunately time is not always patient. I have witnessed your pain and have admired your tenacity and determination to overcome your fear and guilt.

You are now aware of the ordeal to come and you will be ready. Be vigilant and trust your intuition, it is so valuable. You are a beautiful woman in every sense of the word and have touched the hearts of many people at the Abbey. Never worry that your strength will fail you. The healing process and growing self-esteem will increase each day. Do not be afraid, your joie de vivre will infect others and you will be rewarded. Be passionate, expressive and resilient, it suits you and it is your right to be so.

I am your friend...

Signed...

Dr W. Michael

PS If ever you need me, my private practice number is: 020 8353 2424. Your next appointment is on Monday at 10 a.m.

I folded the letter and placed it back inside the envelope. So many thoughts were colliding in my head, but one registered immediately. I wondered why he had put such a wonderful letter on white vellum notepaper and then placed it into a nondescript manila envelope. Was that idiosyncratic for me to pick up on that one small detail, or just me?

Carefully, I selected a hiding place in my diary and placed it by my bed. If that wasn't a message of faith to give me hope, it was close to it. Soon this room would be the haven of another restless soul, but tonight and possibly for a few days next week, it was still mine.

I turned on the bedside lamp, closed the curtains and showered away the last loving aroma of Simon. As I brushed my hair, the reinstated Angelica looked back. No longer the frightened, hollow eyes or the sallow skin of an invalid, but a radiance and eyes that were ready to fight for the right to be free.

Tania came back, carrying a frothy cup of cappuccino and two digestive biscuits as a special treat.

'Now, you have a good, restful sleep and I shall check in on you later.'

She put the tray down and kissed me on the cheek. She had not done that before. Was it her personal farewell? The way my life was shaping up I may not be here next week.

'Night, night, Tania. See you later!'

I was now alone with my thoughts, soon to be asleep and perhaps to dream.

Chapter Seventeen

Saturday, sweet Saturday! No, no, no, go back to sleep. It's all too early. It was only 5.30 a.m. and my body clock had nudged me prematurely.

The room was light and already the birds were chatting away, deciding which spot was going to give up the best worms. I tried to go back to sleep – fat chance – the dawn chorus was like a ghetto blaster on overdrive. Instead, I lay, pondering on what the day might bring. Throughout my life I had pre-empted or acted out the way my day would perform in my head. Today, I had to let the day unfold as it happened.

No longer the marauding ants, marching up my spine, making my head and stomach sick. The face in the balaclava I had identified and it didn't frighten me any more because I knew who it was. John's image still crept into my mind – would he always be my nemesis or would time heal? I loved him once – no, don't go down that road.

Fight or flight, sink or swim, negative or positive, were the lessons we had to learn. Did it have to be one or the other? Why couldn't I opt for something in between? OK, today I'm going to be stronger and more assertive. If there is a situation that I can't handle, I am allowed to walk away from it. Don't be negative, try to be supportive, and what comes next?

No matter what techniques I tried, the stomach curdling began to insinuate itself into my gut. I threw off the duvet at 6.30 am and decided to go for a jog in the woods. Think of a good thought for the day! *Freedom*! Every minute that passed was taking me nearer to hugging my kids, cuddling my dogs, stroking the cats and diving into the wonderfully cool water in my pool. I'm going to give them back their *mum*.

The staff at the nurses' station were quite startled to see me at their door.

'Just going for an early jog to the common and back. Is that OK?'

I didn't wait for a reply as my motor was running and I needed to go. I pushed open the barred doors to the patio and ran. The sky was not blue and not grey, but sort of murky, with a hint of thunderstorm in the distance.

Jogging through the trees in the silence was invigorating and I was surprised at how fit I had become since my arrival. It must have been three weeks – time flies when you are on drugs. The first week passed totally unnoticed; all I did was eat and sleep and have horrific nightmares.

I was pondering on the intervening time when I came to a fork in the path. Shall I go off to the common or forge ahead? Straight ahead was the choice and then I took a left-hand fork, which was overhung with bracken and branches. I hopped, skipped and jumped my way through and had a vague memory of coming this way before. Very soon, almost directly ahead, appeared a double row of metal fencing, barring my way.

I pushed apart the damp bracken and saw statues on the neatly manicured lawn, stone statues of angels and a stone fountain of a fish with water gushing from its open mouth. The grey building in the centre looked very old and from its centre rose a huge bell tower. Only a few yards in front of me was a weathered signboard, anchored to the ground by stout concrete posts. It was the Convent. I had seen it before when I was with Sam, but from a different angle.

An oppressive feeling chilled my bones. I didn't want to be seen spying on them so I retreated. I had a fleeting image of my mother. She had been born into the Catholic faith and her childhood memories of being chastised by the nuns were unpleasant. I had often asked her why she rejected the faith when she married Dad, but there was never a reply. Her life before Dad was a 'no-go' area.

Happily, there were bright splashes of sunlight as I re-entered the bridle path on my return run to the Abbey. Come on *future*, I'm ready for you! With each running step I remembered a face from my past, a sentimental journey through my pictorial scrapbook.

It was still early, only 7 a.m., when I reached the courtyard. Archie Dickens had just arrived and was making himself ready to start at 8 a.m.

'Hello, Archie, isn't it a lovely day?'

I had startled him and he sat back on his chair with a bump.

'Good heavens, Miss Angelica, what a delightful surprise! You must have been up with the larks.'

'I don't know about that, Archie. If they were larks they must have been having a rare old shindig!'

I don't think he heard a word I said, so I smiled and continued up to my room, leaving him to sort himself out.

Sweaty clothes were off and shoved into my laundry bag for home and I was under the shower in minutes. I put a few essential items into my faithful raffia bag, including my diary with the letter from Dr Michael. The clothes I had chosen the night before. For my date with destiny, I would wear pale-cream, crêpe culottes with matching camisole and overshirt. Sporty but comfortable was the order of the day, especially as the colour showed off my tan. It was a feel-good factor.

Yes, Milady, you will do nicely! Where was my Parker, now when I needed him? Did he need me too? I offered him a silent prayer and went down to breakfast.

As I closed the door to room 36, I told it that I would be back, just one more time before I vacated it for good. A promise I hoped that I could keep.

Harvey had beaten me down to breakfast and was absently gazing out of the French doors.

'Morning, Harvey, how are you this morning?'

'Oh, Angelica, hello. I was miles away. I'm fine, thank you. You couldn't sleep either? Too much on my mind these days! Did that curly-headed chap find you yesterday?'

'Yes, thanks Harvey, he certainly did!'

I had a sly smile to myself as I collected my breakfast and returned to sit beside him.

'We missed you at dinner last night, a bit lost without you, you know.' He was so forlorn.

'I'm sorry, Harvey, but something came up.' Oh yes, it definitely did, I mused to myself.

He was extremely distracted, probably dreading having to go home to his brother's house. He had already foretold that it was impending doom. I didn't want my buoyant mood to drop, and, thankfully, Alex arrived, wanting to know all the details about my mystery man.

I gave him a vague outline of last evening's adventure, leaving out the luscious bits, to the accompaniment of much eyebrow raising and winking.

Petra didn't arrive for breakfast and neither did Chris, both mourning the loss of the lovely Claire, so we three were the sole survivors of the Musketeers or the Screwed-Up Squirrels Club.

At 9.15 a.m. I took my leave of Alex and Harvey, as briefly as I could. Harvey was very near to tears and thrust an old business card into my hand.

'Now, remember, you are always welcome at my home and we shall not lose touch, eh?' He was such a dear softie, too gentle for the outside world.

'Bye, Earth Mother, see you tomorrow, perhaps?' Would Alex be able to manage more than twenty-four hours, even now?

'Sunday or Monday, Alex, we'll have a chat then. Take care, you two!' Both rose from their seats, like perfect gentlemen. I had to get out of there, fast! I grabbed my bag and headed for freedom.

Archie took my hand and escorted me to the entrance. He punched in the exit number and opened the white Georgian door with its immaculately polished brass knocker. He patted my hand and gently closed the door behind me.

I looked along the arched windows of the hallway and there they were, Alex and Harvey, grinning and waving like two toy soldiers. I blew them both a kiss and turned towards the entrance to the grounds. Waiting was the hardest part.

It seemed an eternity and I kept checking my watch. At one minute past the half-hour I heard the crunch on the gravel and saw the gleaming white bonnet of Orgasma turning into the car park.

I held my breath, anticipating the nearness of my firstborn.

I could see the outline of his face and his hands on the steering wheel. The car came to a halt and I was rooted to the spot, like an adolescent teenager on her first date.

The driver's door swung open. Everything seemed to stand still. Was this déjà vu?

He stood erect in open-necked white shirt and blue jeans and deliberately folded his arms on the top of the car, appraising me with his grey-blue eyes. He was once a shy, gangly youth with shoulder-length hair tied in a ponytail, and he had become a man. His dark hair was cropped in the American style and he was so handsome. *My son*!

He blew a very slow wolf-whistle.

'Your carriage awaits, Mama! Gee! Mum, you look fabulous!' That's my boy!

Cry! Well, what would you expect, I hadn't seen him for six months. Unashamedly, he cried too, then we laughed and laughed, hugged and danced. He swept me off the ground and deposited me in the passenger seat of Orgasma.

Harvey and Alex were waving wildly and enjoying my reunion almost as much as me. Jason grinned and gave them a naval salute, then swung his lithe frame into the car.

'OK, Mom! Let's go and kick some butt! No papering over the cracks! I'm a big boy now, so you can shoot from the hip!'

'You have been watching too many old movies, Jason! You are unreal!' I nearly wet myself laughing. He can't be serious!

He was looking over his shoulder as he reversed the car, then stunned me with his saucy smile.

'Gotcha! As easy as winking! Who loves ya, baby?'

Chapter Eighteen

Orgasma purred her way home under the deft touch of Jason. I took great delight in watching him drive. He would be eighteen in six months and already had the composure of a much older driver.

He could sense my eyes were studying him and, slowly, the dimples dented the corners of his mouth and his face softened into a smile, which grew from his mouth to his eyes.

'Mother! What are you like? You are devouring me like a predatory cat! Meow, purr, purr!'

'I am just so in awe of my number one son. You look so "Young American". Your Uncle Toby has done an excellent job on you!'

'Gee, thanks, Mom!' Briefly he glanced at me and the smile faded.

'What happened to you, Mum? What made you fall apart? You were always so bubbly, full of life, nothing phased you! There is such an awful atmosphere in the house. It's like some Hitchcock thriller! Is it real?'

'Jason, I wish I could say it is imaginary, but what you feel is actually happening and we are caught up in it. Stop the car for a second and I'll try to explain.'

We were halfway home, almost on the motorway, just ahead was the Strawberry Field car park where he turned off, parked and turned to face me. As unemotionally as possible I described the happenings of the past six months, since he had gone to New York. He sat quietly, not interrupting me, just listening.

The story took only a few minutes, as he already knew about the arrest and his dad's sojourn in prison on remand. I glided over the heinous phone calls from the Voice and the upsetting rejection from some of our friends, concentrating on the cold facts and how it would affect us, today.

It was so important that he understood everything, as I needed him to be strong for me as well as himself. I wouldn't tell him about the false holiday that we were about to have – for the time being he had learned enough.

'I'm so glad that you are my mum!' He laid his head against my shoulder and I stroked his hair as I used to when he needed to feel warm and safe. He was such a beautiful person and I was so grateful to have him with me.

'Oh, I forgot! Look on the back seat! That parcel came for you this morning by special delivery, so I signed for it and threw it into the back.' He started the engine and pulled out of the car park. I savoured every minute of sitting in the comfort of Orgasma and listening to her melody. Soon she would be locked in the garage, waiting for me to return.

I reached over and retrieved the brown paper parcel, noticing it had a London postmark. Nothing prepared me for the contents and thankfully it was benign. Jason was intent on filtering into the lane on the motorway, which gave me time to take in what I had found, unobserved.

Inside there was a small white carton and a handwritten note from Commander Johnson. It read:

> Please read this letter covertly and destroy it afterwards. In the box is a camera. I need you to take as many photos as possible, including a separate one of yourself and each of the children. On your return to the Abbey, take the camera and your passports with you and they will be collected by a messenger from the Royal Mail on Monday morning. Your new passports will be engineered and available by the time you need them. There will be further instructions delivered by the mailman when he collects the parcel from you. I have arranged this handover to be witnessed by Dr Michael. You have a great ally in that man! Don't be afraid, Mrs Reeves, it will all work out fine. Signed C.J.

In an instant I had to fabricate a lie and I smiled blatantly at Jason.

'How lovely! Look what is in the box, Jason! It is a present from Auntie Betty, a new camera for when we next go on holiday.' Did I sound convincing? I screwed up the note and pushed it into my shorts pocket, then dropped the camera into my bag.

'I think Dad has got some news for us, just so that you are prepared for his reliable bad mood. The trial is imminent.'

'How do you know this? Has he told you for sure?' I was unnerved and sweating. 'No, I overheard him on the phone and deliberately listened in. Sorry, Mum, but there are so many secrets, you know what Dad is like.' He shrugged his shoulders and looked defiant.

'Do you know who he was talking to?'

'Yeh! It was his brief. I think he has to see him on Tuesday.'

'Right! Well I am sure he will tell us in good time.'

Inwardly I sighed. At least that was one secret I no longer had to keep. So C.J. was reliably informed, the trial would be on Wednesday if everything kept to plan. Poor, poor John, what a nightmare he was going through. He had created his insular world and only he could tear down the barriers. It was too late for us, but not too late to repair the damage he had inflicted on the children. Stop this train of thought, Angelica! Think sunshine, flowers, green fields and being home!

We were there. The long driveway opened up before us and Jason nestled the car into one of the bays in front of the garage. I gripped my hands together, crunching my knuckles and swallowed the dry lump that was lodged in my throat. Had we been followed from the Abbey? I forgot to look in the mirror! Were we being watched right now?

No time to get nervous. The twins were upon us and almost ripped my door from the chassis. The dogs bounded up in hot pursuit of their playmates and barked their way through a chorus of 'welcome home'. Snoopy, the Schitzu, was like a Chinese cracker, jumping three feet in the air and yapping at the same time, trying to keep up with her canine brothers and getting trampled in the process.

John stood in retreat, waiting for his turn to greet me. The melee quieted and we approached and hugged, then I was dragged around to the back patio to witness the preparation of the lunchtime barbecue. John was a fabulous chef and had converted his workmate bench into a culinary worktable, with dishes of meat and spices, oils and pickles.

'It's a double celebration, Mum, for your homecoming and for

Sean and I having finished our GCSEs. No more school, Hurrah! Oh, and for Jason coming home too!' Bless her sweet soul, she was embarrassed, her face shining and pink.

'Well, sister dear, I'm no genius, but that makes it a treble!' Jason loved to tease and swiftly ducked as Rebecca launched a blow at his head.

I looked at John and grimaced. It was hardly a celebration for him, unless it counted as the Last Supper. When was he going to tell them about the trial, or would he revert to type, walk away, leaving me to apply the healing plaster? I so much wanted to feel love for him, but it was like looking at a stranger. How long had I been hiding behind an invisible door of fear? The time was right to face reality and he and I should do it together.

'Mum, you're miles away! Are you tired? Let's sit and dangle our feet in the pool.' Rebecca took my hand and dragged me across the lawn to the pool. This was the only place we could be free of the dogs, as they hated the water. They would whine as if they were in pain if we attempted to coax them near. So we were alone.

This summer had been extraordinary, I couldn't remember so much warmth and sunshine since the kids were toddlers. I sat on the edge, with my calves and feet swaying in the water. Rebecca dumped her body against me and laid her head in my lap.

'Play with my ears and my hair!' She closed her eyes as I began the rhythmic action, letting her hair slip through my fingers.

'Tell me what's troubling you, poppet, apart from me.'

'Am I so transparent? Sean told me to keep quiet and not to get you upset. He cries you know, when he thinks he's alone, but we're twins, I feel what he feels.' Her eyes sprang open and she stared up at me.

'Mum, you mustn't be shocked and you can't fall off again if I tell you!' she whispered.

'OK! OK! I promise. What is it?' I was willing the gremlins to stay asleep. I had to keep control.

'I had one of those horrid phone calls yesterday.'

I pushed her over so that she sat up facing me and I gripped her arms.

'What did he say? Oh, no, not again, not to you!' I hauled her back into my arms and rocked her, but she fought against me.

'No! Don't rock, Mum! You did that when you were sick. Don't do that ever again! It makes me feel sick! Promise me!'

'I won't, I promise. So tell me what happened. Does Sean know? Does your father know or Jason?'

'Yes! No! Only Sean. We kept it to ourselves until we could talk to you.' 'Was it the same voice? What did he say?'

'Oh, yes, it was *him*! He said I was to warn you not to tell the police or he would arrange a little accident. He said he missed being close to you and hoped you would be back home soon and he said that Jason drives well for a youngster. Mum, who is he? What does he want from us? It's Dad's fault, isn't it? Stupid man!'

Stupid was not the right word, totally out of context, but I could not let any of them know how malevolent these people were and how far they would go to keep John quiet.

'Were you frightened?' I was surprised at her control.

'Not as much, this time, I don't know why. Perhaps it was because I shared it with Sean straight away and Jason was back at home, I suppose.'

'Look! Let's try to forget it today and act normally.' Where was my calmness coming from?

'Oh, yes, Mum! You are really funny! Us – *normal*! What a joke!'

We rolled from the pool, down the bank, landing on the lawn, looking up at the sun, laughing too loud. It was probably hysteria! That was the cue for Rosco and Dino to pounce, followed by their furry familiars. The whole tribe of cats and dogs descended on our patch of turf. It was a true communion of earthly creatures. I was home. I put my finger across my lips and Rebecca acknowledged the sign. I would let her know the true story soon enough. I would let them all know.

I remembered the camera that I had dropped into my bag and thought it was time to start taking a few photos. Jason was in his element as he had suddenly become an expert while under the tutelage of Uncle Toby. His polite attitude to his father was brittle but held together effectively. Sadly, he wasn't interested in his father's dilemma at all, keeping conversation to a bare minimum. This must be hurting both of them.

Jay, as he was now called, very USA, was full of fabulous anecdotes of life in New York and how he couldn't wait to get back there. His stories reminded me of those glass domes, which snowed on the scene inside when turned upside down. After all, that was his life, colourful and unreal.

He was such a tonic! His life with Toby was the medicine he needed to inflate his confidence.

With the motive of getting some useful photos I enthused on his technique, encouraging him to take some outrageous poses followed by a few classic singles of us all close up. Finally, he allowed me to take one of him and another of the family, as a group. John didn't want to be outdone so insisted on taking a snap of the entire Reeves menagerie, to keep him company on cold nights. I promised to send him a copy.

The twins were effervescent, then silent. There was intrigue brewing to rival John's impending trial, we just weren't aware of it. They had received the call from the Voice, keeping it a secret, even from Jason and were still not too sure whether I was really sane or in a world of my own. What courage they had shown.

I had to prove my stability and show moral support to John, as he had no other confidante. He was in obvious distress and would be terrified of the outcome of the trial, which was only a few days away. He knew he would go down. How he would survive with villains and criminals I couldn't pretend to know. He could eventually return to his golf and fishing, but there would be no more driving at 100 mph down the M25 in his Porsche. That beauty had to go.

We bustled around and laid out a superb spread on the patio. Rebecca and I had great fun in assembling the trestle table, seriously hampered by the dogs. They hadn't seen me for weeks and were fighting for my attention. Walking on eggshells is an expression well used, but so factual. Thank heavens for the zealous nature of dogs and their aptitude for seeking out accidents. They kept it real.

The barbecue was a huge success. The men took it in turns to be 'Floyd on Food', sampling steaks, chops and sausages so that every portion served appeared to have teeth marks in one corner and nobody retained the same glass. Lager was the order of the day for the boys. Becca and I drank lemonade. Whether it was the influence of seeing the comradely antics between Sean and John or a softening of his anger, Jason appeared to be more at ease.

The sunbeds were dragged from the pool-house and we relaxed after lunch. I swam for a while, letting the water massage my body and the sun replenished my energy. Was the Voice there somewhere, behind the trees, using his binoculars to spy on us?

John opened a bottle of Merlot for me. I was reluctant to drink alcohol along with the 'mood' tablets, as they were now called, so he poured just an inch, which was topped up with lemonade. It resembled pink champagne.

When you know that your life is about to be completely transformed it is impossible to act normally. All my senses were heightened and laid bare. I wanted to ask so many pertinent questions, but knew I had to keep my own counsel and wait. Every look carried an underlying meaning, every gesture was planned.

I kept my eyes closed for as long as I could, listening to the playful banter of the kids. Soon he would ask me what I intended to do after the trial and I would have to lie to protect the secrecy of the plans. The Commander would tell him that we were safe and why we had to go.

With every ounce of concentration I willed him to be strong and accept what I was about to tell him. I had to hold the gremlins at bay in order to stay in control and begin to play the most important role of my life.

Inevitably, the conversation began. Did I still love him? Was there a future for us together? Would I sleep with him again to give him something to hold on to?

He was a drowning man, looking for a lifeline, and at that moment I wasn't at all sure that he would survive. It was his fear and desperation that gave me strength. I was suddenly filled with an inner calm. I held both of his hands and looked into his eyes.

The voice was mine, but the words were those of someone else. I couldn't have been that eloquent! As I offered him my support and comfort, but denied him physical love, his fingers crushed mine, so I pulled my hands free. He tried to keep control, but the anger grew, turning his face black and there was the venom, the viciousness that always lurked inside. He stood and screamed at me.

'OK! Divorce me then! I don't need you, I don't need anyone!'

He stormed off towards the house and would no doubt lock himself inside his den. I didn't follow. He didn't hear my reply, probably because it was only a whisper.

'Yes!' I said. 'Yes, I want a divorce.'

Jason swam over and hauled himself from the pool.

'Well, that was no surprise! I said he was in a foul mood!'

'Jay, don't be so hard on him, he's up before the court on Wednesday so he has reason to be angry.'

'So, he told you then! He didn't, did he? What a liar he is!' He fell on the bed next to me.

'Look, Jay, we all knew this was going to be difficult. Give him some slack, please.'

'OK! OK! But I wish I hadn't come home! He'll never change. I wish Uncle Toby was my dad!'

I couldn't hold back the tears then. Futile tears.

'Mum, I'm sorry! My big mouth! It's worth all of this just to be back home with you.'

We hugged, which caused Rosco to go berserk as he jumped on top of us. He was so protective of me, silly dog.

'I'm going to lay down for a while. Can you keep the twins at bay for half an hour or so. I don't want to explain, just to be quiet for a spell.'

'Leave them to me. We'll clear up the patio and bring you a cuppa in an hour.

I tiptoed through the conservatory and made my way upstairs. On the landing I checked through the window to see that my offspring were still cavorting in the pool. I shuddered as I peeped into the matrimonial bedroom – ghosts – it was beautifully polished and there were flowers on my dressing table. No, no I couldn't go in there ever again – that was my past.

I walked along the gallery and opened the door into Rebecca's room. Her multicoloured rag doll was sitting in the chair next to the bed and seemed to stare at me as if I was intruding. Becca and I had taken about a month to build this doll, and she stood four feet tall. Her clothes were made from over a hundred pieces of material in every imaginable colour, and we had stuffed her with old stockings and tights. Her face was a masterpiece of beauty and humour, with cheeks as red as cherries, and Becca loved her.

Like a thief I pulled out the drawers of her chest, painstakingly looking for her passport and found it in one of the top drawers. The doll stared at me accusingly. I apologised, 'Sorry, Molly Dolly, but it's necessary!'

Sean's room was as masculine as Rebecca's was feminine. One wall was covered in football pictures of his team – Chelsea FC – and the shelves were adorned with souvenirs and trophies from his own achievements.

The floor was littered with discarded clothes and when I opened his wardrobe door it reeked of cheese! I couldn't help exclaiming aloud – pooh!

Thankfully, the twins were both methodical when it came to storing precious belongings, so I found the passport almost immediately.

Jason was rooming with Sean, using the guest bed, and his perfectly neat case and dressing bag were parked on the bed. I slid my hand down the inside pocket of the case and discovered the third, necessary passport. The three passports were tucked in the pocket of my shorts. I would transfer them to my bag later.

All that was left to do was take mine from the bureau in the study and hope that it was unlocked, as I had no idea where to locate the key. I had many secret hiding places, but it was like playing Russian roulette picking the right one.

The phone began to ring as I stood on the threshold of the spare room, which previously had been Jason's room, so I looked over the balcony into the hallway. Why was it ringing so long? Would it be the Voice? Oh, good, it stopped. Loud noises were still coming from the patio, so I assumed John had taken the call.

Rebecca had filled the room with fresh flowers and the windows were open, allowing the clean air to circulate. This room was directly opposite the master bedroom, across the gallery, with its windows overlooking the driveway. I scanned the front lawns and saw a small piece of rooftop of the deserted cottage peeping through the trees. I pondered on whether it had finally been sold or whether squatters were inside.

There was a small parcel on the pillow of the single bed, wrapped in blue tissue paper with a blue velvet rosebud tied into the ribbon. I knew it was from Rebecca. Carefully, I unwrapped the gift, opening the tiny box to find it contained a packet of flower seeds and a note. She had written:

> One day we will plant these blue poppy seeds in a place where we will be happy and we can watch them grow. I love you, Mum x x Rebecca x x

John and I had produced three wonderful people, who didn't deserve this episode in their young lives. This didn't make me feel weepy or sad; it made the anger slowly grow inside, making my resolve even stronger. Nobody would hurt them ever again, I would make sure of that. I lay on the bed, watching the curtains gently floating in and out, breathing with the breeze, and fell asleep.

'Hey! Wakey! Wakey! Sleepy head! Do you know its 5 p.m.? Would you like this cup of tea now?'

'Oh, you little treasure! Who covered me? I don't recall being under the duvet.'

Jason grinned and pointed his finger at his chest.

'Like I said! I organised the lesser people to janitise the yard and they performed well!'

'Janitise! Where did that word come from?'

'You know the Yanks! If there isn't a word to fit, they make one up.' A voice called from below stairs.

'Honey, you awake? Could you come down and take a look at the casserole?' Jason and I both raised our eyebrows in surprise.

'He sounds happy! Praise be!' Jason was definitely taking on the American way of talking. He left the room and I threw off the duvet. The passports were still there, in my pocket.

We rejoined the others downstairs to help with the setting of the table. As joyous and noisy as lunch had been, so dinner was the exact opposite. With the exception of John, we were usually a demonstrative bunch, always kissing, touching and laughing. Why had it never rubbed off on John? He often seemed resentful of our humour and forever criticising.

Life for him was serious, grey and painful, so tonight we were polite, respectful and totally dysfunctional.

The kids disappeared into the lounge after the silent meal, while John and I cleared the table and ferried the dregs into the kitchen. He apologised for his outburst earlier and enlightened me on the latest news from his solicitor that the trial would be on Wednesday.

I was genuinely sad for him. He thought it would be best if he went to his mother's in London on Monday so that he would be accessible to Lincoln's Inn and his brief. They had to get up to speed with the defence of the said crime. I listened quietly, sitting at the kitchen table, watching him load the dishwasher as he collected his thoughts.

Fear was insinuating itself within me and I fought hard to keep calm. The lights were dimming in my head and again I listened to the other *me*, telling myself to accept the feeling and laugh in its face.

'I need to have a little fresh air. I shall be back in a tick.'

Was I moving normally or was I rushing? I headed for the study and went directly to the bureau. It was unlocked! I pulled down the roller shutter, opened the drawer and took my passport out. I kissed the leather wallet and held it above me.

'Do you *see*! I have it now! We shall be safe!' Who was I talking to? Was I telling God or was I challenging the Devil, the Voice that threatened me?

Across the hallway, there was an ancient *Carry On* movie showing on the TV and the kids were in hysterics. I slid the passport into the pocket of my jacket and wandered into the lounge.

'So! Do you see how the old fogies invented timeless humour?'

'Mum, you are spot on! This stuff is really *bad*!' In teenage language, this meant it was excellent.

John stood beside me, holding out a mug of hot chocolate.

'I thought you might like this!'

'Thanks, John, just what I needed!' Everything had become an effort and my shoulders were very heavy. It had been a long day.

'Hey, Dad, what about us, the little people. Can we have one too?'

Sean bounced over the top of the settee, placed his arm around his dad and walked him back to the kitchen.

That was all I could take for one day. My emotions were confused and I needed to close my eyes. I kissed various cheeks goodnight and climbed the stairs. They had to have quality time to bond and make some memories and I had to have time to heal. Sleep was my reward for surviving another day. As I sank beneath the duvet I remembered Iain, my perfect Parker.

I awoke to a beautiful Sunday morning. The air tasted cool and clean and the rest of the house was very much asleep. I wound back the cover on the pool and quietly slithered into the cold water. It gave me goosebumps. How many lengths I swam, I have no idea, but it sorted out a heap of dross in my head.

Soon I was dry and I found one of my velour tracksuits hanging in the cubical. The hot shower had steamed up the mirror so I rubbed it with my arm. I was shocked to see that the face looking at me hadn't changed – it was still my face. Thoughts can be very rewarding at times. I expected to see an older woman, but it was my face, suntanned and shiny, with unruly hair.

I patted my bag, containing the four passports and the camera. There would be some snaps left on the roll, but I thought I would use them when I got back to the Abbey. They might think it strange that I have my bag with me at all times, so I decided to put it in the car. The dogs had found me and were chasing around my legs as I strolled towards the woods at the end of the property.

'What are you doing, Mum? It's Sunday! You're supposed to lay in bed until lunchtime!' Sean was hanging out of his window. He looked naked, but hopefully something was covering his charms.

A pillow flew past his head and landed on the lawn below. I don't think Jason was too pleased to be woken so early.

'Scrambled egg, bacon and tomatoes will be served in twenty minutes. If you want it, be there!' I yelled back and jogged into the kitchen.

Seventeen minutes later, the table was set and we had a full compliment of bodies ready to eat.

'Mum, you heavenly creature! I forgot that you could cook! Look at those huge, fat mushrooms, too! Yummy!' Jason was salivating.

'Less of your cheek, sonny! *Eat!*'

There was no ceremony at breakfast time, everyone grabbed a plate and helped themselves.

'We are booked in at the pub for lunch, Jeannie and Mike invited us. Is that OK with you, honey?' John was being so very nice, it was unnerving.

'That's lovely, I'm really pleased. We can go and spend some time catching up.'

'I'm glad you agree 'cos Mike and I have arranged a quick round of golf. You don't mind, do you?'

'No, not at all, that's fine.' That was an understatement. I could do with some time to put together a few essential items that I needed to be near me from now on. He wasn't going to change the habits of a lifetime now and the routine of him and Mike together would be good for him.

Breakfast was over and we did what families do – all went off to our separate rooms to do our own thing.

John jumped into the 911 with his favourite friend beside him, his bag of clubs. He waved, dropped the clutch and showered the air with shingle. I returned to the kitchen and was soon joined by Jason, who hugged me from behind.

'How about a long walk in the woods with the hounds and I'll tell you all about New York? Well, not everything!' He mischievously gave a knowing wink.

'Sounds good to me. With or without the twins?'

'Give them the choice. I'm cool whatever.'

He stood in the hallway and shouted like a foghorn. Sean and Rebecca appeared at their respective doors and decided to come too. Everything we did in the next few days needed to be indelibly printed in our memories as it was to be the final chapter of the Reeves family. Who would we be next week and where would we be?

If you wanted to be secluded, separated from the rest of society, this house was idyllic. It was totally cocooned by the woods on three sides and the fourth side abutted other properties sitting on half-acre plots or larger. Our animals were in paradise, whether within the grounds or in the woods.

We trundled down the path, towards the old stables, which led directly to the north boundary of the house. The Dalmatians were frantic with excitement, biting each other to prevent the other from getting through the gate first. Becca had Snoopy in her arms to prevent death by trampling.

The dogs weren't leashed, but we carried leads in case they became over-boisterous with any interlopers. The wood was definitely their domain and they resented sharing their patch with any other four-legged creature. Having to leave them behind was a thought almost too sad to contemplate. I'd have to deal with it when it happened.

When the four of us were together we were one huge voice. We held an honours degree in talking; in fact we were amazing, we could have talked for England. It was a veritable verbal extravaganza.

Jay was the young English star in downtown New York, a great favourite with the fair sex, especially women with available daughters. Toby said he was a mobile honey pot and that his life had definitely become more interesting since the arrival of his charismatic nephew.

Our chat was interrupted by the noise of barking in the distance. The dogs were waiting, impatiently, by the stile at Blewers Field but the horses were grazing, so we had to stay on the path.

As we skirted the field a stranger, walking with a huge boxer dog, approached us. Rosco and Dino growled and barked more at the human than the dog, charging past and sniffing the ground where he had trod. The man was wearing a lightweight jacket, combat boots and a camouflage baseball cap. His face was lowered, appearing to be intent on controlling his dog. As the path was very narrow he had to pull to one side to enable us to pass and briefly he lifted his head.

The twins ran ahead, with the dogs in pursuit and Jason tucked in behind me as we drew level with the stranger. He nodded and slipped back on to the path and was on his way.

'Jay, did you see his face?' I was startled at the coldness in his eyes.

'Yeh! If his eyes were any paler blue they would have been sightless.'

'His hair was white, wasn't it?' I had an urge to turn around for a second look.

'Perhaps he was an albino. Haven't you seen him before?'

'No! He may have moved into the old cottage. Let's go back that way and have a gander. We can play super sleuths!' We both laughed and trotted along the track to catch up with the others.

'Did you see that bloke, Mum?' Becca looked excited. 'He was quite tasty! Looked a bit mysterious, definitely a foreigner with those clothes!' She was intrigued.

'Yes! He was definitely different! I said to Jay he may have taken the old cottage, so we'll saunter past on our way back.'

The rest of the walk was uneventful. Keeping to the outer edge of the wood we eventually had to pass by the semi-derelict cottage. We leashed the dogs and they pulled frantically, wanting to be free. The grounds of the cottage had been cleared along one side and as we walked further we could see that there was a Land Rover parked close to the dwelling, but nobody appeared to be around.

My imagination was running riot. Was there a boxer dog in the cottage? If so, he wasn't barking. Did the stranger with the white hair live here now? Was he the Voice, the assassin chosen to destroy my life, or was this my imagination doing what it does best?

But let's face it! This would be a perfect answer. The Voice could see everything that happened in my home. From this old cottage he could creep under cover of darkness, secreting himself behind the trees. No one would see him, no one would hear him. Jason brought me back to reality.

'You could be right, Mum, perhaps that guy has moved in. It must have been when you weren't around or the others would have seen something, and the ground had been cleared very recently.' Jay had stopped with his hands on the driveway gates, looking very much like a young Sherlock Holmes.

'What are you doing Jay, you're not going inside?'

'That gave you a jolt! Don't be daft. He wasn't friendly, so I wouldn't trespass – unless asked!' He squeezed my hand, laughed and raced along the path to beat me to the gates.

Someone could easily keep us under surveillance from there, I thought.

The twins had let the dogs off the leads and were on their way towards the back of the house.

'OK, folks, let's get ourselves ready for our pub lunch!' This stranger was bothering me and I couldn't put him out of my mind. I felt I knew the man in the woods, but I had never seen him before. Was it the brief eye contact? Oh, for heaven's sake, Angelica, let it drop!

'Mother, are you gonna let me drive?' He was giving me a pleading look. 'Great idea, Jason! It's cramped in the car with four so it's best that you drive.'

I looked at the phone, briefly, wondering whether I should phone anyone. It made me feel nervous, so *no* was the answer. If only I could switch my mind off, just for a while. As I changed my clothes, I tried to remember simple laughter, innocent conversation and the feeling of warmth and comfort, but it wasn't there. Would it ever come back?

We arrived at the pub around 12.30 p.m. and my Jeannie squealed with delight. People were smiling and whispering behind their hands, so I walked quickly to the restaurant. Did everyone know where I had been? Still, if they were gossiping about me, then someone else was off the hook.

Our kids were great pals and disappeared out into the gardens, intending to sit by the river and catch up on Jason's American adventure. Oh, and they had a new goat that had butted the drayman when he delivered yesterday. They had called him Tyson!

'Oh! My one and only Jelly Baby!' Jeannie had gone all soft and female. 'Jeannie, don't get too emotional 'cos I can't handle it at the moment, sorry! Can you leave the bar for ten minutes? It's important.'

'Course I can. Hey, Julie, take over for a while!'

Arm in arm we walked out onto the patio overlooking the petanque pitch and sat facing each other. Where was I going to start? I couldn't tell her too much because the responsibility would have been more than she could cope with, but I didn't want to disappear from her life without an explanation of sorts.

'Jeannie, you and Mike have been so good to John and me. I'll never be able to repay you.' Oh God! I sounded so false. This wasn't what I wanted to say, but I had made a start.

'This is all very deep, Jelly! Do lighten up!' She looked embarrassed.

'Right! This is what I really want to say, but it must go no further – not even to Mike!'

She was intent on keeping quiet and just nodded.

'Please listen to me, but don't say anything! John's trial is on Wednesday and the outcome is inevitable. The kids and I have been placed on a police protection programme and will be assuming new identities, which means living in a different location. I have no idea when or where this will be, but I should know tomorrow. A letter will come to you, from the police, to let you know that we are safe.'

She grasped my hands and looked so sad. I thought desperately, please don't cry – I couldn't bear that. She didn't cry; she was speechless.

Julie popped into vision.

'Jeannie, I'm really quite busy! Will you be long?' She was flustered.

'Yes! Yes! OK! I'll be there in a tick. Just cope for a while. Please! Give everyone a drink on the house. That'll keep them quiet!' She waved Julie away and looked back at me. For a moment the pub no longer existed.

'So! This is sort of goodbye, I suppose. You know all about the threatening phone calls and the constant, creepy surveillance from this vicious crowd of thugs. John isn't aware of how dangerous it has become, so, the man in charge of our case at Scotland Yard has organised our disappearance. Not a soul must know, not Mike or even John. Jeannie, these gangsters are evil and will stop at nothing to get what they want and that is John's silence.'

'Angelica! This is madness! Has the world gone crazy! What can John know that is so important? We are ordinary people living in a sleepy village in Kent. I don't understand!' She shook her head in disbelief.

She dropped my hands and looked past me, down towards the river where our teenagers were larking around.

'Look, Angelica! That's real! Youth, innocence, with their whole lives ahead of them. What the Hell is happening to you? I'm so sorry for you and I won't betray you, ever! How will we keep in touch? We can't let these bloody creeps win, can we?' She touched my hands and face, distractedly.

'Sorry, Jeannie, but you really must come now!' Poor Julie was red-faced and about to blow a fuse.

'You go, Jeannie. I'll go down to the river and bring the tribe back for lunch.' Reluctantly, she let me go.

On her return to the bar she found that Mike and John were back and helping Julie by washing glasses. She had an urge to flush John away with the dregs down the drain, but control got the better of her.

Our lunch table had been laid and reserved in the window balcony and we arranged ourselves in boy-girl order. John had the head of the table and Jeannie was nearest to the kitchen, being a true hands-on publican.

The lunchtime staff had taken over and the wet trade had dwindled as the carvery increased in popularity. Jeannie now had time to relax and I prayed that she didn't hit the bottle after my recent revelations. If looks could kill, she had hung, drawn and quartered John and was finding it difficult to talk to him.

I could feel glances of interest, bordering on intrusion, but every time I attempted to challenge a look, the perpetrator smiled discreetly or looked away. I was becoming paranoid! We were a private party, hosted by the landlords, which always caused speculation.

On my way back from the loo I could have sworn that I saw the albino in the private bar. I threw open the door, but the room was empty. Was I going insane? Keep calm – breath – believe in retribution!

The meal was a great success, sealing a chapter for me. I was safe in the knowledge that at least one friend would defend me if put to the test. I couldn't face another showdown with John so decided to ask Jason to take me back to the Abbey. John looked just as relieved as I felt when I suggested I went back earlier than planned. Perhaps it would help him to keep control if I wasn't around to resurrect the guilt.

We had all talked about the impending trial as if it were a movie and we were the actors. After the final act we would leave the set and resume our normal lives. This was real life, unfortunately.

The twins dived into the Porsche and Jay and I waved as they sped off. Mike came out and hugged me hard. He didn't say anything, just gave me a funny little salute. Jeannie kissed her fingers and blew me a kiss. She was already in tears and only she and I knew why. She would tell Mike, I was certain of that, but hopefully not before we had flown.

Jason patted my hand and smiled.

'Buckle up, sweet thing. You did real good, but the tiredness is seeping through your smile.' I didn't know whether to laugh or cry. Was I so obvious?

'Thanks, Jay. I couldn't have held it together without you! How did you get so grown-up?'

'Life is so easy with Uncle Toby. He treats me as an equal, no patronising or pontificating. My views are just as valid as those of the next man. It really matters, Mum!'

'Has your Dad asked you to take him to your gran's tomorrow?'

'Yeh! I said I would have lunch with them and then come back to the Abbey to collect you for good. You'll never go back there!'

His smile made me feel strong and courageous. It was going to be fine. He parked by the entrance doors to the Abbey and opened the car door for me. I told him to leave straight away and allow me to do the next part on my own.

I pushed the call button and announced who I was. The door clicked open and a female member of the clerical staff popped her head out from the office and waved me through. Inmate number 36 is now in the building!

My feet flew to the sanctuary of my room. I slammed the door and breathed a sigh of relief. Everything was as I had left it. My mellow, yellow haven was mine for another twenty-four hours.

There was a short list of received calls and a sealed note from Dr Michael, reminding me of my appointment at 10 a.m. tomorrow. The calls were from my sister Miriam, my girlfriend Georgina, Simon and a nameless number with a London code.

I knew, instinctively, it was from *him*, the Voice! It was like having an affair with the Devil. I couldn't believe what I was thinking, but I was almost excited, more thrilled than terrified. I was gonna beat this bastard at his own game because I was a step ahead of him. The rules had been changed and he had no idea.

Vivaldi was in attendance next door, gently infiltrating the connecting wall, which meant Petra, inmate number 38, was alive and kicking. It was 6.45 p.m., so whoever was around this evening would shortly be making their way to the second floor lounge for hot drinks and idle conversation.

I sat on my bed, hugging my knees, listening to the *Entrance of the Queen of Sheba* and I began to reminisce. One by one I visualised their faces and mentally bade them adieu, wishing them godspeed to a full recovery.

There were one or two people that I hoped I would see again, especially Parker; Iain was my true mischievous friend who had played my fantasy game with me. Together we reinvented Parker and Lady Penelope, taking them to a new dimension and he made my sexual taste buds salivate almost to naughtiness. I could still see his eyes twinkling and the pulse in his neck bouncing as our mouths drew together – oh! so soft and succulent was that secret kiss!

I chuckled to myself. Here I was, doing it again. The only way I knew how to cope was to envelope myself in lustful, sexual, tantalising thoughts, and how many of those thoughts would become reality? Most of them!

Françoise Le Fevre, just the name conjured the vision of a femme fatale. What a stunning creature she was and such a talent. Whatever life tossed my way I would find the time to see her again. We were sisters in spirit and could enjoy our flights of fantasy in tandem. I believe that my joy in penmanship mirrored her incredible, macabre interpretation of life on her canvasses. One day we would drink a glass of wine together, perhaps in France.

I loved this room. It was so welcoming. I was one of the untouchables, without fear of inspection, while in this place. The Abbey allowed me the freedom to be me. The evening was approaching and the air becoming comfortably warm. Vivaldi had ceased to play and the clock showed 7.25 p.m. It was time to join the others in the lounge.

'Well! It's our princess of poetry, so it is!' The door had opened and Carmel stood there with her hands on her ample hips.

247

'Carmel, I'm so glad it is you! I've written a farewell poem, which I think you'll like, for you and your kinfolk in Killarney.'

'You will be missed, to be sure, but it's glad I am that you're about to go for you should be out there having fun!'

We walked arm in arm towards the lounge and she left me as she reached the nurses' station. Mrs Dighton handed me a cup of hot chocolate and I helped myself to a piece of homemade ginger cake as I had skipped dinner. It wasn't long before Alex, Chris and another man I didn't know entered the lounge.

Alex had only managed twenty-four hours at home and was back here for lunch. Harvey had been collected by his brother and was now somewhere in Surrey or Kent and Alex had moved into his old room only steps away from the lounge. Chris was more affable too, as he had taken over Françoise's room, which was next door to Alex. So the gang, a diminished group of musketeers, was now occupying the same corridor.

I had no idea who the new inmate was and didn't try to find out. Chris had taken him under his wing and was revelling in it. At last he was the guide and not the initiate.

I dragged Alex to one side and we caught up on our day apart. He wasn't getting much nearer to renewing his marital status, but he was overjoyed that they had spent an entire day sulk-free. I recounted the briefest details of my sojourn at home, allowing him to decide what was truth and what was euphemism.

'So this is your last night, Angelica. What are we going to do without your flame?'

'Alex, you must light your own fire! You don't need me, you just need to lighten up – ha-ha!'

'Very funny! Actually that was quite good, double-act material! Seriously, I know you'll survive, once you and the kids have had your holiday.'

'Hey, friend! This is much too philosophical. Has there been any news from Iain?'

'Oh, yes, I forgot, we had letters from him all in one envelope addressed to the "Musketeers".'

He took an envelope from his pocket and handed it to me.

'This one is for you and I'll forward Harvey's on to him.'

'Would you mind if I read this later, in private?'

'Not at all. I know you two had a really special bond, Milady!'

I left him then, promising to meet up for breakfast, and returned to my room. There was too much going on in my brain to be in any company. I was relieved to be alone.

Iain's note was succinct and very sad. He was coping, barely, and missing his friends at the Abbey. He thought that I was the only person who would understand his trauma and begged me to keep in touch. There was no way that I could explain my disappearance so he would have to find another confidante. But if thoughts and wishes helped I would never forget him – my Parker!

Tiredness took me away to my dreamscape very quickly that night and I didn't resist. In the middle of the night I sat up in bed – wide awake. Someone or something was there with me, but I wasn't afraid.

I was standing alone in the woods and from behind a tree he appeared and walked towards me. His hair was thick, short and pure white and his eyes were as light as the palest blue sky. I was rooted to the ground and he was so close that I could touch him. Then he was gone and I was sitting in my bed at the Abbey.

Was it a dream or a vision?

Was he an angel – of life or death?

Was it a warning of something yet to come?

Was he the man in the woods?

Was he the Voice?

All these questions raced through my mind as I drifted back into a dreamless sleep.

Chapter Nineteen

I awoke so refreshed that I believed I could conquer the world. As I inhaled, the air was like a blast of eucalyptus, laying siege to any dead thoughts. I remembered the dream and could make no sense of it – no matter – it was just a dream.

After breakfast I watched Joanna grouping all the joggers together by the reception. I sat, sipping my tea and pondered on her clandestine affair with Dr Raschid and the explicit joining together in room 12, witnessed by the involuntary, captured voyeurs.

I couldn't resist a small chuckle, which expanded into a hearty belly laugh, without any help from me. A pair of strong hands planted themselves on my shoulders.

'Careful, Angelica, we may have to keep you here longer if you show signs of stress – like laughing at nothing!'

'Why, hello, Dr Raschid, if only you knew what I was thinking! This joke really is "for my eyes only".'

He walked away, bemused, looking over his shoulder at me as he disappeared through the doors into ICU. It would have been disastrous if he could have read my mind.

Time to go and see Dr Michael. Fate and the mailman were waiting for me. I tapped on the door of room 10 and was asked to enter. Dr Michael was standing behind his desk and a man wearing a Royal Mail uniform was seated beside him.

'Good morning, Angelica. Do come in and sit here by me.' He gestured to a leather padded chair and not the couch.

I placed my bag on the desk in front of me and took out the four passports and the camera, handing them to Dr Michael. He, in turn, passed then across to the mailman.

'We do not need formal introductions, Angelica. This officer is from Scotland Yard and is here on behalf of Commander Johnson.'

The mailman smiled, accepted the goods and tucked them

into his grey, Hessian satchel, fastening it with two buckles. He had taken out a thick, padded envelope, which he handed directly to me.

'Our business is now complete, Dr Michael. Thank you for your assistance and yours, Mrs Reeves.' He stood, shook hands with the doctor, touched his cap to me and left the room.

I sat, looking at the brown packet and then at the two square, tanned hands that had covered my trembling ones. The dark eyes behind the tinted lenses calmed me and gave me courage.

'It's OK, Angelica, you are allowed to be a little afraid, but I am here to help you. We shall sort this out together.'

He handed me his paper knife, which couldn't have been more ornate if it had tried. It was sheathed in a green leather scabbard and it appeared to be made of gold. The head of the knife was an Egyptian cat, having two green jewels for the eyes. It was so beautifully crafted that it seemed ironic to use it for such a mundane task.

The packet contained three folded pieces of paper and a mobile phone. I couldn't help grinning to myself.

'What is so amusing, Angelica?' Dr Michael was studying my every reaction. I'm sure he would have put a stop to this if he could.

'It's the phone! I really hate mobiles and now it seems that this little gadget is my link to a new life.'

I unfolded the typewritten sheets of paper and a photograph fell into my lap. On the back it told me that the face was of Declan Dennehy and he was an undercover policeman. Probably not his real name but he had a kind face and he looked about mid-thirties. I slid the photo back into the packet.

The first sheet of paper declared itself to be the instructions to the phone, which had been programmed and fully charged. Once activated it should retain a signal for five days or so. The number was unlisted and should be used to communicate with C.J. or numbers which had been entered into the address book for my assistance. I refolded the paper and put it together with the phone, into the packet.

The second piece of paper was headed with a good luck message from C.J. and a brief explanation of the man in the photo. He would become my new friend and bodyguard. It was imperative that we became familiar with this face, as we had to perform like a real family, especially at the airport. He would give further explanations later in the documents.

There was a telephone number of a travel agency, a reference number and a name. I had to speak to a Mr Fullerton, who would chat to me like an old friend in case the conversation was overheard. He would confirm that my four tickets to Tenerife would be awaiting my collection at the Iberia desk at Gatwick Airport for the 8.15 a.m. flight, departing on Wednesday. At 5.30 a.m. that morning a cab would collect us from the house and we would be carrying two cases, stuffed with anything as they would be booked in at the airport in the usual way and never collected at the other end. The cabbie would hand me a packet containing four new passports and four flight tickets. The boys would be travelling to Dublin with Declan Dennehy and Rebecca and I would be travelling to Cork. Four impostors would be flying out to Tenerife.

How many minutes had gone by? I couldn't take my eyes away from this letter. I dare not look up because it would break the spell and I would have to say something. What would I say?

The next paragraph contained a list of clothes we were to buy, which had to be worn on the day of travel without any deviation, as our impostors would be wearing identical clothes. Then he delivered the sharpest shock of all.

> Mrs Reeves, I suggest you have your hair cut off before you travel
> – and you should wear a wig of your same hairstyle until the day
> of travel when it can be passed on to the identical 'Mrs Reeves'
> when we swap you at the airport. Sorry! I know this has come as a
> thunderbolt, but your hair is such a characteristic part of your
> persona and could be a vital piece of camouflage if anyone is sent
> to follow you. Whatever you decide, the wig must be handed over
> and you must look totally different when you emerge as the new
> 'Mrs Callaghan'.

I must have gasped because Dr Michael took my hand.

'What is it? I am so worried for you, Angelica. How can I help you?'

He was so lovely, so understanding, so generous.

'It's OK, please, don't worry! It was just a shock. I think it is going to take some time to take all of this in.'

I folded the letters and held them tight in my hand. Suddenly, I felt protective of this knowledge. Dr Michael was my doctor and my friend, but I had to be suspicious of everyone. To talk to him would be so easy, but I could not encourage his confidence. Who knows who may be listening?

As if he heard my thoughts he said, 'I do not want to know the particulars of the correspondence, Angelica. You must read and digest all of that in the solitude of your room. I am here and my support is here.'

He sat back in his seat, totally relaxed, holding his hands out to me with his palms uppermost. I touched his hand with mine. I so wanted to curl up against him, to give in. Instead I smiled.

'Thank you, you are too good to be my doctor, you should be my Father Confessor, my priest.' Everything had changed between us. I had come of age and I had to let him go.

'Angelica, you have all day to yourself to plan your future. I shall be around if you need me.'

I kissed him fondly on both cheeks, pushed the packet down into my bag and walked to the door. As I had my hand on the handle, I turned.

'I'll never forget what you have done for me. You gave me back my life and there is no way that this arrogant slime is going to take it away. I'm gonna win!'

'You most certainly are a winner already. Take care, Angelica, and call me, even if you just call to let me know you are safe, please!'

He had approached the doorway and watched as I walked away. The time had come to toss aside the gremlins. They had no lodgings with me any more. The word negativity no longer existed.

Callaghan, I wonder why that name was chosen? And *Ireland*, why Ireland?

It was almost 10.30 a.m. as I climbed the two flights of stairs to my room. Most of the patients were either out on the morning jog or involved in some other morning activity, so I was free to wander without distraction.

I grabbed a can of Coke from the refreshment area and went to room 36 to settle myself down to reading the rest of the instructions from C.J.

The words kept repeating themselves in my head – *cut off your hair, cut off your hair*.

I stood for minutes in front of the mirror, pulling my hair back, tying it on top of my head and letting the ringlets fall around my face. My hair had always been wild, abandoned and a major part of *me*. I suppose I used it as an accessory, I could disappear beneath its canopy. There was too much of it to hide under a wig! I grimaced at my reflection and it grinned back at me. It's only hair and will grow again! What the heck! Ricardo, my hairdresser, would love the challenge. Let's do it!

With that decision made, I sat cross-legged on the bed and began to read more of the letter. The balance of page two listed the clothes to buy for each member of the family and C.J. reiterated the importance to detail.

He suggested that we all wrote letters to our favourite people and put them into one large envelope to be given to the cab driver on Wednesday morning. These would be despatched by his office with a covering letter from C.J., explaining how they would be able to contact us through Special Branch.

The last paragraph, of this page, was headed 'Identities'. Angelica Reeves becomes Amanda Callaghan (widow); Jason Reeves becomes Connor Callaghan; Rebecca Reeves becomes Brodie Callaghan; Sean Reeves becomes Liam Callaghan.

There was a brief NB.

This family will be settled in Ireland for the near future, under the protection of Declan Dennehy and his team.

There is no need for further information at this time – *less is best*. I suggest that you organise the safety of your animals as if you were taking a normal summer vacation. We can arrange any prolonged care in a week or two when your safety has been sealed.

That was the end of the second page. *Amanda Callaghan*! Again, I looked at myself in the mirror. Amanda – how do you do? This is too insane! How are the kids going to deal with this? Will they like their new names?

No time to ponder now, they would just have to adjust! It was past 11 a.m., so I would have to read page three, which was the most important of all, after I had made some phone calls. It was our itinerary for Wednesday, the exodus of the Reeves family from Gatwick Airport and the emergence of the Callaghans.

Reluctantly, I put the letter aside and sat the telephone in my lap. Time was ticking and I had to get my appointment made with Ricardo, (really Richard). He was a luvvie and would definitely fit me in as I was still so 'newsworthy'. I phoned Georgina's number and waited.

Georgina was gushing with tea and sympathy as soon as she heard my voice and it was all heartfelt. I had to cut her short.

'Georgina! Please, will you do something for me? Book me in with Ricardo tomorrow, anytime, but it must be tomorrow, an hour appointment and say I want something really special as I am going on holiday, OK?'

'Sure, Angie, sure! I'll see if someone can fit me in too and then we can have a natter. What did you say? When are you going on holiday? I thought that…'

'Look, Georgie, I'll explain later. Could you do this for me straight away and phone me back on the same extension, 36, at the Abbey. I go to lunch at 12.30 p.m. so would you do it for me, please?'

'OK, Angie, I'll phone toute de suite and phone you back. Ta! Ta!'

Thank heavens for Georgina and her dizzy head, she'll charm the appointment out of Ricardo. He'll do it just to stop her talking. Next I had to phone the travel agency. I located the number, dialled and waited.

It took a deal of persuasion to be put through to Mr Fullerton, who was extremely busy, but eventually she caved in. Directly I announced who I was, the brusque tone of Mr Fullerton became Cadbury smooth. I imagined him to have a thin moustache, shiny teeth and overpowering cologne. His voice suggested that he knew me intimately – what a creep! The ordeal over, I thanked him and said goodbye. Whoever he was, I wouldn't have trusted him judging by his voice, but what do I know of the workings of the Special Branch.

I was musing over the conversation, when the phone rang.

'Angelica Reeves, who is it?'

'My Angel, at last! I thought my heart had broken and you had disappeared for ever.'

Oh! His voice always turned me upside down and today I had mercury charging through my inner core.

'Simon, you are right on time! I did get your message but I was exhausted when I got back yesterday and I was about to phone you thirty seconds ago.'

'So, Angel, what is the prognosis? Has Dr Mike given you your marching orders yet and when can I see you?'

'Well, strangely enough, I have just been discharged.

'I am in full working order, the MOT complete. Jason is picking me up after lunch this afternoon.'

'Great! Fantastic! Wonderful! When can I see you?' He really did sound ecstatic, but he was protected by the distance of two hundred miles between us. I didn't want to doubt him, but he did blow hot and cold.

'Simon, I want to see you now, even tomorrow and the next tomorrow but I'm taking the kids away on a surprise holiday. They need to be out of the range of the reporters and media for the next week as the case comes to trial in a couple of days and it could be a real circus! The local press will have a field day!'

'Oh! Sweetheart! I'm so sorry!'

'Look, Simon, don't be too sympathetic because I have to stay focused, after all, we are the victims, not the criminals, and nobody cares about us. We are tomorrow's garbage!'

'Hey! Hold your fire! I'm the good guy! I love you! I'm not looking for glory, just a good lay!'

'You're a bastard, Simon!' I couldn't help laughing.

'Seriously, Angel, when and where? I'll be there. Put me out of my misery!'

'Let me get through the next couple of weeks, Simon, and I'll put you to the test. Could you give up everything for me?' The silence was a passion killer. I could picture his Adam's apple protruding as he attempted to swallow.

'Angel, call me when you get back and we'll make plans.' They were empty words. Nevertheless, it gave us both time to decide.

'OK, Loverrrr! Keep on cutting! We'll meet soon. I must go now Simon as I am expecting a call. Remember I love you. Read *Love on the Line* – read and sigh! Bye, bye love!'

We blew kisses and I cradled the phone. Fresh air, I had to breathe fresh air. All this information was stifling my brain. I was holding the phone in my hands and pacing to and fro like a tiger. The pages were on the bed, beckoning me – *read me, read me, read me now*! A silly picture of *Alice in Wonderland* popped into my head and huge circular sherbet fizzers with the words *read me* instead of *eat me*. Or was it *Alice Through the Looking-Glass*?

'Shit!' I was so involved with my thoughts that the phone ringing was like a bomb exploding in my hands and it ended up on the floor.

'Oh, sorry! Are you there? Hello, I dropped the phone!'

'Angelica, it's me, I've done it! Are you all right?' She sounded quite confused.

'Georgie, you are a treasure! What time is it happening?'

'Late, I'm afraid! He couldn't fit us both in until 4.30 p.m. Is that OK?'

'Absolutely perfect! You have worked a miracle!'

'Don't be daft, it was easy, you know what Ricardo is like, the big drama queen, he just can't wait for you to dish the dirt.'

'What time shall we meet? I've got some holiday shopping to do with the gang. Would you like to come too?' I knew she would.

'What a stupid question! I'll bring Charlie's credit card and give it an airing. How about I pick you all up in the Shogun at about 11.30 a.m.? Then we can have a tacky lunch and go shopping!' She was so enthusiastic. 'Excellent, Georgie! I am so looking forward to seeing you. I've really missed you!' Until I voiced the words, I didn't realise just how much.

'Tell me, though, are you better? Is this the end of your depression? Charlie and I are so upset for you. He wants to take care of you, but he won't allow John's name to be spoken. I think if he got his hands on him he would throttle him! Oh, sorry darling, I'm shooting off at the mouth again. Don't take any notice of me, you know how I go on!'

That last comment started me off. I laughed, sitting on the floor, holding my sides and Georgie joined in, overflowing with mirth and giggles like a fizzing bottle of Moët.

'Georgina, you are such a tonic and I love you for it. Must go now, so see you at 11.30 a.m. tomorrow. Bye, gorgeous!'

She was going to be a nervous wreck when she knew the truth, so somehow I was going to have to play things down. She was volatile enough to become a weak link, but that was a risk I had to take. The Buckinghams were friends I would treasure for life.

It was now time to wander so that I could read and digest page three. I stuffed it into my raffia bag, which I hung over my shoulder and I sought the outside air.

'Hello, sweetie, and how's my Angelica this morning?' Tania was on her way downstairs and put her arm around my waist.

'I'm tying up loose ends, Tania. This is my quitting day. I have been consigned to the "Safe and Sound" brigade and will be leaving about 4 p.m.'

'Well, that's lovely, sweetie. Don't look so worried, you are gonna be fine!'

Her beautiful, black face beamed at me and as she left me on the ground floor I breathed in the warm smell of vanilla for the last time.

I had half an hour to lay on the grass and read C.J.'s note before joining the others for lunch. I was really going to miss this place. Absently, I wondered if other care centres were as good as this one or did it all come down to how much private health insurance was at one's disposal.

I lay on the bench seat under the large oak tree and watched the breeze buffeting the rich green leaves above me.

Almost immediately, my little furry friends clicked their tongues and shimmied across the lawn towards me, jumping onto the bench and diving into my bag.

'Sorry, squirrel cousins, but I have no crisps today, so you'll have to go and forage somewhere else.' They were naughty thieves and continued to rummage the contents, not believing a word I had said.

'Tell you what, buzz off now and I'll bring you some cake after lunch.'

Of course, they totally understood 'human-speak' – *not*! I think they got the message and ran away.

I pulled my hat over my face to shield it from the sun and donned my sunglasses and began to read. He said:

I cannot stress how important it is that you follow these instructions to the letter. Managing all of this at a time when you have been so ill is asking a lot, but I shall support you and your family without deviating from the task. I am your invisible protector. These evil people have to be apprehended and I want you safe.

The cabbie is a Special Branch Officer and has performed this procedure many times. He will give you the package containing the *old* and the *new* passports and the four airline tickets to Ireland. Use him as if he was a genuine cab driver, taking you and your family to Gatwick Airport to go to Tenerife for your vacation.

Collect your Iberia tickets and go collectively to the Tenerife check-in, putting your two suitcases through and showing your *old* passports. When your flight is called, make sure the boys have their *new* passports and tickets (you must retain the *old* passports and tickets to Tenerife to be handed to my colleague later) and send them off to the *toilets* by the *Tie Rack shop*. They must go to the last two stalls, which will say *occupied*, put their foot under the door and they will be let in. The *older* boy must go to the *last* stall. Inside will be their *doppelgängers*, who will walk out as the Reeves boys to join their make-believe mum and sister to take the flight to Tenerife.

Jason and Sean will then change into their other clothes in their backpacks, storing the first set into their bags and exit the loos as *Connor* and *Liam Callaghan*.

They must try to act relaxed, being normal tourists, not attracting any suspicion. As they leave the area, *Declan Dennehy*, their dad for the day, will be waiting for them outside the toilets with an airport trolley stacked with suitcases. He'll take charge of them from then until they see you in Ireland.

Their flight to Dublin will be leaving twenty minutes after the Tenerife flight so they will go directly to the check-in and through Customs without any delay.

As the boys go off to the toilets, you and Rebecca will walk quickly into the *Body Shop* on the opposite side of the concourse, as if you have an important purchase to make before your flight. You will walk directly to the back of the shop and through the *Staff Only* door.

As you pass through the door, you will be met by two women: Mrs Reeves and Rebecca (the pretenders). You will hand over the *old* passports and tickets to the Tenerife flight and your wig to Mrs Reeves. She will wear the wig and, together with her daughter, will leave via the shop to catch the flight to Tenerife with her two sons. These four people will become the Reeves family, vacationing in Tenerife.

Another female colleague will give you both time to change into the clothes packed into your hand luggage and hand you two suitcases containing clothes purchased by this office on your behalf. Please accept my condolences on the choices made, but we did our best. She will then escort you to a walkway, which will lead you to the departure lounge for the Cork flight.

The flight is Ryanair and will be leaving fifteen minutes after the Dublin flight has departed. Go to the check-in desk and book in as normal with your *new* tickets and *new* passports and *new* suitcases. You are now officially: Mrs Amanda Callaghan and Miss Brodie Callaghan.

On arrival at Cork airport you will be met by one of our team, Patrick O'Leary. Unfortunately, I wasn't able to despatch his photo to you in time, but he will display a sign with your name as you go through Arrivals. He is five foot seven inches, thirty years old with dark-blond hair, skinny and scruffy.

He will drive you to your destination, where you will reunite with Connor, Liam and Declan Dennehy. Declan will fill you in on everything else. He will escort you to your new accommodation and stay with you as your personal bodyguard.

In explanation of the two flights, it was because we couldn't squeeze four of you on the same flight. I think it will actually benefit our cause, as anyone suspicious of your whereabouts will be looking for four travelling together.

That's all for now. I am your invisible protector, C.J. God speed.

I folded the paper and held it to my chest. I was still lying on the wooden bench and I closed my eyes beneath the dark glasses and sighed. As I read the words I tried to visualise the action. In forty-eight hours we would be in Ireland and apart from the Irish airport, I had no idea where our final destination would be.

It was a balmy day and after all the intense reading I was willing to succumb to the heat of the sun, but I needed to have some lunch and say a few farewells.

There weren't many patients around as I strolled across to the reception patio and I wondered if it was quiet here in July. Perhaps people didn't feel so stressed at this time of year. Sunshine is such a liberator.

I couldn't concentrate at lunch. I was no longer part of this pageant. We gathered around our usual table overlooking the courtyard and I attempted to join in the conversation, wishing I were lying in the sunshine, planning my future.

Petra looked strange. She had lost her lustre since the departure of Claire and Iain wasn't around either to antagonise her, and as for me, well, I couldn't be bothered to involve myself in her melancholy. Her mood swings were so drastic that I am sure it would have taken a magician to calculate the correct medication for her. She was a real loose cannon. When I told her that I was leaving that afternoon she hardly took any notice, just nodded and carried on eating. C'est la vie!

Chris was full of geniality and extravagant ideas and his new friend looked shell-shocked. If this man had been sent to the Abbey for peace and quiet, he would have to find another playmate, as Chris was suffocating him with anecdotes and exuberance. The man had the look of a child on his first day at school – lost! Alex was seated opposite me and I could tell he was following my gaze around the group. As my eyes locked on his, he grinned.

'You won't miss this, will you?' He was in my head!

'Is it that obvious, Alex? You and I are the last survivors of the

Musketeers! Today I will go and leave you here with this motley crew.'

'No problem! Do you know, I have tackled more in the last few weeks than I have done all year, I'm not afraid of myself any more. I don't always like what I discover, but I hope I won't be long behind you.' He seemed so positive and I believed he could succeed.

'Can we go and find a quiet spot in the garden, there's something I want to tell you.' I needed a sympathetic confidant and his sensitivity would bolster me. Dr Michael advised me to go with my intuition and the lights were at green.

'I'm fit, let's go!' He pulled out my chair and gave me his arm in mock chivalry.

I didn't look behind me as I left the dining room, it would remain etched in my memory, as would the cobbled courtyard, the ancient coach house and art studio. I would remember Ann Amery, at her gentlest, standing behind me, viewing the sad child in the painting of Françoise Le Fevre.

We strolled across the lawn to the shrubbery, deciding to sit among the trellises of roses. He chatted about his wife, Laura, and his little girl and his plans to redecorate the house. He said his job had been held open for him, but he had thoughts of a career change, something with less responsibility.

For the quiet guy, he was breaking the sound barrier. His face was alive and his body liberated. He had climbed the most difficult mountain and was still going.

'Hey, look at me, a virtual chatterbox. You certainly bring the best out in me, Angelica. I hope I don't fall apart when you are gone.'

'Mine isn't the credit, Alex, you did this yourself. If anything, I was just the catalyst.'

'OK, it's your turn now. I've already sensed that something crucial is about to happen, you are so alert and poised, ready for action. So tell me!'

I was relaxed, cosy and warm. We were sitting side by side and Alex had a protective arm around my shoulder and we were holding hands.

How much I told him I cannot recollect, but it was the easiest story ever told. I had thought long and hard and it was all in place.

He sat, silently, without moving as my lips spoke the words of my projected journey into a new life. I didn't reveal where the journey ended, that part had to go unsaid.

Eventually, I finished the story and we were still sitting in the same position. I looked down to see his fingers tracing lines on my hand and knew I had to break the spell.

'Well, that's it, that's what I wanted to tell you. What are you thinking?'

I turned to look into his face.

'I'm gobsmacked! I am up there, floating in a balloon! I know you have spoken the truth, but it's incredible, all you need is for James Bond to appear!' He spun around and grabbed both of my arms.

'How can you be so strong, so positive?'

'Alex, do you remember our first therapy sessions when you decided to join in? I cried and cried and cried, so lonely, so depressed and so afraid.'

'Yes, I remember.'

'Ann Amery, Boadicea, taught me to get angry and to use the burn, become the aggressor and not the victim. Well, I've *done it*! I am the stealthy tiger and I shall fight to save my litter. Those bloody bastards out there are going to lose. There is only one winner – *me*!'

My entire body was tingling with energy and right there and then I knew I was ready. I leapt to my feet and pulled Alex to his. He was stunned and speechless.

'Come on, let's run a few laps around the allotments!'

We wiggled through the 'Kissing Gate' and exploded onto the field like two seasoned athletes. It wasn't long before we were both gasping for breath, so we sat where we stood in the middle of the runner beans and raspberry canes, laughing at the top of our lungs.

The time had come to pack my belongings and reread all three pages of the letter from C.J. Alex left me at my door and walked along the corridor to his room, knowing I would see him when Jason came to collect me.

In the privacy of my room I wasn't quite so buoyant. This little box was my sanctuary, my perfect place for reflection and I was leaving it behind. Where would I run to and whom would I turn to when we had fled to Ireland? How long could I remain this tough? It's got to be for ever!

It didn't take long to pack my things into the case, so I had time to kill and a couple of errands to run. I popped downstairs to the office to sign my discharge papers and had a discreet perusal of the invoice that was about to be sent to my insurance company. It was unbelievable. It was costing them approximately £2500 per week, but I had to say it was worth every penny. I was *alive*!

Strangely enough, the sight of that bill boosted my morale; it made me feel important and zapped my spirit. Back in my room, I read and reread the letter until it became an indelible imprint in my head.

The photo of Declan Dennehy was just a portrait, so it gave me no idea of his stature. His hair was dark and thick, the type you could run your fingers through and hang on to. Behave! You hussy! No lewd thoughts, Angelica, but I was curious as to whether some dimples lurked under the designer stubble. Brr! Brr! Brr! Damned phone interrupting my romantic daydream!

'Hello, this is Angelica Reeves.' I waited and waited. 'Hello, is anyone there? Speak to me or I shall hang up!'

'Hello Angel, you have kept me waiting, so I thought I should teach you a lesson!' It was him, the Voice.

'How dare you call me Angel, my name is Mrs Reeves! Why do you keep phoning me? What do you want?'

'Don't you know Angel? I want you, just like Simon wants you and if you misbehave I shall *take* you, use you and *destroy* you! Bitch!'

'You *bastard*, you evil bastard, leave us alone!'

'Don't hang up, Angelica! Do you hear me? I am very angry with you. Why are you going to desert me to go to Tenerife? Ha! You didn't expect me to know, but I know everything. You should be at your husband's side, not running away.'

'It's none of your fucking business what I do!'

'My, my, my, temper, temper! I thought you were a *sad* pussy-cat, but you are really an *angry* lioness. I would love you to sink your claws in me!'

'You're sick! Get to the point! What do you want?' I was very near to screaming. His voice had changed, no longer slime, it had turned to ice.

'You are becoming irritating, but I shall tolerate this for the moment. I told you not to inform the police and you disobeyed me, no matter. Your police force is dim-witted, with slow feet and has no idea who or where I am. I shall be your shadow and they will never suspect.

'So have your holiday, Angelica, knowing that I am right behind you. Tell them that!' The line went dead.

Had I been speaking to my killer? Would this organisation actually kill four innocent people if John's testimony went against them? What did John know that was so incriminating? Did he know this man? No! I couldn't believe that. It couldn't be true. My head was pounding with so many unanswered questions. I have to tell C.J.!

I tipped my bag out on the bed and there it was, the mobile. C.J. was seconds away and I couldn't wait. I was useless with these things so with the instructions in my hand I turned it on and pressed C.J.'s number. It was ringing, success!

'Angelica, I'm here. Is there a problem?' His voice was terse and irritated.

'I'm sorry to bother you, Commander Johnson, but the Voice has called me and has scared the shit out of me! Oh, sorry!'

'Angelica, you are not to worry. We heard everything. He is very confident, but is bluffing. Trust me, in a little while you and your family will be safe. I am going now, so please be calm. Go about your business and don't forget to turn off the phone. You are not on your own, be confident!' And he was gone.

It's OK for him to say, be confident. What if he was in my shoes? I bet he wouldn't be so brave.

Be calm! Calm! Shit! If he heard everything then he must have heard my conversations with Simon. Oh, shit! I'm not very good at this game so I'll have to learn to be discreet. Call-boxes from now on or I shall have to buy myself a mobile. *Stop now*! If I think any more my brain will malfunction.

It was 3.30 p.m. and Jason would be arriving soon. I sprinted down the corridor to the nurses' station to find Tania. She was sitting on their dilapidated sofa drinking coffee.

'Tania, I've come to say goodbye and to thank you.'

She pushed herself up and placed her cup on the desk.

'That's lovely, my little Angelica. You have been no trouble at all. I wish they were all as good as you!' She folded me into her warm embrace and I relaxed against her for a second.

'Tania, did Dr Michael leave any medication for me?' I was embarrassed to ask but felt sure he would have given me something.

'Not as far as I know, but I'll have a look on your notes. Go and have a cup of tea in the lounge and I'll come to you in a moment.' She hustled me out of her room and I ended up outside Alex's room. I gave one tentative knock and the door sprung open.

'Hey, you! Were you waiting for me behind the door?' He just grinned.

'You caught me out. I was counting the minutes to our farewell.'

'Come and have a cuppa to seal our friendship, Alex. If we sit by the doors into the lounge I shall be able to see Jason as he rounds the stairs.'

We wandered into the lounge, took some tea and found a cosy couch by the doors. The room was having a makeover, with staff coming and going, their arms full of curtains and cushions. Evidently, an anonymous philanthropist had donated funding for both lounges. It resembled a vibrant market place with everyone pitching in.

I was so taken with the scene that I didn't realise Jason had arrived until I heard his voice.

'Hi, Mum. I've come to take you home.' My heart fluttered. Words could not describe how the sight of him affected me.

'I'm ready to go, darling. Do you remember Alex?'

We were all standing and smiling and not quite knowing what to do next. The men shook hands, I hugged Alex and we left him watching our departure.

Jason went directly to my room to collect my case and I went to see Tania. She gave me a small box of sleeping tablets, a letter from Dr Michael and a big hug.

Back in my room we checked that I had forgotten nothing,

closed the door to room 36 and sped down the stairs. All I wanted to do was – go.

The duty manager escorted us to the main door with much pontificating and well-wishing, but it was all flying over my head. I was in limbo. I tried not to look back. I had to have one last glimpse of room 10, where Dr Michael held court. Silently, I said goodbye. *Freedom*! It was the strangest feeling, a cocktail of elation and loss. It wasn't until we had pulled out of the driveway and into the lane running parallel to the woods that it registered how quiet Jason was.

'Jason, you're very subdued, is everything all right?' I was so wrapped up in my own emotions that I had neglected his.

'I need to pull over and talk to you Mum.'

He drove into the first lay-by and switched off the engine.

The face I saw then was the Jason who left months ago for America, staring eyes of rejection and a ghostly complexion of one who had much anxiety.

'What is it, Jay? You are frightening me.' He was facing forward and gripping the steering wheel. Suddenly, I thought of the Voice and wanted to vomit. Had that creature spoken to my son and planted a horrible fear in him?

'It's Dad, I didn't realise how serious things were and how depressed he is. I know I said I hated him, but I don't!' His voice caught in his throat and he desperately tried to keep in control and aggressively rubbed his hand across his eyes.

I dared not touch him as I knew the dam would break and he would be mortified, so I remained quiet and still and waited.

'I drove him to Gran's and we chatted about everything and nothing. Gran fussed around both of us and laid out a lovely salad lunch in the greenhouse. It was just like old times, sitting among the strawberries and tomato plants with that overpowering "green" smell that made you cough.'

He stopped again to focus on what he was going to say next. Whatever came out would devastate him, hearing the words coming from his own mouth and admitting how overwhelmed with sadness he was.

The silence was tearing down my defences. My heart said, hold him and comfort him, but the next throw of the dice was his.

'I can't look at you, Mum, 'cos I know I'll fold, but I have to say this and I know it will set me free.'

'It's OK, Jay, take your time, I understand.' I listened to his intake of breath and watched his knuckles whiten.

'Dad told me so much that I didn't know. It was as if he had accepted that I had grown up. He told me he loved me – and always had – but he was jealous of *me* because you loved me more than him – Oh! Hell!'

The sob had been growing in his stomach for years and was now a living entity, as it belched from his throat, spraying droplets of moisture on the windscreen. Nothing on earth could have stopped the outpouring of grief that followed. He lay across my lap and cried until it was finished.

We didn't move, we had become one being, a huge mound of human emotion. Eventually, he lifted his head, calm but exhausted.

'Oh, Mum, what a mess! Don't look so sad, I'm OK now. The revelation was such a shock, but I feel weightless now, sort of free!'

He readjusted himself behind the wheel and smiled. I told myself not to be fanciful, but he looked as if he was glowing.

'Wouldn't you rather I drove, Jay?'

'No, I'm fine, I mean really fine!'

His face was red and blotchy and I wasn't going to rain on his parade and tell him that he didn't look fine. He pulled back onto the lane and headed for home.

'Are Becca and Sean at home?'

'Yeah, I think so. The mobile is in the glove compartment, why don't you give them a call!'

I phoned and had two of them trying to talk at once, so excited at my re-entry into the Reeves' world. Sean suggested that we stop off and get a Chinese takeaway, which suited my plan admirably.

Tonight they had to discover the truth about the demise of the Reeves family. There was no going back and no more time to wait. I looked across at the profile of my firstborn and said a silent prayer of thanks. He had made his peace with his father just in time. Thankfully, John had admitted his involvement with this crime syndicate and how merciless they could be.

Jason drove immaculately, keeping his eyes on the mirrors and not racing as most of his gang did. He was in his own world, probably chewing over the talk with his Dad and trying to make sense of it all. I was orchestrating tonight's scene in my mind.

They had to understand the need for flight and accept it. This was going to be the hardest test they would ever have to face because we could not fail. Success had to be one hundred per cent.

I remembered the forming of the Musketeers at the Abbey and the code they used in the movies, 'United we stand, divided we fall', but we were not about to fall because that could mean that we would die.

'Mum, I understand now why you became so ill; it couldn't have been easy for you trying to keep our heads above water. Dad is sorry, you know, he said he got sucked in and in the end there was no way out. He knows he is going down. Do you think it will be for very long?'

'I don't know Jason. I haven't had any dealings with the solicitors or barristers as I have no knowledge of the law. A little scaly snake of a man was allocated to your dad in the beginning. He used his guile and cunning to extort a massive amount from your dad and then he was kicked into touch and someone recommended the firm of solicitors in Lincoln's Inn which your dad is using now. I have read most of the pre-trial documents, but it's all gobbledygook to me.'

'Here we are, the Soup Dragon. Shall we go in? I'll park on the pavement.'

My first thought, as we arrived home, was to phone John. His Mother was treating him like her favourite son for the first time in his life and at a time when he needed to be cosseted. My guilt at neglecting him weighed heavily, but it was a burden I had to bear. Perhaps that is why we drifted apart, my priority was the family unit and John's was to have the most prosperous import agency in London.

We chatted like old friends – how sad that we couldn't do it face to face. All too soon mother-in-law called his name loudly, which interrupted our conversation and made us both laugh. It was time for dinner and she had to be obeyed. We said goodbye and I wished him good luck! I meant it too. I had no idea what his defence would be or if he would name names; that information was strictly confidential. That would be the last time I spoke to my husband for many years.

The twins were thrashing about in the pool with some of their mates. When they saw me, Sean blew me a kiss and Rebecca insisted on soaking me with a very welcome wet hug. Their gang accepted that I was home again and ignored my existence, as teenagers do until they want feeding. The dogs went berserk, as usual, eventually calming down and resuming their play-fighting.

I sat on the step to watch for a while. It was humid and the air was heavy and oppressive. The sun was deep red and the sky was such a dense blue it appeared to be painted. I needed a cool drink and time in the shade to plan my strategy for tonight.

Jason piled the boxes of Chinese food into the oven, ready to be reheated in the microwave later. Miraculously, the house was clean and tidy, ready to be camouflaged by dust covers. I heard Jason singing to himself as he started to lay the table for tonight.

On the pretext of keeping cool, I wandered down to the old stables, which were used as storage sheds, and found the carrier boxes for the cats. They would have to be brought up to the house at the last minute, as the sight of them would freak out the cats.

It was a quarter to six and I heard a chorus of voices call out, 'Bye Mrs Reeves! Nice to see you again.' I opened the front door and waved to the crowd as they passed by the house. I looked through the lobby window and saw that the pool was empty, so assumed that the twins were showering.

The phone rang.

'Hello!'

'Nice to see the young ones enjoying themselves, Angelica. How I have missed your naked body!'

'*Scum*! Leave me alone!' I screamed.

The Voice laughed and hung up. Jason was by my side with a face like thunder.

'Was that *him* again? I tell you if I get hold of him I'll *kill* him!' He held me tightly and nuzzled his face in my hair.

'He'll get a shock sooner than he thinks, don't you worry.

Let's open some lager, put on some funky music and eat!'

He looked thoughtful, but had obviously decided not to follow up my remark.

The meal was a blast, like a re-enactment of happier times. We were all devotees of American soul music and R & B and creative exhibitionists on the disco floor. The empty food boxes were dumped in the trash, the candles lit and the lights extinguished. We bopped, shimmied and rocked as the music pumped up in volume.

My chance arrived to test their reaction to the holiday when Sean was replacing the CDs on the deck.

'Before we resume our wild dancing, I've got a surprise for you.'

Three pairs of eyes focused on me with suspicion and dread, each read, 'What now!'

'It's OK! It's a spontaneous, fantastic holiday and we leave the day after tomorrow!' Their reactions were in slow motion. They looked from one to the other, searching for a lead.

'Well, say something!' My heart lurched.

Rebecca broke the silence and screamed, 'Yippee! Where?'

Then there was an avalanche of questions. The consensus of opinion was, they were all in favour of it, but felt sorry that John wouldn't be there too. To heighten their enthusiasm I told them that we would go out the next day with Georgina, their absolutely fabulous adopted auntie, to buy expensive new gear and have lunch at McDonald's.

So far so good, a lie of sorts, but I needed them to be happy and receptive when I dropped Ireland in the frame.

'As it is still very muggy, shall we have a late swim then cover the pool to keep it clean while we are away?' Anything I suggested at that moment was fine as they had the holiday on their minds.

The dogs were settled down for the night, so we snuffed out the candles and danced in procession to the pool-house. The cats resented our intrusion as they lodged there at night and we had disturbed their slumber. They flew through the open window with much hissing and bad humour.

The swim was short but necessary. Jason supervised the fastening down of the pool cover and we tidied away the garden furniture. He kept giving me surreptitious glances, with an enquiring wag of his head. Something else was going on and he had decided to wait and see.

The lights in the ceiling of the pool-house could be regulated and we decided to dip them as low as possible and round off the evening with a game of 'True Confessions'. This was a game we had played for years. I invented it as a way of letting them talk, uninterrupted, to ease any difficult problems they were experiencing. It was always a success and great fun.

'Shall we sit on cushions on the floor making a boat?' Rebecca loved to organise the game and usually had her way.

'Oh yes, let's! Shall we?' Sean took the mickey and got royally thumped for it. I sat at the stern with my back against the wall, Jason sat between my legs, Rebecca sat between his and Sean sat at the prow of our human boat. We clung to each other with our knees, giggling and singing, *Row, row, row your boat gently down the stream.*

'Right! Who goes first?' Jay was ready for action.

'Me, I'm the front man and then we can go backwards to Mum!' Sean led off the game with his confession.

'Do you remember about six years ago when the garage was being built and was surrounded by scaffolding?'

'Yes!' We all replied.

'Well, Johnny and I climbed to the top, with Lawrence making hard work of it, as he was a wimp. I needed a leak and by accident sprayed Lawrence down below. He ran home, crying, and told his mum. She came up and tore me off a strip and ranted at Mum, saying that I did it on purpose and I was disgusting.'

'Yes?' We all enquired.

'Well, she was right, I aimed, fired and scored a direct hit, leaving Lawrence drenched with pee! Ha! Ha!'

Poor Lawrence! We rocked with laughter, gradually quieting for the telling of Rebecca's confession.

'Mine is clean compared with Sean's. Do you remember when I went to the stables to uncover Timothy, after hibernation, and we were surprised to find that the box was empty.'

'Yes, I do! We hunted all over the garden and never found him. You cried for ages, so I took you on my bike to get an ice cream.' Jay was intrigued.

'Well, Sarah and I had already found that he was awake, so we gave him an outing to the big chestnut tree and while we were building our camp he went missing. I am so sorry, I lost him!'

She peeped round at Jay, looking very shame-faced. He ruffled her hair, clicking his tongue and we all pretended to be miffed. Jason broke the chain, stood up and trotted off.

'Won't be a minute, I need the loo.'

'Becca, you little rascal. Do you know I nearly bought you another tortoise, but something stopped me.' I did remember feeling oddly suspicious at the time.

Jason was back and the boat was reformed.

'OK, my confession is next, but before I tell it I want to apologise to Mum. Sorry, Mum!' He squeezed my knees.

'About three years ago, when I was on holiday from boarding school, we had a few friends round for a swim. Mum was out shopping and Dad was at work, so I was in charge. One of Becca's mates had the hots for me, so I devised a plan to keep you occupied while we snogged in the pool-house.'

'Who was it, Jay, not Tacky Tina?' Becca was wide-eyed in disbelief.

"Fraid so! While you lot were swimming a relay race we sneaked inside. It was going to be a quick snog, but she tore off my trunks and seduced me!' He was convulsed in laughter.

'Urgh! Jason! She is a slapper and she's pregnant too!'

'Well, it can't be mine unless she is an elephant!'

'Do you know, I knew it all along. I came back from shopping and found you fighting to put your trunks on and Tina, all pink and flushed, coming out of the loo. Hey, this is too much information for me, Jay, but thanks for the apology.' The room was alive with warmth and humour and my confession was due.

'OK, it's my turn now, but I want to change the venue. Let's go outside, it's become very hot in here.'

Everyone agreed and followed me outside, sitting beside me with our backs against the wall.

'I want to tell the whole story without interruption, if that's OK?' An air of expectancy hung over them and they sat like statues.

'Tonight I told a big, fat lie, not for gain or mischief, but to pave the way for the here and now. You are all aware that only a miracle could save your father from prison. Sean and Rebecca have lived through the arrest, the disgrace of John being on remand in the Scrubs and my collapse. Jason has now been told about most of the nightmares by me, and today, by your dad, and he too has witnessed the fear inflicted by a call from the Voice. As the day of the trial gets closer so our lives are put at risk because of what your father might say. I am not going to overdramatise the situation, but our lives are under threat. As from yesterday we are on the police protection programme.

'I have a letter from Commander Johnson of the Special Branch, which you will all have to read and know in intimate detail. This evil creature, who we have named the Voice, is in fact a hit man for the organisation which has laundered money through your father's company. He has bugged our home, tapped our phone and followed us since your dad's arrest and we have to escape to be free. The holiday to Tenerife is a sham; in fact we are being relocated to Ireland. In two days' time our names will change from Reeves to Callaghan.'

Not a word had been uttered, not a body had moved – my little gang was motionless. We were sitting side by side, still holding hands, staring out across the covered pool. I looked to the sky where the moon shone gold and the face on the moon smiled in sympathy.

Rebecca was the first to break contact and came to sit on my lap. Sean and Jason grew closer and hugged each other. I thought how lucky we were. Blood is strong and love is invincible and we had both. Jason pushed his hand through my arm and Sean slid round to the other side of me and did the same. Still no word was spoken. I had provoked thoughts and disturbed buried memories, blotted out by choice and now their minds were a battlefield.

Sean broke the silence, his decision made.

'So when do we read the letter, Mum? I want to know what my new name is? I do get a new name, don't I?' He squeezed my arm.

'Mum, I'm not going to make a fuss either. We have to go, I know, it doesn't have to be for ever.' Becca kissed me, smiled and twiddled a strand of my hair.

'And what about you, Jason?' I had to know.

'The only problem for me is that Ireland is full of the Irish! Seriously, I'm cool! Don't fret, Mum, we'll give them a run for their money! I didn't tell you before, but I have actually stood beside a young boy who had been shot in the head for being in the wrong place. Uncle Toby said that it happens all the time!' He stood up then and one by one pulled us to our feet.

'Mum, is that why you brought us outside, because you think that the pool-house is bugged?'

'Jason, I don't know, but we cannot afford to take chances. Let's go indoors, turn the music up nice and loud and you can all read the letter. I'm sorry, but from now until we fly there can be no more friends dropping in as we can't jeopardise our plans.'

'That's OK, we understand.' Spoken in chorus.

I couldn't quite believe how well they had taken the news. It hadn't really sunk in and I decided to sleep in Becca's room that night as we would both need the comfort.

'How about Robert Palmer, a session of pumping, raunchy rock!' Jason organised the music and I went to fetch the letter.

Rebecca chose to close the curtains just in case the Voice was viewing us from the woods. When I returned she whispered in my ear, 'Do you think it could be that bloke with the white hair, the one we saw in the woods?'

'It had crossed my mind, Becca, but I can't be sure!' I said it in a normal voice, so she placed a finger across her lips in warning. Hastily, I jotted down a message explaining that we must talk normally to allay any suspicion unless we are referring to our escape. They all understood. In turn they read the letter from C.J. and suddenly it had become an adventure.

Before someone panicked about the animals I told them that Georgie had volunteered to look after them while we were on holiday, so we must bring her back some Duty Free. They agreed that it was a great idea, knowing that it could be a long time before we returned. I think they trusted that I would work some kind of miracle that would reunite us with our pets. Georgie knew nothing of this plan, but she and Charlie would accommodate them for as long as it took. I knew this without a doubt.

Jason pointed to his new name and said.

'Hey Mum, that's really ace, in fact I like it!' He strutted around the lounge mouthing, 'Hello, my name is Connor Callaghan.'

Sean started to play the game too.

'Do I look like one of them?' He pointed to 'Liam', his new name.

'Honey, you can be anything you want, even a movie star!'

'Oh Mum, don't say that, he already thinks he is better than Michael Jackson! Will you just listen to this track, I love it!' And she pointed to 'Brodie' while swinging her hips and blowing me kisses.

She had found the photo of Declan Dennehy and held it possessively against her heart.

'I think I'm in love Mum, what shall I do?'

'Pick on someone nearer your age, darling! I think a George Clooney lookalike is out of your league.'

The tension had evaporated and the music had become far too loud. We dimmed the lights and put on the TV, huddling together, holding hands on the settee. No foreign cretin could beat us, we were of *one* mind.

Rebecca wouldn't let go of Declan's photo, much to the amusement of her brothers. Sean nudged Jason, pointing to the passage in the letter when they first meet Declan.

'Look and weep, sister dear, that one is ours!' They guffawed and she handed over the photo, reluctantly, shrugging her shoulders in defeat.

'OK, you win, but my time will come!'

'Can I share your room tonight, Becca? Perhaps you two boys could put my bed in there for me now?'

'That's great! We can plan what clothes we shall buy tomorrow. Let's do it now, this film is really boring.' She was up the stairs in a flash.

The boys leapt up behind her and had transported my bed across the landing before I had switched off all the lights and closed the doors downstairs.

Becca had every intention to chat into the wee small hours, but with all the excitement sleep took hold of her almost immediately. I tiptoed to Sean's room to find that they had dragged their beds together and were discussing the letter, with the aid of a torch, under the covers.

'Enough is enough, fellas, we have got a busy day tomorrow and there'll be plenty of time to plan your wardrobe.' I hugged them and crept back to my bed. Thankfully, I was too tired to think any more and gratefully went straight to sleep.

Chapter Twenty

Something was ringing in my head and absently I stretched out my arm to stop the alarm. No! It couldn't be the alarm, I don't have one, it was the phone!

Jason had rescued it before it stopped ringing and I could hear him talking. He shouted for Sean and Rebecca, so I deduced that it was John. I prayed that they would remember not to mention the holiday, as it would distress him and blow our cover. I had said my goodbye yesterday and now it was their turn to wish him good luck.

I ignored the chatter from below and focused on the window. The weather had changed. I sat up in bed, hugging my knees, and watched the white clouds scudding across the sky at breakneck speed. There was no time for reminiscing as there was too much to do.

Everyone fought for the shower and we were dressed and ready to go walkies by 10 a.m. Talk was stilted and limited until we reached the shelter of the wood and the dogs bounded off. Jason had C.J.'s letter in his pocket and handed it around once he had reread it. He suggested that we each made copies of our individual shopping requirements, so that the original letter could be kept by me somewhere safe.

I stressed that Georgie must not know anything about Ireland and that I would explain that we might be away for some time incommunicado. All they had to do was enjoy the day and spend, spend, spend! We must look upon the exodus to Ireland as a fabulous episode of discovery.

There was electricity between the three siblings, a bond as indivisible as an invisible umbilical cord. I was amazed at their resilience. They chatted and giggled and chased the dogs through the bracken and the undergrowth, daring each other to explore new paths. Poor little Snoopy kept retracing her steps as the prickly thorns clung to her long hair, impeding her progress, so she finally sat in the middle of the track with her eyes bulging and tongue hanging out, waiting for me to lift her up into my arms.

I was startled by the noise of a sharp crack, sounding like a heavy branch being snapped. Ahead of me the Dalmatians heard it too, bounding out of cover and decreasing the distance between us to stand at my side, both alert and sniffing the air inquisitively.

'Where are you all?' I felt uneasy.

'Coming Mum, Becca has got tangled up in the bracken!' That was Jason's voice and not too far away.

The hairs stood erect on the back of my neck. I spun around and there in the distance was the large boxer dog, sitting on the pathway, staring at me. He was motionless, like a statue. Why was he alone? Where was the white-haired man?

My dogs would normally run off in pursuit, either to play or attack; instead they stood rooted to the spot. Were they afraid of the dog? Did they sense that I had to be protected?

'Back safe and sound! Are we going back?' They were all breathless and still laughing.

'Yes! It's almost 11 a.m. and Georgie could be waiting for us.' I turned around, expecting to see the boxer, but it had vanished. It wasn't my imagination, I was sure of that.

We had less than twenty-four hours to go and nothing must interfere with the plan. We jogged back to the house and settled the dogs into their room next to the kitchen. Georgie hadn't arrived, which gave us time to freshen up and make out our clothes lists.

The Shogun scrunched on the stones of the driveway, followed by a short blast of the horn. Georgie had arrived. There were hugs and kisses and a brief argument as to who would sit where and we were off to town.

First stop was the bank, where I withdrew £5000 to tide us over. The cashier was concerned at such a large withdrawal until I explained that we were going on a spontaneous holiday. Have cash will travel! She automatically gave me an updated statement, which confirmed that I had enough capital to pay all of my direct debits for a while. Thank Heavens for the 'flexible friend'; at least that was one way I could obtain money without arousing suspicions. All the time I was crossing the t's and dotting the i's, I didn't have time to worry.

It was supposed to be a characteristic of the Taurean, excellence in money matters, along with dependability, endurance and most importantly – *lust*! Slip of the tongue, I meant – *love*! Today, the Taurean Temptress was hibernating until her Pirate Buccaneer walked from the sea.

Directly we trundled out of the bank the gang chorused – 'Show me the *money*!' Thankfully, Georgie took control, grabbed Sean's ear, spun him around and kissed him full on the lips. We were gobsmacked and naturally burst out laughing.

'Well, that put a stop to your antics, didn't it!' She was as naughty as ever and Sean blushed scarlet.

'OK! Back to the car, next stop Blue Water Park and lots of shopping!' I was actually looking forward to it too.

Once we had arrived and parked we decided to stay together, tramping from; The Levi Shop to Diesel, Gap and Next. Surreptitiously, my cubs consulted their lists when I had guided Georgie to another part of the shop.

The Levi Shop provided new Nike trainers for each of us, blue jeans for three and white Levis for me.

They selected matching jean jackets and I took a heavy white and navy Levi sweatshirt, everything was strictly in accordance with C.J.'s description.

Gap was next, where Rebecca managed to get a bright red baseball cap, so far so good, but the boys struck out. Diesel was *the* shop for the lads and each bought a very expensive short sweat-top in navy, with the logo – that was imperative. Jason found his NY khaki baseball cap but no luck for Sean.

'That's OK! I can use my old Chelsea cap and with the difference accrued I can have an *extra* pair of boxers from Next!' he said with a flourish. Georgie couldn't contain herself, she was champing at the bit to dive into Zuggi, which needed no encouragement as I loved the shop too. A quick glance disappointingly revealed a mediocre range so we jumped across the aisle to Jane Norman and spent a fortune.

Red was like a magnet to Rebecca and she chose a gorgeous stretch top, which clung to her petite body, my little Aphrodite in waiting. I had seen a white lycra body adorned with silver and gold threads, which leapt into my hands, so I had to have it. As for

Georgie, well! She had Charlie's card and had been instructed to have fun, so she went berserk. After half an hour she walked from the shop, lighter by nearly £250, and she was ecstatic!

Down one level and we found the boys in Next, chatting to Andrew, who was an assistant manager. He and Jason had been friends since primary school, even though he was a year older than Jason. Andrew worked his way through the local education system and Jason went off to boarding school, but they always kept in touch. He was a natural salesman with plenty of charm and the gift of the gab.

By 2.15 p.m. we were finished and exhausted. A table at McDonald's became vacant as we crossed the threshold and lovely Georgie wanted it to be her treat. We came and saw and spent, extravagantly. It had been exceptional therapy.

On the way back to town the kids asked to be dropped off at the house – accompanying the oldies to the hairdressers would be too boring. It was great intuition on their part as it afforded me the opportunity to have an intimate heart-to-heart with Georgie. Sometimes, without any effort, plans slip into place.

Unfortunately, it had become quite chilly; today the sun was sulking behind closed skies. My brood jumped from the car to the front door just as the first drops of rain hit the windscreen. Georgina put the Shogun into fast mode as we now had only twenty minutes to plant bums on seats at Beyond the Fringe. Luckily for us the traffic was light and parking was easy and we arrived with a few minutes to spare.

Beyond the Fringe was in the hub of town and was frequented by many visiting thespians to the Orchard Theatre. To describe Ricardo as a drama queen would have been a trifle harsh, but his studio was definitely his stage.

He was dressed in white silk strides and a very tightly fitted crop top in crêpe silk, exposing a stunning diamond pinned through his navel. Understated was not a word one could use to describe Ricardo or his wardrobe and we loved him for it. He glided over to greet me with kisses that didn't quite touch my face and ferried me to his inspection mirror.

Georgie was lavishly greeted by Poppy, who was as tiny as Ricardo was tall. She had vibrant red hair and lips to match and made a striking contrast to her boss. She seated Georgie at an adjacent mirror.

As it was the end of the day we had the studio to ourselves, which was a blessing. I beckoned for Ricardo to come closer and spoke quietly into his ear, hoping that he would not scream when I told him what I wanted him to do.

'Oh, lovey! It will be my *pièce de résistance*! Let's get you washed!' He was thrilled. I hadn't yet told Georgie about having my hair cut off, or about the holiday which wasn't to be, I was waiting for the right time and it had arrived.

We were seated side by side at the sinks, being draped in coveralls and towels and plied with freshly perked coffee. The juniors were ready to plunge our heads backwards, when I asked for five minutes to drink our coffee. No problem! They made themselves scarce and Ricardo called out to us.

'It's OK, darlings, I'm having a quick fag!' Georgie knew me so well. She swung her seat around to face me and carried on sipping her drink and waited. If you could be closer than sisters and more telepathic than twins then that was the kind of understanding we had. She may have disguised herself as the 'dizzy' one, but as I told her the truth (all except Ireland) she didn't flinch, just smiled, patted my hand and said.

'Darling, don't worry about a thing, and I'm speaking for Charlie and me, we'll tidy the house and check the grounds and take good care of the animals. If you are going at 5.30 a.m. then we'll be around by 7 a.m. with the horsebox to take the menagerie back to the farm. They can all live in the old summerhouse for the time being, so that they don't get lonely!'

I wanted to hug her and was very near to tears, but managed to hold it together, as long as I didn't open my mouth until I had my emotions under control.

'Georgina, you are so wonderful! How will I ever be able to thank you and Charlie? You must take this as a token for now!' I had folded £1000 into a bank deposit envelope and I pushed it into her hands. She didn't protest as she understood how proud and stubborn I could be. This was a very necessary gift or prepayment, whichever way one looked at it.

'Ladies, are we done? My creative juices are becoming addled! I cannot work if I am feeling fractious!'

'Sorry, Ricardo, just one more thing and you can let your scissor hands loose! Do you still have the collection of wigs from the Orchard Theatre?'

'Absolutely darling! Where else would they acquire such artistry and perfection and get them cleaned for nothing? Is there an ulterior motive for this question? Tell me please!' He was clasping his hands and hopping from one foot to the other.

'Do you think you might have something similar to my hairstyle as it is now? It is really important, Ricardo!'

'What! Like a French poodle! It is so necessary for you to get with it, darling, this is so passé!' He pulled at my curls, snapping the band which held the topknot aloft and tussling the hair as it fell to my shoulders.

'I will find something and create a masterpiece while you are being shampooed. It might not be the exact colour, but I shall do my best. Can I ask why you want it or is it a secret?'

'It's a safeguard Ricardo, in case I hate what you are about to do to me!' I giggled and held my face in my hands.

'Bitch! I'll make you eat your words!' He loved games and flounced off to the back room to rummage through the boxes of wigs.

By the time we were seated at the stylists' mirrors, with our second cup of coffee, Ricardo appeared with the 'poodle wig'. It was perfect and at last I could relax a little. He had even tied it into a topknot, mimicking my own hairstyle.

'Ricardo you are a magician, thank you!'

He tossed the wig to one side and approached my chair with a glint in his eyes.

'Now we shall see what mischief or genius I can invent.'

Poppy had already begun to sculpt Georgina's thick, black hair and the cut needed to be perfect. With time to kill Georgie decided to have a manicure too, as she watched my transformation with wonder.

An hour after the first snip Ricardo's creation was complete. I watched silently as each length of hair fell to the floor, trying to envisage my new look and feeling terribly empty. My tresses had been part of me for most of my life, I suppose my hair was my security blanket, my camouflage.

A stranger was peering at me through the mirror and I felt quite weird, I looked about fifteen years old. The transformation was incredible, my hair was so much darker at the roots, resembling liquid chocolate. My reaction was displeasing to Ricardo's sensibilities so he went into raptures of exaggerated pleasure.

'Voila! Aren't you gorgeous! Isn't it spectacular!' His arms were stretched out, overcome with enthusiasm and I was stupefied. Thankfully, Georgie rescued me.

'Angelica, you look like a sixties Mod, all adolescent and inviting!' She was desperately searching for words of comfort, which gave me time to find my tongue.

'I am overwhelmed with surprise, Ricardo. It suits me, I think!'

He swivelled my chair in every conceivable direction, catching a reflection in each mirror.

'Well?' He was standing in front of me with his hands on his hips.

'I do like it, really I do, it's perfect, but to engage the element of surprise I have to put this on.' I grabbed the wig from Georgie and pulled it over my newly fashioned curls.

'You are so hurtful, crazy, after all my hard work! Angelica, I thought you were so sweet, but you're not! I hate you now, I really *do*!' Poor Ricardo was devastated and wanted me out of his sight. He disappeared into the back of the studio without a backward glance.

Hastily, we paid our bills and ran back to the car, dodging the puddles and holding our bags over our heads. Georgie had found time to inspect the contents of the envelope and it wasn't long before she asked that very important question.

'You're not going away for just a couple of weeks, are you?' The car was stationary at some traffic lights and she briefly looked my way.

'No! It will probably be more like months. I am so ashamed that I haven't been honest with you but I am trying to lessen the risk of your involvement.'

She was motoring again and I watched the movement of the windscreen wipers, which helped to calm my palpitations.

'Tonight we have planned to write letters of explanation to our nearest and dearest, hoping that we will be understood and forgiven for any deceit. Being so close to you makes this even harder because there is so much that I cannot tell you – not yet!' I was fumbling for words of defence and wanting to reveal everything.

'Don't fret, there is nothing to forgive. I know that you are going through a desperate ordeal and you *will* fight your way through it! I'm not going to stir the mud but I *am* going to be there for you!' I touched her hand on the steering wheel.

'Thanks, friend!'

We had arrived at the house, she swung into the drive and pulled up by the front doors, she turned to me, smiled and hugged me.

'Go with my blessing – and Charlie's – take care and let me know that you are safe. I love you! Now get out before I cry!' She shoved me out of the car and drove off.

The entrance lights had flicked on and I was standing in the floodlights. Rebecca threw the door open wide, then looked disappointed as she was expecting to see something very different. Hurriedly, I pressed my fingers on my lips as she exclaimed.

'Oh, Mother, you are finally here!' She nodded that she understood, approached me and whispered.

'Luckily you did that 'cos I nearly let the cat out of the bag. I'll be glad to be away from here, where I don't have to keep watching what I say.' She yanked me into the downstairs bathroom and pulled off my wig.

'Oh my! I can't believe it, you are so *cool!*' She made me sit on the lid of the loo and ran out to fetch the boys.

While she was away I fluffed at my hair in the mirror and was amazed at how silky it felt. In fact it was quite cute. I *did* resemble a sixties chick, with tiny flat curls, wild eyes and pouting lips.

The boys' reactions were hilarious, rolling around like round-bottomed weebles, with much hip wiggling and lip smacking.

'OK! OK! OK! My mischievous little cubs, it's not that funny. Let's go and get some dinner. This' – and I pointed to my head – 'may be the cutting edge, but I can make it disappear with a magic illusionary trick!' I winked at them and replaced the wig, reverting to the 'old' me.

'That's very effective, Mum, so how about some food!' Jason circled his arms around me, kissing my cheek.

We worked in harmony, talking about the bogus holiday, our packing and how soon we should go to bed in order to be awake by 4.45 a.m. and away by 5.30 a.m. My light-hearted attitude was wearing thin but not yet transparent. They had relieved my workload by organising and packing all the dog and cat requisites in labelled boxes and Sean had retrieved from the stables the travelling boxes for the cats. One more item to cross off the list.

The kitchen was bright and homely and the best place to unwind. I picked at the salad bowl and pasta and the frivolous conversation ebbed and flowed. A shoebox sat in the centre of the table into which a pile of envelopes addressed to their friends and to John had been put. All I had to do was add mine.

Something began to creep up on me and I couldn't fend it off. A corset was being pulled tighter and tighter, choking my breath, as the panic insinuated itself into my blood. Perhaps, like Samson, my strength had disappeared with my tresses.

Please, not now! This was the wrong time for the gremlins to attack. The banter of the kids was banging in my head and I knew I was losing it! Their faces grew large and their speech was slow and slurred. Blankness took over.

'Come on Mum! That's it, open your eyes!' I was sitting, slumped between Jason's legs on the floor, with my head between my knees. My wig, like a dead rat, was sitting in front of me. Rebecca was kneeling by my side, holding a cold dishcloth to my head and Sean was keeping the dogs from licking me to death.

'Whew, what happened then?' I didn't even try to get up.

'Let's stand up and walk into the cool of the conservatory. I think you just overdid it today.' I crammed the wig back in place as Jason helped me to my feet and we walked across the garden room to the glass doors, which overlooked the lawn.

'I am so sorry, I think I am tired. It has been a stressful week, I'm fine.'

'Look Mum, we are all set to go. You have nothing to worry about, the cases are packed (with rubbish) and we have put our special things in our backpacks,' Rebecca whispered to me in her softest tone.

Meanwhile, Sean put the dogs to bed and killed all the lights except the low lights in the lounge and in the hall. He drew the curtains and put on some mystical music and I could sense the fear retreating as my body rebuilt itself.

On his way back to the garden room the phone rang, so he detoured and answered it. He smiled, putting his hand over the mouthpiece.

'It's Dad. He wants to say goodnight to us!'

That was what I needed, to realise how lucky I was and how unlucky it was to be John.

'Hi, John! All the best for tomorrow! We'll be thinking of you, take care, we all love you!' The receiver was ripped from my hand and passed from one to the other.

I left them and went to the study to find paper and pen to write my letters. I realised it was the tormenting thoughts that sent me squiffy and I had to master this or keep going under. The doors were open, back in the garden room and the rain had stopped. One by one the gang joined me and we sat, quietly, locked into our own space, planning the first encounter of our Irish adventure.

'Anyone for a hot drink before bed?' Becca had volunteered and four drinks arrived on a tray.

The notepad and pen sat alone on the coffee table, so with determination I wrote my letters and put them with the others. The people who needed to know how to contact us would receive a letter and hopefully in a roundabout way we would eventually hear from them. The apology to John was the most difficult, but it was done.

The discipline of writing out my thoughts was the final spoonful of medicine needed to sharpen my resolve. *I was back*!

'Brr! Brr! Brr!' The phone broke the silence.

'That's gonna be for me!' Jason was eager and hopeful. Who did he think it would be?

'It's for you! I haven't a clue who it is?' He handed the phone to me and wandered into the kitchen.

'Hello Angel, I can't see you. Why have you closed the curtains? I'll have you in the end. You will be *naked* and you will *scream*!' The Voice slimed and purred. I could smell the stench of his breath in my throat.

'You are *evil* and *pathetic* and you will rot in *Hell*! You're *scum*! Do you hear me, *scum*!' I wanted this man to die.

'Don't be stupid, Angelica, or I might have to make you regret it. I shall enjoy taking you very, very soon. I am following you!' He finished with a sarcastic, high-pitched laugh and hung up.

They were all staring at me. They knew who the caller was.

'I wish I was Bronson or McQueen and I'd cut that bloke's guts out and stuff them back in his mouth.' Sean was so angry that his face was white. That evil creature had sparked and kindled an inner aggression in him that I hoped I would never see again.

'The *bastard*! Come on, Sean, we know the woods blindfolded. Let's take a look at the old cottage. I bet he's in there!' Bless him, Jason was suddenly an all-action hero about to steam in and slay the villain.

'Hold it, you two supermen! Just think a minute. You don't know who this horror of a man is! You don't know where he is and there might be a gang of them! Tomorrow we are going on holiday and animals like him cannot haunt us for ever! We are all tired and there is nothing more to do. Vermin like *him* will go to Hell, hopefully it will be a Hell on earth, a spectator sport and we can watch *him* burn.'

'You're right, Mum! Someone will get him one day.' Jason and Sean slapped hands in a high five.

'Right now we must go and get some sleep. It's going to be a long day tomorrow.' I took Becca's hand and we climbed the stairs. The stress of the day had worn us out.

Chapter Twenty-One

The morning arrived all too soon. Surely it couldn't be that time. My head was thumping. I still had vivid memories of the indecent call I received from the Voice and the hostile reaction it created in my sons. Rebecca's face peeped out from under her duvet and she grimaced, she was half asleep. I could hear coughing from next door and the shuffling of feet as someone guided themselves to the bathroom.

I used the master bedroom en suite, making a farewell visit to my white and gold Greek temple. Ablutions complete and wig in place I descended to the kitchen, creeping past the dogs' door, as I was reluctant to disturb them. I threw a couple of painkillers down my throat with a slug of black coffee, totally the wrong combination, but needs must.

In the hallway, three identical denim backpacks sat waiting to be picked up and I added my black leather flight holdall to the group. My sleepy band of travellers dressed in their 'C.J.' clothes were sitting, very subdued, on the bottom stairs like three not-so-wise monkeys waiting for the arrival of 5.30 a.m. and the 'special' cab. Thankfully, they were all too tired to make conversation.

I went from room to room, checking that windows were closed and taps were turned off and as I closed each door I was also saying goodbye. As I gently closed Rebecca's door, Molly Dolly seemed to sag in her chair. It didn't seem right that she was being left behind, to be hidden in a box and put into storage. She was Becca's comforter. The secrets that were sewn into her rag body would never be told. My journey continued, half closing curtains and checking the timers for the lights. Peering over the gallery I saw that the kids were still motionless, staring at the front door. The day was light-grey, but at least it wasn't raining.

Back in the kitchen, I sticky-taped Georgie's letter to the worktop and pushed the large brown envelope containing the other letters into my bag to give to the driver. I had written to

Auntie Betty, my confidante, but I really wanted to speak to her before I left; I would try from the airport.

The dogs were waking and I could hear them sniffing at the bottom of the door. I had to hold it together, but my heart was already missing them. How could I leave them behind? Rosco had the heart of a lion and had always been my rock. Don't get maudlin! Look for something to take your mind off them!

Tigga, the mother cat, was stretching her front paws and shaking her long tabby fur coat when she suddenly leapt into action. She moved like a ballerina on tiptoes with her tail full and swaying across the lawn. Coco, her boy, was king of the garden. He had thick, black fur, which made him resemble a bear cub. Tizzie, the tabby sister, with huge green eyes, joined them for their morning exercise, chasing imaginary mice, then springing up a tree like a squirrel. They were survivors and would settle almost anywhere. They would still be missed, especially by Rebecca.

Toot! Toot! Toot! The time for action had arrived.

'Come on, Mum, he's here!' Becca was first to the door.

'Just one more thing and I'm right behind you! Have you all double checked your backpacks? Got everything you need?'

'All together, guys! *Yes*, Mum!'

I flew upstairs and down in a trice, blew a kiss to the house and slammed the front door behind me, sparking off a tirade of barking from the dogs. Bye Rosco, Dino, Tigga, Coco, Tizzie and by no means least, Snoopy! We love you! Bye house – I loved you once upon a time!

Four misty faces looked back as the black cab moved out of the driveway and we gripped hands, smiling.

'Shall I close the gates, Mrs Reeves?' He looked at me through the rear-view mirror.

'No! They have to be open for the horsebox. You see my friends are going to look after our animals while we are away. Thanks all the same.'

'OK! By the way, you can call me Jeeves!' He grinned then slid the glass partition closed.

Rebecca sank against me and closed her eyes. She didn't want to see where we were going. Jason was facing backwards, sitting on a truckle seat, using his eyes as a camera, taking Polaroids and storing them in his memory. Sean snuggled up to Rebecca and plugged his walkman into his ears, hooking his legs over the cases and bags in front of him. We all had our own way of dealing with ghosts. As we passed the old cottage, everyone stared at the grounds, but nothing seemed out of place. We glanced at one another, smiled and decided not to pass comment.

I travelled in a black cab very infrequently and had forgotten how roomy they were. We had four bodies, two cases, four pieces of hand luggage, a carrier bag and my 'kitchen sink' handbag and there was still space to roll around when we cornered. On leaving the lane we all looked back. Just trees and leaves and the woods! No ghosts! Gatwick, here we come!

My fascination for people clicked in. Our Jeeves looked like an ex-military man. He had dark hair, with a few silver sprigs, which was cut on a number two – very short! His shoulders were square and he had a large neck and hands and was neither plain nor handsome, until he smiled and he showed an immaculate set of teeth, which turned his face into 'Interesting'.

'Hey, I've just thought! He hasn't given us our tickets or passports! Jason, knock on the window for me, please!' As I said this it occurred to me that nobody had mentioned driving licences either? Jeeves slid the glass back, with an enquiring grin.

'Mrs Callaghan, how can I be of service?'

'Of course, we are now the Callaghans! Thank you, Jeeves!'

'Yes, and during the journey you had all better get used to using your new names. I expect you are wanting these?' He handed a package to Jason (or Connor), who tore it open exposing four old and four new passports, a set of tickets and a letter from C.J.

The expectation was electric. Becca opened her eyes and sat forward. Sean pulled the plugs from his ears in anticipation and Jason became the 'joker'. He was master of ceremonies and toyed with us while he inspected each photo. His face was deadpan for a second and then creased into laughter.

Pandemonium ensued, as we grabbed the passports from him, even Jeeves was amused. I was pleased that he had kept the sliding glass partition open. Actually, the photos were quite flattering; it was seeing our new names in print that was peculiar. I had reserved separate pockets in my bag for old and new stuff so put them away and settled back to read C.J.'s epistle.

The sentiment was really touching, full of warmth and good wishes, and the last of my doubts flew out of the window. We had become his extended family and I had learned to trust him. Finally, he told me to check that my mobile phone was switched on and reminded me of important things to do at the airport. I wished somewhere that there were words of love, the knowledge that someone was going to give me a cuddle, but today C.J.'s words were enough to get me through.

'For your eyes only, Mum?' Becca was watching me and her curiosity begged to be fed.

'No, sweetheart! Here, you can read it too!'

Jason turned in his seat and spoke to Jeeves.

'Is it my imagination or is that silver BMW following us?' He was not wrong.

'Yes, my man, it certainly is! Well spotted! It, or should I say they, have been with us all the way. They have been so obvious that they want us to know that they are there. It's like being in control, but nothing to worry about!'

'Are you going to let Commander Johnson know?' Jason was intrigued.

'It's OK, he already does! I have to close this now as I have to report in.' He slid the glass closed.

For the last half of the journey we repeated our new names in conversation and double-checked the procedure at the airport. My head was becoming hot, due to the wig, so I had to prod it with a pencil, which gave us the giggles. Clothing change was next on the agenda. Rebecca was going to wear her favourite red jacket when she discarded her cap and Levi jacket. Sean would be in Diesel jacket and sweat-top and losing the Chelsea cap and Jason would be wearing his Yankees sweatshirt and had decided to spike his hair with blond gel. Very USA!

Mine was the easiest. I had a very old cream safari jacket that had seen better days, which would make me disappear into the crowd. And of course my sixties chick hairstyle. We convinced ourselves that we were ready for the challenge. There was no going back.

Jeeves slid back the glass and told us that we would be shadowed by one of the team as soon as we entered the airport, so we wouldn't be alone. 'Look, folks, you are going on holiday so just relax and enjoy and act like neurotic holidaymakers! We are pulling into the drop-off zone, so now is the time to ask any niggling questions!'

'Just one, Jeeves! What are we going to do about new driving licences?' I leaned forward to hear his reply.

'Everything else is being handled by Declan, he'll have it under control!' He slid back the glass, parked and helped us to organise our baggage onto a trolley.

There was no time to panic, as people were pushing and bustling and raising their voices all around us. With a wave he was into the cab and vacating the space for the next vehicle to discharge its contents.

'Iberia desk, here we come! Vámonos, amigos!' We were on our way.

We scooted down the ramps, trying to steer the wayward trolley, then sped along the moving pavement. It was a few minutes before 7 a.m. and the airport was teaming with people. At 7.15 a.m. we were queuing for the Tenerife flight and were all in hyper mode.

Jason (or Connor) volunteered to bring us some orange juice to calm us down and he was back by the time we had reached the desk. The cases were marked and then sent off on the travelator, never to be seen again. I searched through the crowds, looking for the man with white hair, but it would have been impossible to spot anyone and who said it would be him?

With the old tickets and old passports safely tucked in my bag I followed the kids to a set of seats. We traced the flight number on the board, but thankfully it hadn't been called. No time to freak out, as we had to find the changeover points.

'Boys, can you see the Tie Rack shop and the neighbouring toilets?' I was too short to view the shops properly.

'Yeh, Mom, it's cool! Can we have the new passports and tickets now, 'cos we are set to go!' Jason (Connor) had stepped into his adopted role.

'Here you are, keep them safe!'

He took both his and his brother's, looked at me long and hard and turned away.

'I love you, Mum, and I won't mess things up. Don't panic but the boarding lights are up, so we are off. See you in Ireland! Shout at me. Say "Be quick," to make things look real.' Sean (Liam) had taken control. I couldn't believe it was all happening so fast.

'Hurry up, you boys, we'll see you in the queue. Becca and I are going to get some tissues,' I shouted as they disappeared from view.

They were gone, swallowed up in the crowds and I couldn't move.

'Come on, Mum, don't think about it, just get going!' Becca, who was about to become Brodie, yanked me to my feet and we rushed across the concourse. We were bumped and jostled by human animals, forcing their way to the boarding zones.

The Body Shop loomed ahead and hastily we zigzagged our way through. We followed a girl into the door marked 'Staff Only'. Directly the door was closed she turned on us.

'Right, make the swap and follow me to the rear door, quickly!' She carried on walking as she spoke.

We almost bumped into two women, who were standing behind the door. They were our clones. My wig was stolen from my head. They grabbed the old tickets and passports from me and were gone in seconds.

'Mum, they really did look like us, how unreal!' My Brodie, as she now was, was flushed with excitement. She put on her red jacket, turned up the collar and crushed the denim one into her bag, clipping the cap onto the strap.

I snuggled into my safari jacket and stuffed the carrier bag into the space it left.

'Ruffle my hair for me, Brodie, it's sticking to my head!' She obediently preened my hair and kissed my nose.

'Come on sixties chick!'

'Hurry, ladies, no time to loiter!' She clicked her fingers in irritation. She was obviously a policewoman and not a shop assistant.

At the end of a corridor she stopped by a door and turned to face us.

'Mrs Callaghan, could you wait here a second.' She unlocked the door and hauled out two suitcases on wheels, relocked the door, sighed and smiled.

'These are yours, I hope the clothes are OK! At least the sizes are about right! Go to the next door, down there, push the bar and it will open onto the main concourse. You have your tickets for Cork and your new passports, yes?'

I nodded and patted the pocket on my bag.

'Great stuff! Follow the Ryanair signs and book in at the flight desk. I am leaving you now. It's all plain "flying" from now on! Best of luck!' She hurried back down the corridor and was gone. Mrs Callaghan and her daughter, Brodie, were about to take a flight to Ireland.

'So, who's gonna push the bar, Mrs Callaghan? The choice is yours!' Her energy was electric.

'Let's get ready to rumble, Brodie, be my guest! Ireland, here we come!'

We entered the shop as the Reeves and exited into the corridor as the Callaghans.

By the time we had booked in, which wasn't that trouble-free as we got lost, our flight had been called, so we ran straight through to the departure lounge. It wasn't until then that I had time to think of the boys. God, I hope they were safe with Declan. I was somewhere in space as Brodie guided me to Duty Free.

'Retail therapy, Amanda!'

'Respect, Brodie! Respect! It sounds quite good though, does it suit me?'

'Mum, what's in a name? You look so different! I'm glad you had your hair cut, you look great! Don't worry about the boys either, they'll be in the air on their way to Dublin with "Uncle Declan" by now.' She kissed her fingertips and blew into the air, provocatively. Naughty girl, she was definitely my child and growing up much too fast.

I loved duty-free shopping. It was the illusion that you were getting something cheap. CKB perfume for Brodie, Dolce & Gabbana for me and a bottle each of Blue Label Vodka, Jack Daniels and Southern Comfort. Not that I was a drinker, but I did like the occasional tipple.

Someone coughed and it startled me enough to grab onto Brodie's sleeve. Reality was still the sinister threat of being discovered by the Voice. Had we succeeded in outwitting the Organisation? I scrutinised the crowd for white-haired men. I was convinced that I had already met the man who wanted to harm me. Brodie dragged me through the boarding gate and onto the aircraft.

As we boarded the plane I still felt uneasy and it took every ounce of self-control *not* to look behind me. We were trapped now. There was no escape. Was the Voice there with me, waiting to say hello? Too late to run as the doors locked and we taxied down the runway, finally becoming airborne. There were definitely no albinos on board, I had checked!

I sat next to the window and felt the excitement oozing from Brodie. She fidgeted with her seat belt and popped open her table in expectation of food. John's face came into my mind. Please be gentle with him and make him strong! I offered a silent prayer just in case someone was listening.

Brodie touched my hand. 'Mum, it's OK! You have done it! We are on our way to meet the fabulous Declan Dennehy and the boys.'

I peered out of the window and squeezed her hand. The airport had shrunk to the size of a Monopoly board. Then I smiled and laughed silently. OK, you albino bastard, you have lost! The lioness and her cubs have gone to ground.

The tannoy clicked into voice.

'Welcome to Ryanair's flight to Cork! Your Captain is Colin Culloty and on his behalf we wish you a pleasant flight!'

Printed in the United Kingdom
by Lightning Source UK Ltd.
119893UK00001B/6